MYND CONTROL

a novel

Teresa
Widdowson

PROLOGUE

As he shuffled down the dark corridor, Ben Marshall's figure glowed in the luminescence of the moon streaming through the small window at the end of the hallway. He felt the cold hardwood floor through his thin cotton socks. The lights flickering in his eyes made it hard to see. His head was pounding, and the lingering acrid smell of the astringent used to clean the floor earlier in the day didn't help.

The chef's knife he'd taken from the kitchen hung heavy in his hand. The touch of the cold steel handle against his palm sent a shiver down his spine. He heard a noise and froze—but it was just a snore. He breathed a sigh of relief. *Everyone's asleep*, he thought. *It's time to end this.*

He passed the first bedroom and continued down the hall as quietly as possible, avoiding the floorboards he knew would squeak. At the last door, he stopped. His hand shook as he reached forward and pushed the door open. He listened for signs the man had woken, but all he heard was the sound of deep breathing. He continued in, his eyes opened wide as he struggled to take in as much light as possible. Ben's lips curled back into a snarl when he saw the man in a deep sleep. *How can he sleep so soundly?* Ben tried to ignore his splitting headache as the bright lights flashed in his eyes. He forced himself to focus on the man. The voice in his head reminded him the man was a killer. *He's probably dreaming about his next victim,* the voice said.

Ben crossed the small room, stood beside the bed and raised the knife. But his palm was damp from nervous sweat, and the knife slipped out of his hand and dropped with a bang onto the wooden floor. The man's eyes flew open, and he called out, "Who's there?"

He flinched when he heard the familiar cadence and almost lost his nerve. Remember, he told himself, *He's not who you think he is! You know what he does!*

He snatched the knife from the floor and slammed his hand against the man's cheek to turn his face away. He would not be fooled. Ben plunged the blade into the man's heart, stabbing again and again, the voice reminding him he was doing what had to be done. What no one else was willing to do.

The click of a switch behind him caused a harsh light to beam down from above, and a bolt of lightning shot through Ben's eyes and into his brain. He grabbed his head and howled from the pain. He turned. A woman was standing in the doorway. He watched as she stood there, waiting for her eyes to adjust to the light. Her face went white and distorted into a terrified gasp. And she started to scream.

"No!" she shrieked, dropping to her knees and rocking as she cried. She turned her eyes away from the bloody mess on the bed, switched her gaze to Ben and screamed, "Oh my god! What have you done? What have you done?"

The woman wouldn't stop screaming, and Ben looked at her, puzzled. A shock wave hit him like a tsunami when he realized who she was—his wife, Michelle. He stared at the knife still in his hand, blood dripping from its tip and oozing into the cracks between the wooden planks. He dropped the weapon and its tip stuck like a dagger into the floorboards. Then he turned, looked back at the bed and saw his fifteen-year-old son, Nate, blood pouring from his chest and soaking rapidly into the sheets around him as his eyes stared blankly at the ceiling.

A guttural cry emanated from Ben's throat, and he dropped to his knees next to his wife. Then he wrenched the knife out of the floor and sliced his own throat.

1

Looking out her bedroom window, Vega saw the beginnings of another beautiful day. The sky was cloudless and clear blue and the tops of the cedar trees swayed in the breeze at the far end of her small back yard. The temperature was supposed to soar all the way to eighty-seven degrees by late afternoon—ten degrees above normal for Redmond, Washington this time of year. This summer in the Pacific Northwest, or PNW as residents liked to call it, had been warm and dry. Good news for people who played outdoors. Bad for the flora and fauna. It could raise the fire danger to hazardous levels. But at least she hadn't yet had to turn on the air conditioning.

Vega looked back at her computer screen and the article about CORE, the latest application she'd written for her employer, ThinkShop. The CORE program name was an acronym for Consolidated Overview of Body Eudaemonia. She had discovered the word eudaemonia by accident after getting sucked down an internet rabbit hole reading about

Aristotle. It meant the condition of flourishing or living well —having a sense of overall happiness and well-being.

Her CORE mobile application collected biometric data from a user's smart device, whether it be a phone, tablet, watch or health band. Depending on the make and model, the data could include their temperature, heart rate, perspiration rate and chemical composition, and respiratory rate. It may also collect information on blood pressure, hearing capabilities (based on how high they had the volume turned up), color of the sclera (which could indicate liver disease or diabetes), pupil size and oxygen saturation. It could also search their face for irregular, possibly cancerous moles or skin lesions. She had even used the smart devices' new Continuous Glucose Monitor sensor, or CGM, to check for signs of diabetes or alert a diabetic if their insulin level was off.

The program combined the information into one comprehensive view to give an overall picture of the user's health. Then the program compared the data against available statistics of healthy people in the same sex, race, age and regional. This provided the user with a snapshot of their current health status. Then it offered links to trustworthy medical information sites that could recommend physicians and, or lifestyle changes to help the user improve their overall health.

After rolling her CORE program out to the public six months ago, a huge feature was written about it on a health industry news website. She smiled when she thought about it. If people paid attention to it, it could save them from more serious health issues later down the road. And ThinkShop was making a killing from it.

She was positive her boss, Liam, had written the article. In it, he stated that forty-one percent of the health-care mobile app marketing companies had already purchased her CORE program—which Vega had a hard time believing. She didn't know how the industry measured it. But she was glad he was looking out for her. Liam was a good boss. He paid his people well, considering it was such a small company. Flattered as she was, her fame hadn't come with a pay raise. Still, she supposed she should be grateful for the accolades. It wasn't often someone took notice of her accomplishments.

Her pants vibrated, and Vega jumped, forgetting she had put her phone in the back pocket of her jeans instead of her backpack. The screen told her it was a local area code, but she didn't recognize the number. *Probably someone selling insurance or some robo-political call.* She hit the *Dismiss with message* icon and dropped the phone on her desk. Thirty seconds later, it vibrated across the surface and played a three-tone minor chord in E, indicating she had a message. She dialed her voicemail box.

"Hey Vega, it's Liam. Give me a call back as soon as you can. I have some big news to share. It's important."

Liam must have called from his personal phone, otherwise she would have recognized the number. She'd never seen him be dramatic, so he must have big news. She hit the *Call back* symbol.

"Oh, hey Vega. Thanks for calling me back so quickly."

"Yeah, no problem. You piqued my curiosity. What's up?"

"We've been bought."

"What?"

"Neilmann Corporation just bought ThinkShop."

"When?"

"It's been in the works for a while. I didn't want to tell anyone until I was sure it would go through."

"Oh."

"Why do you sound so glum? This is a good thing. They paid a good price—overly generous, as a matter of fact."

"Does this mean everyone's getting a raise?"

Liam cleared his throat. "Not exactly."

"Oh, it's the other option then. Everyone's getting canned?"

"That's unclear right now. I'm sorry. It's out of my hands. But they promised to contact everyone individually and discuss their options."

Vega was pissed off. She did not need this in her life.

"What the hell am I going to do?"

"I'm sure they're going to want to keep you, Vega. That's why I wanted to get that article published about your latest work. Not that you didn't deserve the recognition anyway."

"I was wondering about that. Thanks."

"No problem."

"But I'm not sure I want to work for Neilmann, anyway."

"Why not?"

"They're a marketing company. A *neuro*marketing company, which is even worse. And a *big* neuromarketing company, which is doubly worse. Those ads you see on your phone and computer? Neilmann customers created a lot of them."

"Yeah, I know."

"Then you know they use EEG readings and other biometric data to measure customers' reactions to ads. Their customers are normal marketing companies, you know, the ones that create the ads. It always seemed, I don't know, a little too Big Brother."

"Come on. I would think that would be right up your alley with your neurology background."

"That's not the kind of neurological research I was interested in. What's this mean? Should I even be studying the specs for my next project?"

"No. I've already advised our customers about the change. I've told them we've put a halt to any existing projects. It's up to Neilmann to decide what to do with them."

"What about you? Do you still have a job?"

Liam hesitated. "No. But I guess now I don't need one. The buy-out was more than generous. I won't have to work anymore. You know I've been thinking about retiring anyway."

Vega knew he was lying. He would go crazy if he retired. He'd gotten divorced a year ago, and it had devastated him. Since then, he'd buried himself in his work.

"That's great, Liam," she lied. "What will you do with yourself?"

"Still figuring that out. You shouldn't write them off, Vega. At least hear what they have to say. Who knows? You might enjoy working for them."

"Yeah, I guess. But I'd better go polish up my web profile just in case."

They said their goodbyes, and Vega sighed as she closed the program request specifications proposal she'd been studying and pulled up her resume instead. After working on it for about thirty minutes, her phone rang again with another number she didn't recognize. The call tag said *Neilmann Corporation,* so she picked it up. Might as well get it over with.

"Ms. Swift?" a woman's voice asked.

"Who's asking?"

"This is Dr. Astrid Montgomery. I'm a mobile applications VP here at Neilmann Corporation. Is this Ms. Vega Swift?"

"Yeah, that's me."

"May I ask if you've heard the news about ThinkShop yet?"

"Yes. I heard. Liam just called me a few minutes ago."

"Oh, good. I'm glad. You know, we're all excited to have the talents of ThinkShop join us here at Neilmann. I hope you feel the same way because I think you can contribute a lot to our vision."

"Really? May I ask how?"

Astrid laughed and said, "Right to the point. I like that. I read the write-up about you and the CORE app on one of the health-care websites. That was inspiring work. It's exactly the kind of talent we need at Neilmann. I think you'll be a great addition to a special project we're working on. I'd like to talk to you about it, and if I feel you're a good fit, get you settled in here as soon as possible. I've set aside some time on my calendar for tomorrow at nine. Does that work for you?"

It surprised Vega that the woman simply assumed she wouldn't have a problem moving over from ThinkShop to Neilmann, and frankly, that things were moving so fast. The companies couldn't be more different. ThinkShop was a small software company that concentrated on mobile health-care apps, and Neilmann was a huge corporation of neuromarketing specialists. She had no idea why they had bought ThinkShop and couldn't imagine how she could help promote the company's *vision*.

"Don't get me wrong, Dr. Montgomery. It's not like I'm not interested in keeping my job. But may I ask why you think you need my skills as a health-care app writer at a neuromarketing company like Neilmann?"

"I'd rather not discuss the specifics over the phone. Can I expect you tomorrow then?"

2

Putting aside her resume, Vega pulled up the Neilmann Corporation homepage. She read the generic boilerplate about the company and navigated to the *What is neuromarketing* sub-menu. She was learning about their focus groups when her phone beeped with a text. Trent.

Hey u. Outside. Safe to come in?

Vega texted back.

Door unlocked. Mom watching TV. Come in side door.

No prob. I'll come in front and say hi to mom.

The front door creaked open downstairs, and Vega heard Trent's Doc Martens clomp across the hardwood floor. He mumbled something to her mom, which made Vega smile. Trent was one of the few people who didn't feel awkward around her mother. None of her other friends, not that she had many anymore, would have stopped to talk to her. They would have come through the side door.

His heavy shoes thumped up the stairs, and he strolled into her bedroom without a word. He spread out on the bed and Vega cringed. Her only real expenditure on herself since her father had died, other than the essentials, was the redesign of her bedroom. It had been a requirement, though, if she wanted to keep her sanity. She simply couldn't bear having pink walls and a rosy floral bedspread anymore. As redecorations go, it wasn't a very expensive project, and now she had a place where she could work from home—a place where drugs and wheelchairs were not allowed.

She'd hit all the local yard sales, sifted through Craigslist, shopped at the Goodwill and Salvation Army stores, and finally made a trip to IKEA to redecorate her bedroom completely. The hardwood floor was now covered with a large, shaggy turquoise area rug. It kept her feet warm in the winter and added some color. Trent had helped her paint over the previous soft-pink walls with a soothing cream. She covered one wall with burgundy and purple wallpaper accented by stark white shelves, giving her space for her old books and knick-knacks. The final touch was covering an old metal futon with a soft gray chenille fabric, and the room was transformed from her girly bedroom to a space she was proud of and comfortable in—an oasis away from her normal world. Now she loved sitting at her bright-white modern desk and looking out her large window into the treed back yard. And best of all, no more pink.

"Hey!" she said, smacking his feet. "Trent Loki, you take those dirty things off my bed. Didn't your parents teach you any manners?"

Trent laughed and swung his legs off the bed, settling instead for fluffing up the pillows and propping them behind his head. He leaned back against the wall and stretched his legs so his boots hung just off the edge.

"Awfully tiny bed, if you ask me," he said.

"It fits me just fine."

"But what about me?"

Vega chuckled and pinched him on the leg.

"Ow!"

She'd known Trent since grade school. He and his parents had lived down the street, and he was one of the few friends who had stuck with her through the years. Most of her other so-called friends had bailed when her mother really started going downhill. They changed, suddenly not knowing how to act in front of her mother; make excuses why they couldn't come over. Or worse, they'd keep asking her if they could help and then never follow through. She learned the hard way they didn't really want to help. They were really hoping she would just say, *No, she didn't need their help*. So that's what she learned to do—never rely on anyone else.

Not Trent, though. When he asked if he could help, he meant it. And he stayed and actually helped when he could. But he had his own life to live, and it wasn't really his burden. Vega often couldn't bring herself to ask even him anymore.

Trent gave her a smile. He was a good-looking man, and although she might not be a knockout, she felt she was at least OK. Trent's mother was from Jamaica, with skin as dark as midnight, and his father was from Okinawa, Japan. Trent was lucky enough to come out of their DNA merge and develop into something wonderful. His skin was the color of creamy milk chocolate, and when she went through puberty with disgusting pimples on her nose and forehead, he never had a blemish. Six feet tall with a slim, lean body, he'd gotten his mother's height and his father's metabolism. He could eat like a pig, never work out and still not gain weight. *It was totally unfair*, she thought. His cat-like eyes, with their prominent epicanthic fold, gave him a mysterious and exotic look. They were large and a beautiful light green with specks of yellow. She goaded him all the time about the color.

"Are you sure your mail person wasn't Irish?" she would ask.

No one in his family knew where his green eyes came from, and Trent had decided it was simply a recessive gene he'd been lucky enough to inherit from some distant relative. And those eyes were looking at her right now.

"I saw your text earlier. I guess you're, like, famous now?"

"Hardly," she answered. "But it is kind of cool, isn't it? I've never had anything written about me."

"Not even on the bathroom walls at school?"

"I don't know. It's not like I ever went into the boy's bathroom."

He smiled, a devilish grin on his face. "Maybe it wasn't the boys doing the writing?"

"Funny."

"Come on, no one ever wrote anything? Not even any boyfriends?"

"Boyfriends? What boyfriends?"

"Oh right. Sorry, I forgot who I was talking to for a minute. Doesn't matter. You don't need a boyfriend. They just get you into trouble. Besides, you have me! And yes, I think it's very cool that someone wrote something about you. You're so talented, it's about time someone noticed. Who knows? Maybe you'll get more money because of it?"

"Or maybe I'll get laid off."

Trent sat up. "What? Why do you say that?"

"ThinkShop just got bought out by Neilmann Corporation."

Trent leaned forward. "Neilmann? That big company downtown? Aren't they some kind of marketing company?"

"Neuromarketing."

"Neuromarketing?"

"They study how consumers react to ads. They use EEGs and other methods to see how people respond."

"Wow! Sounds a little creepy. What do they want with ThinkShop?"

"Good question. One of the VPs called me today and asked me to come in for an interview tomorrow. Hopefully, I'll get a job offer. Although, frankly, I'm not sure I want to work for them."

"You mean like a full-time job offer? Like with real benefits and all that other wonderful stuff?"

"I guess."

"What do you mean you might not want to work for them? Yes you do!"

"I never thought I'd work for a big corporation after what happened to my dad, you know?"

"You are not your dad, and Neilmann is not Kipling."

Vega thought about her dad. He'd been full of wonderful talk about the family sticking together through her mother's illness, but he had bailed when Miren's disease progressed quicker than anyone expected. She had gotten to the stage of barely recognizing them anymore when her dad got his two-week notice that he was getting laid off from Kipling, a large retailer where he had worked for almost twenty-five years. No time to prepare emotionally or financially. His choice was to take a small severance package and agree not to sue or go away with nothing. The medical bills had started piling up, and they couldn't live without the money, so he had signed the paperwork.

Vega hated Kipling for it, and swore she would never work for a large corporation. She didn't think they cared about the little guys who actually kept their company going. But she'd never forgiven her father for what he had done afterwards.

Trent snapped his fingers in front of her face and jerked Vega back to the present. "Hey! You still with me? Did you say a VP called you? It wasn't like the assistant or something? Or someone from HR?"

"No, it was a VP of programming."

"Woah."

"I was shocked. I mean, I'm still shocked. You're right. I know it's one of those companies I always said I'd never work for, but maybe it's time to get over it. Maybe I was just young and naive."

"Oh yeah, like you're so old and worldly now."

"Shut up!" Vega teased, kicking the bottom of Trent's shoe. "I can't live without a job right now. Besides, just because a company treated my dad poorly doesn't mean every big company is bad, right?"

"I've been trying to tell you that for like years, you know?"

"I know. And it would be nice to have a job with better insurance benefits. I don't know what to do."

"I'll tell you what you do. You go to the interview and get the damn job! That's what you do."

"You're probably right."

"Of course I'm right! I can't believe you're even questioning it. Go and get the job, and then milk them for everything you can."

"I know. I know you're right. It's just hard going back on everything I always said."

"Yeah, that was before, like, reality set in. I don't think there's any way you could have known you'd end up in the situation you're in now."

"But I'd be leaving my mother alone with a stranger every day."

Trent scoffed with a shake of his head. "You do that sometimes now already. And the nurses aren't like strangers anymore, are they? Don't you mostly get the same ones?"

"There are about three or four that rotate. But I don't leave her with them every day, all day."

"And are you sure they won't like, let you work from home?"

"I don't know yet."

"And it wouldn't be like every day, right? I'm assuming you'd still get weekends free. I don't want to sound rude, but do you really think she like even knows whether you're here anymore?"

Vega picked at a thread on her shirt. "I don't know. But I hope so."

"You keep saying she's going to need more care than you can give her soon, even with the nurses. Maybe you could think of this as like a weaning period?"

"I haven't even met this VP woman yet," Vega said, knowing full well she was dodging Trent's question. "She may not even like me. I may not even get a job offer. Anything could happen. Or nothing could happen."

"But you'll never know if you don't at least go. Just get ready for a string of never-ending interviews. I hear you have to pass like a million of them before you're offered anything there."

"You know someone who works there?"

"How would I know any of them?" he smiled.

"You just said." She grunted. "Come on. You know everyone. Remember, you get out a lot more than I do."

Trent snorted. "That's an understatement. I have met a couple of them. At The Cavern."

"The Cavern?"

"You know, that club in Bellevue I love? Those men dancing in their little cages. Ow! Anyway, I've heard them talk a little shop. They said it took them like two months before they got through all the interviews and got a job offer."

"Wow! That sucks. ThinkShop has stopped everything already. Nothing new coming in for me. The buyout is in full swing. A couple of months sounds like a long time."

"Are you doing OK? I mean, financially? I know you had a few big bills coming up you were worried about."

"Yeah, my car insurance premiums are due next month, and I'm going to need new tires soon. Not that I go anywhere except to the doctors' offices anymore anyway."

"I guess you haven't called your mom's sister in England yet?"

"I can't do it. It's like begging."

"You're so hard-headed sometimes. It wouldn't hurt you to like accept some help every now and then. Does she even know the full extent of wha—"

"I've been managing all these years on my own just fine," Vega interrupted. "I don't need anyone else."

"You are so stubborn! At least you have the nurses now."

"Yeah, I guess I should thank you for prodding me into calling and getting that set up. I don't know what I'd do without them now."

"You're welcome. See, admitting you need help is not that hard. Now what about contacting her sister?"

"Not going to happen."

Trent threw up his hands. "OK. OK. I know. None of my business."

They sat in silence, lost in their own thoughts about their lives. That was something she really liked about Trent. They could sit together and not say anything. Just be with each other and not feel uncomfortable. They didn't have to talk just to fill the empty space. It was easy for her to be herself around Trent. If he wasn't gay, she would have made a move on him ages ago.

"So," he said, "let's talk about what you're going to wear to your interview."

3

Crash!

Vega's eyes flew open, and it took her a moment to orient herself. For a second, she had no idea where she was or why. As she came out of her dream-fog, she finally remembered she'd fallen asleep on the living room couch after Trent had left. Now she realized where the noise had come from, and she jumped up. She ran, stumbling across the room and around the corner into the bedroom, afraid she'd find her mom on the floor with a broken bone or worse. Thankfully, she was still in bed but was in the throes of a seizure. Her teeth were grinding, and her body was twitching. Her right arm flailed, and she had knocked her water glass off the nightstand. Sharp, jagged fragments lay in a puddle of water on the hardwood floor.

A tonic-clonic seizure. That's what the doctors called it. They'd told her they weren't that common. Usually, patients had much milder seizures, and her mother had those as well, but it was a known symptom of her late-stage, early-onset Alzheimer's disease.

It grieved Vega to see her mother like this, but she had no time to dwell on her sadness. Stepping around to avoid the shards of glass, she ran to the bed, lowered the rails, crawled on top of her mother and held down Miren's thrashing arms to keep them from hitting anything else. These spells usually lasted less than a minute, but they always felt so much longer. Her mother's head rolled back and forth, and guttural sounds came from her throat that Vega had never heard before. It seemed there was always something new to hate about this disease. All Vega could do was make sure her mom didn't hurt herself until it was over and tell the doctor later, with the hope she could make some adjustments to her medication.

Finally, she quit spasming and looked up at Vega.

"Sharon?"

"No, Mom. It's Vega. Your sister isn't here."

"Is Cyrus home yet?"

"No."

Miren nodded. "I'm tired."

"Of course you are. You've had a bad nightmare."

Miren turned away from her, and a sharp, acrid smell filled the air. Vega realized with a sigh, she would need to change the sheets. She crawled off the bed, crouched on the floor and surveyed the mess. Lying in the broken glass was a small framed picture of the family—Miren, Cyrus and Vega —in happier times, before her mom's diagnosis. Vega remembered the vacation. They had splurged and taken a road trip to the Grand Canyon that summer. She'd only been eleven at the time, and it was one of her happiest memories of them all together. Mesmerized by the vastness of the canyon and the colorful landscape so unlike the Pacific Northwest, they'd spent an entire week hiking the north and south rim trails, watching the beautiful sunsets and searching for souvenirs to take back home from the visitor center.

Vega held back tears as she picked up the larger pieces of glass. She grabbed the mop and broom from the kitchen, swept up the remaining fragments, and just to be sure, ran a bare hand across the smooth surface of the wood, checking for tiny splinters. The last thing she wanted was to leave minuscule pieces of glass for her mother to cut herself on later. She mopped up the remaining water and threw away the mess. On her way back, she grabbed a fresh incontinence pad and a clean set of sheets.

After cleaning up her mother and putting her in a fresh nightgown, she helped her into her wheelchair and changed the sheets. From the kitchen, she took a plastic glass out of the kitchen cupboard, filled it with water and wondered what had possessed her to use a glass one in the first place. She knew better. She must have been so tired she hadn't been thinking straight. Two hours after the seizure began, Vega helped her mom back into bed.

"Would you like some water, Mom?"

Miren mumbled something Vega took as a *yes* and helped her sit up and take a drink. She struggled to swallow, and after several attempts, managed to take a few sips. Then her eyes went wide, and she pointed to something on the wall.

"Are we at the beach?"

Following her gaze, Vega looked at a framed painting of a rocky beach scene hanging on the wall behind her.

"No, Mom. It's just a painting."

"At the beach?"

Vega gently turned her mother's face away from the painting so she would look at her instead. "Mom, we're still home. We're still in Redmond. It's only a painting."

She offered her another drink to distract her, readjusted the pillow and covers and sat the glass on the nightstand, a little farther away from the bed this time. Miren closed her eyes, and Vega softly brushed her mom's hair from her face.

"Get some sleep, Mom. I love you."

She kissed her forehead, and on the way out, she lifted the painting off the wall and set it in the hallway. She would store it away later.

The sheets dropped into the hamper, and Vega turned to face the mirror over the bathroom sink. Her brown eyes were bloodshot, and her dark bangs badly needed a trim. She'd been cutting them herself for several months to save money, and it was showing. After splashing water on her face, she went back to the living room. The clock on the front wall above the piano read four o'clock. There was no way she was going back to sleep now.

She plunked down on the couch and picked up the remote. The TV was showing a commercial about a moisturizing cream that magically erased dark circles under your eyes.

I could use some of that, she thought.

4

A banging noise woke Vega, and she was surprised to find herself in her bed. She must have crawled up the stairs back to her bedroom during the night. She could hear the raindrops as they plunked onto the leaves of the large rhododendron right outside her bedroom window and threatened to lull her back to sleep. But she rubbed the sleep out of her eyes, threw on her bathrobe and rushed down the stairs. After looking through the peephole just to be sure, she opened the front door.

"Morning."

"Hi," said the nurse, looking Vega up and down. "Bad night?"

"She's been having a lot more seizures lately. Come on in, Julia."

The nurse set her bags on the couch. "Don't worry. I'll take good care of her today. I'll tell the doctor for you and see if she wants to adjust her levetiracetam."

"Thanks, that would be great."

"It's bath day today. Do you have time to help me get her ready?"

"Sure."

They moved her mother from the bed to her wheelchair and rolled it into the bathroom next to the tub. Vega splurged and had the original bathtub replaced with one with a door. It was called a walk-in tub, which Vega thought was ironic since she'd gotten it specifically so her mother wouldn't have to walk in to it anymore. She'd lost so much muscle tone from barely moving, it was difficult for her to step over the edge or to stand in the tub for long. Vega tried to get her to do the physical therapy exercises the doctor recommended, but she would have nothing to do with it. And even if she had been willing, Vega was pretty sure she wouldn't understand how to do them anyway.

Julia rolled the water-proof wheelchair into the tub, and they began the undressing process. At first her mother was combative, holding her arms in close to her body.

"No!" she protested, clinging tightly to her pajama top.

Her mom kept resisting their efforts, so Vega brought her phone into the bathroom and set it on the sink. She flipped through her music app, found the *I'm Breathless* album by Madonna and searched through the songs. She hit play, and the melody of "Vogue" filled the room. After a few moments, Miren smiled, and Vega could tell she recognized the song from one of her favorite albums.

"You like that, Mom?"

Listening to the music calmed her down, and eventually they got all her clothes off. Vega laid a towel on her lap to help her feel less exposed. She knew if her mom was cognizant of what they were doing to her, she would have been mortified. The old Miren would hate being dependent like this, so Vega did her best to make it as stress-free as possible. Music always seemed to help, especially if Vega played songs from Miren's teenage years.

She looked at her mother's now frail frame. It was a vicious cycle. The sicker she became, the less she moved, and the less she moved, the weaker she became, and her difficulty swallowing meant it was hard for her to get enough nutrition. She no longer did anything to strengthen her body.

"All set now?" Vega asked.

Miren mumbled and nodded, which was more of a response than she usually got.

"You OK, Danielle?" asked Vega.

"Sure. I'll let you know if I need you. And it's Julia."

"Oh, god. I knew that. Sometimes I'm afraid I'm getting it too."

"You got it right before. I'm sure you're just distracted. Your memory is fine. You've just got a lot on your mind."

"Thanks."

Back upstairs, Vega pulled out the black pants and long-sleeved, light-blue rayon blouse Trent had picked out for her yesterday. It had been so long since she'd had an in-person interview, that she was happy to let him tell her what to wear. In fact, she was pretty sure the last interview she had been on was when she'd applied for a waitress job at the Gourmet Burger during high school. Compared to most of her friends, she hadn't had very many interviews or jobs. ThinkShop hired her after Liam found her resume online, and it had taken only one video call before he offered her a job.

She got dressed and looked in the mirror. Trent had made a good choice. The outfit was understated but still professional. It surprised Vega how much the interview was starting to matter to her. The most important thing about this job possibility was the insurance. According to their website, Neilmann Corporation had a great benefits package. That's what she needed the most—and a steady paycheck wouldn't hurt either. ThinkShop jobs had not always been predictable.

She had arranged for Julia to be with her mom all day, and there was a lot to do. It was evaluation day—measuring Miren's vital signs like blood pressure, breathing capacity, weight, temperature and heart rate. But she would also check her flexibility, strength and mental capacity.

Alzheimer's didn't always affect people as quickly as it had her mother. Miren had been very unlucky, as if getting the disease at fifty-two wasn't unlucky enough. Originally, the doctors thought her diagnosis meant she would live longer than most people simply because she was younger. They had also hoped her mental deterioration might progress more slowly. But they'd been wrong on both counts. Her mother went downhill fast, both physically and mentally, and the deterioration had only increased exponentially in the last two years. She'd gone from being able to walk with a walker to being in a wheelchair. And although she hadn't usually known where she was or who she was talking to, she at least used to say a few sentences now and then. Now she barely said a word. Vega tried not to dwell on it, because if she did that, she might never stop crying.

The TV was playing in the front room, and she followed the sound downstairs. Mom sat, now squeaky clean, in her chair, not even acknowledging Vega when she entered. Miren's shoulders hung forward, and she looked more feeble than usual. Bath days always took a lot out of her. She would probably fall asleep soon, but for now, her expression was vacuous. She was lost in her own little world. Vega hoped it was a nice one.

But she didn't have time to linger. She gave her mom a kiss, said goodbye to Julia, hopped in her Miata and steered the car towards downtown Seattle.

5

It was a slow drive into Seattle from Redmond. The gridlock of cars on Union Hill Road, the busy thoroughfare out of her area, had been a nightmare. And to top it off, the highway traffic on 520 over Lake Washington and into Seattle was almost as bad. The overnight rain didn't stop just because the sun came up, and everyone was extra careful. It was a good thing, but resulted in a slow commute.

It wasn't that people from the PNW didn't know how to drive in the rain—traffic was slower because rain was what they were used to driving in. They knew, because they'd learned the hard way, not to go too fast. Speeding on slippery wet roads just meant you were in a hurry to get to your next accident. Even though she hated creeping along at a snail's pace, she took it in stride. She'd allowed plenty of time to get there, even if the traffic sucked, so she turned up the radio, immersed herself in the music and tried not to be nervous. When she finally got into downtown and onto Union Street, there were just a few turns before she was on Pine. Halfway between 7th and 8th Street, she saw the tall

Neilmann Corporation building on the left, and her nerves finally kicked in.

Wow, this place is enormous!

She knew about Neilmann. Most people did. It was a huge deal when the company moved its headquarters from San Francisco to Seattle more than ten years ago. But Vega could count on one hand the number of times she'd been downtown since then. She just didn't have any reason to or the money to spend on the ridiculously expensive parking. If she wasn't worried about needing to rush home because of an emergency with her mom, she would take the bus. At least the parking at Neilmann was free.

Pulling her car into a visitor slot in the underground garage, she took the elevator up to the first floor. She rounded the corner to the main lobby, and the greenery surprised her. In large white planters, tall trees of various types stood throughout the lobby exuding a wonderful fragrance of earth and leaves. She felt like she was outside in a park instead of inside a building in downtown Seattle. She stood and gaped for a moment before she realized she didn't even know what floor Dr. Montgomery was on. It dawned on her that she should have looked for a picture of her interviewer when she had researched the company online. She was thinking about that as she walked toward the guard's desk by the elevators when someone tapped her on the shoulder.

"You look a little lost. Can I help you?"

Vega turned to see a woman with a phone in her hand and a red pen behind her ear. A badge on a lanyard hung around her neck, flipped so only its white back was revealed.

"Oh, hi. I'm looking for Dr. Astrid Montgomery's office. She's a VP of programming—"

"Oh, Astrid? Sure. No problem," the woman said with a welcoming smile. "I'll show you. I'm headed that way."

The woman nodded to the security guard at the desk. Vega couldn't help but notice the large gold-hooped earrings, which bounced lightly against her red shoulder-length hair as she walked. Her mid-thigh multi-colored skirt and royal blue turtleneck stood out as they passed people dressed in muted pastel button-down shirts and khakis.

Her boisterous personality and vigor matched her outfit and were infectious. Vega smiled.

"You know her?"

"I do, indeed. You can just follow me up, and I'll show you her office."

"You don't mind?"

"Not at all."

They squished themselves into the packed elevator, and the woman pushed the button for the twenty-third floor. Glancing around, Vega checked out the other people, observing their hairstyles, clothing, demeanor and jewelry. She loved guessing what people did for a living. She supposed it was the same reason she enjoyed reading obits. Some people had the most interesting stories. Most of the men were similarly dressed in slacks and button-down shirts, and only one man wore a jacket. The women's attire was more varied—some with simple dresses, others with pants and flowing blouses, and one with a skirt and jacket. Vega tried not to pigeonhole people when she created her fantasy stories, so she decided the woman in a suit was the assistant for the one in jeans.

Everyone was quiet, and her escort smiled at her as people got off on their respective floors. *What was it about elevators that made everyone mute when they got on? Psychologists had probably done some studies on it. She might have to Google that later.*

The last person exited the elevator, and now alone with the woman, Vega felt uninhibited enough to talk again.

"Do you mind if I ask what you do here?"

"I'm a VP. I manage the senior programmers on a new project we've started."

"Me too. I mean, obviously I'm not a VP or anything, of course." In her head, Vega grimaced. She was making a fool of herself and realized she must be more nervous than she had thought. "I mean, I'm interviewing for a programmer position. What's the project you're working on?"

"I'd tell you, but then I'd have to kill you."

Vega grinned, but the woman kept a straight face.

"Oh, sorry, I just assumed you were kidding."

The woman smiled.

Vega kept her mouth shut. She didn't want to offend anyone before she even got the job.

"My department codes mostly mobile apps," the woman offered.

"Mobile apps? That's what Dr. Montgomery's group does. Are you in the same department?"

"Yes, we are."

Vega nodded. "Do you like it here?"

"Yes."

"I'm not sure I will."

"Why not?"

"I don't know. I'm not really a large corporation person. I've only ever worked for small companies. Not that I've had that many jobs."

The elevator bell dinged, and the doors slid open revealing a short hallway leading to a large room filled with half-wall cubicles. People typed away on computers or talked on their phones, and a few heads peeked over their walls to watch as the woman led Vega through the room and down another hallway.

"What was your last project?" the woman asked.

"I just finished an app for ThinkShop. It's called CORE."

"Oh yes. I read about that. Very impressive."

"You read about it?"

"Not only did I read the article, I made everyone in my department read it."

Vega was in shock. "Wow! Uh, I don't know what to say."

The woman simply smiled, walked toward a large office in the corner and opened the door.

"Oh. I'm sorry. I thought you were taking me to Dr. Montgomery's office?" asked Vega.

"I was. I did."

The woman dropped her pen and phone on the desk, turned and held out her hand.

"I'm Dr. Montgomery. But please, call me Astrid. We're not big on formalities here."

Vega's mouth hung open for a moment before she realized it, and with effort, she shut it and shook Astrid's hand.

"Oh! I, uh…" She was tongue-tied.

"Sorry. But I couldn't resist the opportunity to talk to you less formally before the nerves of an interview kicked in. You were nervous earlier, right?"

"Was it that obvious?"

She gave her a grin. "A little. Don't worry about it. Most people get nervous before an interview. You're not nervous anymore, though, are you?"

"No. Actually, I'm not. Thanks, I guess."

"No problem. Have a seat," Astrid said, motioning to one of the two chairs facing her desk.

Vega looked around before she sat. Astrid had a spacious office, and through a large window, she could see the Space Needle.

"Nice view."

"Thanks. Tell me more about why you're worried about fitting in here."

"Oh, that. I guess I never thought I'd work for a big company, especially not one as large as Neilmann."

"Why not?"

"If I'm being honest, it doesn't seem like they care about the little guys. It's more about golden parachutes and fat paychecks for the C-levels, you know? CEO, CFO, COO, CIO."

Astrid nodded. "I see. Drank the *all big corporations are bad* Kool-Aid, did you?"

"I've had some first-hand experience with it."

"Oh, really? Tell me about it."

Vega bit her tongue. She hadn't meant to bring any of this up, especially since she was still trying to convince herself it wasn't important anymore.

"It's really not a big deal."

"No, please. I want to know."

"Really?"

"Yes, really."

Vega sighed. "OK. My father worked for a big company for twenty years. He was planning on retiring from there, but they laid him off with only two weeks' notice. Didn't even try to place him somewhere else. And at the time, we really needed the money. He was devastated."

"What was their reasoning, if you don't mind me asking?"

"Nothing specific—just downsizing, I think. And later that year, the CEO got a gigantic bonus. That was kind of the final straw."

"I can see how that could alter your view. But you know, contrary to popular belief, not all big corporations are bad.

At Neilmann, we have a policy that no one can make over thirty times more than the lowest-paid employee."

It took Vega a second to do the math. It was still a lot of money, but not as bad as most. "Wow! I'm impressed."

"And if we do downsize, we always try to place the affected people into another area. If that's not possible, they're offered a six-month severance package to give them a bit of a buffer while they look for another job. That's what we're offering the employees of ThinkShop if we're unable to find a position here for them. Of course, the best-case scenario is to never have to lay anyone off. But that's not always feasible."

"Right."

"But of course, you won't be one of those."

"How do you know?"

"You're the creator of the CORE program, which is one of the main reasons we bought ThinkShop."

"Oh."

Astrid smiled at her surprise. "I'm getting the sense this interview is not quite what you expected."

"Not at all. But that's a good thing."

"Neilmann is a great company. Good benefits, fair pay, and you'll find as long as you get your work done on time, the bosses, meaning me in your case, pretty much leave you alone."

"Sounds too good to be true."

"I've found that people usually get more done if I just let them get on with it."

Vega nodded.

Maybe Neilmann could be her lifeline after all?

6

The interview had gone so well that Astrid told Vega the next step in the process was to meet the big boss, Ms. Katya Neilmann, president and CEO. If she'd gotten over her nerves before, they came rushing back now. Like Trent said, she thought she would have to go through multiple interviews, but she didn't expect to meet the CEO on her first one.

Leaving Astrid's office, they walked down the hall and around a corner to the other side of the building to a large reception area. As they got closer, a rich, sweet fragrance filled the air, and she saw a sharply dressed woman sitting at a sleek black desk. On it sat a clear vase of pink lilies, which Vega assumed were the source of the wonderful aroma.

The woman was typing into her computer, and Astrid waited for her to look up.

"Can I help you, Astrid?"

"No need to be so proper, Celeste. I've brought a potential new programmer from ThinkShop, Vega Swift, to see Ms.

Neilmann. I spoke to her yesterday, and she should be expecting—"

"Yes, she told me," interrupted Celeste. She pulled up the sleeve of her crisp white blouse to look at her watch. "It's only ten fifty-two. Ms. Neilmann will see her at eleven. Please have a seat."

Dr. Montgomery turned to Vega. "Good luck."

"Wait? Aren't you going in with me?"

"No. She wants to talk to you alone."

"But—"

"You'll be fine. Just tell her what you told me. Don't be surprised if she doesn't let you go without demanding you sign an offer letter."

With that, Astrid left, and Vega didn't know what to do with herself. Finally, she sat down on the soft butter-yellow couch to the right of Celeste's desk and discovered it was just as comfortable as it looked. Sitting there, twiddling her thumbs, she felt like she was back in grade school, waiting to see the principal.

Celeste went back to whatever she'd been working on at her computer, and Vega tried to look like she belonged there. She felt way out of her league and shifted in her chair, crossed and uncrossed her legs and fidgeted while she looked around at the colorful, modern art on the wall. Finally, she pulled out her phone and started flipping through her email.

At eleven o'clock on the dot, Celeste stood up.

"Ms. Neilmann will see you now."

Vega hadn't seen her check with her boss, but perhaps she was communicating with her via her computer, or maybe she just knew she was free at eleven? *Hell,* she chuckled to herself, *maybe they could read each other's minds?*

Vega took a deep breath and walked through the door.

* * *

If Vega thought Astrid's office was impressive, Ms. Neilmann's blew her away. She'd never been in such a nice executive office, but then she realized she hadn't ever been in *any* executive's office, so she had nothing to compare it to. The far wall was a never-ending pane of glass that showed a clear view of the Seattle Space Needle and, off in the corner, a glimpse of the gray-blue water of Puget Sound. Today was one of those rare days when you could see all the way across the sound to Bainbridge Island.

The office was modern, with splashes of the same yellow as the reception area seating. Two yellow leather swivel chairs faced a streamlined, light-colored wood desk. It reminded Vega of the sleek lines of Scandinavian furniture, but heftier. The same yellow leather covered four chairs and an overstuffed couch in a small conversation grouping in front of a modern, low, rectangular fireplace on the other side of the room.

A huge, brightly colored abstract painting hung above the fireplace. It was at least three feet high by six feet wide. She couldn't quite make out what it was supposed to be. *A group of women, maybe?* The smell in the air reminded her of a bright summer day—freshly cut grass and flowers. Sunlight streamed in from the windows and bounced off the light-beige walls, giving the entire room a warm and inviting glow.

Ms. Neilmann stood behind her desk. Her short, boy-cut white hair peppered with black streaks showed off the strong features of her face. She walked around to the front of the desk, and her sky-blue silk blouse glided softly against her arm when she held out her hand.

"Hello, Ms. Swift," she said. "I'm Katya Neilmann. Everyone here addresses me as Ms. Neilmann. Thank you for coming."

"Thank you for inviting me. Can I just say? Your office is," Vega couldn't think of quite the right adjective for it, "well, it's awesome."

"Thank you. I try to make it inviting. I want people to feel relaxed and comfortable. Executive offices can be intimidating."

"I guess that's true. I'm not sure, since I don't think I've ever been in one. Until now."

"No?"

"I've been working at ThinkShop since I left my residency. I guess you know that already."

"Yes, of course, but there's a lot I don't know about you. Let's get started, shall we?"

She motioned for her to sit and settled in behind her desk, pulling up the pant legs of her sharply creased gray slacks to get comfortable. Leaning forward, elbows on her desk, she clasped her hands together and looked into Vega's eyes. Ms. Neilmann's room may look warm and inviting, but suddenly Vega didn't feel so relaxed anymore.

"How did you become such a good programmer, Vega?"

"I studied."

Vega was mortified. *Why did she say it like that?* Ms. Neilmann was going to think she was rude. To her relief, Ms. Neilmann simply smiled.

"Tell me more about your programming background. What was it that got you into the field in the first place, and how do you improve and keep up with the changes in the field? As you know, it's a fast-moving technology. It's not always easy to stay on top of the latest developments."

"I've always liked computers, especially as an interface to the brain. I minored in neural computational sciences. But like you said, the field changes rapidly, and I discovered that I'd probably be more successful if I picked a specific area and focused on that. So I chose mobile applications. They're short, they usually have one or two major functions, and they're something I can write on my own, which can be rare in the programming field. Usually, you're working on a portion of code that'll fit into a larger program. Not that I don't have to make sure my code plays well with others, and of course there are a lot of different platforms to write for, but mobile apps are what I really enjoy writing. I love the thought that what I create might be in everyone's hands one day."

Vega bit her tongue to shut herself up, realizing she'd gotten on a bit of a rant.

Ms. Neilmann leaned back in her chair.

"I'm pleased you're passionate about what you do. Why did you choose neural computational sciences?"

"Originally, I wanted to be a doctor. I have a pre-med degree with a focus on neuroscience. I was in my first year of residency in neurology when I left. But I got a minor in programming, just in case."

"Just in case?"

"I was worried I might have to drop out, which is exactly what happened. So I went back to my second love, programming."

"Why did you drop out?"

"I couldn't afford it anymore."

"You couldn't get a student loan?"

"I already had a student loan. But I couldn't afford to get another one or to stay away from home as much as the residency demanded."

"Why not?" Ms. Neilmann asked, leaning forward again. "Are you ill?"

Vega realized her answer to this question might make a huge difference in her chances of being hired. *How had they gotten to this topic so quickly?* But now that they were there, she couldn't lie. If she got hired, they'd find out soon enough.

"Oh, no, it's not me. I'm fine. It's my mother. She has early-onset Alzheimer's. We're managing, but I had to drop out to take care of her."

"I'm very sorry to hear that. When was she diagnosed?"

"About five years ago."

"I've heard they've made a lot of progress with this disease. How's she doing?"

Vega had to remind herself where she was and not let her emotions get the best of her. She'd finally learned to accept everything about her mother's condition, but somehow telling this stranger everything—this potential future boss— was making her choke up. She took a deep breath and calmed herself.

"Not well. She's been deteriorating quickly in the last couple of years. She's not responding to many of the medications anymore."

"That must be hard."

"But it won't affect my work," Vega assured her. "I've been dealing with it for a long time now."

"You're her primary caregiver?"

"Yes. My father died three years ago."

"I'm so sorry. You'll be glad to know you can add your mother to your insurance plan, which kicks in three months after your start date. Assuming I hire you."

Vega's shoulders slumped. *Three months!* She struggled to focus on what Ms. Neilmann was saying.

"Where do you do your work now?"

"I work from home, in my bedroom."

"I see."

"I have a good setup there. It's more like an office with a bed in it."

"If I decide to hire you, we'll set you up in a nice space here. The project you'll be working on is too proprietary to allow work on it outside the Neilmann premises."

"OK."

"Do you know what we do here, Ms. Swift?"

"You're a neuromarketing company. You study people's reactions to ads."

"Yes. That's part of it. Specifically, we study the sensory, cognitive and emotional reactions of consumers to a product or an advertisement so we can learn why they make the decisions they do when choosing one brand over another."

Vega nodded.

"And do you know who our customers are?"

"The marketing companies who create the ads?"

"That's who pays us. But the true customer is the user—the person looking at the ad. If the data we provide the marketing companies allows them to create a more effective ad, which results in the user buying the product they advertise, then we're successful."

Vega nodded. "I understand."

"But we live in a lazy society, Ms. Swift. People don't want to do more than simply push a button on their phones and have what they want delivered right to their door, preferably before the end of that same day. They don't want to make hard decisions. Choosing between a multitude of products that look practically identical, for all they can tell from the information they glean online, is overwhelming for them. Our goal here at Neilmann is to make their decisions easier and in our clients' favor—the marketing companies who create the ads. That's a perfect shopping experience for everyone involved."

"Oh."

"I can't tell you all the details about the project you will work on due to its proprietary nature, but I'm looking for a very specific type of programmer. As I'm sure you know, application programmers are easy to find. Hell, kids in elementary school are writing phone apps these days. But what we're trying to do here is very specialized—and difficult, I might add. We need someone who is not only an application programmer but also understands the human mind. Your background in both programming and neurology is exactly what we've been looking for. And your work on the CORE program was very impressive."

"Thank you."

"It is just the type of expertise I need."

Katya got up, walked to the window and looked out, turning her back on Vega.

"We are currently number two in our industry, Ms. Swift." She turned back and looked Vega in the eye. "I expect the rollout of this product you will work on will move us to the number one spot by the end of the first quarter of next year. I'm in a hurry, Ms. Swift. This program needs to be completed and into every consumer's smart device in time for the holidays."

"Oh!"

"So, when can you start?"

7

He felt like a stalker as he sat in the car across the street and watched his wife smiling at their son Lucas, swinging on the playground swing set. Dave Byrne stroked his long red beard, a habit he had developed as soon as it had grown long enough, and thought about his life now.

I am such an idiot! I should have never told Laurie what I did.

He knew that. Now. But he wasn't sure he could have lived with himself if he hadn't. It was a catch-22. It had only been a month since he'd gotten home from the conference, but it felt like a lifetime ago. The divorce was already in progress.

Yeah, he'd had too much to drink, but that was no excuse. He remembered everything he'd done, and he had made a choice. At the time, he didn't think it was a big deal. He suspected there were several people in his office who had one-night stands when they went to out-of-town conferences. He often heard his buddies, Mike and Lamont, in the cube next to him practically brag about it. But Dave was never unfaithful in all his nine years of marriage. And he had never wanted to be. *Why would he?*

They were happy, for the most part. But he knew that if he told her he'd slept with someone else, she would kick him out of the house in a heartbeat. She would divorce him and never let him see Lucas again if she could. In her mind, infidelity was one of the worst sins you could commit in a marriage. He never thought it was something he'd have to worry about. He knew he was a lucky man. His wife may not be beautiful, but she was more of a looker than him. Just ask his mother. She'd tell you. Dave knew he was an average-looking guy with an average-paying job. He never thought he'd be able to snag a woman like Laurie.

So it shocked him, when on his last night in Orlando, Florida, a woman approached him at the bar. The conference break-out sessions were over, and he and Lamont were grabbing a beer after a group dinner. After Lamont headed upstairs and Dave was paying the tab, the woman leaned next to him and ordered a vodka on the rocks.

Then she turned to Dave and said, "Hi, there."

He looked up from signing the tab, surprised. "Hi."

"You calling it a night?"

"Yeah."

"You sure you don't want a nightcap? I... I could use someone to talk to."

It was then that Dave noticed her mascara had smeared and left splotchy dark streaks on her cheeks.

"Are you OK?"

"Why do you ask?"

"You've got some, uh…," Dave said, pointing to her cheeks.

The woman took a napkin from the bar and wiped under her eyes.

"Oops! I'm sorry. I thought I had cleaned that up. I've had a rough night."

"I'm sorry."

"Janice," she said, wadding up the napkin and placing it on the bar. She held out her hand. "I'm Janice. Hi, Dave."

Dave's mouth fell open. "How did you know my—"

The woman pulled up the badge on Dave's lanyard. "Dave Byrne, right? Or did you pilfer someone else's badge?"

"Oh, right," he said with a chuckle. "Yes, it's Dave. Nice to meet you, Janice."

She held his hand a little longer than he expected. "I've been watching you," she said.

"You have? Why?"

"I don't know. You seem like a nice guy. You should find some better company."

"What? You mean Lamont? Do you know him?"

Janice waved her hand as if swatting a bug away. "No. But I know his type. I could hear your conversation. Sorry, I didn't mean to, but he was really loud. I was sitting in a booth right by your table."

"Oh, yeah. Lamont gets a little rowdy when he drinks."

"Someone should remind him to use his inside voice."

Dave laughed. "I may have actually told him that a few times myself."

"Well, nice to meet you, Dave. Maybe I'll see you later?"

"I'm leaving tomorrow morning. Today was the last day. Conference is over."

"Oh."

Dave watched as Janice looked down and sniffled. She picked the napkin back up, wiped her nose and tried to put her hands in the pockets of her pants, finally realizing they didn't have any. She looked miserable.

"Do you want to sit with me for a minute?" Dave asked.

Janice looked up, gently pressing her lip together. "Really? That would be great. Are you sure I'm not keeping you up too late?"

"No, it's fine."

Dave led Janice over to one of the more private booths in the corner of the bar as he wondered what was going on with her and why she had picked him to talk to. After five minutes of trivial chatter, Janice broke down in tears and told him she had found out earlier that her dog had died today. The pet hotel in Apopka, Paws, called her and told her. She was devastated, but she couldn't leave. She was working as a registration clerk for one of the other hotel conferences and couldn't afford to leave. Her company didn't consider the death of a pet qualification for bereavement leave.

Dave learned she lived alone, and her dog, a Basenji named Maelstrom, was her best friend. She'd had him since she was twenty-one, buying him as soon as she moved into her first apartment, and he'd been with her ever since. At fourteen, she knew he didn't have long, but she would have never left if she thought he would die while she was gone. She was guilty and gutted.

Feeling sorry for her, Dave stayed and talked to her until after midnight. They ordered more drinks and shared more stories, and before Dave knew what was happening, they were upstairs in her room, taking off their clothes. When Dave woke up in her bed the next morning, she was already gone. But she'd left him a brief note on the nightstand, thanking him for helping her through a rough night.

He sat alone on the bed, wondering how he had let this happen. Now it was Dave who felt guilty and gutted.

8

Back home, Vega walked in, and Julia was stuffing her book in her purse, getting ready to leave.

"How did the interview go?" Julia asked.

"Actually, better than I expected," Vega said, dropping her backpack on the couch. "But I don't think I'm going to take it."

"Why not?"

"There are a few things I don't like about it."

"If you're feeling guilty about leaving your mom, you shouldn't. Especially at this stage of her illness. It's OK to get on with your life. Miren would probably tell you that if she could."

Vega nodded. She knew Julia was right, and she and the other nurses did a great job, but leaving her mom alone every day? Vega wasn't sure she was ready for that. No one could take care of her mother as well as she could. No one knew her like she did. No one *loved* her like she did.

"I know, and I really appreciate your help. If I change my mind, I'll need you a lot more. But it's not just about feeling guilty, which I do."

"Then why aren't you going to take it?"

Vega didn't really want to discuss it all with her. She hadn't figured everything out yet herself.

"It's a long story, or maybe a short one. I don't know. I have a lot to think about."

"I'm sure you'll make the right decision. I'll be off then," Julia said, wrapping her scarf around her neck and giving Miren and Vega a hug.

Back in her bedroom that evening, Vega thought through her interview at Neilmann. She was shocked when, after less than thirty minutes into the meeting, Ms. Neilmann offered her the job. The pay was great, and the project sounded interesting—at least from the little she knew about it. She was excited, but deep in her bones, she was torn. One problem was the NCA, or Non-Compete Agreement. She knew she'd have to sign one, along with a Non-Disclosure Agreement, or NDA. Companies didn't want her running off to work for a competitor and taking all of Neilmann's secrets with her, and she had signed them in the past. As a matter of fact, she'd had to sign both types of agreements to work for ThinkShop. But because she'd been a contractor and not a full-time employee, the NCA was only for six months, not three years like Neilmann's.

"These are both industry-standard forms," Ms. Neilmann had said. "But you take them home with you and read them over, of course. Feel free to have your lawyer look through them. But don't keep me waiting too long, Ms. Swift. I'm eager to get someone on board."

Three years was a long time. If for some reason she decided she hated working at Neilmann and left after a measly four months, or four days for that matter, she couldn't work for any other company with products or services similar to Neilmann Corporation's for three years. If she took the job, she'd better know damn well she wouldn't be leaving any time soon.

The final blow was the insurance. Ms. Neilmann told her it didn't kick in until three months after she started. That was an extremely long time in her mother's life. She supposed the raise in salary should make that a moot point. ThinkShop had provided insurance, but it was not very robust. Her father's life insurance payout, her mom's Social Security, and Medicaid benefits were keeping them afloat. Once Vega became a full-time employee, though—no more Medicaid. She'd be making too much money and working too many hours, and most of that extra money would go toward paying for more home-nurse care. Without Medicaid, medications and other medical supplies would cost a lot more. Even though Ms. Neilmann had really wanted an answer, Vega had put her off. For all she knew, she might not even have a job offer anymore.

She texted Trent.

Hey. You busy?

Vega waited for a reply, but impatient as ever, after about a minute she couldn't take it anymore. She sent another one.

    Where are you? I need you. Call me. Better
yet, come over.

She tossed the phone on her desk and sat back on her bed, and before she knew it, she'd dozed off.

Thump!

Vega jerked awake, immediately worried her mother was having another seizure. Then she saw it was just her phone, which had vibrated itself off the edge of her desk. She picked it up and realized the sound was still off from when she'd silenced it before her interviews. She swiped the green phone icon.

"Hey, how come you're not answering my texts? Are you OK?" asked Trent.

"Yeah, sorry. I forgot to turn the sound back on."

"What's up?"

"I need some advice. Are you free?"

"Is this about your interview? How'd it go?"

"That's why I need you. Can you come over?"

"Sorry. I have a meeting. I'm headed out right now. I should be done around seven-thirty. Want me to come over after?"

"Yes, please! Who's the meeting with?"

"Ken, the gallery owner from Tsuga. Lots of logistics to mull over."

"Oh, right. You want me to order a pizza, or is he treating you to dinner too?"

"No dinner that I know of. And yeah, pizza sounds great. You know what I like."

"OK. See you then."

"All right. Gotta run. I'm an important guy, you know."

She hung up, ordered a pizza delivery for later, opened her computer and clicked on the browser window. It popped up and displayed the latest *Seattle Times* news. The headline caught her attention.

Father, Son Dead in Apparent Murder-Suicide

Police are investigating an apparent murder-suicide at a home in the Capitol Hill area that left a father and son dead.

The police revealed that 32-year-old Ben Marshall appears to have killed his 15-year-old son, Nate, who died on the scene from multiple stab wounds while sleeping in his bed. The father then turned the knife on himself, slitting his own throat. Doctors suspect he may have had a psychotic break.

His wife, Joyce, is devastated. "He was like a crazy man," sister-in-law Shelly said, who lives with the couple. "Joyce kept telling him to go to the doctor. He'd been having headaches and visions ever since coming back from some study, but he wouldn't listen. Now look what he's done!"

The knife was found...

Vega didn't want to read any more. It was just too sad. She flipped over to the obituary page to see if she could find something more upbeat. She scanned through the postings and found one that looked interesting. Apparently, she'd written her own obituary.

Misty Dawn, Age 45

I, Misty Dawn, and yes, my parents were hippies, was born, I lived my life, and my time was up. If you don't believe what I've written here, just give me a call. Oh, sorry. I forgot. I'm dead.

My childhood was fairly typical, but I do remember some of the most interesting parts. Like the time my sisters hid secret messages all around the house on my birthday, knowing how much I would anticipate the final note that revealed where my present was—a black plastic mummy head, swinging ominously from its scraggly hair, tied to the top of our swing set in the back yard. The time my father dug out a pencil lead from the middle of my palm with his hunting knife. Of course, he had sterilized it under a flame first, so it was almost like going to the doctor. Staring lovingly at the boy who lived across the street because he had longer-than-average eye teeth, and I was obsessed with vampires at the time.

I was a sickly child, and as such, got more attention than I probably deserved, much to the chagrin of my two older sisters—which probably explains the shrunken mummy-head gift.

I had two basic philosophies in life: "Career plans are for the unimaginative," and "Surround yourself with people smarter than you, and maybe it will rub off."

I like to think I was a pretty decent human being, despite what some people may say about me. Don't listen to them. They probably just saw me on one of my bad days.

Please don't have a viewing of my dead body. I don't want a bunch of people gawking at it and talking about how fat I'd gotten. And don't bury me in the ground for the bugs to eat. If you know me, you know I don't like bugs. Burn me to cinders and scatter my ashes over some place cool. Or donate my body to science. Maybe once they cut me open and look at my insides, they'll be able to tell you why I was so weird.

Don't cry a lot, I don't want to mess up your makeup or ruin your day, but a few tears would be appreciated. Now, go live your life before you end up where I am.

Vega chuckled as she read. Some people wrote the funniest things, and every now and then, she needed something humorous in her life.

9

What had she done?

After discussing her job offer dilemma last night with Trent, she still thought it was too much of a risk. She had called Ms. Neilmann's office and told Celeste, who'd been unable to hide the surprise in her voice.

Had she made the right decision? She still didn't know. There were a lot of compromises—three months' wait before the insurance kicked in, the NCA and she would be away from home more. She wouldn't see her mom nearly as much, and she felt extremely guilty about that aspect being kind of appealing. It was getting harder and harder to watch her mother deteriorate—not only because of her decline in mental capacity but also because of the way she was changing physically. When Miren got her diagnosis, she and her dad hadn't realized how much her physical body would suffer. Vega assumed that just because she couldn't remember things, at least her body would still function correctly. Now she knew better.

Coffee. That's what she needed—and to get out of the house and quit dwelling on it. She was hoping to get a call today from a company Liam had recommended. He put in a good word for her, and the director of HR was supposed to call. She didn't need to stay home for that, and the home-care nurse was already here. She grabbed her backpack, told her mom and the nurse goodbye and jumped in the car for some *me* time.

SoulHouse Coffeeshop was her favorite place to unwind in Redmond, and as soon as she walked through the doors, the smell of coffee, tea and pastries mingled with the incense they sold, caused her shoulders to loosen and her mind to relax. The place was eclectic. Near the front door sat weathered but comfy chairs and tables. To the left, shelves of new-age books, tarot decks and crystals lined the wall with a row of hi-top tables against the windows facing the parking lot. In the middle of the space was the kitchen, and a counter where you entered your order for coffee drinks, lattes and teas, or a bite to eat from their scrumptious sandwiches and baked goods' menu. To the right, a few more tables and chairs faced a small stage for local bands, poetry nights or book readings. You could even get your fortune read here.

She walked to the counter, ordered a chai tea latte and a blueberry muffin and grabbed a hi-top by the window where she had a splendid view of people and traffic and the large maple trees planted in the parking lot.

As she sat and drank her tea, her phone began playing a clip of an old electronic song she'd discovered one day while perusing the internet, "Tiny Geometries" by Ray Lynch. When she heard that tune, it meant the caller was not in her contact list. *Probably some marketer*, she thought. She checked the area code—425. It was local. Hoping it was the HR person from the company Liam told her about, she took a chance and answered.

"Hello?"

"Hi, Vega?"

"Yes, who's this?"

"It's Astrid."

"Oh."

"Yeah, remember me? The woman who thought she was going to be your boss soon?"

"Yes. Hi."

"You turned the job down?"

"Yeah."

"Can I ask why?"

"Sure. There are several reasons. The NCA, the insurance and the time away from my mother."

"What do you mean, time away from your mother?"

"Oh, I guess I didn't tell you. She has Alzheimer's. I live at home so I can take care of her."

"Why didn't you tell me during your interview?"

"I guess I was afraid it would impact my chances of getting the job."

"Why's that?"

"Because I may have to leave early, or I might be late a lot."

"It seems your mother's condition would be a reason for you to take this job, not refuse it. That seems contradictory. You would have a steadier, larger salary, right? And we have great insurance."

"Yeah, but your insurance doesn't kick in for three months, and I'll lose my Medicaid as soon as I take the job. I'll be making too much money and working too many hours."

"Did you tell Ms. Neilmann about your situation?"

"Yes."

"I'm surprised she didn't offer you a flexible schedule."

"She told me she doesn't want me working on the project outside of Neilmann. She said it's a security risk."

"She's right, but I can work with you on your schedule."

"OK, but what about the insurance?"

"Don't worry about it. We waive that waiting period all the time, especially at the level you'll be coming in at. None of the upper-management people waited that long for their insurance to kick in."

"Why didn't she tell me that?"

"That doesn't mean she won't try to save Neilmann the cost of three months of insurance if she can get away with it."

"You mean if someone's stupid enough not to ask for it to be waived?"

"That's not exactly what I said."

"Well, that's a relief. But there's still the issue with the NCA."

"What's the issue?"

"What if I don't like it there? What if I get fired? What if I can't stay because it doesn't work out with my mom? I won't be able to get a good job for years!"

"You could have just asked for a modification to the NCA so it would suit your situation better. Plus, if you do have to leave, I can help you through that problem."

"I can do that? Ask for the NCA to be changed?"

"Sure. Those things are just boilerplates. Most people never sign them the way they are. I can't take out anything about sharing Neilmann's proprietary information, of course."

"I wouldn't expect that. But it never dawned on me to ask for changes. I can't believe I didn't know."

"So, you'll take the job?"

"What do I need to do to change the agreements?"

"What are you doing right now?"

"Uh."

"Come to my office. We'll work on them together, get the papers signed, and get things rolling."

"OK. Thank you!"

"Text me when you arrive, and I'll meet you in the lobby."

Astrid hung up. Vega was stunned.

That was crazy!

She couldn't believe Astrid had called her. She felt like a doofus for not realizing she could ask for modifications.

Now that she knew how badly they wanted her, she wasn't just going to ask for changes to the NCA and insurance—she was going to ask for a lot more money.

10

It was her first day at her new job, and when Vega pulled on to Pine Street and saw Neilmann Corporation, she still couldn't believe she was going to work there. She looked at the building and had to admit it was beautiful.

The architecture was modern and artistic, with lots of glass and rich wooden accents. Originally, the structure had been the headquarters of a huge retail chain, but with the proliferation of online sales, large brick-and-mortar stores were becoming obsolete. The company had gone bankrupt and abandoned the building, which had sat empty for several years until Neilmann Corporation moved in.

She had received several informational emails after signing her offer letter, so she knew she had an assigned parking spot. Finding it in the underground garage, she pulled in and made her way to one of the first-floor conference rooms.

After four hours spent learning about benefit packages, getting her picture taken for her badge and setting up her ID and password for the Neilmann intranet, the hiring managers entered the room and took over responsibility for their charges.

"What do you think?" asked Astrid, as Vega picked up the piles of informational handouts and stuffed them in her backpack. "Are you still glad you decided to join us?"

"My brain is in overload. I'll never remember everything."

Astrid gave her a grin. "Don't worry. You won't have to. Most of it is online, and what's not, you probably don't need to remember anyway."

Vega nodded. "That's good to know."

"Ready to see your office?"

"I have an office?"

Dr. Montgomery smiled and guided her to the elevator and pushed the button for the twenty-third floor.

"You'll see."

The doors parted, and Astrid led her down the hall and stopped in front of a door to one of the smaller offices.

"This is you."

"Really?"

"Has a door and everything."

"Nice!"

Vega never expected to get an actual office. She assumed she'd be in one of the half-wall cubicles they had passed earlier. But it wasn't completely closed off. Her door was all glass, so it would be hard to get away with playing solitaire all day—not that she would ever do that. But still—nice digs, and she enjoyed being by herself. She was used to working alone.

"Why aren't I out there with everyone else?"

"They're first-levels," Astrid said. "You're a senior programmer. Besides, everyone on the MYND project has their own office. Ms. Neilmann wants us all to be heads-down working, focusing on nothing but getting this project completed in time for the holiday rollout. She's worried you'll get distracted if you're out there in the jungle. Neilmann has a lot riding on this."

"I see."

"If we succeed, I mean *when* we succeed, it will be a game-changer. So, less distraction, more concentration. That's our motto."

"Sounds good to me."

Vega looked around her office and saw a landline phone on the desk. "People still use these things?"

Astrid chuckled. "It's obvious you haven't worked in a real office in a long time. Everyone does. Cell phone signals can be hijacked and information stolen. Landlines are also more reliable inside buildings. Plus, your battery won't ever die on you."

"Oh. I guess I never thought about all that." Then she looked up and saw the Space Needle from her window. She was so blown away by having an office to begin with, she hadn't even noticed.

"Holy cow! I can see the Space Needle."

"Yeah, we definitely have the best side of the building. Don't get too excited, though. Most of the time, it's so foggy you can barely see it."

"This is great! I thought I'd have to climb the ranks before I got a space like this."

"We're very impressed with the job you did over at ThinkShop. I know I was. Ms. Neilmann has big plans for you."

"Yeah?"

"Of course. You wouldn't be on the MYND project otherwise, and you'd be out there slugging your way through the bog with the rest of them."

The company provided MacBook they told her about in orientation, sat on her desk.

"Go ahead," Astrid said. "Sit down and log in. I want to make sure your ID and password are working. Then I'll give you a tour."

Vega sat down, flipped up the lid and turned on the computer. When she entered her ID and password, the login took her straight to the intranet homepage of Neilmann.

"I'm in," she said, as she started to search around on the website.

"You'll have plenty of time for that later. How about some lunch, and then I'll show you around?"

"OK." She shut the lid of her laptop and slung her backpack over her shoulder.

"No need to bring that if you don't want to. Your office door locks."

"Oh, OK. Let me just get some money," she said, digging for her wallet.

"Don't worry about it. This one's on me."

"Are you sure?"

"Absolutely. My treat. It is your first day."

Vega had pigged out on a luscious cinnamon roll from the breakfast bar at orientation, but she realized she was already hungry. She wondered if being nervous made her hungrier than normal. Not comfortable leaving her backpack on top of her desk, she dropped it in one of the larger bottom drawers and followed Astrid out of her office.

"Don't forget to lock the door," Astrid reminded her.

"Have you ever had things stolen here?"

"Not that I know of. And they wouldn't want *your* stuff. They'd want what they could get at through your computer."

"We shouldn't even trust the people who work here?"

"I hope so. But some of our programs and data are extremely valuable. Our competitors might pay someone a lot of money to steal it."

"Has that ever happened?"

"Not yet. But you get an unhappy employee, for whatever reason, and you never know. And your access level is higher than most."

"So they would break in through my computer and steal it from the cloud?"

"They would try, I'm sure. But we've got some extensive firewalls, and they're monitored constantly."

Vega nodded. "Where's my k—"

Astrid pointed to the door. The key was in the lock.

"Thanks."

"No problem. Come on. I hope you're hungry."

"I have to warn you, I'm not really a big lunch eater. Usually I work right through and later realize how hungry I am."

"I bet I'm going to change your mind about that."

* * *

Vega followed Astrid to the first floor, and as they walked down the hall toward the lobby, they passed several conference rooms. In one, she saw a man talking to a large group. He caught her eye and smiled. She smiled back.

"What's going on in there?"

"It's a focus group session. That's Drexel Hicks, the senior manager of client development, and his assistant, Daphne Hart. You'll be working with them once your program is ready for user testing. You'll meet them later."

"I thought it was top secret, but they're right here where anyone walking by can see them."

"The device isn't a secret. We've been using it for a few years now for our neuromarketing studies. But they run the tests in the labs in the lower level. That's just an orientation presentation for the focus group."

"Oh. Where are we going for lunch?"

"The cafeteria."

Vega groaned before she could stop herself. *Cafeteria food, really? That was the best Dr. Montgomery could do?*

Astrid heard her but simply smiled as she pushed open the door at the back of the first floor and walked inside. When Vega followed her in, she stopped dead in her tracks.

"Holy cow!"

"Right? Is this a cafeteria or what?"

Vega looked around. The place was enormous. She had never seen such a nice cafeteria in her life. The potpourri of aromas wafted around her—the tangy smell of fresh greens, the rich fragrance of cheesy pizza, and the meaty scent and sizzling sounds of a hamburger grill. The room was packed with noisy, hungry people. Lunchtime was in full swing.

There was a sushi bar, a gigantic salad bar and a section called *Flame*, where the grilled and fried food smells originated. The options blew her away, and everything looked fresh and delicious. Different ethnic dishes, vegetarian offerings and breakfast or lunch selections were available, and bowls of fresh fruit sat in the middle of each table.

"How do they know how much fruit you've had?"

"Doesn't matter."

"What do you mean?"

"It's free."

"Everything?"

"No, not everything. Just the fruit. I think they're trying to tell us something. But everything else is really inexpensive. I'm sure the company must subsidize the food vendors. I've never paid much for a meal, and I can eat a lot of food."

"Wow! I should have counted this benefit in with my salary."

"It's definitely a great perk."

But the section that really got Vega going was the bakery. The wonderful yeasty aroma wafted its way toward her as they made their way around the room. She looked at Astrid.

"See. Not your normal cafeteria, is it?" asked Astrid.

"Not at all. Sorry I groaned. It's certainly not what I expected. It's going to be hard to choose."

Tempted to have another cinnamon roll, Vega gave up the idea and took the healthier option instead, deciding on a turkey sandwich and a fresh salad. Astrid zeroed in on the grill area and got a burger and fries. It was all delicious.

After eating, they discarded their trays and came back out to the lobby. Astrid pointed to a set of double doors on the opposite side. "That's the theater. We have our company meetings there. Oh, and they bring in motivational speakers all the time. So if you're into that, that's where they'll be."

They got on the elevator, and Astrid pressed the button for the twentieth floor. "Next stop, the Zen room."

"Sounds like a place to meditate."

"You're close. It's a place where you can go and relax. You know, sometimes you can get in your own way when you're trying to work out a problem. Or maybe you're just having a bad day. So they built a couple of zen rooms so people can chill out and hopefully go back to their desks refreshed and ready to pump out more code or be more productive at whatever they're doing."

The air felt different as soon as they entered the Zen room —more humid, but not uncomfortably sticky. She heard a trickling sound. There were actual trees, picnic tables and benches, and a few beanbag chairs scattered haphazardly around the space. A few feet in, underneath the trees, she saw a meandering, man-made stream running through the room. Now she knew where the trickling sound came from.

"How did they get a stream in here?"

"It's like a continuous water fountain. They reuse the water over and over, and it gets filtered after every pass. The cleaning crew cleans the filters and tops the tank when necessary."

"That is so cool."

The sky-blue ceiling, walls of mottled shades of green, and lighting from large overhead globes covered in a soft white material set the mood of an outdoor park. Illuminated further by light from a full wall of windows, she saw the streets of downtown and all the way to the sound.

Astrid noticed her looking and said, "The windows have a film on them. From outside, it's a mirror."

"This is crazy awesome. I feel like I'm outside."

"There's another one on the second floor near a lot of other fun stuff like the child care and pet care centers."

"I guess I didn't know what I'd been missing out on by not working for a large corporation. I always thought of them as small, boring, gray office spaces. Of course, I've heard of the amazing Google offices, but I didn't realize Neilmann was in that category. I think I could come up with a lot of good ideas in here."

"That's what they were hoping for when they built the rooms. But we're not through yet."

"I can't imagine."

Dr. Montgomery smiled. "I know."

Farther down the hall, Astrid took Vega through a door labeled *Game Den*. The yellow walls, decorated with bright posters of Warhol dogs and soda cans, immediately made her smile. Large, cushioned, comfy-looking chairs, settees and couches filled the room. They looked so inviting that Vega almost sat down, but then she saw the games. Where there wasn't a chair, there was a game—billiards, foosball, air hockey, pinball machines, card tables—it was a game-player's paradise.

"Air hockey?" she asked.

"I know," said Astrid. "Who knew that still existed, right?"

"But you know what I don't see."

"What's that?"

"Gaming consoles."

"They do want you to go back to work eventually. If there were gaming consoles, no one would ever leave. No RPGs or time-consuming games like Monopoly either."

"RPGs?"

"Role-playing games."

"Oh."

"They all take too long. Hard to tear yourself away."

"Good point." She plopped down on a huge, overstuffed couch covered with a material of vibrant, abstract cats. Astrid dropped beside her.

"As it is, I'm not sure I'll ever want to go home!" Vega exclaimed.

"I think that's another point of all these amenities. The company wants you to stay here as much as possible. There's also a dry-cleaning service and a drugstore."

"No reason to go home."

"Exactly. Had enough, yet?"

"I'm not sure I can take any more."

"Yeah, but I saved the best for last."

"Really? I don't know how it could get much better. I think I'm going to like it here."

"I might advise you to hold that opinion until you get the specifications and deadline for your project."

"I've had some tight schedules before. Just because I worked for a small company doesn't mean I didn't have unreasonable deadlines."

"I wasn't implying anything."

"Sorry, I can get a little defensive sometimes."

"I noticed."

"What's this last place you're going to show me? Or is it not a place?"

"Yes, it's a place. I could keep going, but we can visit the gym and pool later."

"There's a pool?"

"Yeah. By the way, do you have any pets?"

"No."

"Well, if you ever get one, you know you can bring your pet to work if you want to? As long as it's well trained."

"I think I remember them saying that in the orientation, but I don't have time for a pet."

"That's OK. In your case, I think you'll find this last stop more interesting than anything else I've shown you."

11

Back in the elevator, Dr. Montgomery pushed the button for LL.

"Going down to the dungeon?" asked Vega. "Is that where the mad-science experiments take place?"

"You'd be surprised."

"What's in the lower level?"

"It's where we do our testing. When Neilmann first began, we took EEG measurements from bulky caps placed on the head with electrodes and wires leading to the electroencephalogram machine. I'm sure you remember those."

Vega nodded.

"People thought it looked a bit creepy, so we didn't want it to be visible to the other employees or visitors and hid everything in the basement. It also has the extra benefit of being a Faraday Cage. Helps to block any disrupting signals."

"The entire basement?"

"Yes."

"I guess that makes sense."

Vega tried to relax, but her mind was going a million miles an hour, and she was a bit jacked up. The coffee she'd had before she left for work, all the sugar in the yummy cinnamon roll and the caffeine from the soda she drank while in the game den were making it hard to stay chill.

The elevator dinged their arrival, and they walked into a small foyer with two choices—back on the elevator or through a door in front of them. On the door was a white plaque with black lettering that read, *Labs*. To the right of the door were a speaker, a palm reader and a black plastic eyecup. Astrid placed her hand on the reader and put her right eye in the cup.

After a few seconds, the computer announced, "Unknown visitor," accompanied by a high-frequency beep.

Astrid smiled. "Oops. Let's try that again."

The second time, the voice said, "Welcome, Dr. Montgomery," and the door clicked open.

"Sorry about that." She laughed off the failure. "Maybe my eyes are too bloodshot today?"

"What if you couldn't get in?"

"Call security. There are ways around it. But if I told you —"

"I know. You'd have to kill me?"

"There's a lot of very sensitive equipment in here, not to mention software. Our consumer test labs and our product testing labs are all down here. You need a special security clearance to get in, unless you're volunteering for one of the tests. But then you're accompanied by an employee. I hope they took your palm, iris and voice print at orientation."

"Yes. I was wondering why everyone didn't have to do that."

"This is why. Most employees don't even know what's down here."

Through the door, a long hallway stretched before them, bathed in a soft-blue glow emanating from recessed lighting in the ceiling.

"What's with the blue lighting?" Vega asked.

"Believe it or not, there have been scientific studies that prove a pale robin's-egg blue color has the most calming effect on humans. We have a lot of volunteers we work with, so we wanted this environment to be as relaxing as possible."

"Why not just paint the walls blue?"

"I know it's hard to tell, but they are painted blue."

Vega put her hand on the wall, but it didn't help. Everything had a blue tint to it. She wouldn't want to look at herself in a mirror right now.

Astrid walked past a door on the right labelled COMA-1.

"What's COMA stand for?"

"Consumer assessment. It's an inside joke. A nod to Robin Cook's novel."

"Oh! Funny."

"It's one of the rooms where we do our focus group testing. But we're going into the observation room first."

Vega followed her into a room, one door down. Several computers and monitors sat on a long table facing a large window on the right wall. It reminded her of movies where cops stand in a room looking through a one-way mirror at a suspect being interrogated on the other side.

"Is that a one-way mirror?"

"Yes. Just like in the movies."

In the COMA testing room, on the other side of the window, were two rows of cubicles filled with people looking at phones and tablets. Each person had a slim, white plastic headband around the top of their head. A man and woman were walking around the room, stopping at each cubicle to talk to the participants. She recognized them as the same people she'd seen earlier in the conference room.

"Those are the MYND headbands, right?"

"Yes. That's our latest version, 4.0. Drexel and Daphne are running a test to check consumers' reactions to some of our customers' ads."

"What does the acronym stand for again? I saw it in my documentation, but I can't remember now."

"It's M-Y-N-D. It stands for Marketing Y-bit Neuro Disseminator. You'll read about it in the package I've prepared for you. Sorry I had to wait for your first day to share it, but I couldn't give you anything ahead of time. Proprietary, as you can imagine."

"Of course."

"Dr. Ryker Fedorov, whom you'll meet later, invented it. Like I said earlier, we used to use the EEG caps, but we needed finer details about specific areas of the brain. We didn't need an entire brain scan. And besides, they were clumsy and time-consuming to set up. So Ryker engineered the headband. He's a genius, if you ask me."

"But haven't those types of headbands existed for years? Like the ZONE and the Focus?"

"Similar headbands have been around, yes. But they either try to measure absolutely everything or focus mostly on the prefrontal cortex and the alpha waves—the conscious relaxation regions of the brain. And they don't provide the level of detail we need. Dr. Fedorov perfected the technology for Neilmann. The MYND headband provides more exacting details of the brain waves in the areas we are most interested in. The ZONE came the closest. Ryker invented that one, too. But I think I'll let him tell you how that worked out."

"Oh, OK."

Vega looked around the room. On the opposite wall was a bank of upper and lower cabinets. A coffee maker with a box of sugar, sweeteners and some stir sticks and creamers sat near a sink in the middle of the lower cabinets.

"What's in the cabinets?"

"Oh, just miscellaneous stuff. Coffee cups, paper plates, paper towels, stuff like that. Some of us are too lazy to go to the break room."

Vega opened one of the drawers and saw medical supplies —cotton swabs, alcohol wipes, syringes, bandages and other paraphernalia.

"What are these for?"

Astrid shut the drawer. "Oh, just a few medical supplies."

It seemed strange, but maybe it was some kind of OSHA requirement. Vega looked back at the volunteers.

"Do you ever have to adjust the headband?"

"Sure. There's an interface on the computer, and Drexel and Daphne have the same app on their phones, so they can tweak the headband parameters, turn it on and off, yada, yada, yada."

"How is the headband communicating with the app? Bluetooth?"

"Yes."

"What's everyone looking at?"

"Those are Neilmann-supplied smartphones and tablets. They're connected to the Neilmann intranet. We have an extensive set of fake sites they can surf. To them, hopefully, it looks just like a smaller version of the internet. We're controlling the ads they see as they surf."

"How do you do that?"

"Through the interface to the Neilmann cloud," Astrid said, pointing to the computer and large monitors on the table. "Drexel periodically changes what ads the subjects see on their screens. Then the headband collects their brain wave information as they respond to the ads and sends the data back to the cloud. The smart devices collect some basic biometric data like heart rate and track their eye movement. There's another testing lab and observation room across the hall, and a couple of smaller rooms, CRT-1 and 2, for individual testing."

"Why would you need to do that?"

"Depends on the types of measurements our customer wants. Let's say they really want to see how females react to certain ads. Maybe even narrow it down further by females from different age groups and or ethnicities? They might want to test them individually and compare the results. We've also determined that people's decisions are often influenced by who is with them in the room."

"Really? Why do you think that is?"

"We're not sure. None of the subjects will admit it affected their decisions, but when we compared the data, it's obvious it did. We think they were worried other people in the room might judge them for what they surfed for or whether a specific ad had caught their attention."

"Why not only do individual testing, then?"

"It takes a lot more time and money to test one person at a time. Some companies don't think it's worth it."

"But they can't see each other in those cubicles, right?"

"We've tried to give them as much privacy as we can without building separate rooms for everybody. But that doesn't seem to matter. All it takes is other people in the room with them."

"Interesting. What's next?"

"I need a caffeine boost. How about you?"

Vega followed Dr. Montgomery out and down to the other end of the hall, into a break room. She eyed the coffee pot and shook her head. She was still flying. Astrid helped herself to a cup and sat at one of the tables.

"No coffee?"

"No thanks. But I wouldn't mind a water."

"In the fridge. Help yourself."

Vega opened a small refrigerator. Filled with sodas, fruit juices, bubbly and flat waters and various types of milks and energy drinks, she grabbed a bottle of boring flat water and sat down across from Astrid.

"Where do I pay?"

"It's all free."

"Wow, OK."

She took a sip and thought about what she'd seen.

"How do the MYND devices work?"

"That's something you'll learn from Dr. Fedorov. You'll be working closely with him."

Vega nodded and took another drink when a stocky man with dark brown hair and a full beard came into the room. A taller, more slender man followed him in, and Vega recognized him as the guy who had been leading the focus group orientation. The bearded man ran his hand through his hair, focused intently on his tablet.

"Looking at the latest stats, Doc?" asked Astrid. "Hey, Drexel."

So engrossed the doctor hadn't noticed them, he jerked his head up and almost dropped his tablet. Drexel walked up to stand beside him.

"Huh? Oh, yes. Sorry. We're just looking over some test results."

"Hi, Astrid," said Drexel.

"Dr. Ryker Fedorov, Drexel, this is Vega Swift, the new senior programmer we just hired."

Drexel leaned forward and shook her hand. "Drexel Hicks. Nice to meet you."

"Thanks."

Dr. Fedorov glanced at Vega, then over at Astrid. "The CORE programmer?"

"That's right."

Ryker slowly looked Vega up and down.

"I see."

"Nice to meet you," Vega said, holding out her hand. For a moment, she didn't think he would take it. Finally, he tilted his chin up, grunted and gave her a weak handshake.

"I was going to call you after I looked over these test results," Ryker told Astrid. "I read Ms. Neilmann's email last night saying someone new came on board from ThinkShop." Ryker turned to Vega. "Hope you're prepared to work some long hours."

"I, uh—"

"Don't let him scare you off on your first day," said Drexel.

"We have a deadline," said Fedorov.

Astrid raised her eyebrows at him, and he added, "But I'm sure Astrid will make sure I don't work you too hard. I guess everyone needs to sleep now and then."

"That's good to know," Vega said.

Astrid shrugged him off. "He's really a nice guy once you get to know him."

Ryker ignored her. "Have you gotten your security clearance yet, Ms. Swift?"

"Yes, I think so, but I haven't tried it out yet."

"I'm sure it's gone through by now," said Astrid. "I should have let you try it out earlier. No worries, though. We'll do it later."

Dr. Fedorov turned and left, and Drexel said, "Guess I'll see you around. Welcome to the team," then followed Ryker out.

Astrid stood up. "Are you ready to get down to the nuts and bolts of what you'll be doing here?"

12

It had been a long first day. Vega was beat, and the long, slow, tedious drive home was making her even more tired. It would not be fun commuting to work, but as she pulled into her driveway and looked at her little house, she smiled. It was good to be home.

It wasn't a large house. In fact, it was the smallest and least expensive house in the Spring Lake community. Vega wasn't positive, but she thought it was one of the first homes built in the area. Then a developer decided they could make a lot of money by building more. She liked their little house, perhaps even more because it was the runt of the lot, even if it did have a few bad memories.

It was a cute two-story, with a little over two thousand square feet. In the back yard, her mother used to keep a garden—half of it filled with flowers and half with vegetables. When she got too sick to take care of it, Vega had let it go to ground, and now the small garden shed in the back was full of neglected tools. She had not inherited her mother's green thumb and didn't have time to deal with it.

Surrounded by trees on all sides, the house was situated off 248th Avenue Northeast, east of Peterson Pond and just west of Patterson Creek. If she walked to the edge of her back yard and peeked between the trees, she could see the creek. The closest neighbor was only four hundred feet away, but felt much farther, because she could only see their house from the main road.

The white frame home was accented with a blue tin roof, and when it rained, which it did often, she loved listening to the sound of the raindrops plinking on the roof. She often stayed awake at night just to hear the rain. It was a mystery to her how people could live in places like Phoenix or San Diego, where it rarely rained. She would be miserable.

One of her favorite memories as a young child was when her parents bought the house. Her mother loved it—set off in the woods in the outskirts of Redmond. Vega remembered running upstairs, seeing her room for the first time and playing on the swing set in the back yard. But her clearest memory of that day was when her dad Cyrus had taken Miren in his arms, swung her around and kissed her in the front yard. They had been so happy then.

They used to be in love. Whenever Vega felt sad about her life, or about her mother's illness, she tried to remember those days. Lucky for her, her dad brought in good money then, and made a huge down payment on the house. So even though things were extremely tight now, at least the mortgage payment was low.

Vega's head was swimming. She hadn't thought her first day would be so jam-packed and was a little worried about living up to the high expectations everyone seemed to have of her. She'd read through the specs Astrid had sent her and talked with her about the crux of the job on the MYND project team. It was easy enough to grasp, but she had a lot to learn about how the headband gathered data and how it married that data with the current smart devices' biometric information.

Ideas were swirling around in her head as she opened the front door at six twenty-nine. She had cut it close. Too close. The nurse was supposed to leave at six-thirty. She wasn't sure if this new schedule would work. With her higher salary, she could afford to pay the nurses to come in daily, and then she would take over after work. She could tell it was going to be exhausting, and it was only the first day.

When she walked in the door, the nurse was rolling her mother's wheelchair into the living room.

"Hey," Vega said.

The nurse looked up and her wearied expression said it all. It had not been a good day.

"Your mom went for a little swim today," said Danielle.

"What?"

"She was swimming in her bed. Thought she was back at some old apartment complex in the pool. I caught her doing some overhead strokes."

"That is really weird. She rarely moves much at all," Vega said.

"She was probably hallucinating. I think she has a UTI again, so I've started her on an antibiotic. I left the pills on the pass-through."

"Is that normal? To have hallucinations from a UTI?"

"Yes, strangely enough, it is. She's also had a couple of muscle spasms today. She's just not moving enough. It's to be expected at this stage."

Miren looked up and said, "Honey?"

Excited to hear her talk, Vega ran over to her. "Mom?"

"Ethel? Where's Theo?"

Vega sighed. "It's me, mom, Vega, your daughter."

"Where's Theo?"

Ethel and Theo were Miren's parents, and had been gone for years now. Vega tried not to be disappointed. At least her mom had said something.

"Theo's not here, Mom."

Her mother looked away, and Vega swore she could see her eyes glaze over as she went back inside her inner world. The brief glimpse of awareness had passed.

Danielle started packing her things and said, "You should really look into putting her into a long-term care facility. She's not going to get any better. I know you want what's best for her. It's just going to keep getting harder for you to do this alone."

"I'm not alone. I have you."

"You know what I mean."

She nodded. "Thanks, Danielle. I'll think about it. Really."

Vega knew she was right, but she couldn't afford it—not any place nice, anyway. At least not yet. Even though she hoped this new higher, steadier income from Neilmann would eventually let her, the thought of moving her mother to a long-term care facility felt like she was putting her out to pasture to die. She didn't know if she was ready to live with that decision.

13

The traffic wasn't nearly as bad today as Vega travelled into Seattle for her second day of work. The smoke-filled, orange-tinted sky from wildfires burning in British Columbia hung heavy—the northerly breeze pushing it down into Seattle. Vega could smell it in the air, even down in the Neilmann garage. Smoke was becoming a normal summer occurrence, making her glad her father had insisted on adding air conditioning to the house many years ago, thinking simply to increase the resell value. They rarely turned it on at first, but over the last ten years, it came on more and more during late summer because of heat and smoke.

She shook off the sad thoughts and unlocked her office door, still surprised it was hers. Today she had a meeting with Dr. Fedorov to dive into the guts of the MYND headband and learn more about the project. She had spent several hours yesterday reading the project specifications, but there was more to get through. She opened the file and started reading.

Absorbed in the document, she jumped when she heard him knock on her door. She checked the time on her computer and saw it was already ten o'clock, surprised two hours had already flown by. She motioned him in.

"Ready to begin, Ms. Swift?"

"Yes. Morning, Dr. Fedorov. Please, call me Vega. I'm ready. Just been reading more of the MYND headband specs. I have a lot of questions."

"Good. Good. But I've made some notes since I wrote the documents you're probably reading."

He handed her a file folder with several printed documents in it. She flipped through and saw lots of handwritten notes in the margins and inside the paragraphs.

"You hand-wrote your changes?"

"I'll have Daphne enter them into the computer later. Jotted down a few notes I hope will clarify some things for you, Ms. Swift. I much prefer to write rather than type. Ready to go to the lab so I can show you around?"

"Sure, Dr. Fedorov," she said, guessing if he wasn't ready to get less formal, maybe she shouldn't be either. "I was wondering about the MYND acronym?"

"I thought you said you read the specifications? Take out the documents."

Vega pulled the pages out of the folder, and he reached in the front pocket of his white button-down shirt and took out a pen. It was beautiful. The barrel was a swirl of marbled deep blues and flashes of deep red and yellow. He uncapped it, revealing a flourished gold and silver nib, and Vega realized it was a fountain pen.

"You write with a fountain pen? I didn't know people still used those."

Ryker shook his head with a smirk on his face. "Lots of people use them. They're much nicer to write with than most other pens."

"Wouldn't it be easier and quicker to just type everything into the computer?"

He snorted. "It's all about the experience, Ms. Swift. Here."

He put the cap back on the pen and handed it to her. "Take a close look. It's a Visconti Van Gogh, in the color Starry Night."

When she looked closer, she could appreciate the swirling mix of colors even more. "Oh! I see. It has the same colors as the painting. What are those things called?" she asked, pointing to the cut of the barrel.

"Facets."

"Right, facets. It's gorgeous."

"You can try it if you like."

"Oh, no. That's OK. It looks expensive," she said, trying to hand it back. "I don't want to break it."

He pushed the pen back to her. "Please. I want you to appreciate the ink as well. I've filled it with a Troublemaker ink called Starry Night Blue."

"Troublemaker. That's a cool name."

She hesitated, but took the pen back. She knew nothing about fountain pens, but she wouldn't mind having one like this on her desk, just to admire it.

"Uh. How do I open it?"

"It's a magnetic seal. Simply pull on the cap. Gently."

Vega pulled off the cap, and Dr. Fedorov flipped the front page of the document to the blank back side.

"Go ahead. Write something."

Not knowing what to write, she finally simply signed her name.

"No, no," he chastised her. "There's no need to press down so hard. It's not a ballpoint. Try again."

This time, Vega wrote with a lighter hand, and the pen flowed like butter across the page.

"Oh! I see what you mean. It feels wonderful."

"Of course it does. Now look at the ink in the light."

Vega held up the paper and turned it towards the overhead light.

"Very nice! It has gold sparkles. And it's a deep blue. I thought it was black. Does it have red in it, too?"

"It has a red sheen."

"It's beautiful."

Ryker smiled. He took back the pen, flipped the document right side up, and underlined the title at the top of the page. "M-Y-N-D. Marketing Y-bit Neuro Disseminator. Have you forgotten already?"

"No, I know what it stands for. But isn't it a gatherer of information rather than a disseminator?"

"Yes, it is a data collector. To gauge user reactions to ads. We used to use the clumsy EEG caps, but my invention is much less cumbersome and provides more detailed information."

Vega realized he had dodged her question, but she let it slide for now.

"How can you tell how well the ads are doing?"

"The brain expends only two percent of its energy on conscious activity, which means it uses ninety-eight percent of its processing power doing things we are unconscious of. The MYND headband measures the five brain waves, which I'm sure you're familiar with—delta, theta, alpha, beta and gamma—but it focuses in fine detail on the beta waves, which are most active during decision-making and analytical problem-solving, and gamma waves, which are associated with heightened perception. It's looking for indications that the user is engaged and observing. I didn't bother collecting the minutiae of the neural oscillation data from every region of the brain. That would be a waste of energy and would bombard us with useless data. We also take data from the frontal and prefrontal cortex and the hippocampus. These areas are also involved in the decision-making process."

"Are you using a specific EEG electrode pattern? I mean, I know you're not using electrodes, but…"

"Yes, I'm mimicking the 10-20 pattern as much as possible. Of course, I'm restricted by the physical shape and area covered by the headband."

"How do you know when these regions are not in their normal state?"

"The headband takes baseline measurements when the participants first come in. But no one is going to wear headgear all day while they're surfing on their phones or tablets, so the next phase is to replace the headband with an application. And that is where you come in, Ms. Swift."

"Oh, OK."

"Your job is to create a program that collects the same data, directly from consumers, without the hardware."

"You want me to eliminate the headband?"

"Yes."

Vega didn't think Ryker looked all too happy about this idea. It was, after all, his baby. "That's quite a challenge."

"I guess neither Astrid nor Ms. Neilmann revealed this in your interview."

"Ms. Neilmann did say I was going to be working on a project that would gather data via smartphones and tablets, similar to my CORE app. But she wasn't very specific. She said she couldn't share the proprietary information with me until my first day at work, and she was leaving that to Astrid, and I guess, you."

He nodded in understanding. "Well, then. Let's get down into a bit more detail, shall we?"

"Sure."

With that, Dr. Fedorov got up, tucked his pen back in his

shirt pocket, and headed down the hall to the elevator, and Vega rushed to keep up with his long strides.

* * *

Once on the basement level, Ryker insisted she try out the palm reader and eyecup for herself, and it worked flawlessly. They walked down the hall past the two COMA labs, and he unlocked a door on the left labelled Engineering Lab.

"This is the engineer testing lab. Did Astrid show you this yesterday?"

"No. She just showed me one of the COMA labs and an observation room."

The room was small, separated by half-wall dividers. He pointed to an empty desk in the back corner behind one of the half-walls. "You can have that spot. I'm at this one," he said, sitting at the front desk.

"You will perform any tests with the MYND headband or app here in the lab. And all the focus group trials get done down here. It's a very proprietary technology. Anything you test down here is safe from hackers. The whole basement is basically a Faraday Cage."

"Yes, Astrid told me. Keeps the signals from going out or coming in. So, every time I test my program, I have to come down here?"

"Not for small tests like compilation error checks, but if you are running the program, connecting to the brain, or the intranet, then yes. There are no exceptions. Also, all the vendor smart device hardware interfaces are down here. And you'll need to test your program across all the different platforms."

Vega nodded. "I see."

Ryker sat at his desk and motioned for her to roll a chair up beside him. He pulled a MYND headband from a drawer and snapped open the cover, revealing the electronics inside.

"I didn't know Neilmann was in the business of creating their own hardware," Vega said. "Astrid told me you also invented the ZONE headband. That's impressive. It's one of the highest-selling meditation bands on the market, isn't it? Why aren't you still at that company?"

"I am."

"What do you mean?"

"Neilmann bought ZONE five years ago. Ms. Neilmann wanted the technology. And she wanted me. She had a vision of the MYND headband and thought I was the one to give it to her."

"Really? I didn't know ZONE got bought out."

"Ms. Neilmann didn't make a big headline splash. She was afraid it would impact the ZONE sales, which are still going strong. I don't think she thought the public would see it as a good fit. And she didn't want our competitors to wonder what we were up to."

"But your competitors found out, surely? I would assume they keep close tabs on what Neilmann is doing."

"Of course. But they still don't know why."

"So she bought out ThinkShop, for the same reason she did ZONE."

Ryker cleared his throat. "Yes, I guess you could say that."

Vega was getting the impression he wasn't as enamored with her as everyone else seemed to be. She bit her tongue and peered inside the headband.

"You never really explained why it's called a disseminator. Doesn't it just collect?"

He shook his head. "Of course not. After gathering the brain wave information, we then disseminate it to our advertising and marketing databases. We combine the EEG data with the user's biometric information collected from their smart devices. Then we take all that data and analyze it, with the goal being to understand how users responded to specific ads.

"Then we take the user responses and determine whether we need to change an ad, or possibly alter its placement on the screen or time of day it's displayed, to improve its efficacy. Generally, we find there are trends among specific types of users, usually based on age, race, sex, etc. We've even found that the time of day a user views an ad, and which state or area of a country they live in, can reveal certain trends in how they respond. Once we adjust the ad or replace it with another, we run the trial again, gather the information and re-analyze it to determine if the changes made had a positive or negative effect on their hit rate."

"In other words, did they now want to click on the ad or buy the product?"

"Exactly. It's a perpetual cycle. But right now, because it's all done with focus group testing, it's a slow and time-consuming process."

Gears were spinning in Vega's head, and then they locked in place. "Oh, I see! I can imagine how much more effective the ads would be if you could make them more appealing in real-time."

"Exactly."

"I hate to admit it, but it's an ingenious idea."

"Why do you hate to admit it?"

"Most people don't like to see ads when they're surfing. Me included. And I hate having to click on those icons to tell the advertisers I don't like an ad. It's like I'm doing their job for them."

"Of course. But what if you didn't have to? What if they weren't all just junk? What if we could manipulate what you saw to be only ads for a product or service you actually needed or wanted? And what if we presented it in a way you found interesting or even stimulating?"

"That would definitely be less annoying. But wait a minute. Once this goes out to the real world, how do you know the user is looking specifically at a Nielmann's ad or exactly which ad they're looking at?"

"We added a marker."

"What's a marker? You mean, like a cookie?"

"Kind of. I'm sure you know cookies are old school. No one uses those very much anymore. Think of the marker as a digital fingerprint attached to the ad. It identifies everything about it—what product or service it's for and what version it is, for example, is it from this year, last year, or last month, for that matter?"

"That is both cool and disturbing at the same time. Was it your idea for the *Buy* window pop up if a person looked at an ad for too long?"

Dr. Fedorov gave her a quick nod. "Very perceptive, Ms. Swift. That was actually Ms. Neilmann's idea. She is determined to make her company number one in the industry again."

"This sounds like an extreme amount of data to sort through and compare. Do you keep this data for every single user for all the Neilmann customer ads?"

"Not every single one. As I said, we try to base our changes on any similarities or trends we find in specific user groups."

Vega was pretty sure she could use a lot of her CORE program code to gather the biometric measurements, but the big obstacle was going to be reading the brain waves— wirelessly.

"This is going to be a challenge."

"That is why we needed you, Ms. Swift. I'm sure there are other programmers who could complete the project, but you are the first one Ms. Neilmann felt had exactly the right qualifications."

"I hope I don't disappoint her. There's a lot to learn in a short time," she said. "I'm not sure the smart devices of today even have the capabilities I'll need to accomplish this."

Ryker shook his head. "Failure is not an option, Ms. Swift."

14

Marie Castle gave the little brown golden-doodle puppy a hug. His fur was soft against her cheek, and he smelled like the dog shampoo she'd just used to wash him. She nuzzled his neck and ruffled the hair on his head, and the dog responded by licking her face with his soft, wet tongue. Wiping off the saliva, she laughed, and the dog gave a little bark. She looked up when the front office door opened.

"Mornin'!" said Ash as he walked in. "You look awfully happy."

His six-foot-two frame towered over her. He wrapped his arm around her shoulder and gave her a quick side hug. "You just win the lottery or somethin'?"

"I wish! Got a call from SmartMart this morning and I got the job! I start next Monday. I'll be working as a cashier at one of the Bellevue stores."

"Oh. Congratulations, I guess."

"Come on, be happy for me," she said. She pushed him away playfully. "I know you don't like it, but it pays way better than the Best Motel did, and now I can take day classes at Bellevue College."

"That's good."

"OK, it's not exactly my dream job, but it's better than that crappy housekeeper job at the motel in Kirkland. And it's second shift."

"Second shift?"

"Five p.m. to one a.m. It's gonna be weird, but like I said, now I can take my vet tech classes in the day. I like volunteering here at the animal shelter, but it's not paying my bills."

"I know. It's all good. But I don't like SmartMart any better than the motel. Maybe less. Doesn't it, like, get robbed all the time?"

"Not *all* the time. And anyway, they have bulletproof glass in front of the cashiers now."

"That right there should tell you something."

"You got another job in mind?"

Ash looked away and knelt down. A weary old mutt slowly strolled up to the front of his cage and sniffed Ash's fingers. He reached out and scratched its head.

"I didn't think so," she said.

"I just worry about you is all."

"I know. But don't. I'll be fine."

Marie wasn't about to admit to Ash that she was a little worried herself, but she had to be strong. Her bank account was almost empty, and she was already sharing her little one-bedroom apartment with two other people. With a fold-down couch in the living room and two twin beds in her bedroom, it was a packed house. She couldn't afford to turn down this job.

"I may not have a better job for you, or like, a sugar daddy to pay for your school and put you up in, like, a nice apartment or anything like that, but I know how you can make some easy money."

"I don't want anything to do with drugs, Ash."

"No, not drugs. I told you, I'm not doin' that stuff anymore and like, even if I was, I would never ask you to like, sell anything. I thought you knew me better than that."

"I'm sorry. You're right," Marie said as she walked toward the end of the room. "How much money? What do I have to do?" she asked, pulling the metal cabinet door open. As she reached in for one of the gigantic bags of dog food, the smell and sound of nuggets made all the dogs go nuts. They all started barking at once, recognizing the meaty chunks were about to come their way.

Ash pulled a folded piece of paper out of his back pocket.

"Look. I found this on the bulletin board in the front office. Not sure who put it there. But anyway, I think you should go with me."

Marie set down the bag of food and took the paper from Ash's hand.

"Five hundred dollars?"

"Yep."

"For two hours of work? And you don't know what we have to do?"

"No, but who cares?"

"Call them right now!"

"I did already."

"What'd they say?"

"We're in!"

"Me too?"

"Of course you too!"

Marie leaned in, gave Ash a big hug and then pulled back quickly. "Wait! When is it?"

"It's next Saturday. You're not workin' are you?"

"Whew! No, I already quit the motel, and I don't have to work on Saturdays at SmartMart."

He gave her a high-five and said, "All right then, let's make some money!"

15

After spending a week with Dr. Fedorov, Vega thought she understood the basics of how the MYND headband worked. It was ingenious really, although she didn't know how she was going to accomplish the same thing without hardware.

They had spent a lot of time going over the mechanics of the headband. Dr. Fedorov was a patient teacher, educating her on all its capabilities and reviewing all the hardware and firmware functions. He even told her about a kill switch he added to enable the headband to be powered off manually in case of an electrical failure or short. "Don't want anyone accidentally getting electrocuted," he had snickered.

She knew she could use the various positional sensors available in smart devices to zero in on specific areas of the brain, but her major problem was how to collect the information wirelessly. The brain's neural oscillations were strong enough to penetrate the skull, barely. She needed to find a way to use the existing smart devices' capabilities to strengthen and localize the capture of those weak signals.

She also needed to identify more biometric parameters to use to fine-tune their understanding of customer responses and reactions. In the focus group studies, they already used a lot of the same sensors she did in her CORE program—basic biometric data like temperature, blood pressure and heart rate. But Neilmann wanted more.

She pulled out her CORE project specifications and the wireless MYND project goals document. She wanted to compare them to see what she could reuse from CORE to accomplish her goals. Next, she opened a document about the sensors available on all but the most ancient smartphones, watches and tablets and read through the list.

General Sensors:

Barometer: measures air pressure; detects weather changes; determines altitude.

Ambient Light Regulator: adjusts brightness of screen based on available light.

Proximity Sensor: uses infrared rays to reflect off objects and determine distance of smart device from the user.

Hygrometer: humidity sensor.

Thermometer: monitors temperature of device and of user.

Position Sensors:

Accelerometer: tracks the movement of the smart device in space to allow device to switch from landscape to portrait mode when appropriate.

GPS (Global positioning system): tracks device's exact location on the Earth.

Gyroscope: electronic-mechanical device that detects changes in smart device's movement in space to aid in determining orientation.

OPM (Optically Pumped Magnetometer): reads/sends magnetic fields and signals.

Digital Compass: indicates Cardinal direction of device.

Communication Sensors:

Transmitter: encodes user's voice and sends to local carrier cell tower.

Antennas: obtains signal to connect to network; Current loop antenna receives or transmits low-frequency signals.

Microphone: captures user's voice and noise in proximity of user.

Biometric Sensors:

Pressure: measures user's blood pressure and the pressure user puts on device when pressing buttons or screen; measures user's body moisture (sweat).

CSR (Conductance Skin Response): measures skin conductance response to determine amount of sweat user produces and its chemical composition.

CGM (Continuous Glucose Monitor): monitors glucose levels in user to detect signs of diabetes or hypoglycemia.

Optical (light): recognition of light color and intensity; reads eye-prints for security, identification.

Ultrasonic (sound waves): uses sound waves to measures short distances to aid in reading facial features for security, identification, mood and state of emotional health.

Capacitive (electronic capacitors): detects change in capacitance on screen from user's touch; primary mode of user interaction; reads fingerprints, pressure and location of pressure.

IR (Infrared): uses infrared light LED and reflection to measure distance; provides three-dimensional face mapping for security, identification; identifies heat signatures.

Electromagnetic (radar): uses radar's electromagnetic waves to detect movement around device.

LiDAR (laser light): uses lasers to judge depth; maps out a space.

CMOS (Complementary Metal-Oxide Semiconductor): image sensor. Converts photons to electrons.

Vega's head was spinning from information overload, and she pushed away from the computer and looked out at the Space Needle, almost completely obscured by clouds. She was positive it would shock most people if they knew how much information their smart devices collected about them.

So far, the goals for her project were impressive, but she had to admit it made her a little uncomfortable. She knew Neilmann studied consumer reactions to ads, but everything she read before arriving here said it was only in test environments. That was true, for now. But when she finished her program, it would read people's brain waves in the real world—without them even realizing. It all seemed a bit too Big Brother.

What had she gotten herself into?

She was deep in thought when a knock came on her door.

"Sorry. You busy?" Drexel asked. "I thought I would drop in and formally introduce myself."

"It's OK. I was just reading over some specs. Trying to put a plan together."

He held out his hand. "I know we met before, but I don't know if you even remember me. Your first day was probably really busy. I'm Drexel Hicks, senior manager of client development." He smiled. "Fancy title for someone who runs the focus group studies."

She stood up and took his hand. "I remember you, Drexel. Vega Swift. Nice to meet you—again."

"You interested in getting a bite to eat at the cafeteria?"

Thinking about how many specifications and project description documents she still needed to get through, Vega almost refused. But apparently, her poker face needed work.

"Don't say you're too busy. If you start working through lunch on your second week, it might become a habit."

He gave her a huge smile, which made her chuckle. She decided he was right.

"OK. You're on. I guess this will still be here when I get back. Hopefully."

"I think it's too early for you to worry about getting fired, at least not just for going to lunch."

"It's never too early to worry about job security."

"Sounds like there's a story behind that. Maybe you'll share it at lunch?"

Ignoring his question, she took a few bills from her purse. "Lead the way."

* * *

Vega wasn't sure if she would ever get used to the Neilmann cafeteria. She wished she could take food home. *Maybe she could?* She'd have to ask Astrid.

They chose a food station, got their meals and sat at a table next to one of the windows at the back of the room. The sky was gray, but it wasn't raining. Yet. Outside, a breeze rustled the hemlock tree branches, and fallen needles swept into piles against the parking lot curbs.

She picked up a fry and dunked it in her ketchup.

"Thanks for the invite."

"No problem. I wanted to talk to you. Since I'm the one who'll be testing your new program on the human guinea pigs, I thought I should get to know you a little. Learn about your exciting life."

Vega shook her head. "I'm afraid you're going to be disappointed. Exciting is not exactly the adjective I would use to describe my life right now."

"What word would you use?"

"Boring would be more accurate."

"Boring? That's hard to believe. You do not look like a boring person."

"I didn't say *I* was boring. I just said my life was."

"Touché. And why is your life boring?"

"It's a long story," she said, brushing him off. "What about you? How did you come to work for Neilmann?"

"Went to a job fair, senior year of college. I sought them out specifically. Always wanted to work here."

"How come?"

"As you said, it's a long story."

They smiled at each other and continued their lunches in silence for a while. Vega found she felt comfortable around him. And she noticed he wasn't too bad to look at either.

After some light conversation about the weather and commuting, Drexel finished his lunch first, wiped his mouth and said, "I'm running one of my focus groups tomorrow. You should sit in and get a feel for it."

"Good idea. I'd like to see one from start to finish."

Vega was also thinking she'd like to spend a little more time with Drexel while she was at it. "Tomorrow?"

"Yes. It starts at ten o'clock in conference room 2A."

"I'll be there."

16

Vega took the elevator down to the second floor and searched for conference room 2A. It was a dark day and the room's dropped ceiling and fluorescent lighting did little to brighten the space. The room smelled musty from all the hooded rain jackets draped over the back of the small dark-blue fabric chairs, and water dripped off them and landed silently on the light gray carpet-tile floor. As she entered, she glanced at the faces gathered around the large table.

Wow! That's quite a long, very red beard, Vega thought to herself as she noticed one man in the group. She watched as he stroked the six inch long beard that was the same color as his scruffy shoulder-length hair.

Everyone watched her, waiting, but she looked away and walked to a back chair. When they realized she wasn't going to say anything, they turned around, and she watched as a few brave people whispered introductions to each other.

After a few minutes of muted conversation, Drexel came in, followed by a short, freckled woman carrying a large box, both donning white lab coats for the occasion.

"Hello, everyone! My name is Drexel Hicks, and I'm the senior manager of client development for Neilmann Corporation. Thank you so much for volunteering to participate in one of our focus group studies!"

Despite the gloominess of the day and the corporate staleness of the room, Drexel's excitement and vigor were infectious and the energy level of the group rose with his animated enthusiasm.

"This is my research assistant, Ms. Daphne Hart. She has a few housekeeping items to get through before we start."

Daphne set the box on the table and pulled out a file folder and a smaller white box from inside. She put the large box on the table and took out blank name-tag stickers from the folder. "Welcome everybody!" She handed out the labels and said, "Please write your name on the label and put it on. And tell me, who are the two people who didn't fill out our online questionnaire or sign the non-disclosure agreement?"

Two young men seated together raised their hands. Daphne stared at them just long enough to make them squirm, and one of them offered an excuse. "Our internet was down."

"No problem. I just happen to have some extra forms right here," she said. She pulled them out of the folder. "Y'all can fill these out while Drexel explains the testing. Do you have a pen?"

The men nodded, and Daphne backed away from the table and sat as Drexel took center stage.

Drexel opened the white box and pulled out a slim, u-shaped white headband with the words *MYND V4.0* printed on the front of the band in a futuristic, non-serif font. Near the back, on the left arm of the band, was a small round power button, and above it was an LED power-indicator light. He held the headband up and rotated it so everyone could see it. "This device measures your brain waves. You will wear this during your testing today."

There were murmurs, and Drexel gave the group a few moments to settle down.

"Wait a minute," said a man, "is this thing gonna fry my brain?"

"No, it's just a reader. It will not cause any damage to your brain."

The man laughed. "That's what they always say!" he said, causing others to laugh as well.

Drexel looked at the front pocket of the man's shirt. "And yet, I see you own a smartphone."

"That's different."

"That smartphone puts out radio, infrared and other types of signals continuously. If you're not worried about your phone, you have no reason to worry about this headband."

"Oh, OK. I was just kidding, man."

Drexel gave the man a look. "Let's get down to business." He handed the MYND headband to the young woman seated closest to him. "Please pass this around so everyone can see."

The woman examined it, handed it to the next person, and the headband made its way around the room.

"Today's test is simple. You will surf on a browser on a smart device while wearing one of these headbands. It's placed on your head like a sweatband. The printing goes in front and the power button in the back. As we asked you in the questionnaire," he said, "please let us know now if you have any problems wearing this for at least two hours."

One woman raised her hand and asked, "It's not tight, is it? I get headaches easily."

"No. It's about as tight as a normal hairband or shower cap. It shouldn't hurt. In the back there's an adapter made of flexible plastic so we can adjust it to fit different head sizes."

A young woman in the back raised her hand. "How is it going to measure our brain waves?"

"There are sensors imbedded in the headband on those multiple rigid bars you see protruding from the band. Those arc over the top of your head, and the sensors read your brain waves."

"Cool!" the woman said. "Is it like one of those ZONE headbands that displays your brain waves on your phone and helps you meditate?"

"Not exactly," said Drexel. "It measures your brain waves at a much more detailed level than something like the ZONE."

There was a bit more mumbling as people examined the device. The headband made it back to the front of the table, and Drexel placed it back in the box.

"OK folks, I know you probably have more questions, but there's only so much we can share since this is a proprietary product. Your participation in this focus group trial is simple. All we ask is that you surf on a browser on a smart device. While you're doing that, the headband takes measurements and gathers data."

"The website said we'd be getting paid five hundred bucks," said a middle-aged man at the end of the table. "That's not much for two hours of my time."

Drexel smiled. "It's certainly your decision whether to take part. If you feel the money's not worth it, by all means, leave now."

The man shifted in his chair. "Yeah, well. I'm just sayin'."

Drexel nodded to Daphne. "In a few minutes, we'll all go down to the lower level to our consumer research and testing area," she said. "Y'all are going to need to place your phones, and other electronic devices, in the box in the middle of the table. You can't have any recording or internet connectivity devices with you during the test."

"We're not going to surf on our own phones?" asked one of the men.

"No, we'll give everyone a Neilmann device for this test. If you need help, we'll be there for you."

The same man who groaned about the money spoke up again. "I have the latest iPhone. I'm not going to leave it here to get stolen."

"We'll take good care of all of your items during the testing," Daphne said. "This box will be locked in a secure location, and we'll give everything back to you once the test is over."

"What kind of phone are we getting?" a young woman asked. "I'm not going to have to use an iPhone, am I? I've never used one of those."

"Don't worry. I'll make sure everyone gets something they're used to," Daphne said. "And I'm sorry, but you must leave your smart devices behind. We must ensure confidentiality."

The man with the latest iPhone grumbled, but took it out of his pocket, placed it in the box, and everyone else followed suit.

"Anyone wearing any smart devices like watches or health bands?" asked Daphne. There were a few head nods. "Y'all go ahead and place those in the box as well, please."

There was another groan as they removed their devices and placed them in the box.

"OK. Thanks everyone. Once we're down in the test area, you'll each get a MYND headband and a smartphone or tablet. These will only have access to the Neilmann intranet. After I—"

"Excuse me, what's an intranet?" asked one of the volunteers.

"An intranet," Drexel said, "is simply a private network limited to a certain business or set of computers and servers, and this one is specific to Neilmann Corporation. In simplified terms, and for our purposes, it's a limited set of websites for you to surf."

"Oh, OK," said the volunteer, nodding her head.

"We want you to browse our intranet," said Daphne. "Just search around and see what interests you. Like Drexel said earlier, while you're doing that, the headband will take measurements while you surf. After two hours, the test will end, we'll return your devices and y'all will all get paid. That's it! Sound good?"

Drexel and Daphne looked at the group and everyone was nodding their heads, saying yes, happy to get five hundred bucks for doing something they would probably be doing anyway. Daphne took the forms from the two stragglers and slipped them into the folder. Drexel said, "All right then, if there are no more questions, please grab your bags and coats and follow us down to the lab."

* * *

Vega was impressed with how Drexel and Daphne kept the group under control during the explanations. Shuffling behind the group, she made her way to the elevator, and in the lower level, followed them through the security door, down to the COMA-1 lab. Inside were two rows of small six foot high, blue-gray fabric cubicles, ten cubicles on each side. Each cubicle contained a red-cushioned rolling office chair, and a MYND headband sat on each of the small desks.

"OK, y'all," said Daphne, "just pick a cubicle. It doesn't matter where you sit. There's a phone or tablet in each cubicle that you'll use for surfing. If you'd prefer a different vendor, just let me know. Drexel and I will come around and check with you individually."

Vega stood near the door and watched as everyone settled in. Daphne and Drexel made the rounds, checking that each volunteer's headband fit securely. They changed their smart devices if requested and made sure the devices were fully charged and the MYND application was running in the background. Then they ensured the Neilmann intranet browser was up and ready for the participants to use.

Drexel whispered something to Daphne and then walked over to where Vega was standing. "Almost ready."

Daphne pulled a phone out of her pocket and started pushing buttons.

"What's she doing?" Vega asked.

"She's starting up the devices. All the headbands connect via Bluetooth to an app on our phone. Allows us to power them off and on. We can also start the brain wave monitoring and change which brain waves the headband focuses on. Oh, and stop or start the transmission of data."

"Oh, I see. Ryker hasn't shown me that yet. We're still focusing on the headband itself."

"I'm sure you'll get to it soon enough."

Vega leaned close to Drexel's ear. "By the way, is Daphne from the south? She sure says y'all a lot."

"She's from Oklahoma. Hasn't lived there in a long time. She thinks y'all is a very convenient word and refuses to stop using it. I've caught myself saying it a few times. Hard for it not to rub off."

Vega chuckled. "It is kind of a handy word. I mean, the plural of you, after all, is just you. But I would constantly bite my tongue, trying not to correct her."

"Oh, yeah? A stickler for good grammar?"

"Yes. Bad habit, I guess. I try not to correct people, but sometimes it's hard. And don't get me wrong, it's not like I'm perfect by any means."

Drexel snickered. "Feel free to correct me anytime you want. At least then I know you're listening to me."

Vega smiled at him, and he grinned back.

"OK, everyone," Daphne said, "are there any last-minute questions before we get started? No? All right then, y'all start browsing!" Daphne waited a few moments and then asked, "Everything good?" A few mumbles, but everyone was a go. "OK. Browse to your heart's content. If you need anything, raise your hand and someone will come to help you."

With everyone set, Daphne, Drexel and Vega went out into the hall.

"Daphne, this is Vega Swift. She's the new programmer Ms. Neilmann hired to eliminate the headgear."

Daphne held out her hand. "Oh, wow! Nice to meet you. I can't wait to see if you can do it."

Vega gave her a warm smile. "Me neither!"

"I've got it from here, Daphne."

"OK. See you in a couple of hours."

Daphne walked toward the elevator, and Vega followed Drexel into the observation room.

"All right then. Time for the fun part."

17

It had been a long night, and Vega was tired. Miren was having a hard time relieving herself, and Vega was worried she was getting another UTI. She had had to change the sheets in the morning after her mom had an accident, and it had leaked through the incontinence pad.

On the bright side, work yesterday was eye-opening. Watching the brain waves of the study participants change as they surfed had been interesting, and it gave her a sense of how Neilmann combined the data with the eye-tracking capabilities of the smart devices to determine where they were looking on the screen. Drexel had observed this in real-time to determine when to display a new ad based on the reactions shown in the users' brain waves.

She had made a breakthrough this morning and was feeling proud of herself. She'd discovered a way to use one of the smart devices' newest chips to map the cranial magnetic fields produced by the brain's electrical currents. This method provided a much stronger signal than just capturing the electrical signals themselves, which were extremely weak. The optically pumped magnetometer chip, or OPM, was used to help determine direction—north, south, east or west—but she was convinced the code she'd written to direct the chip to pick up the magnetic fields around the skull would provide the level of detail she required from the brain wave signals.

She reviewed the brain wave chart to refresh her memory.

Brain Wave Frequencies:
Delta: 1 - 4 Hz, deep sleep
Theta: 4 - 8 Hz, drowsy
Alpha: 8 - 12 Hz, relaxed
Beta: 12 - 30 Hz, focused
Gamma: 25 - 100 Hz, active

She wrote a subroutine so that when the MYND app activated, it directed the magnetometer to search for signals in the one to one hundred hertz frequency range. She was excited about the possibility of finally solving the puzzle of how to read the brain waves wirelessly.

There was a lot to do, and it might take forever if she coded everything herself. She searched through the Neilmann database and found the CodeBot AI program Astrid had told her about. She clicked on the bot app and brought up its interface.

"Let's see if you're as good as Astrid said."

After reading through the specs to figure out how to use it, she started writing the instructions for CodeBot to program a routine that would activate the proximity and LiDAR sensors in the smart device to localize the OPM chip's search area. Next, she told it to boost the magnetic wave information being sent back to the users' smart devices via Bluetooth. Once the program captured that info, the MYND program would upload it to the Neilmann cloud. As a failsafe to ensure the MYND program had continuous connectivity to the brain, she directed CodeBot to add a command to keep the Bluetooth connection active at all times. That way, even if the user turned the functionality off, it would still be available to the MYND application.

It was going to take a while to write out the parameters for CodeBot, but if it could program these subroutines for her, it would save her a lot of time. She created a general list of what she wanted CodeBot to do and set it aside. At least she had a direction.

The next goal was figuring out what other biometric user data she needed to collect. Her CORE program was a good start, but it was originally designed to look for diagnostic information to determine the state of the user's health, not gauge their interest in product ads. And the users activated it voluntarily. It didn't run continuously in the background unless directed to do so by the user. Her thought was to expand CORE's functionality so she could measure not just the physical but also the emotional state of the user. Then she would incorporate the CORE program code into the MYND application to create an overall picture of the user at any given point in time—like when they were looking at an ad.

She started typing a list of information she wanted to include in addition to the basic biometric info the CORE program had originally collected.

<u>Additional measurements:</u>
Track subject's eye movements with the camera to determine if they're looking at an ad.

Count eye blinks per minute to gauge interest. People blinked less often when their interest was piqued.

Combine camera and ultrasonic waves to measure facial movements—frowning, smiling, or neither.

Record positional key points—slumping often equated to boredom; upright, more alert.

Direct microphone to capture voice and measure pitch to gauge excitement—rising or lowering.

Capture keywords in conversation. Neilmann had a database she could access to compare against words and help determine interest in an ad.

She checked the list and liked what she saw. It was a good start. With a little more time, she might determine more parameters she could include to provide an even more comprehensive and detailed picture of the user. She just needed to write all the code. Too bad she couldn't get CodeBot to do everything.

The final goal was to tack the ad marker onto the end of the data string she sent back to the cloud so the marketing group could take that data and adjust the ads in real-time and Neilmann could ensure they displayed the most enticing advertisements to each user. It would be up to the analysts in marketing to decide how to alter an ad or whether to replace it with an entirely new one. Vega was glad she didn't have to worry about that part of the project.

She still wasn't sure how she felt about the whole thing. It made her think of George Orwell's depiction of the future in his book *1984*.

"You know, just in case, I think I'm going to add a kill switch to you, like Ryker did with the headband," she said to her computer. "Never hurts to have an easy shut-off switch."

Vega knew it was silly talking to her computer, but she did it all the time when she was programming. It helped her think. *Surely she wasn't the only one*, she hoped.

Even though she might have her qualms, she had to admit that studying the technology and figuring out a solution was one of the most fascinating things she had ever worked on. Writing the CORE app had been fun and interesting, but the MYND project was light-years more challenging. And if it worked as well as she hoped, it would certainly give Neilmann a leg up on their competitors.

18

Jenny Black stuffed the wad of bills into her purse's zipper pocket, looked in the dressing-room mirror and checked her makeup.

"What cha doin'?" asked her friend Tanya.

"What do you think? Would your mom like this outfit?"

"What chu you talkin' 'bout? I haven't seen my mom in five years. I have no idea what she'd like. Why you askin'?"

"I'm just trying out ideas 'cause I wanna look good, you know, presentable. I'm telling my mom about my job tomorrow."

"You look like Martha Stewart or somethin'."

Smiling widely, Jenny leaned closer to the mirror and rubbed some lipstick off her front teeth.

"Good."

"Why you ruinin' a good thing? They don't need to know nothin'."

"I'm tired of lying to them. Anyway, I can't keep telling 'em I work the night shift at the Amazon distribution center. My mom keeps saying she's gonna come in and take me to dinner one night."

"Didn't you tell her it was in Tacoma?"

"Yeah. She decided it's not that far after all."

"I thought she didn't like to drive at night."

"She doesn't. But she says she's gonna call an Uber. Believe me, I've tried to talk her out of it. She says she wants to meet my boss."

"Did you try tellin' her you only get thirty minutes for lunch?"

"Yeah, I tried that too. I've made up so many lies I can't even remember everything I've told her now. She says she'll bring sandwiches, and we can eat in the break room."

"Shit, girl! You know they're probably gonna disown you."

Slipping her hands into the sleeves of her denim jacket, Jenny picked up her Louis Vuitton bag and turned to Tanya.

"Who knows? Maybe they'll surprise me and tell me they love me no matter what?"

"Yeah, right. Look outside, Jenny."

"What?"

"You heard me. Open the door and look outside."

"Oh—kay," Jenny said, taking a long look at her friend. She walked over, opened the back door and looked into the dark parking lot behind the building.

"What? I don't see anything."

"Look up."

"Yeah, so?"

"You see any pigs flyin' in that sky?"

It took a second for the joke to click. Jenny chuckled. "You're so funny."

"Text me tomorrow? Tell me what they said?"

"Yeah. I may need a place to crash for a while."

"No problem, girl. You know I'm always here for you."

"Thanks." Jenny gave Tanya a hug. "Wish me luck!" she said as she walked out into the night.

***

It was three o'clock in the morning when Jenny got home. She snuck in the back door as quietly as she could, took off her platform heels and slipped down the narrow hall to her bedroom. Slowly, she shut the door behind her, trying to soften the click of the latch. She quickly undressed and walked back across the hall to the tiny bathroom, cinching the belt of her robe around her. As she wiped off the last remnants of her heavy makeup, there was a light knock on the door.

"You in there?" asked her mother, Cecile.

Jenny opened the door and looked down at her mom, who was at least four inches shorter than her.

"I'm sorry. Did I wake you up?"

Her mom reached in and stroked Jenny's arm. "No, baby, it's fine. You know I'm a light sleeper. How was work?"

"OK," Jenny said, praying her mom didn't ask for more details.

"Did you tell that boss of yours I want to meet him?"

"Uh, yeah, about that, Mom. You know, people don't really do that anymore. Parents don't go meet their kids' bosses unless they're a minor or something."

"I don't care. I want to meet him."

Jenny sighed. "You know, tomorrow night really isn't good. We're gonna be doing inventory, and we barely even get breaks on those nights."

"Didn't you just do inventory last week?"

Shit. She needed to start keeping better track of her lies.

"Oh, right. That was just a spot check. This week it's an all hands-on-deck kind of inventory."

"They work you too hard, which is another reason I want to go down there. I'm coming and I'm going to call OSHA on that boss of yours if he doesn't give you the breaks you deserve."

Jenny rolled her eyes. "Mom, it's fine, really. He's a good boss. How about we just make it next week instead?"

Her mom looked at her, and Jenny felt like she could see right through her. Her guilt-o-meter went up several notches. She hated lying to her about her work, but didn't think her mother would understand. And now Jenny was getting cold feet again.

"Nope, I'm coming tomorrow. Don't worry, I promise not to make a scene. I know how much you need this job."

Jenny's mom was right about that. Her father had practically demanded she study management, but after taking out thousands of dollars' worth of student loans, by the end of year three, she simply couldn't take it anymore.

She hated everything about it and had no intention of working in the corporate world living an eight-to-five life with a husband and two kids.

What she really wanted to do was be a dancer, but every audition ended with the same comment. *You're too curvy. You need to lose some weight.* But as much as Jenny tried, she could never seem to lose enough to satisfy them. She couldn't help it if she had tits and an ass. *Wasn't that the way a woman was supposed to look?* She didn't understand this obsession with thinness. It was unhealthy. The only time she'd gotten positive feedback about her weight, was when she'd gone on a grapefruit and cottage cheese diet for a month and she'd lost fifteen pounds. She thought she looked like a stick, but the choreographers loved it. But she couldn't keep it up. She had no energy and ran out of breath halfway through the rehearsals, so they ended up sacking her anyway. Eventually, she admitted she would never be able to support herself as *that* kind of dancer.

Now she just wanted to make as much money as she could to save up enough to pay off her student loans, get out of her parents' house and move to France. She had always loved the idea and had taken several semesters of French as electives. It had been the only thing that made all those management and business classes bearable. Her dream was to live in Paris in a cozy place near the Champs-Élysées and sit outside at a little cafe and eat croissants with her skirt flowing in the breeze. She became obsessed when she'd discovered the show, "Emily in Paris." She'd streamed all the seasons in one week. If she couldn't dance for a living, she would settle for dancing on the sidewalks of Paris.

"Let's just play it by ear, OK?" Jenny asked. "If it's a bad night, I'll call you at eight and let you know."

Cecile shook her head. "No. No more excuses. I'm coming."

Jenny sighed. She knew her mom meant it. She would go down to Amazon tomorrow and realize Jenny didn't work there. There was no backing out now. She took her mother's hand.

"Mom, there's something I need to tell you."

19

The sun reflected off the windows at the top of the Space Needle and Vega realized how easy it was to forget about the view when she was so absorbed in her work. But she was pleased with her progress after a full month at Neilmann. She turned to leave, and Drexel was standing inside her office, watching her.

"Oh! Sorry. I didn't hear you."

"I know. You were a little absorbed. I was wondering how long it would take before you realized I was here."

"How long was it?"

"I don't know. I forgot to check."

She laughed at him and said, "Then that little experiment led to no conclusion."

"I'll have to work on my concentration next time." He smiled at her and shrugged, admitting his failure. "How's the project going?"

"It's not a simple task you guys have given me."

"I know. That's why we wanted you on the team. What do you think? Now that you've had a chance to get your head around it, do you think you can do it?"

"I think so. I definitely don't have it all figured out yet, but I'm enjoying the challenge."

She got her backpack out of her drawer and grabbed her coat.

"You have time for a drink before you leave?" asked Drexel.

"I would like that. Really. But I've got to get home and relieve the nurse, and I don't want to stress out about it all the way home."

"What time do you need to be home?"

"Six-thirty."

"You know you have an hour and a half."

"Oh! I thought it was later than that. What am I doing? I should still be working."

"You've stopped now, so let's go get a drink."

Vega hesitated, then thought about what waited for her at home.

"You know what? OK. But nothing alcoholic because I still have to drive home. How about we just go to the cafeteria? Get a soda or something?"

"Trying to stay away from something that feels like a date?"

Turning red, Vega adjusted her backpack on her shoulder so she had something to look at other than him. He was exactly right. "No! That's not it. I just want to do something quick."

"OK. Let's go to the cafeteria then."

Vega nodded. "Thanks."

The cafeteria was not very crowded, since there was only a skeleton crew left from the busy hours of breakfast and lunch, and they grabbed a drink and chose a corner table.

"So," Drexel started, "tell me about your progress."

"It's good. I've been learning how to use CodeBot."

"Are you finding it helpful?"

"Yes. Should shave a couple of weeks or more off my coding time. I hope."

"No kidding?"

"And I have an idea about how to read the brain waves wirelessly that, hopefully, will pan out."

"Yeah? How?" he asked, leaning forward.

Vega played with the straw in her drink. "I'd rather not say anything."

He backed away and looked at the table. "Oh. That's fine if you don't want to tell me."

"Oh, no! It's not that. It's just…I don't want to jinx myself by saying it out loud."

"Superstitious a little?" he joked.

"Not usually. But I've never tried to do anything like this and I'm afraid if I tell you, and it doesn't work, you'll wonder why they hired me in the first place."

"Don't be silly. From what Astrid tells me, they bought ThinkShop mainly so they would get you and your CORE program."

"Yeah, I've been told. Talk about being flattered, and you know, no pressure or anything." She looked up at Drexel, who was smiling.

She heard a jingle play and pulled her phone out of her back pocket. "Not me."

He looked at his phone's display, frowned and looked back at her. "Sorry. I should probably take this." Getting up, he put some distance between himself and Vega and tried to talk softly into the phone. But she could still hear him.

"Hello, John. … Yes, I got it. … "I already told you. I'm working on it."

She saw Drexel's jaw clench as he listened to the caller talk. "Don't patronize me!" he spat out. He glanced over at Vega, took a deep breath, gave her a small smile and, in a more civil tone, said, "Look, I'm a little busy right now. Can we talk about this later? … Fine."

She watched as he smashed his finger on the screen to end the call and slammed his phone into the back pocket of his pants. "Sorry about that," he said as he sat back down.

"That's OK. Is everything all right?"

"Yeah. It's just…It's my father. It's fine. I'll talk to him later."

"OK. Sure. I didn't mean to eavesdrop."

"Kind of hard not to." He stared down at the table and shook his head. "It's nothing."

"It's obviously something. I could share something about my father, if it would help."

"Yeah? What's that?"

"Never mind. I don't know why I said that."

"No, I want to know. If you're willing to share."

Vega looked at the table, took a deep breath and whispered, "He killed himself."

"Oh, shit! I'm so sorry!" he said, reaching over to touch her hand.

She looked up and saw the pity on his face. "He said he couldn't stand to watch my mother, the love of his life, deteriorate in front of him anymore. He'd just been laid off and I think they let him go because he spoke up about something in the office. I think he felt like a failure."

"Can I ask what happened?"

"He drove his car off a cliff—well, a mountain, to be exact—Mount Rainier."

A shocked look came over Drexel's face. "Shit! That's, uh, inventive."

"He left me a note and told me he'd put the brakes on first so it would look like an accident—to make sure we got the insurance money."

"That's horrible! I'm so sorry."

"Not your fault."

"No, I mean—"

"I know. Sorry. I don't know why I told you. I haven't told many people. Never even told my mother, not that she would understand now anyway. When it happened, she was still cognizant enough, but I didn't want to break her heart. I'm sorry. I didn't mean to unload on you."

Drexel reached over and touched her arm. "Don't worry about it. People tell me I'm easy to talk to."

Vega gave him a smile. "Yeah. Maybe that's it."

They sat in silence for a moment, and Drexel gave her a grin. "Enough about fathers. We should go out some time. I mean, for real."

Vega nodded. "I'd like that."

Their drinks now empty, he stood and picked up their empty cups.

"I'll take care of this. I imagine it's time for you to go now. Thanks for having a drink with me, even if it was just a soda in the cafeteria."

He leaned over and gave Vega a kiss on the cheek.

"See you soon," he said, walking away before she could respond.

She watched him the entire way as he walked across the cafeteria, threw away their cups and left. Not a bad view.

Vega thought back to his phone call. *It was strange*, she thought, *that he called his father by his name instead of Dad or Father*, but then, she knew nothing about him. Yet. She caressed her cheek lightly with her fingertips.

She liked it here more and more every day.

20

Dave stroked his long red beard as he followed Dr. Montgomery into the elevator. After he'd finished the focus group study, the facilitator guy had pulled him aside and asked if he would be interested in earning a little more money by participating in an individual test, and really needing the extra seven hundred bucks, he'd said yes right away. He was staying in the cheapest hotel he could tolerate and was working more hours at the bar, but the bills were still racking up as he continued to pay for Laurie and Lucas to live in their twenty-seven hundred-square foot house, and he was stuck in a crummy hotel room.

He had finally gotten the call from Neilmann and was now back in their basement. He stepped out of the elevator.

"I forgot about all the blue."

"It's supposed to produce a calming effect. You're not nervous are you, Mr. Byrne?" asked Astrid.

Dave looked down as he followed her. Lucky for him, her white lab coat didn't quite cover her short red skirt. Her long muscular legs were showing, and he was enjoying the view. *Hell*, he thought, *if I'm going to be divorced for having an affair, I might as well enjoy myself.*

He shrugged. "I guess so. I don't know why you wanted me to come in by myself, but I'm glad you did."

"Good," said Astrid. "And thank you for agreeing to do an individual study."

"Better for me. I get enough of people at work."

"You work with a big group?"

"I'm a bartender."

"Ah. You have a busy weekend ahead?"

"Yeah, I'm workin' more hours so I can get a better place."

"You're moving?"

"If I can afford it. Staying in a crappy hotel right now. Gonna look for a slightly less crappy one."

"If you don't mind me asking, why are you staying in a hotel?"

"My wife kicked me out. She wants a divorce."

"Sorry to hear that, but no worries, Mr. Byrne. I'll make sure you're out on time." Dr. Montgomery stepped into the CRT-1 lab, and he followed her in. "Please, take this seat," she said, motioning to a desk with a phone and headset already set out.

"Thanks. And please, call me Dave. No one calls me Mr. Byrne."

"OK, Dave, just like in the group session, that phone is your tool today, and you'll simply surf the intranet, like you did before."

Astrid pulled a prepared syringe from her lab-coat pocket and popped off the cap. That's when Dave got nervous.

"I didn't know I was getting a shot."

"Just a little something to help you relax."

"I was relaxed before you pulled out that needle."

She chuckled and said, "It was in the agreement form you signed. Didn't you see it?"

"Honestly, doc, I didn't read the whole thing."

Her face spread into a grin, and she nodded. "Most people don't. But you have nothing to worry about, Mr. Byrne—I mean, Dave. This will wear off before it's time for you to drive home. We want the results of the study to be as accurate as possible and we've learned from experience that many people get nervous, especially in our individual studies —even if they don't realize it. So now, we give every participant a small dose of midazolam before the test. Your questionnaire answers stated you had no allergies. Is that accurate?"

"Not that I know of."

"Would you prefer a pill form? If so, we'll have to wait about thirty minutes for it to take full effect before we can start the test."

He shook his head. "No, a shot is fine. I'm starting to understand why you're offering more money for this one."

Dave took off his jacket and hung it on the back of his chair, glad he'd worn a short-sleeved t-shirt. She pulled out a small foil packet from her pocket and ripped off the top. Removing an alcohol wipe, she cleaned an area of his upper arm, inserted the needle into his muscle and pressed the plunger. She removed it quickly and covered it with a small bandage stored in her other pocket.

"Not so bad, huh?"

Dave shook his head. "Piece of cake."

"This should take effect quickly. In the meantime, let's get you prepared for the test, shall we?"

"You always carry drugs in your pockets?"

She gave him a smile. "I came prepared."

After turning on the phone, she entered a password, flipped through some screens and opened a browser window. She picked up the headband and pushed the power button near the back.

"OK, Dave, I'm going to put this headband on you now. I might need to adjust the fit, so bear with me for a moment."

"Sure thing."

A few minor adjustments to secure a snug fit, and everything was ready. She handed him the phone and said, "You're all set. All you have to do is surf the internet for topics that interest you. How are you feeling?"

"It's kicking in, Doc. I'm not gonna lie. Feeling pretty good."

Astrid gave him a smile and nodded. "Excellent. It may take a few more minutes for you to feel the full effect."

"Got it."

"I'll be back in two hours, but if you need anything, just wave your hand and someone will help you. We'll be monitoring to make sure you're OK and the data collection is performing properly."

"OK, thanks."

"Happy surfing."

Dave got comfortable, looked at the phone and began browsing.

* * *

Astrid closed the door to the lab and walked into the observation room next door, where Drexel was already sitting at the long table in front of the one-way mirror. He was typing on a keyboard in front of three large monitors.

"Hey," she said.

"All set?"

"Yes. Everything ready to go?"

"Got the ads lined up."

Astrid looked through the glass and saw Dave, absorbed in his phone, oblivious. "You need anything before I leave?" she asked, lightly touching his arm..

"Nope," Drexel said. "I've got it. Thanks for helping me out."

Astrid rubbed his arm and gave it a little squeeze. "No problem. You know I would have gladly handled everything for you, right?"

"I know."

"How'd the meeting with your dad go?"

"Oh, you know there's no pleasing that man."

She nodded. "I remember."

"It's all good, though," Drexel said with a smile. "And thanks again. I've got it from here."

"Call me if you need anything."

"Sure thing. How's your sister doing, by the way?"

"Her last results were good, and she's almost done with the chemo, but we won't know the results for a couple of months. Thanks for asking."

"That's good to hear. Go on, now. Get the hell out of here."

"OK. See you later."

Drexel walked her to the door and gave her a smile as she stepped into the elevator. Back in the observation room, he locked the door, looked at the computer screen and chuckled when he saw Dave had entered a search for *do birds have tongues*.

One monitor revealed Dave's surfing activity, and periodically, Drexel changed the ads Dave saw as he surfed. Another monitor displayed his physical responses gathered by the phone he was holding, which included his heart rate, blood pressure, eye-movement tracking and temperature. But the most important measurement was the EEG line graphs of his brain waves. The headband constantly monitored his gamma, beta, alpha, theta and delta brain waves but took the finest details from his alpha, beta and theta waves. The background apps and numerous sensors had already taken Dave's biometric baseline measurements when he had first picked up the phone.

Drexel picked up his smartphone from the table, connected to the Neilmann intranet, opened the MYND headband interface app and flipped through the options. When he found the *Actions* icon and hit select, it revealed Ryker's new subroutine. Back on the Neilmann computer, he chose another ad from the database and hit display. Then he pressed the *Stimulate* icon on his phone and watched as Dave's brain waves began to change.

21

She worked all day trying to get the communication link on her program to stabilize, but with no luck. Vega looked up when Drexel poked his head in her office, smiled and pointed to his watch.

"Hey, you at a good breaking point? I know it's early, but I also know you said you can't be late getting home, so I thought I'd take a chance. Want to go grab a drink? A real one this time?"

Vega knew she needed some relaxation time after being heads-down for hours, and she probably wasn't going to figure out the solution to her problem in the next hour, so she shut the lid on her computer and stood up.

"Sure. Why not? Let's go before I change my mind."

An afternoon with Drexel sounded better than she wanted to admit, so she grabbed her backpack and followed him out. They walked outside and into the domes, right in front of the building. A lot of the downtown businesses had copied Amazon after they'd built theirs. Some simply put gardens on the roofs while others put enclosed spaces in front filled with trees and other natural elements. Neilmann had done a good job of populating their domes with trees, bushes, grass and flowers—a little extra nature in the heart of downtown Seattle. Peering up through the trees, she saw the sun was already low in the sky. Fall was quickly approaching.

"It's really beautiful here."

"Yes, it is," he said, looking at her instead of the scenery.

Sure she was blushing, but pretending not to notice his gaze, she continued, "I wish I'd come down here before I started working for Neilmann. I love this area and they did a great job of creating a little oasis downtown. I've just been too busy."

"With your mom?"

"Yeah, mostly."

"How is she, by the way?"

"Not so good. She has another UTI and the antibiotics aren't working yet."

"I'm sorry."

"No reason for you to be sorry. I've been dealing with this stuff for a long time."

"That's rough, though."

They walked up to a little sidewalk bar hidden behind several Japanese maple trees whose feathery green leaves were just turning yellow, and Drexel motioned to the short menu behind the counter.

"They don't have much of a selection, I'm afraid—wine or beer."

"I didn't realize there was a bar here. We can drink liquor outside?"

"It's still considered a part of Neilmann, even though technically, it's outside of the main building. It's only open to employees."

"How do they know we're employees?"

"Curtis knows me, don't you?" he asked, nodding to the hefty man behind the bar.

"Yep. He's a regular."

"Don't be telling her my secrets."

Curtis zipped his lips shut. "Beer or wine?"

"If he doesn't know you, just show him your badge."

"I see," said Vega. "Beer is fine," she said. "Unless it's an IPA."

"Don't care for IPAs?" asked Drexel.

"Too sharp for me. Too much bunny."

Drexel raised his eyebrows, and Vega grinned. "Sorry. Learned that from a friend of mine. I mean, hops."

"Funny."

"Just a little inside joke."

"Between you and whom?"

"My friend, Trent. We've known each other since grade school."

Curtis took their order, handed them their beers in plastic cups, and they walked deeper into the domes.

"I've never heard you mention him before. In fact, I've rarely heard you talk about anyone except your mom."

"Sadly, there aren't many people in my life. Mainly just Trent, my mom and all the doctors and nurses."

"Is that by choice?"

"No, well, yes." Vega sighed. "Honestly, I don't even know anymore."

She took a sip of her beer and it was good—not too bitter, but with a little complexity—just the way she liked it.

"It's hard to socialize," she answered. "I feel bad enough about having a nurse with her every day, so now I try to spend as much time with her as possible when I'm not at work."

"How often did they come before you got this job?"

"Usually once a week, but sometimes they came an extra day, depending on what I needed to get done."

"And you do everything else?"

"Yeah."

"Why?"

Vega kept her answer simple. "Money," she said.

"Oh."

"No, that's not totally true."

"It's OK. You don't have to tell me your life story."

"No, it's fine. Honestly, I don't enjoy relying on anyone else. If it wasn't for her almost burning the house down, I probably would have never called the nursing service."

"What happened?"

"She put sugar water in a pan on the stove to make hummingbird food, but she went back to her bedroom and forgot all about it. When I came home, the smoke alarm was wailing, the kitchen was filled with smoke, and the bottom of the pan had practically burned through. I was so freaked out, I just stood there and stared at it like a zombie. But thankfully, I came to my senses, pulled the pan off the stove, turned off the burner and threw open all the windows. I was lucky the fire alarm sprinklers hadn't come on. That would have caused major damage. But I can't imagine what would have happened if I had come home five minutes later. I found my mom in the back yard wandering around with her hands over her ears, crying."

"Holy shit! You were really lucky!"

"I know. And the kicker was that we didn't even have a hummingbird feeder anymore. The bears liked them too much and were constantly pulling them down, so we hadn't had one in years."

"Then you got the nurses?"

"Yes, but what a pain in the butt! So much paperwork and so many questions. It took me more than a month to get through all the bureaucracy, and it was humiliating. After all that, once they started coming, I almost had to cancel them anyway."

"How come?"

"My mom would not cooperate. It's one of the traits of Alzheimer's. She used to be so loving and sweet, but by that time, she'd gotten argumentative and stubborn. She kind of reminded me of how I used to act when I was a teenager."

"Oh, you were the rebellious type?"

"For a little while. Anyway, the nurses did their best to make good with my mom, but the first time I left her alone with them, she went into her bedroom, locked the door and didn't come out all day. I took the lock off her door after that—something I should have done long ago. It took two months before she let the nurses take her blood pressure and temperature and start giving her shots and medications. I was never sure whether she finally decided to cooperate or her mental state had just deteriorated so much she couldn't tell if the person helping her was me or a nurse."

She looked at him. "Sorry, I didn't mean to blather on."

"It's OK. I'm glad you feel comfortable talking to me. I want to know more about your life."

"Enough about me. What about you? How long have you been at Neilmann?"

"Four years. I always wanted to work here."

"How come?"

Drexel hesitated. "It seemed like a good place to move around. I thought I would never get bored because there are a lot of different departments I could work in."

"Hmm. That's an interesting reason. I never would have thought of that."

Vega was feeling a buzz from her beer. *I'm a cheap date*, she thought, and then realized it actually felt like a date. They walked to a small grassy area where she sat down on the soft grass, and Drexel dropped beside her, his shoulders touching hers.

"Not a bad way to spend the afternoon, huh?" he asked.

"Not bad at all."

They sat in silence for a while, and eventually, she broke the trance, stood up and dropped her cup in a nearby recycling bin.

"Thanks for the beer, but I should really get going."

He hopped up and asked, "No time for another one?"

"No. I need to get home."

Drexel looked at his phone.

"It's barely five. Could I entice you to another beer if I give you a glimpse of my living quarters?"

"Your living quarters?"

"Yeah, I have a loft right around the corner—in the Titan building."

"I didn't know you lived so close. That sure makes for an easy commute. How do you afford to live downtown? Neilmann must pay their bosses well."

"It was a gift."

"I'm sorry. That was rude of me."

"I don't mind."

"In that case, from whom?" she asked.

"My dad. And nice grammar, by the way."

"What?"

"Whom."

"Oh, thank you very much. Remember, I'm a bit of a grammar snob."

Drexel chuckled and gave her a smile. "I remember. Why do you think I complimented you?"

"Call me impressed, then. Great memory."

"What grammar faux pas bothers you the most?"

"Hmm. I guess it would be when people say, in regards to."

"What's wrong with that?"

"It should only be one regard. In regard to."

"Oh. I didn't know that. I probably say it."

"I try not to correct people, but my tongue gets sore a lot."

"Huh?"

"From biting it."

Drexel laughed, and said, "I didn't realize you had such a sense of humor."

"I didn't realize you were rich."

"Technically, *I'm* not."

Vega really wanted to know what his parents did for a living to make so much money, but she'd already been rude enough, asking how he afforded his place. She always wondered how the hell people could live in downtown Seattle. *It was so expensive!* Maybe he'd tell her once they got to know each other better.

"What do you think?" he asked.

"Sure, why not? You're right, I've got a little time. Show me your lair."

* * *

Vega had always wanted to live in downtown Seattle—not that she didn't love their little house in Redmond—but she wanted to experience the hustle and bustle of living downtown. She envisioned starting her mornings by heading down to Pike Place Market, getting a yummy pastry and hot coffee, and then enjoying them both as she took an invigorating stroll beside the water. In the evenings, she would simply walk down the street and pop into a cozy nightclub, where she'd listen to a local band while having drinks with her many friends.

Her perfect place would be a huge loft apartment with lots of exposed brick, big metal ductwork and large windows overlooking the sound. She knew she'd never be able to afford a place like that, but she could dream.

They rode up to the top floor, and Drexel unlocked the door to his loft. Vega followed him in, running into his back when he came to a dead stop.

"What are you doing here?" she heard him ask.

She prodded him forward, shut the door and came to his side to see a man sitting on a black leather couch.

"Can't a father come to see his son?"

"Of course. I'm just surprised." He turned and said, "This is Vega. She works with me at Neilmann. Vega, this is my father, John."

She walked forward and held out her hand. "Nice to meet you, sir."

John stood up and looked down at her, standing easily a foot taller. He brushed out the wrinkles in his tailored, dark navy-blue jacket, adjusted his red silk tie and then grasped her hand, squeezing a little harder than was necessary.

"Manners. Hard to find these days, son. Vega, you say?"

"Yes, sir," she said, deciding to keep the formality going since it seemed to impress him so much.

"And what do you do at this little marketing company?"

"It's not a *little* company, John."

"Ah, yes, I forgot. Proud of it, aren't you? I could buy it next week, son. If it's not a formidable adversary, then it's a *little* company."

Vega tried to ignore the obvious tension. "I'm a programmer, sir."

"Just a programmer?"

"A *senior* programmer, to be specific."

"I see. And how long have you been with them?"

"Only a couple of months."

"You have time to climb up the ladder. My son has worked there for four years, and he's still only a senior manager."

"I'm working on it, John."

"You've been saying that since you first started there, and you've only been able to move up one level. When I was your age, I was already a VP. I can see now why you're not advancing any faster. Perhaps if you spent more of your spare time on your work, and less on your extracurricular activities," he said, looking at Vega, "you would already be further in your career. When I was working my way up at —"

"John, stop it. Can we not do this right now?"

John smoothed back his thick salt-and-pepper hair and jingled the keys in his front right pocket.

"Very well. But I'll be back tomorrow, and I expect to be brought up to date on your plans to get your career back on track."

He nodded at Vega. "Miss, I trust you will not be a deterrent to my son's future." He pointed at Drexel. "Tomorrow." Then he walked out the door without a look back.

22

Drexel shut the door behind his father and stood there. Vega wasn't sure what to do with herself.

"Maybe I should go?"

He turned around. "No! Don't go. Sorry about that. I just wasn't expecting him."

"He has a key to your place?"

"Yeah. He bought it for me, so I guess he feels like that gives him carte blanche to come and go whenever he feels like it."

"Oh."

Vega tried to relax and looked around the main living area. It was like Drexel had read her mind and found the loft of her dreams. The west wall was a large bank of windows that provided an unobstructed view of the glistening water of the sound. It was one of those few amazingly beautiful pre-fall days in the PNW—clear and brisk. Boats from large to small bobbed on the calm water, and she watched as a jet ski bounced across the small waves.

The opposite wall was exposed red brick, and large, silver ductwork hung from a high ceiling. It was perfect.

"Your place is great. I admit I'm a little jealous."

"Thanks. I love it, but there's not a lot of privacy—only door is the one to the bedroom, and I guess the small half bath in the corner there. But I like the openness of it."

"That's why I find lofts so appealing. They seem large, even if they're not. And your view is stunning."

"The only thing better would be if I had bought it myself. Then John wouldn't feel so entitled."

"I don't mean to be nosy, but why do you call him John?"

"Let's just say he's not the type of man you call *dad*. I guess you noticed he's a little formal."

And a little too fixated on your career from the sound of it, she thought. "Yes. Anyway, none of my business."

She walked to the window and looked out. "Do you go to Pike Place Market every day for fresh fish and flowers?"

Drexel shook his head and smiled. "I had visions of doing that when I first moved in. You know, cooking some just-off-the-boat tuna or swordfish every evening; bringing home vegetables to grill in the summer; buying fresh flowers for the house every week. I do that, but not nearly as often as I thought I would. Other things in life keep getting in the way, or probably, I let them get in the way. And it's so busy in the summer with all the tourists. I guess we set our own priorities."

"That's true. It's taken me a long time to realize that, though. I always thought I didn't have time for things. But I think if we really want to do something, we make the time."

"I agree. And you know what I want to do right now?"

"What?"

"Have another beer. How about you?"

"Do you have anything non-alcoholic? I still have to drive home."

"Right. How about a soda?"

"Yeah, that sounds good."

While Drexel was in the kitchen, Vega walked over to a large bookshelf and browsed through the titles: *Understanding the Brain*, *The Psychology of Today*, *Programming for Beginners*, *How to read Body Language*, *Understanding Emotions from Facial Expressions*.

He handed her a can of soda. "Do you mind a can?"

"No, I prefer it. Otherwise, the ice just melts and makes it too watery. Interesting book collection you have here."

"I have a lot of varied interests."

"I imagine some of these help you understand people better. Have you been able to use anything you've learned to help you run your focus groups?"

"I'm not sure I could say that. But I do enjoy learning how to read people better, and I'm interested in what we're doing and how the MYND headband works—how someone's actions can be better understood and measured from their biometric responses."

She picked up a book on programming and flipped through a few pages. "Are you also a programmer?"

"I dabble a bit."

"I'm surprised you have hard copies. Haven't you heard of this thing called e-books?"

"Sometimes I prefer a physical book, you know? It can be annoying to pull out an electronic device and sort through a bunch of menus just to read something." He took the book from her and ran his hand across the paper. "And you know, I know it's old-fashioned, but I kind of like the feel of actual paper."

Vega nodded. "No, I understand. I have a few *real* books myself."

He closed the book, slid it back into the bookshelf and took her hand. "Come on. You can delve into my deep, dark secrets later."

They sat on his couch and looked out the window.

"To your future success," he said, holding his beer out for a clink.

She tapped his bottle with her can.

"Thanks."

Vega took a swig of soda and leaned back into the couch, allowing herself to relax and sink deeply into the plush, soft leather. She couldn't remember the last time she'd been at someone else's place or even spent an evening with someone other than her mother or Trent. She could get used to this.

Drexel mirrored her lounging posture and put his feet up on the coffee table. They turned to each other to say something, found themselves inches apart, and he took advantage of the closeness, leaned in and kissed her. She didn't pull away.

"I've wanted to do that for a while," he admitted.

"You have?"

"I was waiting for the right opportunity. I didn't think it would be nice to lay one on you in the cafeteria."

"You were ready to kiss me so soon?"

He grinned, and she grinned back. "Does Neilmann frown on employees fraternizing with each other?"

"Fraternizing?" He snickered at her wording. "No. But…"

"Maybe I shouldn't have let you kiss me?"

"No?"

"But it's too late now."

"That's true." He pulled her closer. "In that case, why don't we do it again?"

"I like the way you think," she said and kissed him, this time a little harder, a little deeper. There was more feeling behind this one. She pulled away. "Is that really still a thing?"

"What?"

"Romances in the workplace being frowned upon. Is that really still an issue?"

"I don't think so. It's not like it's spelled out in our employee guidelines or anything. And I don't really see much harm in it, except I guess, when things go awry. Then you still have to work with your ex. That's not always very pleasant, and it makes things awkward sometimes."

"I can't imagine having to work with my ex after we split up."

"That bad?"

"You don't want to know. Jay was clueless. There's no way I would still want to be around him."

"By ex, do you mean ex-husband?"

"God, no. I've never been married. I was talking about my ex-boyfriend and our last date together, except I left him alone, so I guess we weren't together much that day. For our six-month anniversary, he took me to a mud-bogging race, which, for some reason, he thought I would enjoy. That's how well he knew me, and that's the day we broke up."

"Mud bogging?"

"Yeah, it's where a bunch of jacked-up trucks race around a track made of sloppy, wet mud. Let's just say, don't wear your Sunday best because it will never be clean again."

"I know I don't know you very well yet, but I can't see you enjoying something like that."

"See, you already know me better than he did." Vega said. "So, back to that kiss…"

"You're not worried about us breaking up later?"

"Just don't take me mud bogging."

"I promise."

"And, I guess if we start this…"

"We'd better not end it."

"Does that mean we have to get married?" she asked.

Drexel shifted on the couch, took her can from her and set it on the coffee table and leaned in close.

"No need to think that far ahead."

23

To prepare for her first night shift, Maria had tried to sleep in the afternoon, but she was having a bad evening. She only got about four hours of shut-eye and had a splitting headache. But after taking all the aspirin she could stomach, aching head or not, she had to get to her new job. She couldn't afford to screw this up.

Maybe some yogurt would help coat her stomach, she thought, grabbing a carton out of her refrigerator. She scarfed it down and swallowed three more aspirins with her coffee before getting on the road.

The rush-hour traffic was busy as usual, but luckily, 520 was still moving at a decent pace. She tried not to lose her temper at the asshole who cut in front of her, but her head was pounding, and before she knew what she was doing, she looked over at the offending car and screamed, *Asshole!* Then she flipped the driver the finger. Shocked at her own behavior, she pulled her hand down quickly, hoping he hadn't seen it. She looked up to the sunny sky and saw bright, sparkling lights. *Lightning?* It wasn't even raining.

But when she looked back at the road, the lights were still there. She shook her head, trying to clear her vision, and in her rearview mirror, noticed a large black SUV right on her tail.

She sped up, but the SUV stayed with her, and she panicked, pressing her foot down on the gas, and zigzagging through small gaps in the traffic. The flashing lights now filled her eyes, melding together as she watched the headlights of the car behind her getting closer and closer. Then she realized who it was—*her old boss! He wasn't going to let her go! Was he following her to her new job? He was going to abuse her there, just like he'd done at the motel!*

She turned, and the lights of the SUV behind her were so close, she couldn't understand why the car hadn't hit her back bumper yet. Her brain was splitting in half from the pain and in an involuntary reflexive movement, she screamed and jerked her hands up to her head. Her legs stiffened, and she pressed the gas pedal down to the floor. There was a crunching sound as her car lurched forward and plowed into the car in front of her, and with the pedal still down, she kept moving, shoving the damaged car into the next lane over. She heard more smashes behind her as she continued forward, fighting to regain control. Her brain felt like it was on fire. She grabbed the steering wheel and turned it left, away from a second car she'd just hit, but another shock of pain seared through her cranium, and her hands left the wheel again.

She barreled into car after car, and so many lights now flashed in front of her eyes, she could barely see. Her brain felt like it was pushing its way out of her skull, and she didn't know why her head hadn't exploded yet.

By the time it was all over, Marie had crashed into a string of cars all the way from Northrup Way, along a six-mile stretch to the West Lake Sammamish exit. When she finally hit the concrete highway divider head-on, the only thing that saved her from instant death was her airbag. Seventeen wrecked cars lay in her wake.

24

What had she been thinking? Vega was furious at herself for not checking the traffic before she left Drexel's because apparently, there was a huge accident on 520, and traffic was backed up for miles. It was five thirty, and at this rate, it would take at least an hour to get home. If she could just make it to the next exit, she'd take the back roads.

She hit the call button on her steering wheel and rang the nurse.

"Hello?"

"Julia? Hey, it's Vega. I'm running a bit late. Can you stay a little longer tonight?"

"Sure. When do you think you'll be home?"

"It will probably be another hour."

"OK. I'll be here."

"Thanks. I really appreciate it. I'll be home as soon as I can."

She didn't know why she'd gone off with Drexel to his loft. She should know better by now than to try to have a social life, but as she thought back to their time together that afternoon, she smiled. It was all good, and it had been nice to feel relaxed and wanted. Jay had never treated her so gently or cared about her satisfaction the way Drexel had.

* * *

She made it home by six seventeen—a whole thirteen minutes to spare. Coming in from the carport, she hung her coat on the rack in the mudroom and walked to the living room at the front of the house. Julia was sitting on the couch reading a book with Miren next to her in her wheelchair watching *The Golden Girls.* It had always been one of her favorites, but Vega was pretty sure her mom had no idea anymore what was happening on the screen. She kissed her on the forehead, but her mother swatted her away like an annoying fly and she stepped back. It was one of the little things her mother did now and then that broke Vega's heart.

"Don't let it get to you," said Julia.

Vega looked over and said, "Yeah, I know, but. Anyway, hi. Thank you for waiting for me. How'd it go today?"

"OK, but you may want to talk to the doctor."

"Why?"

"You know she's been having a much harder time swallowing lately?"

"I noticed that."

"I heard about a new drug that just got approved by the FDA, and it's supposed to be good at helping with that."

"Is it covered? Will my insurance cover it?"

"I don't know, because it's an out-of-network drug, and it's new. It's not available in a generic form yet, so you'll have to check."

"Probably not," she said. "And it's probably two hundred dollars for a thirty-day supply."

"More like three hundred and forty-seven."

"Jesus, I was kidding!"

"I know. Sorry," Julia said.

"Are you sure it would help? Will she be able to get something down for a change?"

"I don't know. You know, with this disease, nothing is a sure thing, but it can't hurt to check with the doctor. I think it's shown improvement in a lot of cases."

"Three hundred and fifty dollars?"

"Forty-seven."

She rolled her eyes. "Oh good. I'll have enough left over for a coffee."

Julia looked like she wanted to pat Vega on the head. "Sorry. Just think about it, OK? I can talk to the doctor about it if you like."

"No, I'm sorry. I don't mean to take it out on you. It's not your fault," she said with a sigh. "Wait, can you ask for some samples first?"

"I don't know, but I'll try."

"Did she have any other problems today?"

"Nothing I couldn't handle," she said, putting on her coat.

After the nurse left, it was dinner and time spent with her mom, then laundry duties and cleaning. Miren barely noticed as Vega rolled her wheelchair into the bedroom, parked it next to the side of the bed and locked the brakes. Her mother's frail feet were covered with pink and white polka-dot socks with white plastic grips on the bottom, and Vega gently picked them up and swung the chair's footrests out of the way.

"OK, Mom, here we go."

To get her into bed, Miren was so weak now Vega had to support almost all her mother's weight. It was times like these she was thankful her mother didn't weigh more than she did.

"One, two, three!"

Her mother moaned and said, "Time to get up?"

"No, Mom. It's late. It's bedtime now."

She checked to make sure her mom's bum was on top of the mattress. Then, after five more minutes of scooting her around, adjusting the sheets and covers, and positioning and repositioning the pillows, Miren was finally comfortable. She raised the side bed rails and stored the wheelchair at the rear of the bed. Vega didn't like the rails. They seemed so confining—like they turned the bed into a jail. But her mom had fallen out of bed several times already this year from seizures or loss of muscle control, and now the rails were a necessity.

"I'll be in my bedroom if you need me," Vega said.

But Miren didn't seem to hear her, and her eyes looked at her blankly. Vega smiled weakly, stroked her mother's cheek and gave her a kiss on the forehead. At least this time, her mom didn't swat her away.

Back in her bedroom, she took off her bra, changed into some sweats and a long-sleeved t-shirt, opened her laptop and started browsing. But instead of focusing on the screen, she found herself daydreaming about Drexel.

25

To get the last box stuffed it into the car, Jenny had to smash it down a bit. Thankfully, it was mostly clothes. Tanya put her hands on the trunk and asked, "Is that the last one?"

"That's it."

Tanya slammed it shut, and Jenny looked back at her childhood home and saw her mom peeking out the living room window, quickly stepping back and whipping the lace curtain closed when she saw Jenny looking at her. Wiping tears from her eyes, she sniffed and asked her friend, "You mind driving?"

"No problem," Tanya said, taking the keys from Jenny's hand. "Anything else you gotta do before we go to my place?"

"No. Let's just get out of here. I don't wanna be here when Dad gets home."

She nodded, scooted into the driver's seat, and Jenny waited until they were halfway to Tanya's apartment before finally breaking the silence.

"I can't believe she kicked me out."

"I thought you kinda expected that?"

"I know that's what I said, but I didn't really think she would do it."

"I hate to say I told you so, but, you know, I kinda told you so."

Jenny sat on her hands and stared out the windshield.

"I really thought she'd understand. It's not like the Kitten Club is all nude. Hell, a lot of quote, professional dancers wear skimpy outfits too, so what's the big difference? I mean, I'm not a prostitute!"

"Yeah, but you know that's what most people think, don't you? Soon as you tell 'em you're a stripper, that's the first thing they go to—stripper equals prostitute. They don't get it."

"Yeah, but to be fair, we both know some of the girls are taking tricks on the side."

"Yeah, I know. But that ain't you, and it sure as hell ain't me. And anyhow, your mom oughta know you better'n that."

Jenny played with the cross on her necklace, swishing it back and forth along the chain. "Yeah, I really thought she would get it. I mean, I'm making so much money! You know, just another year, and I might have my student loans paid off. I thought she would be happy about that, but it just made her more upset. Like, then she was sure I was a prostitute!"

She pounded her fists on her head. "Stupid, stupid! Why did I tell her?"

"It's gonna be OK. Don't worry. You can stay at my place as long as you need to."

Reaching over, Jenny wrapped her hand around Tanya's on the steering wheel. "Thanks. I don't know what I'd do without you."

Tanya chuckled. "Yes you do. You'd be callin' Kirk right now. He'd take you back in a heartbeat."

Jenny cringed at the name, but she knew her friend was probably right. She'd met Kirk at the club, but the management had a policy about not going out with customers, and she didn't want to lose her job, so she blew him off. But eventually he broke her down. She went out with him anyway, and it was good, until it wasn't. As soon as things started to get heavy, he wanted her to quit her job. He said he couldn't stand all those other men looking at her body. So she cut him off, and he never came to the club again. But she knew if she called him, he would come back to her. At least, that's what she told herself.

"I don't need him. You're here."

"That's right, girlfriend!" Tanya said, with a high-five.

After they unloaded her boxes into the front room of Tanya's one-bedroom apartment and dug out a few of Jenny's essentials, they made up the pull-out sofa, poured themselves a glass of wine and sat back on the pillows. They clanked their glasses together.

"To your new life!"

"To my new life!"

Tanya leaned over to set her glass on the table next to the couch and picked up her phone. "Oh! I forgot to tell you!"

"What?"

She flipped through the apps on her phone and pulled up a screenshot from an Instagram posting and showed it to Jenny.

"Saw this the other day. I don't know what it is exactly, but it's from that big company in downtown Seattle. I'm sure you've seen their building, Neilmann Corporation?"

"Oh, yeah. It's a marketing company."

"Look at you."

"Hey, I didn't go to college for nothin'!" Jenny joked.

Chuckling, Tanya said, "Well, that marketing company is lookin' for volunteers, and they're payin' five hundred smackers for two hours!"

"What?"

She yanked the phone out of Tanya's hand and read it.

Volunteers needed!
$500 for two hours of your time.
Group sessions.
Time: Saturday, September 8, 9:00am
Location: Neilmann Corporation, 721 Pine Street, Seattle

"Wow! But surely they've already filled the spots?" she asked. "They probably have hundreds of volunteers by now. That's a lot of money!"

"No! Get this, I sent a DM to the poster, and they wrote back and said they were lookin' for twenty people in a certain age range, had to be local, and they needed two more. He said he was gonna delete the post as soon as they had enough, so I signed us up, and as soon as I did, the post was gone!" Tanya said with a big smile. "I hope that's OK."

"What? Of course it's OK! Are you kidding? Five hundred dollars for two hours? What do we have to do?"

"I don't kow. But who the fuck cares? Can't be any worse than strippin' at the Kitten Klub. Like you said, they're a marketing company. It's not like they make torture devices or somethin'."

Jenny laughed and said, "You're right. Who cares?" She held her glass up for another toast. "To making money!"

"Hell yeah, girl!"

26

Vega was writing ideas for the base code for the MYND application when Astrid stuck her head in the door.

"Hey, you busy?"

"Just jotting down some thoughts about how to stabilize the program's connection. Any ideas?"

"If I knew how to do that, we wouldn't have had to hire you."

Vega sighed. "Right. What's up?"

"Are you at a good stopping point?"

"I could use a break," she said, rubbing her temples.

"How would you like to go to lunch with me today?"

Rolling back from her desk, Vega shut the lid on her laptop. "Sure. When?"

"How about right now?"

"OK."

"The whole time you've been here, all we've done is talk about work, and I think it's time we talked about something other than brain waves."

Vega laughed. "You're right. Sounds like fun. I would love to! Cafeteria?"

"Hell, no! I know the food there is good and all, but let's get out of here for a while. You do remember that we work in a city with a lot of great restaurants? But since it's short notice, why don't we go to the Crab Shack? They have outside seating with heaters and we can enjoy a lunch by the water. What do you think? Do you like seafood?"

"I love it. Where is it?"

"By Pike Place Market—on the water."

"Sure. Why not? My brain could use a rest, and my body could use a nice walk. I sit too much working here."

"Don't we all?"

* * *

The day was chilly, gray and wet for September, but it was only drizzling, and the thought of being by the water was enticing. The walk down Pine Street toward Pike Place Market was invigorating, and they took their time strolling slowly past Westlake Park, watching people hurry to their next destination donned in their light jackets and sweatshirts, faces obscured by hoods. In the PNW, you didn't pull out an umbrella unless it was pouring, and usually when it rained, it was more of a hard drizzle than a downpour.

Astrid turned to Vega. "Are you enjoying it so far?"

"Yeah, I am. More than I thought I would. Honestly? It's kind of nice to get out of the house."

"You stayed home a lot, taking care of your mom?"

"Almost every day."

"How old is she?"

"She's only fifty-six. And she's pretty far gone—rarely knows who I am or what year or day it is. I don't even think she knows where she is anymore. She barely talks."

"God, I'm so sorry to hear that. Who takes care of her while you're at work?"

"There are several nurses who come in. They're good. They know what they're doing. But it's still hard to leave her every day. I mean, it feels so good to get away, but I feel so guilty for doing it."

"I can't even imagine."

"Anyway, let's change the subject."

"OK. Sorry."

"No, don't be."

They walked the rest of the way in a comfortable silence, and as they entered Pike Place Market, Vega could smell the briny smell of fresh seafood and hear the slap of fish landing as the vendors tossed them back and forth to each other, much to the enjoyment of the tourists. It was late summer, and the place was still crowded. Voices of excited vacationers broadcasted through the aisles. She looked to the right and saw the long row of booths selling fresh-cut flowers, the soft fragrances barely making a dent through the odor of seafood.

They meandered their way through Pike Place Market, continued down to Elliot Way, and when they arrived at the restaurant, Vega smelled the salt of the sound and the rich aromas of melted butter and boiling crabs. People placed their orders at a small formica counter, and next to it, live crabs in a glass tank crawled over each other, searching feverishly for an escape route. Near the water sat several wooden picnic tables with a plexiglass divider keeping out the worst of the biting wind whipping off the sound. Strategically placed heaters provided warmth. The place was small, but the crabs looked delicious.

They put in their orders, picked up their drinks and found an empty table.

Sipping their drinks as they waited for their food, Vega asked, "How did you end up working at Neilmann?"

"They held a recruiting event at our college. I always wanted to work in downtown Seattle, and I had one more semester before finishing my computer science degree, so I went. And hell, if they didn't hire me!"

"Where did you go to school?"

"UW."

"Me too!"

"Yes, I know."

"Right. Of course, boss."

Astrid smiled. "Your degree in medicine with a concentration in neurology is why we hired you. Oh, and your programming skills, of course."

"Thanks. I can't remember if I told you, but I was studying to be a doctor. I was focusing on neuroscience because I was hoping to help people like my mom."

"Makes sense," she said with a nod.

"What about you? Have you always wanted to be a programmer? Well, I guess you're a manager now."

"Yeah, I like it. I like programming, but I like being a manager of programmers better. Believe it or not, I find it less stressful. I prefer helping people get their projects done on time rather than being responsible for doing the actual coding myself. I guess I've discovered I enjoy working with people more than coding. Maybe I should have gone into marketing? Taken Drexel's job?"

"I don't know. You're good at what you do."

"Thanks. How'd you like working for ThinkShop?"

"I liked it. But it's nice to have a constant paycheck and real insurance for a change. Since they were a contracting service, they didn't offer a lot of benefits. I'm enjoying the ones at Neilmann, for sure."

"Yeah, they are nice."

"But it gave me a lot of flexibility to take off when my mom needed extra help."

"I can always work something out if you need time off for that kind of thing."

"I know. Thanks."

"How are you getting along with Ryker?"

Vega rolled her eyes. "It's fine. He's a bit of a weird bird, though. I don't think he likes me."

"Nonsense. He's just hard to read."

The conversation halted as their food arrived, and the server placed plates of large, steaming crabs in front of them.

"This looks great!" Vega exclaimed as she admired the plump, luscious-looking crab and inhaled the aroma of hot, melted butter.

After a few minutes of cracking open their crabs, devouring the largest chunks of meat, and licking butter off their fingers, Astrid asked, "Are you seeing Drexel?"

Vega caught some food in her throat and coughed.

"Sorry. Too forward?"

"No. It's fine," she said. "Why did you think so?"

"I saw you two hanging out the other day."

"Oh."

"I know you're working with him, but come on, you can tell me. You guys looked awfully cozy. Seemed like a little more than a simple work meeting. Are you hooking up?"

"Hooking up? I don't really like that term. It makes it sound like all you're doing is having sex."

"So, you are having sex?"

Vega's mouth fell open, and she was glad she'd just swallowed her bite of crab.

"Sorry. Should have warned you. I've been accused of not being very subtle."

Vega stalled and took a sip of her drink. "I do like him."

"You are, aren't you?"

Sure her face was turning red, she replied, "I plead the fifth."

"Kind of a gamble to date someone at work, though. Might not turn out well, and then you're stuck looking at them every day," Astrid said as she dug out a juicy white lump of meat and dunked it in butter.

"Yeah, I thought about that."

"And he's not looking for anything long term. Just so you know."

"How do you know? Did you and Drexel date?"

Astrid took her time chewing her crab and took a drink before she answered. "It's been almost a year ago now. No big deal."

"What happened?"

"Difference of opinion."

"About? Oh, sorry. I don't mean to pry. It's really none of my business."

"No, it's fine. After all, I'm the one who brought it up. I guess I got too fucking heavy for him."

Astrid chuckled and put a hand over her mouth. "Oops! Sorry, again. You're also going to learn that I have a bit of a sailor's mouth when I'm not at work."

Vega shrugged. "Don't worry about it. Nothing I haven't said before myself."

"Oh, thank goodness. Anyway, back to Drexel. He wanted something light. I'm ready to settle down and start a family, you know?"

She nodded. Vega understood the pull to have kids, although it was pretty much the furthest thing from her mind right now. She had enough responsibility. They dug into more crab, and she said, "I get it. Sometimes the timing isn't right. But you seem like you get along fine with him now."

"Yeah, it's OK. I learned to push everything down. You know what they say, *fake it 'til you make it.*"

"You still have feelings for him?"

"Yeah, well. I'll get over it."

"Crap, I'm sorry, Astrid. Is this weird?"

She waved her off. "No! I didn't mean to make you feel guilty or anything. If you and Drexel are a thing, I'm fine with it. Don't stop seeing him because you're worried about hurting my feelings or something. Really. I'm sorry I brought it up. I just wanted to get to know you a little better."

Astrid stood up and threw her demolished crab shells in the trash. "Come on. We'd better get back before Ms. Neilmann sends security after us."

Vega smiled. "OK. This was fun, though. We should do it again soon."

"Absolutely."

As they walked back to Neilmann, the drizzle gave over to rain, and rushing through the streets made it difficult to talk. Astrid gave her a quick hug as she got off on the third floor, saying she still needed a little time in the zen room before going back to her office.

Vega felt bad. It was clear to her that Astrid was lying. She obviously still had feelings for Drexel.

27

Vega woke with a start and looked at the clock—five thirty. She'd been having a nightmare about her mom choking as she tried to swallow, calling for her. But bogged down in some kind of quagmire, Vega was moving in slow motion and couldn't get to her fast enough. She shivered, shook her head to try to shrug it off, and rubbing her eyes, pulled off the covers and swung her legs over the side of the bed.

It was too early to get ready for work, so she wrapped her flannel robe around her, slid her feet into her sheepskin slippers and went downstairs to check on her mom and make herself some coffee. Her mom was still sleeping, so she took her steaming cup of java back upstairs, opened the *Seattle Times* website, and a bold headline caught her attention. She read through the article.

Four Dead in 520 Fatal Car Pile-up

At least seventeen cars were damaged yesterday after a woman lost control of her vehicle traveling east on 520.

The accident took place around 5:30 pm between the Northrup Way and West Lake Sammamish exits.

One observer stated, "It looked like she had her foot on the gas."

At least 4 people died.

Her car was speeding at 85 miles per hour when it struck the first car in the 60 mile per hour speed zone. Two victims died on the scene, and two others were rushed to nearby Overlake Hospital, where they passed away later that night.

According to the King County Chief Medical Examiner, Dr. Akshay Kumar, it's believed the driver, Ms. Marie Castle, suffered a mental episode, causing her to lose touch with reality.

"Possibly her muscles stiffened, and she pressed the gas pedal to the floor of the vehicle," said Agnes Maynord, King County Sheriff. "We believe she was in a confused state at the time of the accident."

Maynord also claimed Marie spoke incoherently at the scene of the accident before she died at the scene, insisting a large, sexually crazed man from Best Motel had been chasing her in his black SUV. However, no sign of a vehicle matching that description was discovered in CCTV footage.

"She was OK when I saw her last week," said close friend, Ash Walker, who worked with Marie at the

Bellevue Animal Shelter. "We had gone to this test thing together to make some extra money. She was fine!"

Marie's parents refused to comment.

Twelve people were injured in the series of crashes. Two have now fallen into a coma and are in ICU at Overlake.

"There were comments made to the EMT by Ms. Castle," said Dr. Kumar the next day, "that were consistent with psychosis. It has now been supported by forensic findings that, at the time of the accident, she was in the middle of a psychotic episode."

Vega wondered what had caused the woman to have a psychotic episode while she was driving. *Had she been off her meds?* She couldn't imagine why someone in that state of mind would get behind the wheel and endanger everyone's lives.

Not interested in reading any more depressing news, she closed her laptop and got ready for the day.

* * *

Vega spent the whole morning in the lab, skipped lunch and was head-down coding and testing all day trying to solve the ongoing connectivity issue with her program. She was headed back upstairs to her office when her cell phone rang, and her heart sped up when she looked at the caller ID.

"Hello, Danielle?"

"Vega, thank god! I've been trying to reach you all day. I had to call an ambulance to take Miren to the hospital."

"What? Why?"

"Her UTI has gotten much worse, and the antibiotics aren't helping. She was having major hallucinations, and they had to give her a shot just to get her in the ambulance. I've been trying to call you all day long."

"What do you mean?" Then it hit her. "Oh, shit! I'm so sorry! I forgot to give you guys the phone number for the lab, and the cell phone service doesn't work down there! Oh my god! I totally forgot. I'm so, so sorry! OK, I'm on my way!" Vega started to hang up, but heard Danielle yelling at her from the phone.

"Wait! Vega!"

"Yes?"

"They've got her on an IV because she was dehydrated, and they switched her to a different antibiotic, so hopefully, her UTI will start improving soon. And like I said, they had to give her something to calm her down, and she's asleep right now, so there's no reason for you to rush over."

Vega took a deep breath and tried to calm down. "Are you sure?"

"She wouldn't even know you're here. I think she's going to be asleep for a few hours."

"OK. OK," she said, trying to calm her racing heart. "Will you stay with her until I get there? I don't want her to wake up and be alone."

"Sure. I would be at your house with her anyway. So, it doesn't matter. The doctor said she'll probably sleep for at least a couple of hours, so there's no hurry."

"OK. I'll come by after work then. Is she at Overlake?"

"Yeah. Room 203."

"OK. Thank you! Thank you so much! I don't know what I'd do without you."

"You're welcome. And don't worry. I'll make sure she's well taken care of."

"Thanks again. I should be there around five thirty."

"All right. See you then."

Vega hung up and put her head on her desk. She couldn't believe she'd forgotten to give the nurses the number to the lab. *What was wrong with her!* Thank god it was just hallucinations from her UTI—like that wasn't bad enough. This was her mom's fourth one this year, and it seemed like every time she got one, they had to put her on a stronger antibiotic and keep her on it longer. Now the latest ones weren't even working anymore. *What would the doctor do if none of them worked?*

She lifted her head and tried to shove her concerns aside. There were a couple of hours left in her day, and there was nothing she could do right now anyway. Might as well get some work done. Ms. Neilmann had told her she wanted the program running by the end of the week. Vega didn't know what the repercussions would be for her if she couldn't get it ready in time for the holiday rollout, but she really didn't want to find out.

* * *

Purple veins rose like little mountains, and the IV line sticking out of Miren's thin hand looked huge. A blood pressure cup was wrapped around her tiny arm as she lay sleeping in the hospital bed. It broke Vega's heart to see her mother like this. She looked so gaunt and helpless. Not knowing what else to do with herself, she refilled the water glass and cleaned off the remnants of the meal that were still on the bedside tray. Hardly a morsel had been touched. Just as she sat down, a nurse entered the room with an IV bag in his hand.

"Hi."

"Hi," Vega replied.

"I'm Andrew, Miren's nurse today."

She stood up and extended her hand. "Vega. Her daughter. How is she?"

"She's doing better than when she first got here. But she has a severe UTI. We'll have to keep a close eye on her."

"Is the doctor coming by today?"

"No, sorry. He's already made his rounds for the day. But he'll be back tomorrow around ten o'clock."

"OK. Can you tell me anything?"

"Your mother came in very dehydrated, so as you can see, we're giving her IV fluids."

"You put her on a new antibiotic?"

"Yes. I guess you already know her UTI is proving very virulent against the usual ones, so the doctor put her on one of the strongest ones we have. It's called Avycaz."

Vega nodded. "OK. How long will she need to be in here?"

"All depends on how she responds. A lot of these UTIs have become very antibiotic resistant, so the doctor is hoping this one will do the trick. But your mom's going to need to be in here at least a week, possibly two."

"Two weeks! Why? Can't she just come home and take the antibiotics?"

Andrew shook his head. "It's not a pill. It's given intravenously, and that's the standard timeframe for Avycaz therapy."

He went about changing the bag on Miren's IV pole as she watched, still in shock from what he had revealed about her mother's condition. *Two weeks!* There was no way she could afford that. Just when Vega was thinking she might get out of debt in a couple of years with the higher pay from Neilmann. She would never get her mom in a nice place.

"Her condition is very serious," he reiterated. "But I should let the doctor tell you more. It's not really my place."

"Please don't make me wait until tomorrow morning. I've been through a lot of these with her already. Just tell me."

She watched as he drew his lips in tightly, but he gave in. "The doctor said she has pyelonephritis."

"What's that?"

"It means the UTI has spread upwards, into her kidneys. It's not a condition to be taken lightly."

"Are you saying she could die? From a UTI?"

She watched as he clenched his mouth shut, and then he said, "You'll have to talk to the doctor. I'm sure he'll be able to give you more information. I promise we're going to do everything we can for her while she's here."

What the hell was going on? Pilo-what? She bit her lip. She didn't want to cry in front of the nurse.

"Can I stay here with her in the hospital tonight?"

"We don't usually let family stay overnight unless it's a hospice situation."

"Please? I'll sleep in the chair. I don't want her to wake up and not have someone familiar with her."

Andrew gave her a quick nod. "I understand. I think we can make an exception in this case. My shift ends at eight tonight. Lori is on next but I'll let her know."

"Thank you so much. I really appreciate it."

Bag replaced, he checked Miren's blood pressure and temperature and started to leave the room.

"When do you think she'll wake up?" Vega asked.

Andrew checked his watch. "She should wake up any time now."

"OK. Thanks again."

The nurse left, and she sat down in a chair, pulled out her phone and sent a text to Trent.

Hey. Mom in hospital. You busy?

Waiting for him to text back gave her time to think. *Would Mom have gotten this sick if I'd been home with her every day instead of at work?* She'd done her best to make sure her mother got enough fluids and nourishment, but a few days ago, the doctor had recommended she take Miren off solid food and change her diet to baby food and nutrition drinks, which Vega thought was disgusting. But her mom didn't even seem to notice her meals were any different from what she had been eating before. The doctor said the foods would be easier for Miren to swallow, they would still give her the nutrients and vitamins she needed, and that it usually bothered the relatives a lot more than it bothered the patient. But even with the change in her diet, her mom struggled to get things down and often refused to eat at all.

Sometimes Vega simply didn't know what to do to help her. She felt guilty and powerless and pissed off. All at the same time.

28

The next morning, Vega woke up early and changed into the clothes Trent had brought her last night. She was bleary-eyed and tired when she went into the office, but at least it was a shorter commute. The good news was that she was close to making the MYND app a reality, but she was still having problems stabilizing the connection. After lunch, she decided she needed a change of scenery, so she closed her program and went down to the zen room to look over her notes. Sometimes, simply stepping away from her code and reading through the specs helped her discover glaring errors.

In the hospital last night, she'd stayed awake late, making notes and jotting down ideas. It had been impossible to sleep anyway, with nurses coming in the room constantly to check on her mother. When she finally almost dozed off, she had one of those light-bulb moments. Somewhere she had read that scientists had determined most of our thoughts are actually subconscious, and these ideas we get right before we go to sleep, had probably been stewing around in our brains for days. When our minds had an opportunity to relax, the solution crystallized, bubbled up to the surface and popped out. She believed it because it happened to her all the time.

Just as she was about to close her laptop and head back up to her office, Astrid came in and sat down on the beanbag chair next to her.

"Hey, how's it going?"

"Good. I think I may have solved one of my major problems."

"That's great! Has it even been three months yet?"

"Saturday was my three-month anniversary, at least by the calendar. But I guess by actual work days, it's today."

"Tell me you're still loving it."

"I am."

"Why don't you sound convincing?"

"No, I do. I just wish I could get my program stabilized."

"You'll figure it out."

"I hope so."

"So, what are you doing in here?"

"Trying to think about things differently."

"That's the point of these zen rooms. They're good, right?"

"Yes. And honestly," she said, "sometimes the view in my office is a little too nice."

"I could have some blinds installed for you."

Vega laughed and shook her head. "No! That's OK. I spend enough time in the windowless test lab. I was kidding."

"All right. I'll hold off on ordering the blinds," she said with a smile. "You're in here brainstorming?"

"Yes. I think I've figured it out, but I haven't tested it yet, so I could be wrong. I'm going to run a simulation tomorrow."

"Good. I'll let everyone know."

"What? No! I mean, I don't want an audience. I don't even know if it will work yet. There are issues with the connection. I can't keep it stable. That's what I'm trying to fix. And I haven't finished all the biometrics yet."

"I'm sure it will be fine, and besides, I'm down here because I was looking for you. Ms. Neilmann has been demanding an update on your progress. I've been giving them to her every week, but she's very eager to see the program in action, so I'm getting Daphne to set up an in-person meeting. She would be ecstatic if you could show her a working program. Tomorrow at ten?"

"Uh." Vega hated showing her program to other people, especially bosses, and especially since she didn't know if it was stable yet.

"As long as you don't think she'll expect it to—"

"Ms. Neilmann wants to see what you've done. I'm sure she won't expect it to be perfect yet. I'll get it set up."

"OK. I'd better get to my office then and start coding."

Vega pushed herself out of the beanbag chair and hurried

back to her office to try out her latest idea. She didn't want her first demo to crash and burn.

* * *

The system squawked *unknown visitor* and emitted an annoying high-frequency beep when Vega tried to get through the lower-level security system. She was nervous and wondered if her sweaty palms and bloodshot eyes were messing with the program. She tried again, but it failed again. Everyone was probably already in the conference room waiting for her. It would be embarrassing if she couldn't even get into the lab area. The third time, the reader finally announced, *Welcome, Vega Swift.*

In the hallway, Drexel was waiting for her. He leaned into her ear and whispered, "I know a work-around for that silly system."

She raised her eyebrows. "Yeah?" Astrid had told her one existed, but she didn't think she was supposed to know what it was.

"I'll tell you later. Are you nervous?"

"Yes. A little. It's been a long time since I've given a presentation, and I really didn't expect Ms. Neilmann to come to my first one."

"Are you kidding? She wouldn't miss this for the world. This project is her golden egg."

"No pressure then."

Drexel smiled and squeezed her arm. "I'm sure you'll do fine."

They entered the conference room, and as she suspected, Ms. Neilmann, Dr. Fedorov and Astrid were already there.

Everyone chatted for a while, and after a few minutes, Ms. Neilmann said, "Are we exchanging pleasantries all day or are we going to get down to business?"

"Yes, sorry," Vega said. "I think I've finished the base program of the MYND app, but I have to preface this presentation by stating that I have not yet had a code review or a chance to—"

"Fine, fine," Ms. Neilmann waved her off. "I understand it's not perfect yet. Let's get on with it, shall we?"

"Can't wait to see what you've accomplished," said Dr. Fedorov.

She looked around the room. At least Drexel and Astrid were smiling at her. "I've downloaded the app on my phone, so I'm going to project it to the screen so everyone can see what I'm doing."

Lowering a large screen covering the side wall, she powered up a small projector on the ceiling. After unlocking her phone, she went into her settings panel, started the share program, and everything on her phone displayed on the screen. She opened the MYND app, and the main menu appeared with its five selections: *Calibrate, Connect, Capture, Analyze* and *Terminate*.

"I'm going to be using myself as the guinea pig for this demonstration."

"Wait a minute," said Drexel. "How will the program know it's only reading your brain waves? Won't it get confused with all of us in the room?"

"Excellent question, Drexel," said Katya.

"Because first, as you'll see, I'm going to run a calibration routine so the MYND app can differentiate my brain from others in the area and connect only to my brain. When I press the calibrate icon, twenty-five pictures of random items will display on my screen, each for one second. I chose each picture to elicit activity only in a specific area of the brain, allowing the MYND program to pinpoint the exact location of each region. It will simultaneously take measurements of my brain waves so it can set a baseline from which to measure future activity. I selected the images from a study conducted by the National Center for Biotechnology Information. A good starting point, I thought."

"Excellent idea," said Dr. Fedorov.

Vega smiled at Ryker. It was one of the few times, other than when he was showing her his fountain pen, that he'd said something positive to her.

"I must reiterate that this is my first test. I would normally do this on my own before bringing everyone in, but Astrid, I mean, Dr. Montgomery, convinced me to go ahead."

"Yes, yes. You said that already," Ms. Neilmann complained.

Dr. Fedorov added, "You should never start out a presentation with a negative statement, Ms. Swift. You have already set our expectations too low."

"Oh, sorry."

Asshole, she thought. *Just when I thought he was being nice.* "All right. I'm going to calibrate the MYND app to my brain now." She pressed the *Calibrate* icon, and a slice of pizza, a house, a bear, and other seemingly random words and pictures appeared on the phone's display as she watched. When the images stopped, the screen displayed *Calibration Complete.*

"OK. Now that the calibration is done, I can start the connectivity routine."

She hit the *Connect* icon, and in bright green letters, the word *Connecting* displayed and began flashing. After a few seconds, the message changed to *unable to stabilize connection.*

"Hang on. Let me double-check a few things," she said. She could feel everyone watching her as she flipped through the app's menu. She scrolled down into the settings and tweaked the calibration parameters and then navigated back to the main screen and hit the connect symbol again. The connecting message displayed again, started flashing, and after a few seconds, it changed to bright green letters stating, *Connected*, and Vega breathed a sigh of relief.

"Looks like it connected this time," said Dr. Montgomery.

But before the words were out of Astrid's mouth, the green message flickered off, turned to red and said the connection had dropped.

"That's weird," she said. She tried again, but the same problem occurred, and after five attempts, Astrid stepped in.

"I think you need to go back to the drawing board, Vega. It's just your first test. Don't get discouraged."

"Yes, I guess you're right," she said, closing the MYND application and stopping the projection. She was mortified that she had failed in front of everyone—especially Ms. Neilmann.

Why hadn't she been firmer with Astrid and demanded she let her do the first test on her own?

"Sorry everyone."

Ms. Neilmann stood up and gave Astrid an icy stare. "Don't waste my time again until you know you have something that works."

Vega watched her as she turned and walked out of the room.

"Maybe in the future you should conduct these trials on your own time before calling us in to watch a failed experiment? Some of us have important work to do," said Ryker, who abruptly got up and followed Katya out of the room.

Vega turned to Astrid and hissed, "You told me they would understand!"

"It's fine, Vega. They're just looking forward to you being successful. Don't take it personally. Lord knows I've learned not to."

Drexel tried to boost her mood. "Don't worry about them. You'll figure it out."

Vega stuffed her phone in her back pocket and walked to the elevator with them.

"Don't beat yourself up," said Astrid. "It was just your first test, and frankly, no one really expected you to have it finished so quickly."

"Really? It didn't sound that way. I know I said it wasn't ready, but I at least expected the connectivity to work. I thought I had it figured out. I'm not sure what went wrong."

"Do you want to bounce some ideas off me?" she asked.

"No, I want to look it over first. I'm hoping it's something simple. I would really hate to have to start all over."

"Surely it can't be that bad," Drexel offered.

She knew they were trying to make her feel better, but it wasn't working. She was pissed off, mainly at herself for letting Astrid talk her into going through with showing it to everyone when she knew it wasn't ready.

The elevator couldn't get there fast enough.

29

It was Saturday morning, and after burying herself in her office yesterday working on her program, she thought she'd finally found the problem and, hopefully, the solution. She decided to go in and test it out since she didn't need to worry about calling in the nurses with her mom in the hospital. It would be great to have the lab to herself, and she knew Ryker rarely worked on weekends.

She walked through the lobby to the elevator, and the place felt so deserted it was almost creepy—like a zombie apocalypse had occurred, and she hadn't gotten the memo. Most people were probably out with their families or significant others doing something fun. The only plan Vega had lined up for the weekend was to visit her mother in the hospital. *My life is pathetic*, she thought.

When she got to the security panel, she lifted her hand to the palm reader and stopped, remembering the little secret Drexel told her the other day.

"We built a back door," he said.

"But then anybody can get in."

"No. The only people who know are those who already have security clearance. We don't think it will be a problem, and besides, we change it every month."

"You change what?"

"The system has a speaker, as you know, but it also has a microphone. So, we created a password. It's always just one word."

"What is it this month?"

"Galimatias."

"Galimatias? Is that a real word?"

"It is. It means confused or unintelligible talk. Leave it to Fedorov to think of a word like that."

"I just say the word?"

"That's it. Simple as pie. Oh, another benefit is that it doesn't respond with that obnoxious welcome message, which means you are incognito."

"Oh!"

"We wanted to keep it easy."

Vega still couldn't believe they'd added such an insecure feature, but it wasn't her decision, and this was the perfect time to try it out. She looked at the palm reader, said, "Galimatias," and the door clicked open. She didn't know why it surprised her when it worked. It just seemed like a silly thing to allow when they spent so much money on the other high-tech security measures.

Down in the test lab, she went to her desk and looked through a technical document on the workings of the optically pumped magnetometer chip, double-checking the notes she'd taken the first time she read it. She futzed and tweaked with her code, and after a couple of hours, she stood up and stretched. Her idea was good. She had rewritten some of her code to direct the OPM to boost the electromagnetic waves before capturing them. Hopefully, that would stabilize the program's connection to the brain so it would quit crashing.

Before she ran the test to check out her changes, she needed a little caffeine boost. She walked down the blue hallway towards the break room, but stopped when she heard something. It sounded like voices coming from inside the CRT-1 individual testing lab. Someone probably came in while she was at her desk. Stepping closer, she looked through the small glass window in the top of the door, but all she saw was the back of someone sitting in a chair. She moved around, trying to get a better look, stepping lightly to keep her sneakers from squeaking on the tile floor. She wasn't sure why she felt the need for stealth mode. It wasn't like she wasn't supposed to be here. But she was curious about what others were doing here on a Saturday. *Maybe they simply didn't have real lives either?*

She tried to listen, but it was hard to hear. It sounded like a woman and man talking.

"She's getting close," said the woman. "I think she's…"

Was that Ms. Neilmann? She couldn't quite hear the entire conversation, and they were just out of her range of sight. She heard the woman speak again.

"And were you…stimulate the nucleus accumbens?"

"…did whatever we wanted him to…," said a man's voice.

Was that Ryker?

Vega gave up trying to understand the whole conversation, and she couldn't quite tell who they were. They kept just out of her view, and the door muffled their voices, but she could see that the person in the chair was a woman. She saw a man's hand take her arm and give her a shot.

She pulled away from the window quickly.

What was going on in there? And why were they talking about stimulating the nucleus accumbens?

Vega thought it must be an individual testing session. *But why had they given the woman a shot?* Then she overheard another snippet of conversation.

"…sure you can replicate…have to tell her…"

Rushing silently back across the hall, she packed up her stuff. It wouldn't affect the schedule that much if she waited and ran her test on Monday. She was pretty sure they didn't know she was there, and she wanted to keep it that way.

She didn't know what they were doing in there, but maybe she wasn't supposed to.

30

It was Monday, and her latest test had failed. The code swirled in front of her as Vega's concentration failed. She couldn't quit thinking about the strange conversation she'd heard in the lab on Saturday. *What were they talking about? And what was that shot for?* She tried to convince herself to let it go—that she'd only heard part of it and was probably being overly imaginative and taking everything out of context.

But try as she might, she couldn't do it. She couldn't. She had to know, or she'd never get any work done.

Sighing in frustration, she pushed her chair back and walked down the hall.

"Hey, Vega. What's up?" said Astrid, glancing up from her computer.

"May I sit?"

"Sure."

Vega shut the door. "I have to ask you something."

"You're making me nervous."

"Don't be nervous. I'm sure it's nothing. But, well…"

Astrid waited.

"I saw something this weekend, and I'm not sure what to think about it."

"OK."

"I came in on a Saturday to test out a solution to the connection problem I've been having with my program."

"You came in on the weekend?"

"Yes."

"I'm glad you're taking the deadline seriously."

Vega gave her a little smile. "Yeah, well, I was embarrassed by my failure."

"It's fine. Everyone understood that—"

"Yeah, I know. But still."

Vega continued, avoiding Astrid's eyes. For some reason, she felt like she had done something wrong by eavesdropping on the conversation, even though it wasn't like she'd meant to—initially, anyway.

"Anyway, someone was in the CRT-1 lab—two people—no, three. I think the third person was a woman, maybe a test volunteer, but I'm not sure. Someone gave her a shot. But they were also talking about—"

"Stop right there. I know what you're going to say," Astrid said.

"You do?"

"You're wondering why Drexel would give someone a shot for an individual trial."

"I didn't know it was Drexel, but yeah."

"I'm sure it was him, and he gives most of the participants in individual trials a very mild dose of midazolam before each study. He used to give them a pill option, but it took too long for those to take effect."

"Why give them anything at all?"

"After studying the brain waves of the individual participants, Dr. Fedorov discovered the MYND headband struggled to maintain a stable connection with some of them. He said their right hemisphere beta waves were in hyper-mode, which meant they were stressed out. Maybe they were nervous about being in an individual test? He wasn't sure. But it was a very common occurrence, and it affected the headband's connection. He suggested we give them a light sedative to relax them a bit before starting the test."

Vega sat back in her chair. "Oh! I thought. I don't know what I thought."

"Sounds to me like you thought something evil was happening in our deep, dark basement."

Embarrassed, she looked down and a nervous laugh escaped. "I admit, I did go there first."

"Maybe you've been watching too many horror movies?"

"No. Not into those, but I do love a good psychological thriller."

"Same thing. Just less blood and guts."

Vega stood up. "I'm sorry I bothered you. I feel so silly now."

Astrid waved her off and gave her a grin. "Don't worry about it. You're only human, and it's kind of nice to know you care enough to say something when you think someone may be doing something questionable."

"Thanks." Positive her face was beet red, Vega hung her head and shoulders dramatically and slunk towards the door. She gave Astrid a snicker. "I think I'll go work on my program now."

* * *

Back in her office, Vega felt like an idiot, but then she remembered she forgot to ask about hearing them discussing stimulating the nucleus accumbens. She shook her head and decided they had probably been talking about various areas of the brain, and there wasn't much to it—just like the shot.

She thought about what Astrid said—that Fedorov determined putting the user in a more relaxed state resulted in a better connection with the headband.

Holy crap! That's it! Why hadn't they told her about that sooner? They knew she was having connectivity issues.

She flipped open her laptop.

Relaxation. Maybe that was the key? And what brain waves increased when a person was more relaxed but not asleep?

Alpha waves.

Opening her files, she dove deep into her research on brain wave patterns and their indication of the subject's mental state.

If she could figure out how to increase the user's alpha waves when the app started, maybe she could put them in a more relaxed, receptive state so the connection would stabilize? She couldn't give them a shot of sedative every time, but maybe there was another way.

She pulled up the smart devices' list of sensors and capabilities and scanned through the possibilities.

Maybe she could use the current loop antenna?

Invigorated, she delved into the technical specifications and couldn't type the code in fast enough. She missed lunch, ignored her emails, and four hours flew by before she thought she had figured it out.

Rolling her chair back, she stood up and walked over to her window. It was so cloudy and rainy that she could barely make out the Space Needle, and the fog feathered the crisp lines of the iconic shape, giving it an ethereal quality.

She felt confident in her code and was excited about running another test. It might still need some tweaking, but she felt she was on the right track. She did not want a repeat of the last fiasco. This time, she would do all her testing alone until she was positive the program was running problem-free. She called the lab to see if it was empty.

Dr. Fedorov answered, "Lab."

Damn!

"Hey, Dr. Fedorov, I was hoping to come down and test out some changes to my program. Are you going to be there long?"

"Why? Am I going to be in your way?"

"No, sorry. I just kind of wanted to test it out on my own."

"I see. OK. I'll leave."

"OK. Thanks, Ryker. I really—"

Ryker had already hung up.

Vega looked at her phone. She didn't know what it was about him, but she didn't think he liked her very much. Although she had to admit, she'd never seen him be that warm and cozy with anyone.

* * *

When she opened the door to the testing lab, Ryker was already gone, and she breathed a sigh of relief. It wasn't that she didn't want him to be there necessarily, she just didn't want her program to fail in front of anyone.

She sat her laptop on her desk, navigated to the MYND program files and opened an interface to the cloud. After starting the program, she selected *Users*, and when the hamburger drop-down menu displayed, she selected the only name listed, hers. She pressed the *Connect* icon, which caused oscillating sine waves to pop up over a transparent blue image of a 360-degree rotating brain.

Her new subroutine ran as soon as the app started, zeroed in on the prefrontal cortex area, and sent out a signal in the alpha wave range, using the phone's current-loop antenna. After a couple of seconds, the app displayed *Connection Established*. But before she even had time to wonder if it would stabilize, the connection dropped.

She flipped through her notes, made some changes, and after two more failures, thought she'd found the issue. She fine-tuned the signal to fluctuate between eight and twelve hertz rather than simultaneously sending the entire range and ran the program again.

Her fingers tapped on the desk as she waited for another minute to pass, and the connection stayed solid. She breathed a sigh of relief, but then the connection crashed again.

"Damn it!" She was sure her last change was the fix she needed. The only good news was throughout the testing, she hadn't felt a thing. Not that she should, but part of her thought it was strange knowing her brain waves were being manipulated, and she couldn't even tell.

But maybe it had done nothing at all?

She pulled up her documentation and read through the current loop antenna's capabilities and the alpha wave details but couldn't find a problem. *Maybe she needed to change tactics?*

Another few hours of research, and she had a new idea. She looked at the clock and freaked out. *There was no way she could get home in time before the nurse left!*

She shut her laptop and started shoving things into her backpack before she realized her mom was still in the hospital. There was no need to rush home. She sat back down. *Was she relieved or sad?* A little of both, she realized.

Since she didn't have to leave yet, she opened her laptop again and went down some rabbit holes, learning as much as she could about how to increase alpha waves. Then she found an article in the National Library of Medicine titled *The impact of monochords on the bioelectrical oscillations of the brain.* She read through the document and found the conclusion very interesting. The article stated:

"In the MC (Monochord) group, alpha band spectral power and posterior theta waves were shown to increase with a decrease in mid-frontal beta waves and posterior alpha bands. This clearly suggests that monochord sounds are quite effective as an inducer of relaxation, even with only a single session."

Maybe she could mimic Ryker's sedative shot using sound? Could it be that easy?

Vega jumped down a few more rabbit holes, learning as much as she could about monochords, how they affected brain waves and the keys and ranges of the most effective chords.

She started coding again.

31

Old urine and cigarette smoke permeated the stale air of Dave Byrne's run-down hotel room. On the ceiling above him, he saw splotches of black, which he was positive were some kind of mold. He flung the cold compress off his forehead and pushed himself out of the small, creaky bed. When he pulled the thin beige curtain to the side and looked out the smeared glass of the front window, he saw no one. He unlocked the cheap deadbolt and chain lock, opened the door and looked out.

"Who's there?" He looked around at the empty parking lot. "What do you want? Leave me alone!"

When no one responded, he slammed the door shut, vibrating the front window inside its frame. He turned back into the room, sat down at the small round table in front of the window and took a sip of his now cold coffee. His hope that the caffeine in the instant slop would help his headache had been for naught. Vaguely, he recalled driving from work back to the hotel yesterday, but it felt like a lifetime ago.

He poured the coffee down the sink and flopped back down on the too-soft bed. His brain was on fire, making it impossible to focus. *How did I end up here? All because of a silly, meaningless one-night stand. Why did I even tell her?*

"Get the gun. Everything will be OK."

Dave's head shot up from the pillow, and the quick change of position caused the blood to rush to his head. He cried out from the sharp pain and looked around the empty room.

"Who said that?" he asked.

He stood up, looked under the bed then threw open the door to the small closet and slammed the clothes aside, causing the metal hangers to screech painfully as they slid across the rail. He squeezed his eyes shut and covered his ears.

"Why is everything so goddamn loud?"

"Get the gun, Dave. It's the only way out," said the voice.

"Who's in here? Come out, you coward!"

But the small, vacant room revealed no one. There was no place to hide.

His thoughts were muddled, and he scuffled slowly back to the bed, staring at the rickety wood-veneer nightstand. He sat down and touched the handle on the drawer, knowing what was in there—the Glock he had bought but never planned to use. He pulled tentatively, and the drawer scraped open in jerks.

"That's right. Go ahead. You know it's the right thing to do."

A knife jabbed itself into the center of his brain, and he sucked in his breath and dropped his head between his legs.

"I can't. I won't!" He sucked back tears when his hand reached inside and pulled out the gun. He stared at it as if some alien metallic object had magically sprouted from his palm. *If Laurie were here right now, she'd be chastising me for not putting it some place where it would be impossible to get at quickly.*

In a fog, he remembered the day he'd come home with it after his buddy had taken him to a shooting range and talked him into buying it.

"Think of your family, man!" Jake had prodded. "You gotta be able to keep 'em safe!"

"I don't know. I don't like the idea of having a gun in the house with my son."

He was never a fan of guns. He'd only agreed to go to the Wood Hill Shooting Club in Bellevue because it was Jake's birthday. But after a little more goading, Jake had talked Dave into taking one of the metal monstrosities home with him.

Laurie had not been happy, but he had reiterated Jake's argument that he had bought it simply to be able to protect his family.

"How am I ever going to protect you and Lucas if I don't have something to fight back with? What if someone breaks into the house?"

But now, thinking back about that day, his argument was lame, and he knew it. He knew his intentions weren't that honorable, and he'd only bought it to impress Jake.

His wife's retort was logical as ever. "Think about it, Dave. What are the odds of us being attacked in our home and you having enough time, foresight and courage to go and get the gun? I mean, come on, we both know you're not the bravest man in the world."

That had hurt. He hated it when she put him down like that. *And hadn't she been doing a lot more of that lately?* he asked himself. He struggled to think, but was having a hard time even remembering what she looked like right now. *Was he really married? Did he even have a son? And would he ever be able to see him again?* He started to wonder if it might all be some kind of sick joke. *This* was his real life—alone in a crappy hotel with his demons and a splitting headache.

The voice appeased him.

"Go ahead, Dave. Do it for Laurie. For Lucas."

He turned his head and finally saw where the voice was coming from—his dad, sitting right by him on the bed. He wasn't even shocked that he'd been alone in the room just a moment ago. He knew all along the voice had been his dad's —the one person in the world Dave could never fool. His father told him, when he'd married Laurie, that she was too good for him—that he would never be able to keep her.

"Laurie deserves better than you. You know it and she knows it."

"I can't do it."

"Yes you can. Show her you're the brave man she never thought you were."

He cringed and cradled the gun in his hand, weighing its heft. Then he turned and looked at the bed. This would be messy. Laurie would be disappointed in him.

Better do this somewhere easier for someone to clean up.

His clarity of thought surprised him and he smiled, knowing his wife would be happy he had thought about someone else's needs at the very end.

With the gun in his right hand and his left holding his aching head, he rose slowly from the bed and scuffled into the bathroom. The knife sliced deeper into his brain, and white flashes flickered in front of his eyes, creating jolted lightning bolts in front of him. He leaned on the wall to steady himself and slowly stepped into the stained bathtub, the tarnished rings rattling against the metal rod grating in his ears as he closed the moldy shower curtain.

"Good thinking, son. I'm proud of you. Let's finish this, shall we?"

Holding on to the edge of the tub, he lowered himself down and tried to lie back, but his six-foot-one frame wouldn't let him. So he sat up with his back pressed against the cracked, peach-colored tiles and put the gun in his mouth. For a split second, he thought he couldn't do it. But then he heard his father's voice for the last time.

"It's for the good of the family, son. Come on. It's time for you to join me."

Dave pulled the trigger.

32

Judy Grant, 92

Judy Grant passed away in her home, peacefully. It's believed that it was due to her trying out her new, uh, sexual gadget. Perhaps it was a little too effective, because the doctor said her heart simply gave out. Hopefully she hadn't been left on the edge, if you know what I mean.

She left behind a bunch of junk for us, her kids, daughter Julie, and son Raymond, to sort through. So if you're looking for an old CRT monitor from the seventies, a box full of knitting supplies (lovingly played with by her cat, Edgar), a 1978 Ford Pinto (kaboom!), or a glow-in-the-dark black velvet painting of Jesus shaking hands with Elvis, get in touch with us after a compassionate amount of time has passed. A couple of days is fine.

Judy was a great mother and grandmother who leaves behind a normal, dysfunctional family taught by the "school of hard knocks," and reminded daily about the fifteen-mile walk she had to take to school every day in the snow. So suck it up, children! She had a bit of a farting problem and had no qualms about letting them rip, regardless of the setting. She constantly reminded us that it was, after all, a normal, human biological release.

She loved to cook for us, but we did not love eating her meals, having learned over the years that cooking, to her, meant making sure nothing bad was left in the food. Burnt meant dead germs. The advantage of dining at home was, we were never overweight.

Judy will be sorely missed and is survived by us two kids, her brother George…

Vega sat back and chuckled. It was just what she needed this morning. She didn't think obituaries could be so entertaining, but they often were, especially when she discovered one like Judy's. It was amazing what people could come up with. She just hoped someone would be as inventive with hers when she died, and she could write one that was just as interesting for her mom when the time came. Miren would like that.

It was her dad who had gotten her interested in reading them. He joked with her once and said, *"I read them to make sure my name isn't there."* But she knew he was really looking for names of old friends from the army whom he'd lost touch with years ago, secretly hoping he wouldn't find them.

He hadn't been in the military for long—only two years—mainly, he said, so he could take advantage of the GI Bill and afford to go to college. But he said he made some of the closest friends of his life there. Unfortunately, not all of his buddies had come out unscathed, and he'd lost touch with most of them.

When she'd first caught him reading obits, it seemed like a macabre habit. But when he showed her a few surprisingly humorous ones, she'd gotten hooked. She hadn't realized people wrote those kinds of obituaries, expecting them to all be sad and boring. Now she searched them often, looking for the hidden gems.

She spent the morning in her upstairs bedroom-slash-office, the same one she had slept in since she was twelve. She could not have imagined she would still be sleeping in it when she hit thirty, which she had done just a few days ago. There had been no celebration for making it to that landmark age, unless she could count her best friend Trent buying her a cinnamon bun.

Looking out at the back yard, she saw the rusty, red swing set, its chains twisting in the slight breeze. Quickly, she looked away, but it was too late. The memory came flooding back—the afternoon that would change her life forever—she just hadn't realized then by how much. Her parents had called her inside from where she'd been sitting on the back patio, reading. She could still see the look on their faces as they shared the news, her father holding their hands and promising them that together, they would get through it.

"Yeah. Right," she said to herself, remembering how he'd abandoned them.

After the insurance company paid out for his *accident*, Vega took over the family finances and care of the house and her mother. At the time of her father's death, Miren was still talking, although repeating herself a lot or talking about life as if it were twenty years earlier.

"Everything will be fine," she recalled her mother telling her in one of her more lucid moments. "We have money in the bank. We can live simply. I don't need much. You go ahead and get what you want."

But her mother was wrong. Miren needed a lot—doctor appointments, drugs, therapy, canes, wheelchairs, a new bathtub and then home-nurse care. And soon, Vega knew she was going to have to put her in a long-term care facility, whether she wanted to or not. But there was no way she could afford to do that right now—not in a nice one, anyway. She didn't know how she was ever going to afford it.

Dying was expensive. But dying slowly was *really* expensive.

* * *

It had been a week since she'd admitted Miren to the hospital, and although her mom was slowly improving, the tab was racking up, and Vega was worried. The doctor said she should think about moving her to a long-term care establishment because it might be cheaper. Her mother was out of the woods for now, but she needed another week on the UTI drug, and because she kept pulling out her IV, she required round-the-clock monitoring.

A year ago, Vega had researched facilities—done a cursory scan, trying to prepare for the inevitable—but her heart hadn't been in it. She thought Miren would have at least a couple more years before she needed that level of support. But it looked like she'd been wrong. So for the last few days, Trent had gone with her to check a few of them out, and together they'd decided Sunrise Center was the best one for the money. And thankfully, it was on her way home from work, so it would be easy to visit every day. The Northrup exit was right off 520, then it was a short drive down 124th to Sunrise Center and a quick jaunt east to put her back on the highway toward home. It was a busy traffic area, but at least it wasn't out of her way.

When they'd visited, the staff looked overwhelmed, but at least they smiled at her. The rooms were clean, and some patients were in a small recreation room, socializing. Everyone wasn't hiding away in their individual rooms.

But it was a large place, and Vega knew there wouldn't be much time for personalized attention. The bedrooms were little postage stamps, and there was no outside area to speak of. She knew her mom may not understand where she was or what was happening to her anymore, but she often perked up when she sat outside in the fresh air. They told her they would get her out of her room often, even if an IV pole might be trailing behind her.

Sunrise Center wasn't the worst place she'd seen, and it was one of the few that would support Miren's round-the-clock antibiotic care that Vega could afford—barely, and not for long. She could have extended the home-care nurse schedule to cover twenty-four hours, but that was even more expensive than a room at Sunrise, and she was starting to worry that she might eventually have to refinance the house or sell it and move into an apartment.

The nurse, Andrew, had her mom dressed and ready to go when she walked into the hospital room. The IV attached to Miren's wrist was now secured to her arm with a medical wrap bandage so she couldn't pull it out. He was helping her out of bed and into a wheelchair. Vega was glad it was someone she knew.

"You're doing great, Miren," he said as he got her seated in the chair. "Look, your daughter is here."

"We're going on a trip to a new place, Mom. I think you'll like it there."

Miren looked at her with questioning eyes. "Are we going home now?"

Happy that at least she had talked to her, Vega squelched the tears that threatened to fall and said, "Not yet, Mom. We're going to a nice place so people can watch out for you all the time and make sure you're OK. Doesn't that sound good?"

"We're going home?"

"No, Mom. Soon though."

Vega straightened up and looked at the nurse. "Might as well go now, I guess. Hopefully she'll be OK."

Holding her mom's hand, she walked beside Andrew as he wheeled her down the hallway and out the large doors at the front of the hospital. A Sunrise Center van was waiting for them, and Vega's stomach churned. She was mentally wrecked, feeling like she had failed her mother. When Miren was still cognizant, they had discussed her fate, and all her mom had asked was that Vega put her somewhere fun.

Sunrise Center did not look very fun to her. It looked sad and lonely. But it was the best she could do for now.

The van's hydraulic lift gently guided her mom into the back, and Vega climbed in and sat on a fold down seat inside. A man was reading Miren's hospital band, matching it to his records. She thanked Andrew and watched him walk back inside the hospital. The van pulled out, and they began another chapter of her mom's life.

33

It had been a week since her program failure, and after a ton of testing, Vega was almost ready to present her finished program to the group. But as she sat at home on Saturday, waiting for a load of laundry to finish, she refused to think about work anymore. She pulled up the obit section of the *Seattle Times*, scanned through them, and one finally grabbed her attention because the picture looked familiar. She read the obit.

David Byrne, Age 51

Loving father and husband, David Byrne was a people-pleaser, having learned the art of making people laugh by working as a bartender for more than 20 years.

Dave loved an adventure and telling a good story to his family and friends around a campfire on their many trips to the great outdoors. A stranger to no one, he could make friends with anyone and was always ready to offer a smile and a hand to someone in need.

He is survived by his wife Louise, son Lucas and his beloved golden retriever, Bones.

Funeral services will be held…

The obituary was pretty ordinary—short and sweet. But she couldn't quit staring at the picture. David Byrne looked so familiar to her. *Maybe it was the red hair?* She walked down the hall to the tiny sitting area on the other side of the stairway and dug out her old school albums from the bottom of one of the bookshelves. But after flipping through them all, she still couldn't find him. Finally, she went back to her room and did a search on her computer. She picked the *images* option and found a more recent picture on a YouTube video of him teaching viewers how to make a Sidecar cocktail. His hair and beard were much longer.

Then she remembered.

He was the guy she'd seen in the conference room when she watched her first focus group session. He was memorable because of his hair. It was so red it almost looked unnatural, and his matching beard hung down to his chest. She was sure it was him.

Now that she had spent so much time trying to remember who he was, she wanted to know what had happened. The obit hadn't said, so she went back and expanded her search for news articles published right before his death. Of course, he may have simply died from a heart attack or cancer and there may be nothing to find.

After thirty minutes of fruitless surfing, she decided to take another direction. She signed on to the *Propinqui* genealogy website, where she already had an account and was building a family tree. In the site's search engine, she entered Dave's first and last name, his birth and death dates and state of residence. She narrowed her search to the *Life Records* database and hit return. Five potential matches displayed, and she clicked on the one best matching her parameters. A list of census records and birth and death certificates popped up. Sifting through them, she eventually found the right David Byrne, clicked on the death certificate image and searched through the information until she found the line for cause of death.

Suicide.

Below, in the *Underlying Cause* area, was a note that said: *Affective psychosis.*

* * *

As she drove down Union Hill on her way to see her mother, Vega noticed the leaves were starting to change on the maple trees. Even though living where she did in Redmond Ridge meant a long drive into Seattle, it was worth it. She loved the area. A lot of housing developments were built over the last few years, but there were enough trees left that Vega felt like she lived in the woods, and this week, the weather started to leave summer behind and leap into fall—her favorite time of year. The highs of the day had dropped to the low seventies, and the clouds were increasing. She was glad the eighties were over.

When she arrived at Sunrise Center and walked through the sliding glass doors, it was the smell that hit her first. Even though she'd been here many times, the odor still surprised her. *The smell of dying.* That's what it made her think of. Even with the astringent sharpness of ammonia the staff used for cleaning, there was a lingering smell of urine and human waste—and sometimes vomit—and the musty smell of body odor and bad breath. She had been surprised to learn through her studies of Alzheimer's, that older people really do smell differently. She couldn't remember exactly, but it had something to do with bacteria interacting with skin. Something called 2-nonenal. And then there was the food. Not the yummy aroma of nicely charred burgers or baked bread, but the flat odor of tasteless, mushy food and nutritional protein drinks.

But it wasn't just the miasma that hit her, it was the humidity and heat. The staff told her elderly people were often colder, usually due to having less body fat, but also because their bodies' internal temperature control mechanisms simply did not work as well as they used to. The combination of the smells, heat and humidity was like walking into a dirty sauna. She stood for a moment, tried not to grimace and let herself acclimate.

Looking around, she saw too many patients and not enough staff. It wasn't dirty, per se, but it wasn't sparkling clean either. She watched as a man sleeping, she hoped, slumped over in his wheelchair while drool escaped from the corner of his mouth and dripped in a continuous line onto the linoleum floor. Nearby, a caretaker, oblivious to his plight, was trying to hold a woman down who was determined to walk out the front door in her nightgown. Vega felt bad for the employees. It wasn't their fault they were understaffed and underfunded.

She checked in at the visitor's desk, slapped her name tag sticker onto her blouse and turned down one of the narrow halls.

Propped up against a stack of pillows in her bed, Miren was watching TV. The IV was gone, and she looked much better, but the doctor said she still wasn't eating, and he wanted to keep her at the center for at least another day. Her mom didn't even look at her when she entered the room.

"Hi, Mom. What are you watching?"

There was no reply, so Vega scooped up a chair from the corner and sat next to the bed. The TV was on, but Miren wasn't looking at it. She was staring into space.

"I wish you would talk to me."

She knew her mom was in some other universe, and sometimes, Vega wished she could join her there, temporarily anyway. At least she could talk to her then. The nurse at the front desk told her it had been a good morning, but since leaving the hospital, she was less and less talkative, barely responding when Vega came to visit each day.

A family picture sat on the small chest of drawers, and she smiled when she looked at it. She had tried her best to make the place feel like home.

Vega could tell her mom was continuing to lose weight, and the doctor had said she may have to put in a feeding tube soon. If she did that, instead of going back home, Miren would move back to the hospital. It didn't matter anymore about the expense, because she really had no choice. She would just have to deal with the consequences of the costs later.

It made her mad just thinking about it.

Why did the world spend so much money traveling to space, when they could use it here on Earth figuring out how to rid the world of Alzheimer's? She loved the idea of traveling to another planet as much as anyone, but maybe we should concentrate on fixing all the things wrong on our planet first?

She knew she was probably jaded and partial, and there were worse diseases that were also incurable, but this was the one affecting her and her mother's lives right now—the one that mattered most to her. Often, when she watched people pray over their loved ones to get better, it infuriated her. It probably wasn't fair of her, but she couldn't help but wonder how could they continue to believe in a god? No god would let their people suffer like this.

Vega tried to quit thinking so negatively, but she was mad. Miren did not deserve this. *Why didn't this disease only affect bad people?* She was already starting to question if it was cruel to keep expending so much time and energy to keep her mother alive. *Did she even still want to be here? We treat our pets better than we treat our fellow humans*, she thought. *We don't let them linger. When they're suffering, and there's no hope, we end their lives for them.* The problem was, since Miren couldn't tell her, Vega had no idea if she was still enjoying her life.

She sat with her mother for an hour, trying periodically to get her to talk to her. Every now and then, Miren would mumble something incoherent, and Vega would try to get her to say more. Finally, she put the chair back where it belonged, pulled on her coat and kissed her mom's forehead.

"Bye, Mom. I'll see you tomorrow."

* * *

Back in her bedroom at home, she read the news article again about Marie's accident. She couldn't get it out of her mind, and remembering Dave's obit, there seemed to be a lot of psychosis going around. It was probably coincidental, but it made her think back to the conversation she'd overheard in the Neilmann CRT lab about stimulating the nucleus accumbens. She had learned during her neurology studies that evidence suggested a connection between the septal area and some mental disorders like depression and schizophrenia. *What had they been referring to in their conversation in the lab?*

She had an idea and called Trent.

"Hey, you," he said. "You called me instead of texting. How old school."

"Yeah, well, I didn't want to type all this."

"You know you could just turn the microphone feature on?"

"Yeah, I know. Do you want to talk to me or not?"

He laughed at her stubbornness. "Yeah, OK. How's the corporate whore doing?"

"Trent!"

"Sorry, I've been waiting for the right opportunity to ask that ever since you got your new job. But it never quite presented itself."

"She's doing fine. Still working on my program."

"Can you tell me what it does?"

"Not exactly, but I'll give you a hint. It has something to do with marketing."

"Funny! Since Neilmann is a marketing comp—no, sorry, a neuromarketing company."

"I've been thinking…"

"Uh oh. Watch out."

"No really, listen. Have you read about all these psychotic breaks happening lately? I think something weird is going on."

"What do you mean?"

"I have this feeling they're connected to our focus group tests."

"What's that?"

"Volunteers come in and have their brain waves monitored while they surf the internet. A headband measures how people respond to customer ads that display while they browse."

"Why do you think they're connected?"

"I'm wondering if the headband is causing psychosis somehow."

"Where did this come from? I haven't heard anything about psychotic breaks."

"I've read some articles and obits in the *Seattle Times*. Remember that big pile-up on 520 the other day?"

"Yeah."

"The woman was having a psychotic episode. And there was another one a couple of weeks ago about a man who killed his son and then himself—another psychotic break."

"Weird."

"Oh, and then there was this guy, Dave. He committed suicide after he also had a psychotic breakdown. I had to research that one."

"How did you find out he had a breakdown? Was that in the paper, too?"

"No. I had to look him up in Propinqui. You know, the genealogy website? It lets you look things like that up if you have a premium subscription."

"Why did you look for him in the first place?"

"I saw his picture in his obit. I was curious because he looked so familiar. Then I remembered I'd seen him in one of the focus group tests."

"You and those obits."

"That's three people who've died lately from psychotic episodes."

"And you jumped to, Neilmann is behind it all?"

"No, I also overheard a strange conversation in the basement. Astrid told me it was an individual test. They were talking about stimulating the nucleus accumbens."

"The what?"

"It's complicated. Look, I know I probably sound a little crazy, and maybe I am, but I have an idea."

"I'm listening."

"How would you like to help me with a clandestine mission?"

"Doing what?"

"I want to see if I can find some proof at Neilmann, but I need a lookout."

"Don't you work there?" Trent asked. "You still do, right?"

"Yes, but I'm not going to *my* office. I want to get into Ryker's files."

"Who's Ryker?"

"He invented the headband."

"What are you looking for?"

"I don't know. I'm hoping there's something in one of his drawers—maybe notes he doesn't want to store in the cloud where everyone can see them."

"OK. When do we do this?"

"Sunday. Are you game?"

"Let's see, hang out here and watch reality TV, or do something in real life that is exciting and maybe even a little dangerous? I'm in."

34

When Sunday rolled around, the sky was blue with just a few small clouds scattered above. It was only supposed to hit sixty-nine degrees—a beautiful day. Vega put the car in gear and turned it toward downtown with Trent in the seat beside her. She really appreciated his help and knew he wouldn't be sitting at home watching reality TV. He would be painting or whatever else he needed to do to prepare for his gallery showing.

Her employee card swiped through the reader, and the garage door into the lobby of Neilmann Corporation clicked open.

"That was easy," he said.

"I do work here. It's not like I'm not supposed to be in the building."

"How do the visitors get in without a key card?"

"It's only locked when there's no lobby receptionist—on the weekends and after hours."

"Am I going to get a tour?"

"Not today. If someone spotted us, I'd have to explain your presence, and that would kind of negate the whole point."

"You have to at least show me your office," he said. "I want to see this fantastic view you have."

"We're on a mission here. No side trips."

He crossed his arms in mock anger.

She felt a little guilty since he was helping her, so she said, "I'll show you some other day. I promise."

"Maybe when you're not spying on your co-workers?"

"Exactly."

Vega had only been in the office one other time on the weekend, and was almost empty then. Neilmann offered a ton of amenities to encourage their employees not to leave on the weekdays, but few people talked about working on the weekends. There certainly weren't many cars in the garage.

They walked to the elevators, their footsteps echoing through the lobby.

"Wow, nice trees!" Trent exclaimed, walking around them, peering up into their branches.

"Yeah, aren't they great?"

He followed her to the bank of elevators, and once inside, she hit LL.

"We're going down to the dark, scary basement?"

Vega laughed at his comment, remembering her first time there. "You sound exactly like I did when my boss, Astrid, took me down here, but it's definitely not dark. The whole floor is blue—blue walls, blue lights. You'll see. It's kind of bizarre. She claims it's calming."

"What's down here?"

"We're going to the test lab where Dr. Fedorov's office is. Well, it's not really an office. It's just a desk. I can't look at the files on his computer. It's not like he's shared his password with me, and he locks his main office. But I know he keeps notes on paper with a fountain pen, and I'm hoping some of them will be down here."

"How quaint. And with a fountain pen? I didn't know people used those anymore."

"Apparently, it's a big thing with some people. There are clubs devoted to them. He goes to one of their meetings every month."

"Huh. Who knew?"

"I'm hoping there will be something in his files."

"What exactly are you looking for?"

"Proof."

"Of what?"

"Honestly? I don't know yet. I'm just winging it here."

Vega walked up to the palm and eye reader and simply said, "Pareidolia."

The door clicked open.

"What was that word you used?"

"Pareidolia. It means the ability to see shapes of pictures where there are none—like when you see faces or animals in the clouds."

"Cool. Why do they have all those contraptions by the door if that's all you have to do to get in?"

"That's the official security system. The password I used is a backdoor—a way to get in if you have a problem with the system, or can't use your hand or eye for some reason. It also doesn't log you in when you use it, and I don't want anyone to know I was here today. Not that there's anything wrong with it, but just in case."

Vega cracked open the door to the testing lab, peeked inside, and seeing it empty, motioned Trent to follow her in and walked over to Ryker's desk. She opened a couple of drawers, but all she found were pens, paper pads, staples and other office supplies.

The other small drawers revealed nothing significant either, so she tried the large bottom drawer and found it locked. She dug a lock-picking set out of her purse and sifted through the tools.

"Since when do you know how to pick a lock?"

"I watched some YouTube videos."

"And now you're an expert?"

"It looked easy," she said with a mischievous grin. "I tried it out on our garden shed door first. Wasn't too hard."

"Why does he lock his drawers if he's already in a secure area?"

"Can't be too careful, I guess," she said, tucking her hair behind her ears as she started picking. "The MYND headband is proprietary. There's nothing else like it on the market, and once I replicate its functionality with my app—oops!"

"What happened? Did you get it?"

"No. I just told you too much. I need to quit talking."

"What did you tell me? I didn't hear anything."

Vega grinned, heard a satisfying click, tugged at the handle, and the drawer glided open revealing a row of hanging paper file folders. "Bingo!"

"You did it? I'm amazed. Look at all that. I thought everyone was going paperless."

"Not everyone, thank goodness, because drawer locks are a lot easier to pick than trying to guess computer passwords. But there might not even be anything useful in here."

Vega started flipping through file folders but then stopped and turned to Trent. "OK, time to play lookout. I don't want to get caught sifting through Ryker's files."

"What do I do if someone comes?"

"Just come back and tell me."

"What if they come in here?"

"Hopefully, we'll be out of here before that happens."

He walked back and took post at the door, keeping an eye on the hall through the small window. She got to work.

Sifting through the files, she found something that looked promising and pulled out a thick file folder labelled *MYND Lab Tests*. There were several pages of details of tests conducted with the headband showing exactly what she expected—the results of reading the volunteers' brain waves to determine their reaction to Neilmann customer ads, but there was also a section of data that showed they had tested *sending* signals from the headband back to the user. That was interesting.

She flipped through them quickly. It looked like they'd started with gamma waves and worked their way through the various awake frequencies. But the wording of Ryker's scribbled notes in the margins—*not effective, no measurable results, no change*—indicated nothing had created the effect they were looking for. It wasn't until they tried stimulating the nucleus accumbens directly, that his notes indicated satisfaction. Vega knew stimulation of that area could result in feelings of pleasure and reward. It was basically the part of the brain that told us; *you want this.*

On each test results' page was an area that noted side effects and she noticed that as they increased the electrical stimulation to the nucleus accumbens area, it took the subjects longer for their brain waves to return to their normal state.

Maybe she was right about there being a connection? Perhaps the side effect wasn't as temporary as they thought?

She laid the pages on top of the desk, pulled out her phone and took pictures.

The earliest dates of the testing showed they'd started two months before they hired her. They'd been working on this before she even came on board.

Continuing her search, she found something she wasn't expecting at all—a brochure advertising the MYND application.

Maybe the marketing group had sent it to Dr. Fedorov to proofread so it would be ready when she finished it?

She looked it over and was shocked. It described the app's ability to stimulate the nucleus accumbens to convince customers to buy a product or click on an ad.

Did Neilmann think the ad agencies wouldn't care that the app would alter people's brains to manipulate them into buying their products? When were they planning on telling her this? Were they expecting her to code this capability into her program somehow?

She took pictures of the brochure, and just as she clicked off the last one, she heard Trent's shoes squeaking on the tile floor.

"Someone's coming! The elevator's moving!"

"We should go to the break room!"

Vega shoved the files back into the drawer and took a quick look to ensure everything was as she'd found it. A glance through the door's window told her the elevator hadn't opened yet, so she grabbed Trent's hand, yanked him with her down the hall and rushed into the break room.

They both froze and listened as the elevator dinged and heels clicked on the floor and headed towards them. She took a chance and peeked out the breakroom door window.

"It's Ms. Neilmann and Ryker," she whispered.

"Is that important?"

"Shhh! They're coming down the hall."

She sighed with relief when they turned into a testing room and closed the door. Poking her head out, and seeing it clear, she rushed down the hall and pulled him with her into the elevator.

Back in the car, Trent asked, "Did anyone see us?"

"I don't think so," Vega said.

"That was close."

"I don't know if I like being a spy."

"Yeah, but you have a reason to be here."

"But I'd have to explain you being with me, and I definitely shouldn't be showing you the basement. I wonder if she knows what they're doing?"

"Who? What are they doing? Did you find something about psychotic breakdowns?"

"Not exactly. I shouldn't say anything."

She saw his eyebrows raise. "I was just your lookout while you broke into someone's desk."

"I know, and thank you, by the way. But I can't show you what I found."

"All right, but you better find a really good way to thank me. My heart's still beating like a Blue Man drum. I think my days as a lookout guy are over."

Vega chuckled and started the car. "I hope it was worth it."

* * *

Back home, Vega transferred the photos from her phone to her computer and took a closer look. She opened the picture of the advertising brochure that touted the new MYND application and read a bullet list of promised capabilities:

Strengthens memory retention of your products

Focuses consumer attention on your ads

Enhances pleasure emotions as your ads are viewed

Increases intent to purchase

Results in increased sales and volume

At the bottom of the document was a footnote:

The world's first multi-channel electroencephalogram (EEG) application known to not only read brain waves but also stimulate the nucleus accumbens. The MYND application promises to tap deep into your customers' brains and activate and stimulate their emotions to motivate them to select and purchase your products and services. Studies have shown that strong emotional memories have long-lasting power and may positively increase purchase intent over time.

Vega was shocked. She hadn't even finished writing the program yet, and that capability was definitely not in the specs. Then there was the side effect she'd read about in the test results that as the signal strength increased, it took longer for the subjects' brain waves to return to a normal state.

Were they already doing this with the headband?

The more she read, the more she began to believe there was a correlation between the recent psychotic breaks and the focus group testing.

She didn't know if she was right, but she knew she was going to find out.

35

The next day at work, Vega pulled into her normal spot in the parking garage. On the drive in, she'd been contemplating what to do about the information she'd discovered in Ryker's files. As she walked toward the elevator, a young woman approached her.

"Excuse me," said the woman. "Are you here for the testing?"

"No, I work here," Vega said.

"You do? Great! Maybe you can help me? I'm looking for this group," the woman said, pulling her phone out and scrolling through screens. "I have an email, and I think it said I'm supposed to go to the third floor, but I can't remember. Should have put it in my calendar." She shook her head and chuckled. "Tanya's always telling me I'm calendar-challenged. She's my best friend. She was supposed to come with me, but she got food poisoning last night."

"Ooh. Sorry to hear that. I've had that before. Not fun."

"No, it's not. She was up all night shooting stuff out of every hole she has." The woman smacked her hand over her mouth. "Oh, god. I'm so sorry. I'm not usually so crass. Tanya's starting to rub off on me."

"That's OK. I get the picture."

She kept scrolling through her phone as they waited for the elevator. "I know I had it here somewhere."

"Maybe you can check with the lobby receptionist? I bet he'll know." Vega thought the woman looked nervous. "Is it a focus group test?"

"I don't know. The posting just said some kind of consumer testing. Probably tasting some yucky food or something." She stuck her tongue out, grinned broadly and put out her hand. "I'm Jenny, by the way. Jenny Banks."

Vega took her hand. "Vega Swift. I don't think it's food tasting. That's not what we do here."

"Oh! All I know is it's a marketing company."

"They don't do the type of marketing you're probably thinking about. They're a neuromarketing company."

The garage elevator dinged, and they walked on.

"Neuromarketing? I've never heard of it. What's that mean?"

"They use eye-tracking, EEG readings, things like that, to determine customer reactions to ads."

"EEG? Isn't that something to do with your brain?"

"It's a way to measure your brain wave activity."

"Oh man, that sounds kind of cool. I didn't know there were companies that did that kind of thing."

"It probably sounds a little strange, but it's not invasive."

"I don't care. They're paying me five hundred bucks for just two hours!"

"Wow! That's a lot."

"Whatever it is, I hope it doesn't hurt."

"I don't think you'll have to worry about that," Vega said, not bothering to tell her about the sedative shot she might be getting.

"Oh, good."

On the lobby floor, the doors parted, and Jenny stepped out.

"Good luck with the testing," Vega said.

"Thanks!"

* * *

As she walked down the hall towards Astrid's office, she could feel the sweat from her armpits dampening her blouse. She took a deep breath and tried to calm down.

Her door was open, so Vega leaned in. "Hey, you got a second?"

"Sure. Got a meeting in about ten minutes. What's up?"

She shut the door, and Astrid said, "This must be serious."

"Yeah, actually it is."

"What's wrong?"

"It's about the MYND program."

"Oh, shit! Please don't tell me you can't get it to work. Ms. Neilmann will kick us both to the curb!"

"No, nothing like that. Remember when you told me why they give the individual volunteers shots?"

"Yes."

"I never got to tell you what else happened that day, that I overheard them saying something about stimulating the nucleus accumbens. And I… I found these documents."

"What documents?"

"They were in Ryker's files."

"You went through his stuff?"

"It's not like they were hidden," Vega said, not revealing she had picked his drawer lock. "I took some pics."

"You took pictures? Why not just save the files to your folder and send them to me?"

"They were paper files. You know how he is. And I didn't want to remove them, in case he needed them."

Astrid shook her head. "OK, then. Let's see these documents."

Vega opened her photo gallery and showed her the files. "Look at this last one," she said, navigating to the image. "It's a customer brochure for the MYND program and it brags about its capability to stimulate the nucleus accumbens to make users want to buy."

"I see what you mean."

"And I've researched a couple of people in the area who've had psychotic breaks, and I think they both participated in the focus group tests. See the stimulation side effects detailed in the test documents? And look at the dates."

Astrid looked at the pictures of the documents on Vega's phone and leaned back.

"You're sounding a little crazy. Are you telling me you think the headband is causing psychotic breaks? Is that what you're saying? That we're purposefully hurting people?"

"Maybe not purposefully, but…" Vega waited. "I know it sounds ridiculous, and I don't have any proof, but it seems coincidental, don't you think?"

She saw disbelief on Astrid's face, but she wasn't ready to give up. "OK, maybe there's no connection, but what about the stimulation of the nucleus accumbens? It's not ethical. Are we really doing that? We have to do something."

Astrid looked at the time on her computer. "Not right now we don't. I don't, anyway. No time. I have a code design review meeting in about thirty seconds. Tell you what. Let me talk to Ms. Neilmann and see if I can get to the bottom of everything."

"No! Don't do that! She might be part of it!"

"Part of what? Now you're saying there's a conspiracy? I have to go, but I promise not to do anything until we talk again. I'll stop by after my meeting, and we'll put a plan together. How's that sound?"

"Sure. Thanks."

Vega went back to her office, hoping she hadn't just made a huge mistake.

36

Astrid hadn't seemed to take Vega's findings seriously. *Could she be part of this whole thing too?* No, it was too hard to believe. She didn't know her that well, but surely, she wouldn't be involved in something like this. Deciding to put it out of her mind for a while, she worked on finishing the final touches on her program. She would quit dwelling on it until she heard back from Astrid.

She was looking out her window, thinking and waiting for another compile to run, when the ring of her landline split the silence.

"Hello?"

"Ms. Swift, this is Celeste. Ms. Neilmann would like to see you."

"Ms. Neilmann? Why?"

"Not my job."

"OK. When?"

"Now."

"What—" Vega quit talking, because Celeste had hung up. She couldn't imagine why Ms. Neilmann would want to see her. *Maybe Astrid had talked to her after all, and she wanted to see the documents for herself?*

Celeste was ready for her when she arrived. "Go right in. Ms. Neilmann is waiting for you."

She opened the huge door, entered the office and it had the same impact on her as the first time she'd been there. She assumed it had something to do with the warm colors and cozy fire burning in the fireplace—even if it was fake. Vega felt immediately more relaxed until she saw Astrid sitting in one of the yellow chairs. Astrid smiled awkwardly, and Vega's warm and fuzzy feeling turned cold.

"Ah, Ms. Swift. Thank you for coming," said Ms. Neilmann from behind her desk. "Please, have a seat."

"Thanks," she said, looking over at Astrid who looked down at her hands clasped together in her lap, thumbs circling.

"So," said Katya as she leaned back in her chair, "Astrid tells me you have some interesting information you've come across."

"I guess she told you already." She looked over at Astrid. "I thought we were going to talk about it first but, good. I guess this is good."

"You guess?" asked Ms. Neilmann.

"Yes, I mean, I wanted to tell you, but I thought I should talk to Astrid first."

"Yes, she did come to me—" Astrid started.

Katya held up her hand to Astrid like a traffic cop, still looking at Vega. "Of course. You did the right thing taking it to your boss first."

Vega cleared her throat and asked Astrid, "Did you tell her what I found?"

"Yes, I—"

Holding her hand up again, Ms. Neilmann stared her down. "I'll let you know if I want your input, Astrid."

She sunk back in her chair.

Ms. Neilmann turned back to Vega. "She said you've come across some disturbing documents, but she didn't show them to me, so I'm not sure what you think you've found." She leaned forward with hands clasped together and looking unblinkingly at Vega. "And I'm very interested in hearing how it is you came to find them."

Ever so slightly, Vega scooted back in her chair, worried by Ms. Neilmann's change in tone. She glanced at Astrid who was looking at her lap again.

"The more I think about it, it's probably nothing," Vega offered. "Really. I shouldn't have bothered her with them, and I'm sorry I wasted your time."

"Such a quick change of tune for something so important?"

"It's just…" she took a deep breath and dove in. "OK. One of the documents I found is a brochure that states the MYND application will send a signal to the nucleus accumbens to influence users' decisions."

"I see," said Ms. Neilmann, leaning back in her chair. "Well, I was really hoping to reveal this information to you later, once you had the main program working, but I guess there's no sense in waiting now."

"What infor—"

"Please let me finish, Vega. There is another functionality I need you to include in your program."

"OK."

"I need the program to do exactly what that document you found says—send a signal to the nucleus accumbens. Stimulate it, you might say."

"Oh."

"Dr. Fedorov will give you the specifics, some kind of signal. You're already doing that, right? Astrid tells me you're working on sending a signal to calm the subjects before the program begins."

"But that's not the same kind of signal. And it's not really relevant because I couldn't get it to work. I've gone a different direction."

"Oh, well, it doesn't matter. You still need to replicate what Ryker's doing but without the headband. I guess you'll just have to start from scratch."

"You're trying to make sure the users select the right ad?"

"Exactly. We're giving them a little nudge to encourage them to click on *our* customers' ads and hopefully, buy their products."

"We simply want to have a little more influence on their decision," Astrid said.

Vega looked back and forth at them. "Are you both serious? You're trying to alter their brains to *make* them buy a product or click on an ad?"

Katya laughed her off. "Oh, please, Vega. Don't be so dramatic," she scoffed. "We're not *altering* their brains. We're just temporarily sending them a brief spark to improve our odds. Marketing companies have been trying to do this since the beginning of time, but the technology hasn't been there to do it until now. Unfortunately, it won't affect everyone because there is only a small percentage of people on which this technique is effective. Ryker hasn't narrowed down the differential, but the numbers are still large enough to make it worth our while and give us an edge over our competitors."

"You're controlling them."

"We're not *controlling* them. We're giving them a prod in the right direction."

Vega didn't know what to say, so she said nothing.

"Why don't you and Astrid go back and talk about this? I'm sure she can clarify everything for you, and then you can work with Dr. Fedorov to add in the feature. Yes?"

Ms. Neilmann stood up, signaling the discussion was over.

* * *

"I don't get it," said Vega, sitting in Astrid's office. "Why didn't you just tell me? Why did you have to go to Ms. Neilmann? I thought we were going to talk it over first?"

"I had to check in with her to see if it was OK to tell you. We were going to tell you, eventually," she said, "but everyone thought it was better to wait until you had the guts of your program working. We wanted you to really understand what we're trying to do. I know you think it's a bit unsavory, but it's not like we're hurting anyone, and it's going to help put Neilmann back in front."

"Unsavory? It's unethical! I can't believe you all agreed to this. Surely, it's illegal?"

"No. Not illegal at all. Neuromarketing is still considered a simple marketing tool, and frankly, it's a bit misunderstood. There are no regulations around it that would cover anything like this. Think about it this way. With the changes we're making to the ads based on what we learn from the focus group studies, and eventually from your real-time collection of data with the MYND app, we'll already ensure the users have a strong interest in what we display to them. They'll already *want* to click on the ad or buy the product or service. We'll be targeting the users with the most proclivity to buy that specific product to begin with. We're simply giving them an extra push."

Vega was nonplussed. She couldn't believe what Astrid was telling her. "Whose idea was it?"

"What?"

"Whose idea was it originally—to stimulate the nucleus accumbens, Ms. Neilmann's?"

She saw Astrid's eyes widen. "Pffft! Oh, please. Ms. Neilmann couldn't think of this. No, it was Ryker's. He was supposed to get a promotion for it once he got it working. She promised him a VP level."

"But he's not a VP, is he?"

"Not yet, and he's not happy about that."

"I don't even know what to say."

"Like Ms. Neilmann said, if Dr. Fedorov has already done it, surely it can't be that hard."

"Doing it wirelessly is completely different. He's probably using electricity."

"I'm sure you can figure it out. He's been testing it with the MYND headband for a few months now."

"On humans."

"Of course on humans. How would he know if it worked otherwise? That's what the focus groups are all about now."

"I just don't think it's ethical."

"Yes, you keep saying that."

Vega shook her head. "And besides, I'm not even sure it can be done."

Astrid leaned forward. "We have faith in you, Vega. You're almost finished with the MYND program, right? Eliminating the headband completely?"

"Yes."

"I'll have Ryker send you the full specs," she said, typing on her computer. "If you have any questions, get together with him. Give me a call after you've looked through them, and let me know what you think."

By the time Vega got back to her office and opened her mail, Ryker's specification file was already in her inbox. She started reading, and despite her distaste for the whole idea, after scanning the details of what he'd done, she couldn't help but be intrigued. It was ingenious, and she found herself already thinking about how she could accomplish the same thing with her program.

It was near the end of the day, and after spending several hours reviewing the information, she called Astrid.

"Hey, it's me. I've read through the specs."

"And? Can you do it?"

Vega hesitated. If she said yes, she was practically agreeing she would. If she said no, she would probably be packing her bags and going home. She decided to play it safe, for now.

"I think so."

"How long do you think it will take to add the functionality?"

She was just guessing, because she wasn't sure what she had in mind would even work. But she did some calculations in her head. *Maybe two weeks, no, at least three with testing*, she thought to herself. *But she had to add in her two-plus-half buffer.* Whenever she gave anyone a finish date for one of her programs, she always started with her estimate of how long she thought it would really take her to complete it. Then she took that number, multiplied it by two, and finally, added in another half—just to be sure. That way, when she finished ahead of schedule, which she usually did, she impressed her employers with how fast she could code. She got the idea from watching old reruns of the original Star Trek where the ship's engineer, Scotty, used the same calculation to estimate how long it would take to fix something on the ship. Captain Kirk always thought he was a genius.

"I could probably get it done in nine weeks, which includes testing. *If* I can figure out how to do it."

"If?"

"I don't know how, or if, I can replicate that signal wirelessly."

"I see. That's a little too long, though. If I tell Ms. Neilmann you're going to miss the Christ—"

"But I won't do it," Vega said, surprising herself at her abrupt decision.

"Why not?"

"I already told you. It's not ethical, and it *should* be illegal."

"Maybe, but it's not. And don't you think our competitors would do it in a heartbeat if they could?"

"I don't know. I hope not."

"We need an edge, Vega. We've been number two in the industry for too long, and Ms. Neilmann is not happy. She's been looking for a way to get back to the top ever since Seichō surged ahead."

"There's more to life than being number one."

"I don't think she feels that way, and it's not just about being number one. You probably haven't heard, but word is, she's fighting off a hostile takeover."

"What?"

"That's what Ryker says."

"I thought Neilmann was doing really well?"

"We were. But for the last several years, Seichō has been eating our lunch."

"I remember reading about them when I was researching Neilmann before my interview, but I didn't see anything about a takeover."

"It's not public yet. Ryker told me our board of directors is giving Katya 'til the second quarter of next year to turn things around. If not, they're going to seriously consider a buyout from Seichō, and honestly, I think they'll just take us over anyway if we can't get our numbers up."

"I had no idea."

"That's another reason this MYND project is so fucking important. Why Ms. Neilmann is always on my ass about it. This is her lifeline."

"I'm sorry, but I just can't do it."

"You mean you *won't* do it. You just told me you thought you could."

Vega stayed quiet.

"You'll probably lose your job."

"So, what? You're going to fire me?"

"Not me."

"Ms. Neilmann."

"Yes, and I wouldn't be surprised if she sends me out with you."

"She wouldn't."

"Oh yes she would, and I need this job."

"You'd continue to work on a project even if you knew it was hurting people?"

Vega saw Astrid take a deep breath, probably trying to keep herself composed. "I'm trying to be reasonable. I cannot let you take me down, too. I can't afford it. Anyway, nothing is happening! I know Drexel and his team check on the volunteers after the testing. Everyone is fine, OK? So, just drop all the conspiracy bullshit!"

"Fine!"

There was a moment of silence, and then in a calmer voice, Astrid said, "It doesn't have to be this way. Stay. Finish the program, and when you're done, you can move on to something else—another project. I'm sure Ms. Neilmann will agree to that."

Looking out the window, the clouds were heavy, and the rain, although light, was constant. Hundreds of tiny drops streaked on the huge panes, little copies of the adjacent buildings reflecting in them as they trickled down on their way to the ground. Vega was torn. Astrid wasn't the only one who needed her job.

"Think about it," Astrid said. "Take the night, and mull it over. I know you need this job too."

"You're right. I do."

"How's your mom, by the way?"

She tried not to get emotional when she answered. "I had to put her in a long-term care facility. She has a serious UTI and is on an IV antibiotic therapy."

"I'm really sorry to hear that."

"Yeah, it's not good, and it's eating up my bank account."

"In that case Vega, you need to think about your mom."

"That's low, Astrid."

"I'm just trying to help you see your situation clearly."

It took every amount of self-control she had to not simply scream, *I quit!* Instead, she said, "All right. I'll think about it."

"I can give you one night. If your answer is no, I'll have to tell Ms. Neilmann your decision tomorrow."

37

Vega locked the door of her office, replaying her conversation with Astrid. She didn't know what to do. She knew what she *wanted* to do, but she also knew sometimes she let her emotions get the best of her and that led to rash decisions she later regretted. *Maybe I'll stop by on my way out and ask Drexel? See what he thinks.* He'd been at Neilmann much longer. Surely, he would agree what they wanted her to do was wrong.

When she got to his office door, he was on the phone, so she waited in the hallway, leaning over the railing trying to see the lobby, twenty-two stories down, but the large green leaves of the Ficus and Japanese maple trees obscured her view. Astrid told her they brought them in soon after Neilmann moved into the building, and the entire lobby had changed from a stark, empty space to a lush garden area. The maple trees were already changing to their fall colors of red and yellow.

As Vega waited, she couldn't help but overhear Drexel's conversation.

"I'm not meeting you tomorrow. I have a plan in motion that will all but guarantee me a promotion. Get off my back! … I'm not moving over to One— … I said I would— … Yes, John. I know. How could I forget that I owe you everything? You bring it up every fucking time I talk to you! … Yes. Fine. OK. Tomorrow."

The conversation stopped, and she was pretty sure she knew who he'd been talking to. It sounded like he needed a moment to cool off, so she waited a few minutes before she tapped on his door.

"Hey, you," she said. "Bad time?"

"I always have time for you."

"Thanks. I have something I need to talk to you about."

"OK."

Vega sat and reiterated the chain of events and conversations that led to Astrid's ultimatum.

"I can't believe they're asking me to do this. Astrid told me the whole thing was Ryker's idea. Why am I not surprised?"

"Yeah, it was. He told me since decision-making is focused in the nucleus accumbens area of the brain, he thought if he could figure out a way to stimulate it, it might increase how often a user clicked on our customers' ads.

"Now, periodically in the trials, we direct the headband to send a signal to that area after we display a new ad. We try to make it random so we can tell if it really makes a difference. Ryker added a command into the interface to the headband so we just press an icon and it sends the signal.

"He said he got the idea from an article about an experiment with rats that were fitted with special EEG caps and trained to hit a button in their cage which stimulated the nucleus accumbens. I guess the rats really liked it, because once they realized what the button did, they quit eating or drinking and just hit it until they dropped from exhaustion, or died. It's kind of fascinating."

"Oh, my god, Drexel!"

"Don't worry. He said the effect is not nearly as exaggerated in humans, and it doesn't affect everyone to the same degree. But it worked, and it must feel pretty good, because we've had a lot of volunteers that were very unhappy when the testing ended. They kept asking when the next session was, and I had to tell them they couldn't do another one for six months. We want to get random samples of customers. They were not pleased."

"I can't believe everyone is on board with this."

"I don't know why you're so surprised. If our competitors could do it, they would."

"Astrid said the same thing."

"For all we know, they're already doing it."

"I understand now why she didn't tell me right away, because I might not have taken the job."

"Please don't let this drive you away. If you don't do it, they'll just find someone who will."

"Gee, thanks Drexel."

"Come on, you know I think you're brilliant, but no one's irreplaceable. Not even me," he said with a smile.

She knew he was trying to lighten the mood, but it wasn't working, and she was having a hard time not crying. She hated that she always turned to tears when she was angry. It kind of negated the whole point of being mad about something because she couldn't debate. All she usually did was crumble.

"Why don't you come to my place for a while? Is your mom back home?"

"No. She's still at Sunrise Center and it's sucking up every penny I have. I can't afford to leave Neilmann now. I can't live without this salary."

"I didn't realize how bad things were."

"Yeah, well, that's life, right?"

"Come on. Come to my place. I think you could use a drink."

* * *

Once in Drexel's loft, Vega found herself relaxing as she sat on his couch and looked out the window at the view.

Why should she care if people were coerced into buying things? It probably happened all the time in ways she had no clue about. Who was she to do anything about it? She was no one. Just one of many people in this world trying to do the best she could for her and her mom.

She should know better than to get involved. Her father had drilled that into her after he was laid off. *If it doesn't affect your life directly, don't get involved*, he would say. She didn't know exactly what had happened to him at work, but apparently sticking his neck out had gotten him laid off, just as it would her now if she didn't do what they wanted. Unlike him, however, she wasn't going to bail out on life just because things got tough. But she *was* going to allow herself time to be pissed off.

Drexel handed her a beer. "Maybe you should quit dwelling on it for a little while?"

She took a swig. "Yeah. It's just making me upset. I can't believe I'm trying to convince you I shouldn't do it, when it doesn't seem to bother you at all."

"You're taking it all too personally. It's just business and I think it's a good idea. I don't know if you realize how badly Neilmann needs a win."

"Yeah, Astrid told me. I had no idea."

"Oh, she did? I imagined you sitting in bed at night reading the annual report. But you know what? I can think of something a little better to do in bed," he said with a questioning look, holding out his hand.

She gave in, smiled back and took one last sip of her beer. Taking his hand, she let him pull her into his bedroom. As much as she wanted to be mad at him for all this, for going along with it, she couldn't do it. It was too hard to look at him and stay upset when all she could think about was getting his clothes off. And he was right. There was more than one way to get her mind off her troubles.

But instead of cuddling into him as she usually did afterwards, she rolled on her back and looked at the ceiling, her thoughts going back to the lingering effects of the stimulation she'd read about in the documents. *Should I tell him?* She looked over at Drexel.

"Have you seen the news lately about all those deaths and suicides linked to psychotic episodes?"

"Uh. I don't think so."

"Remember that major pile-up that happened on 520?"

"Yeah."

"The ME said the woman had a psychotic break. That's why she crashed into all those cars. She thought someone was chasing her."

"Wow. That's awful."

"There are other incidences. I've read the obituaries."

"Why are you reading obituaries?"

"It's a hobby."

"That's kind of morbid."

"No it's not. My father got me into it. Sometimes people write some really funny ones."

"Okaaay, but what's your point?"

"It's another reason I think this whole thing is a bad idea. I think some of these deaths I've been reading about are people who took part in the focus group trials. Now that I know what Ryker's been doing with the headband, I think I know why."

Drexel sat up and looked down at her. "I know you're upset, so I'm going to take that with a grain of salt."

She propped up on a pillow. "I may not have anything positive, but I think I know of at least two people who were involved in the trials who've died. One was a suicide, and the other was that accident."

Drexel shook his head. "You think?"

She turned away from him, swung her legs over the side of the bed and started to put her clothes on. "I'm not saying anyone specific is responsible. I just think there's a connection."

"What led you to this conclusion? Just seeing some obituaries and news articles?"

"No. I remembered one of them, because I saw him in that first group test you invited me to. Then I saw his picture in the obituary."

"And the accident?"

"In the newspaper article about it, Marie's friend—Marie was the lady who caused the accidents—talked about them going to some kind of test before she died."

"So you assumed it was our focus group test?"

Vega shrugged.

"Did Marie say anything?"

She looked away as she pulled on her top.

"Vega?"

"She said a sexually crazed man from her previous job was chasing her in his SUV. I know she was having a psychotic break, and I admit it sounds strange, but…"

"Strange? It's bonkers! The test probably had nothing to do with Neilmann. It could have been anything."

"If I could look at the customer key file, get the real names of the participants, I could follow up. See if she was in one of the trials."

"I can't believe you. Don't you think I've already done that?"

"Astrid said you did follow-ups, but…"

"We do them after every test to make sure there are no lingering side-effects—which by the way, there haven't been."

"Maybe you could let me look at them?"

"Why? Don't you trust me? Anyway, I can't. They're proprietary. When someone signs up for a session, Neilmann guarantees anonymity. Access to that file is on a need-to-know basis and you are not on that list." He sighed. "You haven't told Astrid or Ms. Neilmann what you're thinking, have you?"

"I mentioned it to Astrid, but she blew me off, just like you. I haven't even decided if I'm still going to be working there tomorrow, but even if I'm wrong about the stimulation hurting people, we're altering their brains, Drexel. Don't you care?"

"We're not altering their brains. It's just business. You think if what Neilmann is doing was hurting people, no one would care? I wouldn't care?"

"Of course, I think you would care, but I don't think you believe me. Surely Ms. Neilmann would care?"

"You're right. I don't believe you. But I'm also not sure Ms. Neilmann would care, even if you were right."

"What? You can't be serious."

"I think all she cares about is her company."

"Really?"

Slipping into his jeans, Drexel walked over to the window and looked out. Vega couldn't help but be stirred by his strong profile, silhouetted by the soft gray sky. It was obvious he had gone off into deep thought somewhere.

"Drexel?"

He turned to her and said, "She's my mother."

She was floored. She walked over and stood next to him by the window.

"Why didn't anyone tell me?"

"No one knows. She doesn't know."

"How could she possibly not know? I think she'd remember if she'd given birth to you."

"She was a teenager—sixteen, I think. I'm sure she felt like she was too young to raise a kid, but what do I know? She put me up for adoption as soon as she had me, and it was closed. They won't share any information."

Vega sat back down on the bed. "How did you find out then?"

"I hired a private detective."

"Do your adoptive parents know?"

"No. I didn't tell John, and who the hell knows where my mother is."

"You don't know?"

"She left us a long time ago."

"Your father's divorced?"

"I wouldn't know. He doesn't exactly talk to me about anything other than work. I never saw my mother again."

"She doesn't come to see you?"

"I haven't seen her since I was eight years old."

"Oh, wow! I'm so sorry."

"Yeah, whatever," Drexel said, looking away.

"Your father never re-married?"

"No. I'm sure he must go on dates, but he's never brought anyone back to the house. He says she was the love of his life and I think he blames me for her leaving."

"Why?"

"I was quite a handful as a kid, I guess. I get the impression my loving mother, Sarah, thought being a mother would be easier. My opinion? The only reason she ever adopted me was to complete the happy family picture for her neighbors and friends to see," he said with a sneer. "I don't think she ever really wanted me."

"That's horrible!"

He shook his head. "It doesn't matter."

"Why haven't you told her?"

He sat down beside her. "I'm not sure she would want to know, and I don't think she'd be happy about it."

"Is that why you work for Neilmann?"

"Yeah. I wanted to get to know her—find out what kind of person she was before I decided if I was going to tell her."

"Have you found out what kind of person she is yet?"

Drexel shook his head. "I shouldn't have said anything. I don't really want to talk about it anymore."

"I'm sorry. I didn't mean to pry."

"By the way, that other stuff? I think you're jumping to conclusions. It's not like you have any proof, do you? People do have psychotic breaks all on their own. Most people don't need any help with that. I'm sure it's all just a coincidence."

"I'm not sure I believe in coincidences, and I think you're being naive."

"And I think you're looking for a conspiracy where there is none."

She put her hands on her hips, and said, "And I think you have blinders on!"

Drexel yanked his shirt up from the floor where she had peeled it off him earlier and threw it on, buttoning it with more force than necessary.

She watched him and tried to calm down. He was right. She didn't have any proof of anything. Yet.

She took a deep breath and said, "I'm sorry. You're right." Walking over to him, she moved his hands away from his shirt and finished buttoning it. "I understand how hard it must be for your mother to be right there and you not feel comfortable enough to tell her who you are."

"I doubt that."

"What are you waiting for?"

"I don't know. And quit trying to be nice. I'm not through being mad at you."

Gently, Vega took his chin in her hand and moved it toward her so she could look into his eyes.

"I'm sorry. Really. I'm sure you're right. Maybe I'm just seeing connections where there are none."

"You should do it. Do what Ms. Neilmann wants. It's not hurting anyone. And anyway…"

"What?"

He cleared his throat. "I don't want you to leave."

He leaned in and kissed her, and she stood on her tiptoes to bury her lips into his. They fell back onto the bed, and she started removing the shirt she had just so carefully finished buttoning for him. She laid back on the sheets and when he climbed on top of her and kissed her neck, she let all her concerns melt away again. Her only worry at the moment was how hard she was falling for him.

38

The front door opened, and a man's voice cried out, "Drexel! Are you in?"

Vega rushed to cover her naked body with the sheets.

"Is that your dad?" she asked in a whisper.

Drexel flung himself out of bed and quickly slipped on his jeans. He yanked a t-shirt out of a drawer, pulled it over his head and turned back to her.

"Stay right there. I'll get rid of him."

Oh my god, she thought. *The man really does just come and go as he likes.*

Drexel left the bedroom and shut the door behind him, but because of the open ceiling, she could hear everything.

"Were you in bed, son? A little early to hit the sack, don't you think?"

"No. Just changing clothes."

A pause and then his father understood.

"You're having sex in the middle of the day? I can smell it all over you. Sarah would be ashamed of you. Don't you have more important things to do?"

Vega couldn't believe the audacity of the man. She pushed herself out of bed and started putting on her clothes. For all she knew, he would come in the bedroom with no warning just to see who Drexel had been sleeping with. She couldn't help but listen as the conversation continued.

"What do you want?" asked Drexel.

"It's time for our planning session about your future. I've brought the notes from our last meeting, so let's sit down and look over them and see where you stand on some of these goals I laid out for you last time."

"Now is not a good time, as you noticed. And anyway, I'm doing just fine. There's no need for you to review my progress."

"You wouldn't say that if you had nothing to hide. Things at work not going as well as you expected?"

"John, please! Can we talk about this later? I have company."

Vega heard his father snort. "I see. So, you *are* putting your social life ahead of your career goals. Just what I was afraid would happen."

"They were never *my* career goals. They're yours! Everything I have is yours!"

"Of course, everything you have is mine. You're my son. This Neilmann thing is simply a training ground for you. If you think this is hard, you're certainly not ready to move over to OneVision. Perhaps I need to escalate your goals."

"Maybe I don't want to work at OneVision? Have you thought about that? Have you ever even asked me what I wanted?"

"What's come over you? I thought we had an understanding?"

"Yeah, the understanding that you can come into my place any—"

"You mean my place, don't you?"

"Fine! Do you want me to move? Would that make you happy?"

"What would make me happy is if you quit whining like a little boy. I can see I'm going to get nowhere with you today. Get yourself together. I'll be back tomorrow and we'll go over everything then."

"I'm busy."

"Then reschedule. I'll be here at five o'clock, and I expect you here."

The door slammed, and Vega sat on the edge of the bed. She wasn't sure if she should go in and comfort Drexel or just leave him alone. She didn't want to embarrass him, so she went into the bathroom and freshened up, and when she came out, he was sitting on the bed.

"Sorry about that."

"It's fine. Don't worry about it."

"I'm sure you heard everything. One of the downfalls of having this modern, exposed ductwork and open ceiling. Looks cool, but there is absolutely no privacy."

"Yeah. I couldn't help it. Are you OK? Does he just come in like that all the time?"

"He feels like he can, since he owns the place. I'd be better off having a normal landlord. At least there are laws against them entering your residence without warning."

"I thought he bought it for you?"

"He did buy it for me, but he didn't *give* it to me. He just lets me live here rent-free, as long as I follow his rules and meet his expectations."

"I know it's none of my business, so please tell me if I'm out of line, but what was he talking about? Are you looking for a job at OneVision? Is he planning your career path? He talked about planning sessions with you the last time he was here, too."

Drexel laughed at her naiveté. "He's been planning my career path since he adopted me."

"He works at OneVision?"

"He owns OneVision."

"Oh! Holy crap! I had no idea. They're the biggest media conglomerate in the U.S.!"

"Yes, I know, and he never lets me forget how he worked his way up from nothing to be where he is today."

"You didn't really want to work at Neilmann because you could move around in the company, did you? Why aren't you working at OneVision? Just because of your mother—I mean, Ms. Neilmann?"

"No. He wanted me to prove I could make it on my own first, and frankly, I don't want to work for him. You see what he's like. He's overbearing and manipulative—a micro-manager."

"Maybe once you were there working with him, at his company, he'd lighten up?"

"Not likely."

"I don't know. After everything that's going down at Neilmann…"

"That's different."

"How? Everyone's willing to manipulate people to make the company successful."

"They're already going to buy things. We're just helping them buy the things that will make Neilmann more successful."

She shook her head. Maybe he wasn't as different from his father as he thought he was.

"Let's not argue again," he said. "I know what we're doing is not the most ethical thing, but if we don't do it, someone else will. Of that, I have no doubt. The technology is there. Someone will take advantage of it eventually, and I'd rather it be at Neilmann so we can control how it's used. Wouldn't you?"

Sighing, Vega gave in. "I guess you have a point. At least this way, we know what it's used for."

He pulled her to him. "Good. I don't want us to fight. I want you on my side."

She snuggled into his lap. She still wasn't totally with him and with what Neilmann was doing, but he made some good points, and she was tired of swimming against the tide.

39

Jenny had been on edge for the last couple of weeks. She had a headache that wouldn't quit and insomnia to boot. She couldn't seem to turn her brain off. *Maybe it'll be a good thing? Maybe I'll get some great tips tonight? I'll certainly look energetic and willing.*

In the back of the Kitten Klub, she pulled into the parking lot, running late, as usual. She hurried in through the back door of the dressing room, and Ronnie was there, tapping his foot and looking at his watch.

"Where the fuck you been, Juicy?" he asked, using her stage name. "You're late—again."

"How do you know?"

"I'm lookin' at my watch," he said. He pulled a knife out of his pocket, flipped it open and started cleaning his nails.

"You know that thing's not accurate. Why don't you come into the modern age with the rest of us, and check the time on your phone like a normal person?"

"Ha! I like this watch. That other shit's too complicated. When I wanna know what time it is, look," he said, showing

289

her the gigantic face of his watch, "all I have to do is turn my wrist, and voilà! I can see it! I don't have to turn anything on or nothin'. It's like a fuckin' miracle or somethin'."

"Uh huh. Anyway, I'm not late. I've got five minutes before I go on. I'll make it. Don't worry about it."

Ronnie set his knife down on her dressing table and pointed his finger at her.

"You bet your sweet ass you'll walk onto that stage on time, or you'll be walkin' back out the door. And don't let a fuckin' hair on your head, or any other place on your fuckin' body, be out of place."

"Yeah, yeah. Get outta here. We're tryin' to get dressed," said one of the other women.

"Like I don't see it every fuckin' day." He glared at Jenny again. "You got four minutes."

Ronnie left, and she threw off her jeans and t-shirt, and pulled on her red sequined G-string and matching bra. Slipping her feet, with their bright red toenails, into a ridiculously high pair of clear platform heels, she walked over to the mirror, and in two minutes flat, glued on her false eyelashes, teased her hair and glammed up her makeup. She looked at the clock above the mirrors, and with one minute to spare, she rushed out of the dressing room, stood behind the curtain and peeked out to let the DJ know she was ready.

When he saw she was there, he started his barking.

"And tonight, our hot and sexy lady is here to keep you entertained. Give it up, gentlemen and ladies, for our lovely, luscious, Juicy Lucy!"

Consisting mostly of men, the crowd hooped, hollered and clapped, and Jenny pranced onto the stage into a dense, white cloud created by a tucked-away smoke machine. The smoke flowed across the floor, and she started her gyrating dance moves under red spotlights and a sparkling disco ball. The DJ spun the tongue-in-cheek classic, "You Can't Always Get What You Want," by the Rolling Stones.

Jenny started dancing and spinning, stroking and pulsing on the gold stripper poles, but soon she found that the cacophony of sounds and disorienting lights and smoke, all began to merge into a single swirl of confusion. The music seemed louder than normal and continued to rise to an almost ear-splitting volume the longer she danced. The swirling cloud from the fog machine flooded her vision, and the reflections bouncing off the disco ball created bizarre patterns on the faces of the crowd. Everyone began to morph and warp, their expressions contorting into surreal, freakish Picasso-like distortions.

Suddenly, flashes of light sparked in front of her eyes, and someone jammed an ice pick into her brain. She screamed and held her hands to her head, twirling around in circles, and at first, the oglers thought it was part of the act. Even the DJ joined in.

"Looks like Juicy Lucy is getting a little crazy for us tonight, folks!"

But when she didn't stop screaming, the bouncer ran up onto the stage, picked her up and swung her over his shoulder and hauled her back to the dressing room. Not missing a beat, the DJ jumped right into his spin. "Don't worry folks. Juicy Lucy may be a little too loosy-goosey tonight, but keep those ten-dollar bills handy because our next lovely lady is coming up soon." There was a moan from the crowd as the DJ started playing some bass-thumping hip-hop music.

Back in the dressing room, still screaming, Jenny squirmed one hand free, grabbed Ronnie's knife from the dressing table and stabbed the bouncer in the arm. He screamed.

"Bitch!" he yelled as he dropped her to the floor and back-handed her across the face. Her head flew back, banged against the wall with a crack, and she crumpled to the floor.

"Fuck! My head!" she screamed. "My fucking head is splitting open! I can't see! What are all these fucking lights?"

She took the now bloody knife and stabbed it repeatedly into the side of her head as she screamed.

"Make it stop! Somebody make it fucking stop!"

By the time the paramedics got there, Jenny was already dead.

40

Against her best judgement, Vega conceded to adding the final capability to her MYND app and had given up worrying about the ethics of it all. She needed the money too badly, and everyone had almost convinced her that if Neilmann didn't do it, someone else would. But before she could start working on the additional functionality, she needed to get the main part of the program working. Then she could focus on how to stimulate the nucleus accumbens.

For the past week, she'd been heads-down, working like a madwoman, and had just left the lab after a successful test of the program's functionality on the iOS platform. Part of her couldn't believe she had done it, and she knew who she wanted to share her accomplishment with first.

Drexel's door was open, and he looked up from his computer and motioned her in.

"Hey!"

"Hey, yourself," she said. "Guess what."

"What?"

"I finished my program."

"Everything?"

"Well, not the last piece, but the main program is working," she bragged, practically bouncing on her heels. "No more connectivity issues, and I just finished testing it on all the different vendor platforms."

"That's fantastic!" Drexel exclaimed, giving her a hug.

"Thank you! I have to admit, I'm excited. After talking to Astrid a couple of weeks ago, I had a brainstorm. I didn't realize you gave your individual study participants drugs before the tests."

"You make it sound like I'm shooting them up with heroin or something. They actually—"

"I know. Astrid told me all about it, and it gave me an idea."

"Yeah?"

"That maybe if I could do the same kind of thing with my program, I could get the connection to stabilize."

"How did you mimic the effect of a sedative?"

"I used a monochord."

"A what?"

"I'll explain it later. All that really matters is that it worked. Want to see the results? I have the output on my computer."

"Of course I want to see! Are you kidding? Don't you want to let Astrid in on this?"

She took his arm and smiled at him. "I will. But first, I want to show you."

He squeezed her hand, and they went back to her office, where she pulled up the result files on her computer. It showed her brain wave fingerprint was confirmed and calibrated, and that the connection was stabilized. There was a graph of the activity of her brain waves, and to the right, a display of all the biometric data collected for the time period.

"I ran it for two minutes."

"This is great. I know they hired you specifically to write this program, but if I'm being honest, I didn't really think you could do it."

"Gee thanks."

"No! I didn't mean it that way. I didn't think *anyone* could do it. It's kind of mind-blowing, and I really want to know how you did it."

"It's kind of complicated."

"Don't think I'll understand?"

"That's not it. It's just, it's detailed, and I'd rather wait until I tell everyone at once so I don't have to go through it multiple times. I mean, if you don't mind."

"Of course not. You know, Ms. Neilmann is going to go nuts when she sees this."

"I hope so. Assuming nuts is a good thing."

Vega smiled when he leaned over her shoulder to look at her computer screen. He smelled especially good today—a mixture of woodsy and fresh—and for some reason, it made her wonder if he still had this effect on Astrid.

As if reading her mind, he asked, "When are you telling Astrid?"

She checked the time. "I guess I'll have to wait until tomorrow. I forgot she's out of the office this afternoon. Something about her sister."

"Oh, she didn't tell you?"

"No. What's going on?"

"Her sister has lung cancer. She's been getting chemo and Astrid takes her to her sessions."

"Oh, no! She never said a word."

Vega felt bad. Almost everyone in the department knew her struggles with her mother, yet Astrid had her own medical drama to deal with and never even mentioned it. She had no idea anything bad had been going on in her life.

41

The next day, Vega showed Astrid her working program and a meeting time was arranged for her to reveal it to Ms. Neilmann. She was excited, and this time, she got there a little early, but when she walked into the conference room, Astrid was already seated at the table.

"Hey."

"You ready?" asked Astrid.

She took a deep breath. "I think so."

Astrid offered her a smile. "You're going to do fine. And Vega, I'm so glad you decided to stay."

Vega gave her a little smile as Ryker came in.

"Hello, Dr. Fedorov."

"Ms. Swift. Looking forward to seeing a good demo this time."

"Yes. I promise you won't be disappointed."

Ms. Neilmann entered next, followed by Drexel.

"I'm glad you're still with us, Vega, and I'm impressed with how quickly you've been able to complete this project. I guess there's a reason your last name is Swift," Katya said, chuckling at her own joke.

Internally, Vega groaned. She'd heard that joke a few hundred times already in her lifetime, but she simply smiled and said, "Thank you, Ms. Neilmann. I admit to using the CodeBot AI program to help me with some of the smaller subroutines."

"That's what it's there for," Astrid assured her.

Drexel gave Vega a little squeeze on the shoulder when he didn't think anyone was looking and sat down across from Ryker. She smiled at him and told herself not to get distracted. Once everyone settled, she began.

"Thank you all for coming. I want you to know I've already tested the program on every vendor platform, and I've worked with the marketing group to ensure the outgoing data is in the format necessary for their collection and analysis. Just to be clear, the app will only be available on smart phones and tablets. No one shops on their fit bands and watches."

"Of course," Ms. Neilmann agreed.

"I'm going to be the guinea pig for this test, just like the first time."

Vega started the share program, so everything on her phone showed on the conference room screen.

"If you remember from my first demo, I began with a simple calibration procedure. Since then, I have greatly enhanced that procedure. Now it uses every location assisting sensor available on smart devices to help the

MYND app calculate and maintain an extremely accurate location of the user's brain during both the calibration and connection phases. Some of the capabilities I used are the accelerometer, gyroscope and the LiDAR capability."

"Wait a second. Can you please explain? What's an accelerometer?" Ms. Neilmann asked. "Sounds like something that speeds things up. And LiDAR? Never heard of it."

"Of course. The accelerometer measures the motion of a smart device in three-dimensional space. The gyroscope is a tiny electronic-mechanical device that measures changes in the smart device's orientation, and LiDAR, which is an acronym for light detection and ranging, is a laser light that judges depth and maps out three-dimensional space.

"I also used the ultrasonic function, which uses sound waves to read facial features, the IR, which is an infrared capability, and the electromagnetic radar sensor. By using all these sensors in conjunction, I was able to get a very detailed map of the location of all the different areas of a user's brain.

"Oh, and I almost forgot. I also used the CMOS chip, which stands for Complementary Metal-Oxide Semiconductor, to enhance the brain wave images. It converts photons to electrons. It's usually used for optical character recognition."

"Wow, I'm glad you know what you're doing, Ms. Swift," said Ms. Neilmann. "I honestly didn't realize our smart devices did all that."

"Most people don't. And using all those different sensors is what's ensuring the MYND app knows where the user's brain is at any given time. Without them, I could never collect the level of detail required for this project."

Ms. Neilmann nodded. "I see. Please, continue."

"I also added a functionality so that if the MYND app detects there is a measurable distance from the device to its owner, all data collection is halted. This will further ensure the app is reading only data from the owner of the smart device, in case, for instance, they hand their device to someone else for a moment or the device is set down, and accurate readings can no longer be obtained.

"So now you know what's happening behind the scenes when it calibrates and connects."

She ran the calibration routine, and the screen displayed various pictures and words and then announced *Calibration Complete.*

"Now, the connection phase."

As she selected the connect option from the MYND app's main menu, Vega said a little prayer. To whom, she didn't know, because she was not at all a religious person—just to the universe in general, she supposed. In a few seconds, the application displayed *Connection Established*—and it stayed connected. She let out a breath she didn't realize she was holding and relaxed her tense shoulders.

"The app has now established a solid and stable connection with my brain. And just so you know," she said, smiling, "throughout this whole experience, I did not feel a thing."

The group chuckled, and she continued. "Next, I'll start the data gathering."

"Wait a minute," said Ryker. "How did you finally get your connection to stabilize?"

"If you noticed, when the calibration and connection routines ran, a musical chord played in the background. That chord is called a monochord. It's often used in meditation and consists of one note with overtones and undertones. Think of Tibetan throat-singing but staying on a single note."

"I've never heard of Tibetan throat-singing," said Astrid.

"You should check it out. It's very interesting. I don't know how they do it. Monochords have been proven to have a relaxing effect, hence the use in meditation. They often result in an increase in the posterior theta waves, a decrease in the mid-frontal beta waves and a slowing of the posterior alpha bands resulting in a decrease in anxiety levels and a more relaxed state. I determined that the time it took for the calibration to complete and the connection to establish was long enough for the monochord to have the desired effect and stabilize the connection."

Looking at Ryker, she said, "I came up with the idea after learning we used midazolam to relax the subjects in the individual trials. Of course, I don't have that option, so I did some research and decided to try using a monochord." She looked over at Ms. Neilmann. "I also thought we could use the monochord as a marketing tool. It could become forever associated with the MYND app, or maybe if we don't want the app to be front-and-center, with Neilmann Corporation. Kind of like the F-sharp major chord that has become perpetually associated with the power-up of an Apple computer."

"Interesting. Is there any other way to accomplish the same thing?" asked Katya.

"I did explore some other ideas, specifically using the current loop antenna, but using the monochord was by far the less complicated method. However, if you don't like it…"

"Let me think about it," she said. "Astrid, why don't you talk to the marketing group? See what they think?"

"Sure," she replied, making herself a note.

"But how are you able to read the brain waves wirelessly?" Ryker asked.

"I'm using the OPM."

"Magnetic field communication?"

"Yes. Of course, I needed a frequency range from one to one hundred hertz—the frequencies of all the different brain waves—so I directed the OPM to search for signals in that range. Its reach is not that far, but it's enough for my purposes."

Ryker smiled, "An ingenious idea, Ms. Swift."

Vega's eyebrows raised. Ryker had just given her a compliment and smiled at her. She smiled back, but then watched as he looked away, lowered his head and jotted something down on his notepad with his fountain pen.

"OK, I give," said Drexel. "What's an OPM?"

"The OPM is fairly new in smart devices," answered Vega. "It used to be a simple magnetometer and focused on compass-related applications, and it's still used for that. But within the last few years, almost all smart devices—phones, tablets and even most of the watches and fit-bands—have all been upgraded to the OPM chips or optically pumped magnetometers."

"That's a mouthful," said Ms. Neilmann.

"Hence, the acronym. Think of it as a very specialized magnet. The technology has been in use for years in hospitals. It was added to smart devices for contact tracing to gauge users' distances from people known to be infected with monitored contagions. There are, I'm sure, other plans for future uses. But in my case, I'm using the technology to do exactly what it was originally used for in the medical field, to read brain waves."

"But what about interference?" Ryker asked. "How have you been able to isolate the brain waves from the rest of the environmental noise?"

"Yeah, that was a difficult problem. It's easier with the headband because it's got the latest EEG noise-cancelling technology already built into the hardware. But I don't have that luxury. So, I requested and reviewed ten years' worth of brain-pattern neuronal-discharge data, which I obtained from MIT. I then wrote a pattern-recognition routine to review the information in that data and wrote an algorithm to differentiate brain-wave signals from the rest of the cacophony."

Ryker's mouth dropped open. "You wrote an algorithm? I would very much like to see that. Perhaps we can—"

Ms. Neilmann held up her hand, stopping him in his tracks. "I think that's enough technical explanation for now, Dr. Fedorov. Let's let Ms. Swift continue with her demonstration. You guys can get into the minutia later."

Vega was relieved. She had no problem explaining everything to him, but she would rather not have to spell it out so that everyone else in the room understood. It might take a few hours.

"Thank you. As I said, now that my connection is stable, I can start gathering data."

She selected the *Capture* option, and a small oscillating brain-wave image displayed on the screen.

"How often are you taking samples?" asked Dr. Fedorov.

"I have it set to capture five hundred per second, but I think I could push it higher if you felt you needed more data."

"Good," he said, nodding as he made a note.

After a couple of minutes, she said, "That should be long enough." She selected *Terminate* from the main menu.

"Now we can look at a summary of the activity the program collected and drill down to look at the brain waves themselves."

She selected *Analyze,* and a page titled *Brain Wave History* popped up on the screen:

VEGA-1:
Brain-wave fingerprint: Confirmed
Connection: Established 10/13; 15:28
Timeframe: 10/13; 15:32 - 15:34
Gamma: 25 Hz - 100 Hz
Beta: 14 Hz - 20-25 Hz
Alpha: 7 Hz - 14 Hz
Theta: 4 Hz - 7 Hz
Delta: .5 Hz to 4 Hz

"There's a graph of the actual waveforms as well. This is the numerical information. You can click on any of the names or visual brain waves to examine finer levels of detail."

"What about the biometric data?" asked Astrid.

"I made quite a few changes to my original CORE program and incorporated that code into the MYND application. The gathered biometric data syncs with the brain-wave information from the same time frame. This will provide a full picture of the user's response to ads or products as they view them."

She swiped back to the main menu, selected *Biometrics,* and a list of available files displayed.

"This list shows all the biometric data files for the user."

Vega clicked on one of the files to show the details.

<u>Biometric Data:</u>
Blood Pressure: 134/92
Blood Glucose: 100 mg/dl
Heart Rate: 82 bpm
Oxygen Saturation: 99%
Pupillometry: 64mm
Blink Rate: 14.6/min
Perspiration: Normal
Perspiration Comp.: H20: .99, Na: .03, CI: .04, K: .3
Temperature: 97.6 degrees

"The MYND app uses this data in real-time to determine reactions to ads. However, I thought it would be useful to have a periodic footprint. And of course, this data will be uploaded constantly to the Neilmann cloud."

"But wait, you didn't say anything about the ad information," said Ryker.

"Oh, right. I tack the ad marker information onto the end of every string of data sent back to the cloud so the marketing group can associate the exact ad with the user's current state—both physical and mental—and hopefully, determine which ad will get a better reaction next time."

He nodded and Ms. Neilmann chimed in, "This is really excellent work, Ms. Swift, but I see you haven't yet added in the last feature we discussed."

"Thank you. You're right. I needed to get the connection stable and ensure the base program worked before I added in the new functionality."

"I hope this is not just a stalling tactic."

"No, of course not. I realize how important the additional feature is to you and the company."

"To *us*, Vega. You are part of the Neilmann family now."

She nodded. "Of course."

Ms. Neilmann stood up and said, "I'm anxious to see the final program running—soon. Pedal to the metal, Vega. Winter is coming."

42

It felt like déjà vu all over again as Vega parked her car and took the elevator to the third floor of the hospital. The doctors had finally broken down and transferred her mother back to the hospital so they could put in a feeding tube. It went in through her mom's nose, which Vega thought looked terribly uncomfortable, but she hoped Miren would at least start gaining some weight back now.

But the first thing she noticed when she entered her room was how thin her mom looked. The second was that the feeding tube was gone. Shocked, Vega turned out of the room immediately to go find a nurse. Since her mom was back in the hospital, she hadn't expected her to be neglected so badly.

She found a nurse in the hallway, and trying to keep her voice steady, asked, "What happened to my mother?"

"Who's your mom?"

"Room 319, Miren Swift."

"I don't know. She was fine the last time I saw her."

"You need to come look at her again, then," Vega said, rushing down the hall back to the room, the nurse sprinting behind her.

"Did she fall?" The nurse asked, following her into the room.

"No." She pointed to her mom. "But look at her! She's so thin! And where's her feeding tube? Aren't you feeding her here?"

Vega watched as the nurse pressed her lips tightly together and took a deep breath. Then she said calmly, "She probably looks thinner because the nurse from the last shift had to put her in a size large hospital gown. The staff delivered the wrong size to the room, and the nurse didn't think it necessary to get a smaller one. And, yes, we are feeding her. That is, we are *trying* to feed her."

"What do you mean?"

The nurse sighed and walked around to the side of the bed where Miren's feeding tube lay. She picked up the tubing and wrapped it around the IV pole.

Turning back to Vega, she said, "She's obviously pulled her tube out—again. We've been discussing restraining her. I believe—"

"Restraining her? No! Absolutely not. I will not agree to that."

"I believe the doctor is still making her rounds. Let me see if I can get her for you."

She glared at the nurse as she left, then turned to her mom, who was looking out the window, oblivious to the argument.

"Mom, it's me, Vega. How are you feeling? Are you hungry?"

Her mother glanced at her, then turned away and looked back out the window.

She sighed, hating feeling helpless. She stroked her mother's arm, not knowing what else to do.

"I love you, Mom."

Vega was looking out the window, remembering better times, when the doctor came in.

"Hello Ms. Swift. You have some questions?"

"Yes, Doctor Kavali. I'm so glad you're here. What's happening with the feeding tube? The nurse said you're thinking about restraining her."

"As the nurse showed you, we're having trouble with your mother pulling the feeding tube out. And yes, we discussed restraining her, but that would be a last resort. I'm thinking about switching to a gastrostomy tube."

"What is that?"

"I'll just make a small incision in the abdominal wall and insert the tube directly into her stomach. It will be easier to secure it in place so she can't extract it. Many patients with Miren's condition don't like things on their face."

"But is it even helping? She looks so thin."

"You remember we talked about the risks when she first came to us a few weeks ago?"

"Yes. Pneumonia, bleeding, infection. Let's see, nausea, blockage."

"Exactly. Many of these issues are much more likely when the patient tampers with the tube, and Miren is still regurgitating some of the food we have been able to get into her. Hopefully, once I move the tube, she'll leave it alone, things will level out, and she'll start gaining back some weight. But if not, it may be necessary to restrain her."

"What do you mean by restrain? Like tie her to the bed?"

"We use softly lined cuffs, but basically, yes."

"No way! I will not allow you to tie my mother down like some animal!"

"The cuffs aren't tight, Ms. Swift. And we will do everything we can first, to ensure that's not necessary."

She shook her head, walked away from the doctor and looked out the window.

"I can't believe this. It was just a UTI! How has it developed into this horror show?"

Doctor Kavali walked over, stood beside her and placed her hand lightly on her shoulder. "Ms. Swift, it was never just a UTI. You know this. Miren has been going downhill quickly this last year. I know these things can be shocking, especially when you don't see her all day, every day, like you used to."

Now Vega just felt guilty.

"You're right. I know. It's just…she looks so bad."

"She has lost some weight, it's true. But her vitals are good for now. If we can get her feeding situation settled, I'm hoping to see some improvement. Are you willing to let me try moving the tube?"

"Yes, I guess. But…I hate to sound callous, but how much is this going to cost?"

"It will be a bit more than the first insertion. This is a very minor surgery. Just a small incision and the procedure of guiding the tube into place. We should be able to do it in a twilight sedation."

"Twilight?"

"Not a general anesthesia. It's a much milder process, and she should recover much quicker." She added a little softer, "Less expensive as well."

It didn't matter that the doctor hadn't told her the cost. Vega knew it would be a lot. *But what other choice did she have?* She gave the doctor permission to go ahead with the procedure and thanked her. Walking back to the bed, she looked at her mom, now curled into a fetal position. She leaned down and kissed her cheek, and Miren moaned.

Vega could barely stand to see her like this anymore, but she felt too guilty to leave. She sat down in a chair by the bed, pulled out her phone, opened the *Seattle Times* app and navigated to the obits. Flipping through them in search of a gem, she came upon a picture of someone who looked familiar. This was the second time lately. *How strange.* She read through the obit hoping something would spark her memory.

Jenny Black, 22

Beloved daughter of James and Sheila, Jenny Black, will be remembered for her kind eyes and easy laugh. Jenny was a very independent child, and when she was five years old, her father nicknamed her Wild Child because she loved to run in the woods behind our home.

She adored dancing and dreamed of being in the Pacific Northwest Ballet. Jenny's favorite saying was, "I want to dance through life, happy and free."

A water lover, she could often be found at the coast, dipping her toes in the ocean…

Vega finished reading the obit and studied the picture next to it of Jenny. *Hadn't she seen her somewhere before?* She sat back and thought about it. *Did she see her at the SoulFood Coffeehouse?* No, she didn't think so. She didn't go that many places—home, work, Trent's place, the grocery store and now the hospital and Sunrise Center—and Drexel's. She smiled, thinking about him. Except for her new job, her life was so boring she rarely met new people. Then it came to her. *The parking garage at Neilmann! Wasn't she the woman who volunteered for one of the trials?*

Vega studied the picture again and was positive. She remembered her talking about her roommate who had wanted to come with her but had gotten food poisoning. *Weird.*

The obituary didn't say how she had died. But she was only twenty-two. *Must have been some kind of accident.* She looked at the date for the service—Saturday at Lewis Funeral Home in Bellevue. Before she could change her mind, she texted Trent.

Hey, what are you doing Saturday?
Prep work for opening. U?
Have time to go to a funeral?
????? Someone U know?
No. Tell you about it later.
OK. What time?
Pick you up at 10.

Trent was probably wondering why the hell she wanted to go to a funeral of someone she didn't know, but she was curious. Another person who had been in one of the MYND focus group studies who was now dead.

43

The wind was blowing hard, and the feathery tops of the Western red cedar trees bent in the breeze as Vega drove north on Avondale Road. Watching the branches sway, she wondered if they were in for another Strait of Juan de Fuca wind surge. It had been a few years since they had a bad one. The fifty to seventy mile or more an-hour winds had caused havoc in the past—downing trees onto homes and cutting the power for days. She made a mental note to check the forecast later.

Turning west on 165th and north at 188th Place took her right to Trent's townhouse. The street looked completely different than it had just a couple of years ago. What was once a suburban road of single-family houses was now filled with townhomes. When they had first started building, Vega was worried they would simply bulldoze the heavily treed area and stick up some rectangular boxes. But thankfully, she had been wrong. The townhomes were architecturally interesting and spaced generously apart from each other between the trees, most of which were still standing.

Although modern, the buildings somehow still looked appropriate amidst the red alders, Douglas firs and Western hemlocks.

Being an early buyer, thanks to some down-payment help from his parents, Trent had gotten his choice of homes. He'd chosen one set on a small peninsula which jetted out over the edge of the water of Cottage Lake.

She parked the car, got out and took a moment to look across the lake. It wasn't a big lake. In fact, it was more of a large pond. Even so, the view was pretty. And today, the strong breeze sent ripples across the top of the water, distorting the reflection of clouds and sky, and reminding her of the painting by Kathy Ferguson, *Flow*. Vega sighed, realizing it was only because of her mother that she knew the artist's work.

As she walked up to his door, she took a deep breath and enjoyed the pleasant earthy scent of trees and soil. She reminded herself she needed to take advantage of these moments, especially since the rest of the day might not be so pleasant.

She knocked, and Trent swung the door open and motioned her inside.

"Hey you," he said.

"Hey you, back."

Trent's place had a superb view of the water, and Vega liked what he had done with the space. The large windows and sparse furnishings made the small room seem more spacious. A low, cushioned, neutral-beige L-shaped sectional enclosed the family room, and the soft light-brown grass-cloth wallpaper added texture. She had asked him once why he decorated in such neutral colors and painted in such vibrant ones. He'd said the neutral colors showed off his artwork better, and he could change out his pieces without worrying about them clashing with any of the furniture or decor.

"You ready?" she asked.

"What time did you say it started?"

"Ten o'clock. I don't want to be early, though. I want to sneak in and find a seat in the back."

"What's this all about? Whose funeral is this?"

"It's actually not a funeral. It's a viewing. Then they have the funeral—which we are not going to. Grab your jacket. I'll tell you all about it in the car."

As they pulled out of the parking lot, Trent tried again.

"OK. Fess up. What's going on?"

Steering her car west onto Woodinville-Duvall Road, she said, "You're probably going to think I'm crazy."

"Try me."

"OK. I met this woman, Jenny Black, in the Neilmann parking garage a couple of weeks ago. It's her viewing."

"She works at Neilmann? You've never mentioned her."

"She doesn't work there. I'm pretty sure she was volunteering for one of the focus group studies. I only talked to her for a couple of minutes."

"Then why are we going to her viewing?"

"She's the third person I've known who's taken part in one of the studies, who's dead now."

"In how long?"

"Just since I started working there."

"Wow! That seems like a lot of people."

"Doesn't it? I'm not crazy, am I? It's only been a few months, and three people have died."

"Are you sure their deaths had something to do with the focus group thing? What did she die from?"

"I don't know. Her obituary didn't say. That's why I want to go."

"What about the others?"

"OK, there's Dave. He committed suicide, and the death certificate had a note about him having a psychotic episode. He shot himself in the head."

"Fuck! I'm almost afraid to ask about the other one."

"Marie Castle. She had a psychotic break while she was driving. Remember I told you about her being the cause of that big accident on 520 a few weeks ago?"

"Yeah."

"I don't have any proof she was in a focus group, but she had a psychotic break, like Dave, and her friend said they'd been in some kind of test together. Oh, and before I even started working there, I read this news article about some guy who killed his son and then himself. They said he had a psychotic breakdown. Not sure if that one's related or not. But still..."

"This is all horrible, but what does it have to do with the focus group studies?"

"They've been testing a new feature. I first learned about it in those documents you helped me find. Sorry I didn't tell you, but it's part of the project I'm working on. I can't tell you everything, but I think the new capability of the headband is messing up people's brains."

"Damn!"

Vega sighed. She wished she could tell him all about the MYND project, but she had signed the NDA. "I'm still trying to figure it all out."

"You're hoping to talk to someone and find out how she died."

"Exactly."

"But you didn't even really know her."

"They don't know that. Does your family know about all your friends?"

"Good point. OK. As long as I don't have to be the lookout guy again."

* * *

Vega and Trent stepped into the funeral home, and even though it was a gray day, it took them a few seconds for their eyes to adjust to the dark lighting inside. They were in a small lobby. A sign-in book sat on an ornate wooden table off to the side.

"Should we sign in?" whispered Trent.

"I don't think so." But as soon as she said it, a short man dressed in a dark, crisply pressed suit came up to them.

"The family would appreciate it if you signed the book. They want to have a recording of all of Jenny's friends who came to pay their respects," said the man, picking up the pen and holding it out to her.

Vega nodded, "Of course." She took the pen, signed her name and then handed it to Trent. "It's a nice gesture."

Trent gave her a look but took the pen and jotted down his name.

"Please, feel free to sit anywhere. Take your time. The viewing will end in two hours."

She thanked the man, and they walked in through the double doors to the viewing room. It was brighter and larger than she expected. The beige-painted walls held a row of golden sconces and paintings of scenic, idyllic places. About ten people sat whispering in the rows of dark-red upholstered chairs in the middle of the room. On a dais in front of the chairs, a polished wooden casket with glistening gold handles sat, surrounded by large flower wreaths and vases of lilies. A few people quietly whispering to each other, sat in cushioned chairs positioned against the side walls.

The casket was open, and a woman, tissue in hand, stood beside it looking down at the figure inside, obscuring the view. Vega was relieved because she really didn't want to see Jenny's body. She just wanted to talk to someone and find out what had happened.

Trent gripped Vega's arm, and she led him to one of the chairs in the back row. He leaned over and whispered, "I thought we were going to be able to blend in? There's hardly anybody here."

"A viewing isn't like a service or something. People trickle in and out all the time. Anyway, it's not like I didn't know her at all. We'll be OK. Just follow my lead."

Trent raised his eyebrows and shrugged.

"We'll just sit here a while and see how it goes," she added.

After a few minutes, a woman came up to them.

"Hi. Thank you for coming. Did you know my niece well?"

Vega stood up and smiled. "Hi. I only knew her for a short time. I'm so sorry for your loss."

"Thank you so much. I'm Lydia, her aunt."

"Vega. And this is Trent."

Trent stood up. "Nice to meet you. I'm really sorry about Jenny."

Vega took a chance. "Can I ask what happened? I'm sorry, I didn't hear. I only knew because I saw the obituary online."

Tears began to fall, and Lydia pulled a tissue out of her dress pocket and dabbed her eyes. "I… We didn't want to say anything about it in the obituary. It's just too horrible."

"I'm so sorry," said Vega. "You don't have to tell me."

"No. It's OK. The family didn't want to make a public announcement about it, but I don't think her mom would care if I told her friends. And, I don't know, maybe you can help us understand why?"

Vega simply nodded, hoping Lydia would continue.

"She had some kind of breakdown, I guess. She must have. It's the only thing that makes any sense." Lydia sniffled again and wiped her eyes. Leaning in close, she whispered, "She stabbed herself in the side of the head with a knife. Over and over again. It… It went into her brain."

Vega cringed.

"Holy shit! That's gruesome, man," Trent blurted out and then immediately covered his mouth with his hands. "Oh, god! I'm so sorry. I didn't mean to—"

"No, you're right," Lydia said. "It was gruesome. We almost didn't have an open viewing, but… It was on her dressing room table—the knife. She was working in that awful place, and we didn't even know! The knife wasn't even hers. It shouldn't have been there! She shouldn't have been there!" Lydia was crying fully now. "They said she just kept stabbing her head and screaming about a headache and flashing lights. There was blood everywhere! She died… She died before the paramedics could even get there!"

Lydia collapsed into a chair and dropped her head in her hands. "Why? Why would she do that?"

Trent and Vega gasped simultaneously. "Oh, my god! I'm so sorry," Vega said. "I shouldn't have asked. I'm really sorry!"

She sat next to Lydia and put her arm around her. She looked up at Trent in desperation just as an older woman sat on the other side of Lydia.

"I'm sorry," said the woman. "She's distraught. We all are, as you can imagine." She helped Lydia up and turned to them. "Thank you for coming," she said, pulling Lydia close to her. "Come on honey," she comforted, "let's go outside and get some air, OK?"

Vega stood up.

"I think I just found out everything I needed to know."

"Holy shit!" whispered Trent. "What the fuck?"

Vega pulled him out of the row and headed toward the door.

"Let's get the hell out of here."

44

It was hard to concentrate, because she couldn't quit thinking about what happened at Jenny's viewing. Now Vega was almost certain there was a connection between the psychotic breaks and the headband, but she didn't have time to look for proof right now. She had to get this last piece of her program finished before Ms. Neilmann fired her. As much as she hated to admit it, she was enjoying the challenge. Because of her background in neurology, she understood what Ryker had accomplished was remarkable.

Diving deep into his design documentation revealed Ryker had programmed the MYND headband to send an electrical signal directly to the nucleus accumbens, one of the pleasure centers of the brain. But the headband was not automatically sending the signal based on biometric information received from the user. It was being manually activated by a human, usually Drexel or Daphne. They wanted the stimulations to be random, not happen on every occurrence of an ad.

Vega began brainstorming ways to replicate the type of signal the headband was sending, wirelessly. Obviously, she couldn't send an electrical signal wirelessly, so she had to find another way to stimulate the area, and after racking her brain and researching for hours, she was at an impasse. *Maybe it simply couldn't be done?*

She hated to ask for help—it felt like admitting defeat—but flipping through old contacts from her college days at the University of Washington, she found who she was looking for. She checked the website first, just in case he wasn't even there anymore. But when she found him on the faculty page, she discovered he'd been promoted from professor, to the chair of the entire neurology department. Doubting he would take the time to talk to a former student, she took a chance anyway and dialed his number.

"Doctor Amazi's office," said a man's voice.

"Hi, I'm trying to reach Doctor Jermaine Amazi, please."

"May I ask who's calling?"

"Vega Swift. I'm an old student of his. He used to be my advisor."

"I see. Let me see if he's free. Please hold a moment."

Vega drummed her fingers on her desk while she waited. She would be surprised if he remembered her.

The line clicked, and a deep voice said, "Ms. Swift! It's so nice to hear from you."

Vega was surprised it had been so easy to reach him now that he had moved so high in the ranks.

"Hello, Doctor Amazi. I can't believe you remember me."

"Of course, I remember you. You were a standout student."

"Thank you. I see you've moved up in the department."

"Ah, yes. I was lucky to get the position last year when it opened up."

"I imagine luck had nothing to do with it."

"Thank you. So nice of you to say. What can I do for you?"

Vega described what she was trying to accomplish, without telling him who she worked for or why she needed to solve this particular puzzle.

"Hmm," he pondered. "That is quite a conundrum you have. What are the other modalities of neural stimulation aside from electrical currents? Have you thought about rTMS? You do remember the technology, I hope?"

"Yes. Repetitive transcranial magnetic stimulation. Of course! Why didn't I think of that?"

"I'm sure you would have, eventually. We have a system here at UW. Got it donated just last year. Do you need access? I'm sure I could arrange a temporary pass for you."

"No, thank you, doctor. My problem is a little smaller scale than that."

"I'm not sure if you've seen the new devices, but they've shrunk quite a bit in the last few years."

"I'm not surprised. I'll let you know if I think it will help me."

"Please do that. I hope you'll be able to share with me what you're working on when you're finished. I would love to hear more about it. But I'm sorry. I don't have time right now. I have a meeting to attend."

"Of course. I won't keep you. Thank you so much for taking my call, Doctor Amazi—and for your brilliant idea. You are a lifesaver!"

"You're welcome. Any time. I always love hearing from my former students."

They hung up, and now ecstatic, she pulled up her list of smart device chips and sensors again, thinking she might be able to replicate the actions of an rTMS system by using the OPM. She had used it in the MYND app initially to capture the brain wave signals, but she thought she could also use it to send magnetic pulses. And the program shouldn't have any problem focusing in on the nucleus accumbens area since it already knew its position due to the mapping completed in the calibration and connection routines.

She had a plan, and excited, she pulled up *Google Scholar* and researched the available scientific articles about using the rTMS to induce changes to the nucleus accumbens. Already leery about what the MYND headband was doing, she did not want to mess this up.

It made her feel guilty exploiting unsuspecting people this way, but it was so intriguing she almost convinced herself to waive her concerns. Almost. Regardless of her enjoyment of the work, the whole thing made her angry.

Maybe she was being naive. Maybe all the other companies would do this if they could, or maybe they were already doing something worse?

45

It was four o'clock, and Vega's brain was fried. After hours in the lab trying different parameters to get the OPM to stimulate the nucleus accumbens, she had finally gotten the results she wanted, but she still had a lot of testing to do. The lab phone rang, and Astrid was on the other end.

"Hey, are you almost done for the day?"

"Yes. My brain is toasted."

"Good. Let's go out—get a drink."

"Right now?"

"Yeah. I feel bad about how things have been lately between us. You know, I didn't mean to leverage your mom's medical condition. I was just trying to think of what was best for you. I hope you know that."

She wasn't sure if she did know that, but if she was going to stay here with Astrid as her boss, she needed to keep the fences mended.

"I know, and thank you. I still don't like what we're doing here, but Drexel and I talked about it the other day, and I guess I'm glad we're the ones with the technology rather than our competition."

"Exactly! And you know, I need this job too, right?"

"I know. I've been meaning to tell you I heard about your sister's cancer. I'm really sorry."

"Oh! Who told you?"

"Drexel. It just kind of slipped out, I think."

"That's fine. It's not like I try to keep it a secret. It's just not something I like to talk about."

"Believe me, I understand."

"So. Let's go get a drink. What do you say?"

Vega couldn't remember the last time she had gone out with a girlfriend for drinks—well, not counting Trent—and she did count him as a girlfriend. But their last outing had been to a funeral home. This sounded much more inviting.

"Sure. Why not?"

"Really? Yes! I expected you to turn me down."

"Usually, I would have. I'm normally running home to take care of Mom. It's weird not having to rush out, and hell, I could use a drink too. Besides, I really want us to be friends."

"Good. Me too. So wrap up whatever you're doing, and I'll meet you in the lobby in ten minutes."

* * *

When they stepped outside the building, the sun was already low in the sky and would soon be hidden behind the hills of Bainbridge Island. It was chilly, and the wind whipping off the sound, its force concentrated between the buildings, packed a punch by the time it reached them. She stuck her hands in the pockets of her jacket as she walked down Pike Street with Astrid.

"What's the name of this place?"

"Urban Apocalypse. I don't know what kind of drinks you like, but they make a great tootsie roll."

"What's a tootsie roll?"

"Oh, good! You've never had one? Just wait. You're going to love it!"

They made a left on Fourth Avenue, and a few blocks down, Vega saw a worn gray metal sign hanging above the sidewalk with the name *Urban Apocalypse* stamped on it. The outside façade of the bar was gray concrete, with several small prison-like windows placed high along the front. Faux, but realistic cracks painted on the front made it appear as if it had suffered through an earthquake. The large black door would have been more at home in front of a bank vault, but was apparently not as heavy as it looked because her boss pulled it open effortlessly.

The place was dark, and it took a few seconds for their eyes to adjust. But Astrid seemed to know her way around, and Vega followed her as she walked toward the back of the bar.

The warm, slightly humid air pressed against her face as she looked around and took in the scenery. The walls and ceiling were also concrete, or at least they looked like it. For all she knew, it was wallpaper. Apocalyptic-themed pictures covered the walls and various pipes of all shapes and colors —brass, silver and patinated copper–hung from the ceiling. Shelves, stacked full with more liquor bottles than she had ever seen together in one place, sat behind a dark wooden bar that ran along the entire side wall. A pleasant sharp musky smell—like steel, liquor and leather—swirled together in the air. Round metal stools lined up in front of the bar, and hi-top tables sat along the opposite wall. Dark brown button-tufted leather booths hugged the back wall. She followed Astrid to one, and they sat.

"This place is awesome," Vega said.

"I know, right? And the drinks are fantastic. I have never ordered anything they didn't have. I swear they have every brand of liquor available in the world. Not that I know much about it. But look at that stock!"

"Yeah, I saw that. I've never seen so many different types of liquor."

"Sometimes they bring in local bands," Astrid said. "But the place is kind of small, so it sells out fast."

"Where do they put them?"

"Up at the front, under the windows."

"It looks too small to have a band there and still get many people in."

"Yeah, I've never seen more than a three-piece in here. And they're never loud. Never any speakers or anything. It's always acoustic."

"That sounds nice."

"I've only been here a couple of times when they've had music, but yeah, I like it."

"Tell me more about this tootsie roll. I haven't ever heard of it. But then, I'm usually just a wine or beer kind of gal. What's in it?"

"It tastes exactly like a tootsie roll," Astrid said. "The bartender told me there are a lot of different recipes, but he said he makes it with root beer, orange juice and Kahlua—a coffee liqueur. I still don't understand how that combination ends up tasting like a tootsie roll. Is there orange flavoring in those?"

"Not that I know of. But it sounds great. I think I'll have one."

"All right. Let's do it. I'll get the first round."

Right on cue, a server dressed in a dark-gray jumpsuit with a compass hanging off one of his belt loops, a Swiss army knife on a thick, rusty-looking chain looped around his neck and a gas mask on top of his head, came up and took their order.

After he left, Astrid turned to Vega. "So, are you and Drexel still a thing?"

She looked down. She really didn't want to talk about Drexel with her. Vega was pretty sure Astrid still had feelings for him, even if she didn't admit it.

"You don't really want to talk about Drexel."

"Why not? Sure I do. Come on, don't be shy. What's been happening?"

"Are you sure?"

"Yes, please."

Vega could only think that since Astrid wasn't with him anymore, she got her fix by hearing about his life from other people. It didn't make her feel good, but she didn't want to argue about it.

"OK. I guess we're a thing now. I have to ask. You dated him. Did you ever meet his father?"

Astrid rolled her eyes. "Yes. What a fucking nut job! Always on Drexel's case about making something of himself."

"Did he ever just, uh, come in to his place? Uninvited?"

"Not that I remember. But he came over—all the time. Never seemed to leave Drexel alone. Why?"

Vega shook her head. "No reason. Just curious."

"Yeah, right. Come on. You can tell me."

"It's not important."

"You can't do that! Now you have to tell me!"

Vega sighed and gave in. "OK. the other day we were—"

The waiter interrupted with their drinks, and Vega took a sip. "Wow! You're right. This tastes exactly like a tootsie roll! I could get myself in trouble with these. It's like drinking candy."

"I know, right? It's so good I have to keep track of how many I've had so I don't overdo it. Don't get sidetracked. You were saying, the other day?"

"OK. We were in bed—"

"In the middle of the day? You naughty girl!"

"It was after work. Not exactly the middle of the day."

"OK. OK. Keep going."

"Anyway, his dad just walked in."

"Fuck! Into the bedroom?"

"No, thank goodness—the front door. Didn't knock or anything. I'm pretty sure he has a key, or maybe Drexel didn't lock the door. I'm not sure. And you know Drexel's place. The ceilings are all open. I was afraid he was going to charge right in. But Drexel got up and talked to him and he left, finally. But I was dressed by then. I didn't want him to barge in and see me naked."

"Jesus! Yeah, that would be fucking embarrassing!"

"You think? And like you said, he was harping on him about getting a promotion. Moving up in the company. Drexel said he wants him to move over to OneVision after he's proven himself. Sounded like they have planned meetings to discuss his future. He seems very controlling."

"He is. I don't miss that. He owns Drexel's place, you know."

"Yeah, he told me. Enough about Drexel and his dad. How's your sister doing? I'm sorry. I don't even know her name."

"That's OK. Not like I told you. It's Shelly, and the last session really knocked her down. They're going to run tests next week to see how effective the treatments have been. Did Drexel tell you she has lung cancer? She has fucking lung cancer! And she's never smoked a day in her life!"

"Oh, my god! That's horrible! I'm so sorry. I hope the treatments help her."

"Me too. It's just so fucking unfair." She took a sip of her drink. "See, you're not the only one who is desperate to keep your job. Shelly's never had a job with good insurance, and our parents don't make enough to help her. And Violet, my older sister, has a husband and two kids to worry about. They're putting every spare dime they have into a college fund for the kids. Shelly's too old to be on our parents' insurance, so I helped her find a plan she could afford. But it still doesn't cover everything, and she's not well enough to work, so guess who's paying for her insurance? Me! It's fucking expensive to be sick in this country."

Vega nodded. "I know. Believe me."

"I'm sorry for going on about this—and you with your mother and everything. I'm sure it's much worse for you. I can't imagine what you're going through."

"I try not to dwell on it."

Astrid nodded. "I get that." She took another drink and sighed. "I'm sorry. Didn't mean to be such a drag. I wanted to unwind and have fun, not complain about my life."

"It's fine. Sometimes you just need to vent. Maybe we should just call it a night?"

"Hell, no!" Astrid exclaimed, tipping her glass up and jiggling the ice cubes to lap up the last bit of her drink. "We're just getting started."

Vega looked down and saw her glass was almost empty, too. "My turn," she said, waving the waiter over.

While they waited for their drinks, Vega took a chance.

"I've been wanting to talk to you again about the psychotic episodes."

"Oh, god! Not that again. Just drop it, OK? And please, let's not talk about the last part of your program. Ms. Neilmann is just trying to save the company. You do remember that Seichō is trying to buy us out, right? We need every advantage we can get."

Vega nodded.

"Can't we talk about something else?" Astrid pleaded.

She could tell it was a losing battle, so she gave up. "OK. You're right. I'm sorry. What do you want to talk about?"

"Thank you! OK, I know this is still work related, but…"

"What?" she asked, just as the server came back with their drinks.

Astrid took a sip and asked, "Did you know Ryker is Japanese?"

"No way."

"Half anyway. His mom is from Okinawa, and his dad is from Nebraska."

"But he doesn't look Japanese at all."

"I know, right? I knew you'd be surprised."

"Was he adopted?"

"No. But he's the spitting image of his dad. He showed me a picture. I guess his mom's genes got squashed by those powerful, corn-fed, mid-western, all-American ones. I mean, you would never know, right?"

"No! Wow! That's a shocker!"

"He was born there. They moved to the States when he was a baby. He has dual citizenship."

"How did this come up?"

"We had a big celebration when he finished the MYND headband, and Ms. Neilmann took the project team out." Astrid cocked her head. "Ryker had a little too much to drink and started spewing out his whole childhood story to me. His real name is Rikuto. But he said everyone always made fun of it, so he Americanized it to Ryker."

"I am so surprised. How did they end up in Seattle if his dad's from Nebraska?"

"I didn't get the full story, but his dad was in the military. They moved around a lot. He was stationed at the Fussa Air Force base in Japan when he met Ryker's mom. I think he was last stationed in Seattle. I'm pretty sure he's retired now."

"Did he tell you anything else interesting?"

"Oh, I think he likes you."

Vega was floored. "Did he say that?"

"No, not exactly. But trust me, he does."

"He does not. I don't think he likes me at all. As a matter of fact, I think he *dis*likes me."

"No he doesn't. I've seen how he looks at you when you're not watching. And yeah, he may have resented you at first, but I guess he got over it. Remember, I told you he was supposed to get a promotion after creating the MYND device? It's been two years now. But Ms. Neilmann still found the money to hire you."

"Oh crap. I had no idea. No wonder he hates me."

"He does not hate you. I'm telling you, he is into you. I guess he finally realized it's not your fault. I think he admires you."

Vega laughed, not believing her. "Astrid, you are crazy."

"No, I'm serious! You've taken his invention, which he is extremely proud of by the way, and made it obsolete!"

"Then he *should* hate me."

"No, he's impressed." Astrid took a sip of her drink and shook her head at her. "You're attracting all the men in our group. Which is it going to be, Ryker or Drexel?"

Vega laughed even harder. "I don't think that's going to be a hard choice. And anyway, you're dreaming. Ryker has no interest in me. The only time he's been nice to me was when he showed off his fountain pen."

"Yeah, he is really into those. But don't tell me I didn't warn you when he finally asks you out on a date."

"Right."

"Oh, and I think Ms. Neilmann likes him."

Vega almost spit out her drink. "No!"

"Yeah. But I don't think it's reciprocated," she said, chuckling. "If you watch him in the meetings, he always sits as far away from her as possible. Maybe he's afraid she'll jump him right there in the middle of the meeting!"

Vega was worried she was going to pee her pants from laughing so hard, if Astrid didn't stop revealing things. "Stop it!" She caught her breath and took a few sips of her drink. "Man, this is so good."

"Second one. We need to keep track," Astrid said, twirling her ice cubes. "Ms. Neilmann got pretty tipsy at that party as well, and I swear I saw her make a pass at him. She also told me quite a secret that night."

"What?"

"I probably shouldn't tell you."

"OK."

"Wow! You give up fast."

"Oh. If you want to tell me..."

"OK, OK. Quit twisting my arm!"

Vega laughed and threw up her hands. "I did nothing!"

"She got pregnant when she was really young, sixteen, I think she said. She said she was raped by a classmate, but even so, she wanted to keep the baby. Said it wasn't the baby's fault. But her family made her give it up. She's been trying to find out where he is."

"Holy shit! That's awful!" Vega bit her tongue. Astrid obviously didn't know Drexel was Katya's long-lost son. *But why hadn't she been able to find out if Drexel could? Was he lying?*

"Did she hire a private detective?"

"No. I asked her the same thing. She said she was afraid word would get out somehow. Didn't want to tarnish her reputation in the business world. But she said it was a closed adoption, so..."

"Would people really care that she had a baby at sixteen?"

"Who knows? I think she was more afraid they'd find out she was raped. I'm sure she doesn't want that to be public knowledge. She didn't tell me much more. I think she forgot who she was talking to and then came to her senses and clammed up. She's never been very talkative with me since. Maybe she's embarrassed that she told me. Or maybe she just went back to her normal relationship with me," Astrid said with a grin.

Vega was torn. *Should she tell Astrid? Or Ms. Neilmann?* But now she was worried Drexel was mistaken. *What if she told them what he'd said, and it turned out to be wrong?* She almost wished he had never said anything.

Then she thought back to what Astrid said about Ryker.

"Wait a minute. Seichō is based in Japan, right? Did Ryker ever work for them?"

"Not that I know of. Like I said, they moved when he was just a baby. But they go back there all the time to visit relatives. He speaks fluent Japanese."

"Huh."

"He told me when he was growing up, his parents spoke only Japanese at home. They wanted him to be fluent in both languages."

Vega was barely listening as Astrid moved on to another subject. Ryker had ties back to Japan, the country where Seichō was based, and he was unhappy about not getting promoted. He had created the MYND headband in the first place and should know if it was harming the users. And he was also capable of tweaking it to ensure that it did.

46

The next day back at work, Vega stared at her program and took a deep breath. Yes, she'd been able to get it to do what Ms. Neilmann wanted, but there was still some fine-tuning and testing she needed to do before she could show everyone.

After spending several hours adding in the last few changes, she saved the newly compiled program along with the specifications document. She wasn't sure if she wanted to tell Astrid she had finished. Once it went into production, there was no turning back.

She procrastinated, opened her browser, and a news article popped up on the screen. The ads displayed to the right seemed to know all about her. *Hell*, she thought, *they were probably Neilmann customer ads*. She tried to ignore the one for new plastic dishes, which was kind of creepy, since she had searched for some just this morning, and read the news blurb from the *Seattle Times*.

Brain Abnormalities Linked to String of Recent Deaths

A 41-year-old dad kills his child and then himself. A car accident in Bellevue leads to 12 injuries and 3 deaths. A 32-year-old man commits suicide.

What could these deaths possibly have in common, you ask? Normally nothing. But the recent string of unusual deaths and suicides in the Seattle area, have raised an alarm at the Medical Examiner's office.

"In the last few weeks, we've discovered some very disturbing findings in the frontal cortex, septal area and thalamus of several victims of unexpected deaths," said Dr. Akshay Kumar, Chief Medical Examiner of King County. "We believe these abnormalities in the brain are responsible for the psychosis which occurred before the victims' deaths. All I can say is we are taking the matter very seriously, and further investigation is underway."

This statement was prompted by an uncharacteristically high number of murders, suicides and self-harm incidents linked to psychotic episodes in King County over the last few months. The Examiner's office has presented the information to the…

She continued reading. The piece stated that within the last month alone, there had been twelve reports in King County of people with no former mental problems, having spontaneous psychotic episodes. Three episodes led to suicides, five to the person harming themselves or those around them, and one person was accused of murder and was in a mental facility now. The psychiatrists didn't know what to make of it. Apparently, the MEs were now conducting detailed brain autopsies on victims of suspicious deaths linked to psychotic events.

Vega wondered how they knew these people used to be normal, and for that matter, how they knew they'd had a psychotic break.

So far, she'd found no reason what Ryker was doing with the headband, or what she had now recreated with her MYND application, should cause people to have psychotic episodes. But she had a gut feeling there was a connection.

Could she really just stand by and watch as Neilmann rolled her program out to the masses?

She texted Trent.

```
 Can you come over tonight?
```

Still waiting for a reply, Vega shut her computer, grabbed her stuff and was almost to her car when he answered.

```
Wassup?
Tell you tonight. 7? I'll get food. My
place?
I'll b there
```

* * *

On her way home, Vega stopped at one of her and Trent's favorite Thai places to make up for not showing him the documentation after being her lookout. She took the 520 exit to West Lake Sammamish, made a left and pulled into the little strip mall where Bangkok Basil resided. The food was great, and the place was small but adorable. Colorful artwork displayed on the brightly painted walls, and they'd strung twinkling fairy lights across the ceiling. She had called ahead and ordered the dish they both loved—avocado curry with chicken.

Back home, she poured the creamy green meal into bowls, and the spicy smell of curry filled the air.

"You got our favorite!" Trent exclaimed.

"I owed you."

"Yes, you did," he said, smiling.

"Beer?"

"Sure, why not?"

She got the beers, and they clinked their bottles and dug into their food.

"I finished my program," she said.

"Congratulations!"

"Thanks. Did you read the paper today?"

"No, why?"

"Pull it up, and click on the *Medical* section. There's a brief article in there about autopsy abnormalities. The ME has noticed the same thing I have."

"What? Hang on." Trent pulled his phone out of his back pocket, and Vega waited while he read through the article.

"Holy shit!"

"I know! I swear the problem is related to the headband. And I'm writing a program to do exactly the same thing it does. As far as I know, it might cause the same problem."

"Holy crap!"

"But the article doesn't say anything about Neilmann," Vega added. "And I doubt anyone will ever put it together if I don't do something."

"What are you going to do?"

"I don't know yet."

"I thought you weren't supposed to tell me all this."

"I don't know if I care anymore. And anyway, it's not like you know how I did it. And it will be obvious my program exists once Neilmann doesn't use the headband in their consumer focus groups anymore."

"Now what?"

"I can't do anything until I get some kind of proof. I need to be able to show that the people having the breaks are the same ones who are in the trials. It's a blind study. But there has to be a key somewhere—a list that matches the participants to their real names. I need that key."

"Shouldn't it be in the Neilmann computers, or maybe their cloud?"

"Yes. But I've been looking, and I can't find it anywhere."

"Why don't you just ask Drexel? Didn't you tell me he runs those focus group thingies? And I mean, you are doing him, after all."

"Trent!"

"Well, you are, aren't you?"

Vega sighed, giving him a face. "Yes. But I can't."

"Why not?"

"I already tried. I brought it up with him, and he doesn't believe me. He doesn't think there's a connection. And besides, I'm not sure he would want to do anything that would put Ms. Neilmann, the CEO, in an unpleasant light."

"Why not? Does he feel, like, some kind of loyalty to her or something?"

"There's certainly some loyalty there. She's his mother."

"What?"

"Yeah. She doesn't know."

"Oh! This is starting to sound like one of those old soap operas. How could she not know she had a son? Was she comatose for nine months? Or no, wait. What was the other storyline they always used? Oh, I know. She has amnesia!"

"No, none of the above. The reason she doesn't know is she was a teenager when she gave him up, and it was a closed adoption. According to Astrid, she's been trying to find him. But Drexel tracked her down using a private investigator."

"This is all just too weird. If he could find her, why hasn't she found him?"

"She didn't hire a professional because she's afraid it will leak to the public. She doesn't want anyone to know about the baby, because they might find out she was raped."

"Oh shit! This just keeps getting better!"

"I know. I'm still having a hard time wrapping my head around it all. Oh, and guess what else I found out? Astrid told me Ryker is half Japanese. And our main competitor, Seichō, is based in Japan. What if he's working with them?"

"Geez! This is a shit show! You can't just sit back and do nothing," said Trent.

"Watch me."

"Vega! You should call the press, or write a blog or something."

"One minute I feel guilty, and the next, I don't want to stick my neck out. Why should I do anything? Like my life isn't hard enough already. Look what happened to my dad. He spoke up, and it ruined his life. I'm never going to get my mom into a decent place if I don't have a job that pays the kind of money I'm getting at Neilmann. And I signed an NCA. No working anywhere, even remotely similar, for two years. At least I got it reduced. It was originally for three years! And you know I love my mom, and would do anything for her, but I'm not going to have a life of my own for a long time."

"At least you get to have a life. The poor people using your program may not have a life at all—good or bad."

"Thanks a lot. I don't even know yet if my program will cause the same problem."

"You just told me it does exactly the same thing as the headband!"

"It actually does that and more. But I don't know what's wrong with the headband, so…" Vega put her head down on the counter. "Jesus, why does life have to be so hard?"

"It's not. It's an easy decision. You have to tell someone."

Vega looked at Trent. "I've tried! No one believes me! Besides, Neilmann would just tell anyone that did, that I'm a disgruntled employee. Then I'll for sure get fired."

"So, you're not going to do anything?"

"No. I think I'm just going to put my head down and do my work like my dad always told me he should have done. Maybe he would still be here if he'd done that. I'm trying to learn from his mistakes."

47

Driving into work the next day, Vega made the decision to show her finished program to Astrid, and ultimately, Ms. Neilmann. *If she wasn't going to do anything about her suspicions, what was she waiting for?*

Despite everything, she was proud of it and was positive there was nothing else like it out there. *If only they weren't using it simply to make people buy things.* She was already thinking about how, with a few tweaks, they could use it in the health-care industry. The nucleus accumbens was involved in neurodegenerative diseases like Alzheimer's and Parkinson's, so *maybe there was a way they could use the program for something good? She could approach Ms. Neilmann? Start a new group focusing on medical applications for it?*

She laughed at herself. *Right.*

The map app told her traffic was backed up on Union Hill, so she detoured from her usual route. When she stopped at the red light at Novelty Hill, she noticed her brakes felt a little spongy. *Great*, she thought. *She'd have to take it to the shop now*. Something else to suck the money out of her already dwindling bank account.

Forcing herself to think about something nice, she noticed more trees starting to change colors. For some reason, the Katsura trees in the parking lot by Starbucks were always some of the first to turn, and once they started, their summer green leaves quickly evolved into yellow and then a beautiful red. It was her favorite time of year, and she was looking forward to a drop in the temperatures so she could pull her sweaters and warm scarves out of the back of her closet. You could tell when summer was truly over in the PNW by when the rains kicked in again. She really loved the rain. People always thought she was out of her mind when she told them that, but she found it was calming and soothing and added a softness to the atmosphere. And the way it sounded when it hit the metal roof of her little house felt comforting. Often, she would open her bedroom windows at night just so she could hear the raindrops fall and bounce off the rhododendrons outside her window.

Her thoughts went to Drexel. She knew she didn't need the complication of a relationship right now, but for the first time in what felt like forever, she thought there might be something great there. She could count on one hand the number of men she'd gone out with in the last five years, so she probably had no idea what a potential long-term relationship felt like.

The light turned green, and she steered her car onto the main drag of Novelty Hill Road. Thankfully, the traffic was light today. Friday-light, everyone called it. She didn't know if the traffic was lighter on Fridays because people worked four-day weeks, because lots of people simply took Fridays off, or what, but it was always a pleasant surprise not to see a line of brake lights in front of her.

From the peak of Redmond Ridge, the road went downhill at a nine-percent grade for almost two-and-a-half miles. When she came to the intersection at 208th Street, the light was yellow, so she put on the brakes. But they grabbed for a second, and then nothing happened. The light was deep red as she passed under it, narrowly missing a school bus that was already halfway through the intersection. The bus honked, and Vega stood on the brakes to try to slow down, but it had no effect.

She swerved the wheel to the left as she almost hit the car in front of her on one of the sharper turns. Now in the opposite lane, she steered even farther to the left, and with the two driver-side tires rumbling over the dirt and rocks of the left shoulder, narrowly avoided hitting an oncoming car. Thankfully, the traffic was next to nothing in the opposite lane. She steered back into her lane and pulled up on the emergency brake with all her strength. But again—nothing. There was nothing she could do but try to avoid hitting anyone. The brakes were worthless.

It was like being on a bumper-car carnival ride as she whipped the steering wheel back and forth trying to keep from crashing into other vehicles. She leaned on the horn, and drivers swerved off the road to try to avoid her. Before she knew it, her car had jumped over the high curb, and after a teeth-chattering screech of concrete against the metal undercarriage, it came to an abrupt stop half-in and half-out of the center island of the roundabout at the bottom of the hill. Her seatbelt tightened abruptly, strangled her chest to the back of the seat, and the airbag inflated right before Vega's head whipped forward. Her face slammed into the hard white fabric, and she passed out.

* * *

When Vega woke up, the first thing she heard was the noise of radio static and someone calling her name. Slowly, she opened her eyes and saw she was inside the back of an emergency vehicle lying on a gurney with a brace around her neck. A man was looking down at her, his stethoscope dangling from around his neck, swinging in front of his long-sleeved dark blue shirt.

"Ms. Swift, are you awake? Can you hear me?"

"Yes. I… What happened?"

The man was reading her driver's license. "Is your name Vega Swift?"

"Yes."

"I'm Rashon. I'm going to be taking care of you, OK? You ran into the roundabout. Do you remember?"

Vega started to sit up. "I have to get to—"

The man pressed his hand lightly on her shoulder to keep her down. "Woah, just lie back. You've been in an accident."

It took Vega a second for her head to clear. Then she remembered.

"My brakes went out. I couldn't stop. All I could think to do was aim for the center of the traffic circle. I was trying not to hit anyone."

The man nodded. "Good thinking. Don't worry. You didn't hit anyone. Do you know what day it is?"

"Friday."

"That's right."

Vega tried to sit up again. "I'm feeling OK. I'm just a little in shock."

Rashon tried to press her back onto the gurney again, but she gently pushed his hand away.

"Your airbag went off, Ms. Swift. You took quite a hit. I really recommend you let us take you into the hospital and have you checked out."

Vega turned, swung her legs over the side of the gurney and took off the neck brace.

"No. I'm fine. Really. Can't you just check my vitals or something?"

"Yes. We did that. Your heart rate and blood pressure are a little elevated. And I suggest you get an x-ray of your neck."

She moved her neck around.

"I really don't advise—," he tried.

"I'm OK."

He sighed. "Do you mind if I check your vision?"

Vega nodded.

"OK, please follow my finger," he said, moving his finger up and down and around to track her eye movement. "Everything seems fine, but you should really let us take you in."

"No. I don't have time for that. I've got to get to work. Thank you, but I can't afford to go to the hospital."

He shook his head. "I can't make you go, but you may have whiplash or a concussion."

She was a little stiff, but otherwise, was sure there was nothing really wrong with her.

"No. I appreciate your concern. But, I can't."

He nodded and asked, "Is there someone I can call for you?"

"Where's my purse? I guess I need to call a tow truck."

Rashon handed her driver's license back and then reached under the side bench for her purse.

"It was in the passenger seat."

"Thanks."

Vega looked out of the emergency vehicle and saw her car stuck in the center of the roundabout. A police car she hadn't noticed before was parked farther down on the narrow sidewalk. "It's totaled, isn't it?"

"Sorry, I couldn't tell you."

"It doesn't look good though, does it?"

"No. It doesn't. Are you sure you're OK?"

"Yes. Can I just sit here a second while I make a few calls?"

"Sure. We need to fill out some paperwork and get you to sign a release form stating you refused to go to the hospital. OK?"

"Sure. Whatever you need."

"Oh, and that policewoman needs to talk to you."

She looked back up Novelty Hill, and could see she had caused a huge backup. Friday morning was light no more. She shook her head and sighed.

The policewoman came over, got the details and went back and started directing traffic again. Finally, Vega called a tow truck and her insurance company. Her next call was to Astrid.

"Hey, Astrid, it's Vega. I'm going to be late today."

"You're already late. I was starting to worry about you."

"I've been in an accident. But I'm fine."

"Oh, no! What happened?"

"My brakes went out. I couldn't stop my car. Not even with my emergency brake. I don't know what happened."

"Oh, shit! Are you hurt? Did you hit anybody?"

"I'm fine. And no, thank goodness. Just me against the roundabout. I think my car is totaled, though. But I can take an Uber in."

"Don't be silly. Take the day off, and take care of yourself. I'm just glad you're OK. Do you need anything?"

"No, the tow truck is coming, and I've already called my insurance company. They're going to deliver a car to me tomorrow."

"Do you need a ride?"

"No, it's OK. I have a friend who lives nearby. He'll give me a ride home. But thank you."

"You're sure there's nothing I can do?"

"No. I'll be fine. Thanks."

"Of course. I'll see you on Monday. Take care of yourself."

"OK."

Vega hung up and called Trent. But it went straight to voicemail. Then she texted him, but there was no reply.

She sat for a minute and thought about who she could call. It was pitiful how few friends she had. *Maybe I should call Astrid back?* But then she had a better idea.

She took a deep breath and punched in the number. He answered on the first ring.

"Drexel? It's Vega. Are you busy?"

48

Drexel was more than happy to pick her up. He parked his car on the shoulder just south of the roundabout, and after waiting for the policewoman to clear a path for him, walked over to the emergency vehicle where Vega was sitting. Rashon had refused to leave until her ride arrived.

Vega stood up, and Drexel gave her a big hug.

"Are you hurt?" He released her. "I'm not hurting you, am I?"

"No. I'm fine. Just shaken up a bit. Thank you for coming to get me. I hope it wasn't too far."

"What's wrong with your face?"

"What do you mean?"

"You have a couple of shiners."

Vega touched her face.

"It's probably from the air bag."

Drexel hugged her again. "Looks like it hurts."

She touched her eyes again. "A little. Mostly I have a terrible headache."

"I'm just glad you're OK."

Vega leaned into another hug, took a deep breath and allowed herself to let go. Eventually, she pushed back and looked over at Rashon.

"You can leave now. Thank you so much for all your help."

"You're sure you're OK?"

"Yes, I'm fine. I'm sure you have more emergencies to take care of."

Rashon nodded, and Drexel led Vega back through the traffic to his car.

"Do you mind if we just wait here for the tow truck? They should be here any minute."

"Of course. Whatever you need."

"Thanks. I guess now that I think about it, I really didn't need you to come get me. I could have just ridden with the tow truck to the car repair place."

"And then how would you have gotten home?"

"Oh, right. Good question."

"Do you know where you're going to have it taken?"

"Uh, now that you mention it. No."

"It's OK. I know a good place. And I'm glad you called me. I would have been upset if you hadn't."

"Thank you. I'm glad I did too."

After a moment of silence, Drexel finally asked, "What happened?"

"My brakes went out. I'm lucky I didn't hit anyone."

"That's weird. Just like that? No warning or anything?"

"No, well, they felt strange earlier this morning. But I just thought I needed brake fluid or something. I was mentally preparing myself to have to take it to the shop."

"How old is it?"

"Ten years. I think."

"But you get the regular check-ups done, right? They should have caught something wrong with the brakes."

Vega examined her hands. "No, I can't afford to do those regular check-ups. I'm just happy I can put gas in it. I can't remember the last time I took it in. It's been a good car—until now."

"I'm really sorry you're having so much money trouble. Do you need any help?"

"No, it's fine. I mean, the new job has really helped. But I've had to pay for more nurses, then my mom got the UTI and now the hospital, Sunrise Center, new drugs that aren't on our plan, the feeding tube and all that—it's a lot. And now I'll probably have to get a new car. I was barely making it before. I thought the extra money from Neilmann would make my financial situation better. But it seems like everything is blowing up at once."

Saying out loud everything going wrong in her life, Vega started to get emotional. She didn't want to cry in front of Drexel, but tears came anyway. She hid her face in her hands, unable to hold them in.

"God, Vega. You should have said something. You know I would help you."

She tried to stifle her tears. She didn't want to drag Drexel into her messy life. It was nice having him separate. Her time with him was like an oasis away from her normal problems. Looking out the window trying to think of something to say, she was grateful when she saw the tow truck driving up the road.

* * *

Her car was a mess. Sitting in the waiting area of the car repair shop with Drexel, Vega saw it through the glass door raised on the lift in the garage. She waited for the mechanic to come and tell her the damage.

A man in a dark blue jumpsuit walked into the waiting area.

"Ms. Swift?"

Vega stood up. "That's me."

They walked up to the counter to hear the verdict.

"Hi, I'm Oscar. We looked over your car, and I'm sorry to tell you, but we can't do anything. It's totaled. The frame's bent."

"Crap! I knew it!"

"Mind if I ask what happened?"

"I ran it over a roundabout. The brakes went out. I was going down a hill. It was the only thing I could think of to do to not hit everybody else on the road."

"She's lucky to be alive," Drexel added.

The man nodded. "That's what I thought."

"You could tell I ran over a roundabout?"

He shook his head. "No. But I could tell your brakes went out. Someone work on your car recently?"

"No. I haven't had it in a shop for months. Why? Was something wrong?"

"Yeah. It looks like your brake lines were cut. Well, maybe sliced is a better word."

"What?" Drexel asked.

"Sliced?" asked Vega. "What do you mean? When? I mean, wouldn't that just make them not work?"

"I don't know when, but it couldn't have been that long ago, else the brake fluid would have completely leaked out. And the lines weren't cut through. There was just a small slit in 'em so the brake fluid must've leaked out slowly. Have you gone over some rough roads lately? Maybe some back mountain roads or something like that?"

"No."

Drexel turned to Vega. "Have you left your car somewhere? Maybe someplace it could have been vandalized?"

"No. I pretty much just go to work and back. Well, and to the hospital. Sometimes to my friend's house. All city roads." She looked back at Oscar. "You think a bad road could have caused it?"

He cleared his throat. "Honestly? No. The only thing I can think of that would cause something like what I saw in your lines, was that someone cut 'em."

"You mean someone intentionally cut my brake lines?"

"That's what it looks like to me. I mean, feel free to take it somewhere else, but I've been working on cars a long time. Those cuts in the brake lines, they didn't look natural."

"That can't be right," said Drexel.

"What the fuck?" Vega put her hand over her mouth and glanced around the waiting room. "Sorry."

"Do you have some enemies you haven't told me about?" asked Drexel.

"Not that I know of. But now I'm starting to wonder."

"Anyway, like I said, I'm sorry, but your car can't be fixed. And if someone offers to do it, you just walk away. They may say they can repair it, and it'll be good as new. But don't listen to that. Your car's not safe anymore. We'll send the information to your insurance company."

Vega nodded. In a daze, she signed the paperwork and thanked him.

Walking out to Drexel's car, she said, "This sucks. I knew it was totaled. Now I have to get a rental."

"Or I could just be your chauffeur," he said.

"Thanks, but I wouldn't do that to you. You're too far away to come over every time I need you."

"I don't know. It would give me an excuse to see you more often."

Vega smiled for the first time since the accident. "Thanks for offering. But you don't need to do that just to see me."

She gave him another smile, but frowned again as she started thinking about the logistics and costs of the next few weeks. And then she realized her car was the least of her problems. What she really needed to worry about, was who the hell was trying to kill her.

364

49

When Vega showed up at her office the next Monday, Astrid was already there, waiting at her door.

"Morning. How are you feeling?" Astrid asked. "Oh, holy shit, Vega! What happened to your eyes? I thought you said you were OK?"

Vega had tried to cover up the bruises with makeup, but it was a losing battle. She smiled. "Yeah, my face had a run-in with an airbag. They're just bruises," she said, opening her door. "I look worse than I feel. But my car is another story. It's totaled."

She decided she wasn't going to tell anyone about her slashed brake lines until she found out who was behind it. *Maybe it wasn't anyone at Neilmann, but who else?*

Astrid followed her into her office. "Well, that sucks. Are you in a rental?"

"Yeah, until I find time to hunt for a new car—a new *cheap* car."

"Isn't the insurance paying for it?"

"Yeah, but they only give you the current value of your car, and my car wasn't exactly new."

"If you need someone to go car shopping with, just let me know. I love looking at new cars."

"Thanks, but I'm sure I won't be looking at new ones."

"Doesn't matter. It'll still be fun. I'm just glad you're OK."

"Thanks."

Vega sat at her desk, and Astrid took one of the guest chairs.

"How's the program going? Since you were out Friday, I didn't get to check in."

"I'm finished," Vega said, deciding she might as well get it over with.

Astrid jerked her head back. "You are? Why didn't you tell me?"

"I was kind of busy this weekend."

"Right, of course. This is fantastic, Vega! I can't wait to tell Ms. Neilmann! We need to have a demo. Wait a minute. Who did you test it on?"

"Me."

Astrid laughed. "You did? After everything you said about the headband causing psychosis?"

"I didn't feel comfortable testing it on anyone else."

"OK. Could you feel it? When you stimulated your brain?"

"No, actually. It was weird. I just got this overwhelming urge to press an icon on my phone. It was just a dummy icon I'd created to test the program, but still… It was very unnerving."

"We'll get a volunteer in to test it out so everyone can see it working. This is so exciting!"

"I guess."

Astrid slapped her on the leg. "Quit being so down on yourself. This is impressive work. Ms. Neilmann will be so happy to be able to release it in time for the holiday buying rush."

"I'm surprised it doesn't take at least a year or more between the time a program is finished to when they roll it out on the smart devices."

"The timelines are getting shorter and shorter. Especially when it's just software we're talking about. Hardware or firmware is a totally different story." She stood up. "I'm going to go tell Ms. Neilmann. This kind of news is better delivered in person. I want to see the look on her face. I'll call you later with a date for a demo."

Astrid left and Drexel came in right behind her.

He shook his head when he got a good look at her. "You look like an old boxer."

"Gee, thanks."

A large grin spread over his face. "Did you get my messages?"

"Oh, sorry. No. I'm behind on everything. I have to admit, I slept a lot this weekend. I was sore and tired. Almost took today off, but I have too much to do. I want to make sure everything is ready before the final demo. I just told Astrid I finished it."

Drexel was beaming. "I'm so proud of you!" He walked over, picked her up from her chair and hugged her. "You can delete all my messages. I was just groveling, making sure you were OK. I was worried about you."

"We talked on Friday night."

"I know. But then I didn't hear from you all weekend."

Vega drug him into the corner of her office, glancing outside to make sure no one was in the hallway, and kissed him. "I missed you."

He kissed her back and gave her butt a squeeze.

She squealed. "Drexel! Not here."

He kissed her again and whispered in her ear, "Later?"

She pushed him back with a grin and walked back behind her desk. "Get out of here, please. I have a lot of work to do. Astrid's going to set up another demo. She's getting a volunteer so I can show my brain control program in action."

He laughed. "You are such a drama queen!"

She said with a snicker, "Shut up! Go! I've got work to do!"

"All right, all right. I'm leaving." He walked out, then leaned his head back in. "But when you go car shopping, I expect you to call me. I'm sure Astrid will want to go with you, but I can confirm she knows nothing about cars."

"And you do?"

"No, but I'm more fun," he said, winking.

Vega smiled as she watched him leave. Maybe everything would be OK after all. She wasn't going to worry about the rest of the world. For once, she would think about herself.

* * *

Down in the lab, Vega ran through tests of her program's interface to various vendors' smart devices. She had to verify they all worked correctly before the rollout. Waiting for one of her runs to finish, she was reading an obit on her computer when she heard someone come in. She glanced over the top of her half-wall and saw Dr. Fedorov sit down at his desk, his back to her. She started to say something but heard him pick up his landline phone and decided to leave him alone while he made his call.

"Hey, it's me," said Ryker. … Yeah, I know. But it didn't work out exactly as I had planned. … Yeah, yeah. I'm sorry about that. I was expecting it to work."

She was trying not to listen, but couldn't help it. *Was he talking about one of his devices?*

"Yeah, well, I'm not giving up yet. I'll try something else. … I don't really want to take such drastic measures yet. … I know you're paying me. You don't have to remind me. … I'll take her out, don't worry. I'll get it right next time."

Holy shit! Was he talking about her? Is he the one who cut her brake lines? Is he going to try to take me out a different way?

Vega didn't know what to do. She sat there as quietly as possible to see if she could catch more of his conversation, but he was quiet for a long time. *Who is he talking to? Someone else at Neilmann?*

He started talking again. "Yeah, good idea. Maybe I'll give that a try next week. Hopefully, the outcome will be better. … Thanks for the idea, and sorry to disappoint you."

He hung up the phone, and she froze, not wanting him to know she had heard him. Dr. Fedorov was behind it all. She'd been right all along.

50

For once, Vega was the first person to arrive. She had only been there a few minutes when Astrid came in with a young woman.

"Hi, Vega, meet subject number 321. She's volunteered to help with the demo today."

"I'm Vega," she said, leaning forward and shaking her hand. "Nice to meet you. Thank you for helping us out."

Smiling, 321 said, "You're welcome. I've volunteered here before in one of the headband studies. I'm kind of excited about this, though. Dr. Montgomery told me you're going to read my brain waves without a headband or anything. How do you do that?"

"It's a little complicated, but hopefully, it won't feel any different than what you've done before. Did you ever have any problems during or after participating in a headband study?"

"No. No problems at all."

"Great. Just out of curiosity, can I ask if you were a part of the group trial or the individual one?"

"The group trial."

Vega nodded. *Maybe the problem with the headband only occurred in the individual trials?* She didn't know, but she breathed a sigh of relief anyway. She really hoped she wasn't about to ruin this woman's life.

"Good. You will do exactly what you did in the group trial—browse the internet just like you would if you weren't here. You'll just be doing it without the headband."

"Cool."

Vega handed the phone to 321 and helped her through the calibration and connection routines. Then she brought up a browser and told Astrid, "OK, she's all set."

"Thanks." Astrid motioned 321 to the door. "OK. Follow me."

Ryker, Drexel and Katya came into the room, and they exchanged greetings. Then Vega said, "Astrid is taking our volunteer to the CRT lab. I've already completed the calibration and connection routines. You wouldn't have noticed anything different, but just so you know, I added more areas of the brain to my data gathering. Because of the physical headband restrictions, Dr. Fedorov was mimicking the 10-20 system, but the MYND app is closer to the 10-5, or the five percent system, which picks up more signals from a larger area of the brain. There's really no reason I need to stick to a specific pattern at all since I'm not restricted by a physical apparatus. So if it's determined a slight adjustment would result in more detail, or a stronger signal pickup, I can easily change the program's points of focus."

"Ten twenty, five ten? I don't understand these numbers," said Ms. Neilmann.

Ryker explained, "The easiest way to think about it is that the numbers represent where the electrodes are placed on the subject's head. There's no need to delve into the details of the numbers right now."

Ms. Neilmann nodded, and Vega continued.

"Thank you, Dr. Fedorov. When the app goes public, these calibration and connection actions will be conducted automatically when a user gets a new phone or a software update that installs the MYND app. Of course, these demo phones don't have it installed at that basic level yet.

"I've already advised the marketing group, and they have everything set up for this test. All the brain wave, and other biometric data from subject 321, are sent automatically to the cloud where her response to the ads are analyzed and changes made accordingly in real-time so we'll get an accurate view today of how the entire process will work once it's released out to the real-world."

"Excellent," said Drexel.

"As you can see, I've already set the screen up to show what our test subject is doing on her phone."

The screen displayed the volunteer was already browsing. Astrid came in and joined the group. "She's ready when we are."

Vega turned back to everyone.

"I'll let this test run for about twenty minutes so there is enough time for various ad types to pop up in the volunteer's browser. Then we will send her to the break room while we analyze the data. If we feel we have everything we need, we'll let her go back to her life, and then we'll be one step closer to putting the program into production!"

Vega smiled. She couldn't help it. She was proud of herself.

"There won't be much for us to see on the screen," she continued. "We'll be able to tell when she clicks on an ad, but we won't know if she did it because the MYND program stimulated her nucleus accumbens or not until we look at the data. The application is running continuously in the background and will automatically execute a stimulation if it detects an ad has attracted her attention. After she's clicked on the ad, it will then stimulate her right inferior frontal gyrus, which is associated with decision confidence. In that way, the program reinforces her decision so she's not questioning her choice immediately afterwards."

"How does the app know when she's interested in an ad?" asked Ms. Neilmann.

"I used a lot of the smart device's biometric sensors to help gauge the user's interest level. I used the optical sensor and infrared functionality, in conjunction with the camera, to determine how often the user blinks. People generally blink three times less than normal when they're viewing a computer screen, phone or tablet, and that rate may be even lower if they find something on the screen that really interests them. Through the optical sensor and camera, I'm measuring pupil dilation. Larger than normal dilation, unless drug induced, usually means more interest in what someone is looking at. I'm also tracking the user's eye movement to determine where they're looking on the screen, for instance, are they looking at an ad and for how long. I'm also using the ultrasonic capabilities to aid in the reading of facial features and determine if the user is smiling or not."

"Good ideas," said Ryker. "Is that it?"

"No, I'm also using the CSR sensor, or conductance skin response, paired with the pressure sensors, to measure how much the user is sweating and the chemical makeup of that sweat. The largest number of eccrine glands is found in the palms and the soles of the feet. So the palms offer a lot of information. Also, as stress reduces, the amount produced and the protein and lipid levels in the sweat, often decreases."

"That's interesting," said Astrid. "Good thing there's not an antiperspirant for your hands," she snickered.

Vega smiled. "And, of course, I'm using the pressure sensors to measure the amplitude of the heart rate and collect blood pressure information, and the infrared sensor is furnishing an optical reading of the nail beds to determine oxygen saturation. All of these indicators provide details about the current excitement level of the user."

"Very impressive, Ms. Swift," said Katya.

"Thank you, but there's more. I also took advantage of the recent introduction of the CGM, or continuous glucose monitor sensor, and directed the program to measure the user's glucose levels. More glucose is released into the bloodstream by the liver when a person becomes excited."

Ryker was making notes as Vega talked. He looked up. "This is remarkable, Vega. A very broad spectrum. We should get some excellent results."

Stilly wary of him, Vega had a hard time looking him in the eye, but she replied, "Thank you."

"So every time they see a Neilmann customer ad, they'll click on it, or buy the product?" asked Drexel.

"No. Not every time. I hope that was not the goal because the user may go bankrupt or never put their phone down. But combining all this biometric data with the brain-wave analysis should give the MYND app an excellent indication of the user's state of mind at any moment. That will help ensure the stimulation occurs only when their interest is genuinely piqued. I toyed with the idea of stimulating the prefrontal cortex to try and mimic utilization behavior, but decided it was too intrusive."

"Utilization behavior?" asked Astrid.

"It's a disorder where a person, when they see an object, has an impulsive desire to use it, whatever it is. For example, if they saw a stapler, they would staple things until the stapler was taken away. And they would do that regardless of where they were or whether there was anything logical available to staple. My plan was to disrupt the prefrontal cortex when a Neilmann customer ad or product showed on the screen. But I was worried it might be difficult to turn that desire off once it was stimulated, and it would be hard to direct the behavior toward a single ad."

Ms. Neilmann nodded. "Vega, I'm very pleased with what you've put together here. This is a lot more data than I expected you to gather. Of course, the proof is in the pudding, as they say."

"Right. Nothing is one hundred percent accurate, but I believe this large combination of data should give the MYND app a good indication of when to send the stimulation and incite the user to select the ad or product."

"Has it been twenty minutes yet?" Astrid asked.

Vega checked the time. "Another five minutes. When the test is over, we can compare when the volunteer's measurements showed interest, if the program activated the stimulate command and if the stimulation caused her to click on the ad or product. And when we examine the brain wave information, we should easily be able to see where in the patterns the stimulation occurred."

"All of this is really interesting, Ms. Swift," said Ryker, "but what no one has asked you yet, and what I really want to know, is exactly how are you stimulating the nucleus accumbens? You can't be using electricity."

Vega had been wondering when someone was going to ask her that question. She wasn't surprised it had come from Ryker. She found despite her mistrust of him, she was excited to reveal her solution.

"I turned again to the OPM chip. The OPM is not just a reader. It can also *transmit* magnetic waves. I adjusted its parameters so it would perform like an rTMS system."

"RTMS?" Astrid asked.

"Yes, repetitive transcranial magnetic stimulation. One of my old college professors suggested it."

Ms. Neilmann's eyes widened. "You told him about the project?"

"No, of course not. I just gave him a theoretical problem to solve. Of course, the rTMS systems used in hospitals and doctors' offices are much larger machines, but for my use, a strong, repetitive signal for a long duration was not required. I just needed short bursts for tiny units of time. It's how I'm stimulating the nucleus accumbens without electricity. I directed the MYND program to command the OPM to send hundreds of low-intensity magnetic pulses immediately to the nucleus accumbens when a stimulation is deemed appropriate. It's harmless, and the user will not feel a thing. And I can vouch for that because I tested the program on myself."

Everyone looked at her like she was speaking Greek, except for Ryker, whose mouth was hanging open.

51

It had almost been a week since Vega's car adventure, and her bruises were pretty much healed. But she was still in a rental. She hadn't taken the time to go car shopping yet, but she needed to hurry. The insurance company wouldn't pay for a rental car forever.

Her presentation had gone even better than she'd expected, and now she was working with Drexel to test her program on more volunteers before it went into production. So far, everything had gone smoothly, and there were no adverse reactions. She knew because she had insisted on conducting the follow-ups herself. Her program would be installed in smart devices in time for the holiday-buying rush, and Ms. Neilmann was ecstatic. Vega still didn't understand why, so far at least, her program didn't have the same issues as the headband. She was really hoping it wasn't some kind of delayed reaction. As proud as she was of her work, it also kind of scared the hell out of her.

Maybe she'd been wrong all along, and there was never any connection between the headband and the recent psychosis increase?

Either way, she'd decided last night that she was going to confront Ryker and see how he reacted. Holding her breath as she walked into the lab, she rounded the corner and saw him, oblivious to her, engrossed in something on his computer. Vega cleared her throat, and he spun around. "Oh, hi Vega."

"Hi. Am I interrupting you?"

"No, it's fine. Just proof-reading the specifications for my next project."

"Oh, yeah? Can I ask what it is?"

"I'm working on changing the firmware in electronic shelf labels so they can interface with the MYND app."

"You mean like the ones at the grocery stores?"

"They're not just at the grocery stores. They're everywhere."

"Are they all electronic now? I really don't pay any attention."

"No. Not all of them. But they're getting there. I'm starting with the U.S. version first. Not all countries use the same type of labeling, of course. That would be too easy."

"The shelf labels are going to talk to the MYND app?"

"Exactly. That way, when someone is physically shopping in a store, we can gather their EEG and other biometric information and measure their proclivity to buy. It's basically another interface for your program, but instead of online ads that are read on a user's smart device, it will be the shelf tags. Same procedure, different interface, assuming they have a smart phone with them. That allows Neilmann to hit both marketplaces. Online and brick and mortar."

"Another input to the MYND program."

"Exactly. Could be your next project. My job is just to put the interface firmware in the labels."

"Even more customers to persuade."

He gave a weak smile. "That's what we're all about, isn't it? I'm also working on a design for integrating an EEG interface into heads-up displays."

Vega was shocked. Ryker had smiled at her. *How could he act like nothing had happened? Like he hadn't tried to kill her?* She was starting to question everything. She put her attention back in the conversation.

"For gamers?"

"No. The gaming industry is already working on something similar. This is for the military. It needs to be extremely robust. The first target market is the Air Force. I want to measure their stress levels while they're conducting missions—give the pilot a warning if they're about to lose consciousness or their anxiety levels accelerate to a point where they may compromise the mission. For starters. Who knows? Maybe I'll incorporate your monochord trick so we can bring up their alpha waves before their stress reaches dangerous levels."

"I didn't know we had military contracts."

"We don't. Yet. Ms. Neilmann wants to expand. She doesn't want to keep all her eggs in the consumer basket."

"Huh. I'm not sure I like the idea of us being involved with the military, but I can understand why she wants to expand our customer base."

"Why not?"

"It's just…anything war-related. I just, I don't like war."

"No one likes war."

Vega wasn't sure that was true. She kept her mouth shut, but in her head, she was scared shitless. *What if they used her MYND app on soldiers? Or used it against our enemies somehow?*

Ryker continued. "That's why we have weapons. The way I look at the world is if we show our might, no one will want to fight."

"Hey, you made a rhyme," she said, unable to stop herself.

"I wasn't trying to be funny," Ryker said with a straight face.

"Oh, sorry. It's just—"

"What did you need?"

Their conversation had started out so well. Obviously, Ryker was not one for jokes, and so far, she hadn't perceived a whiff of guilt from him. Maybe her next topic would reveal the truth.

"Right. I'm sorry I interrupted your work, but I wanted to talk to you about something I discovered. I know the MYND headband is your baby, but, uh—"

"Just spit it out."

"OK. I think the MYND headband is hurting people."

"What? How?"

"Look," she pulled a chair up, took her phone out and showed Dr. Fedorov the news article about Ben. Then she swiped to Dave's obit and told him what she'd found on the online genealogy site about his suicide. Finally, she told him what she had learned at Jenny's viewing. "I know at least two of these people were in the tests. Oh, and there's Marie," she continued, showing him the article about Marie's accident. "I can't prove she was in one of the tests, but I could if I could see the customer key file. You know, so I can match up the subject numbers to their real names. If I could —"

"Hang on. You're saying you think the MYND headband is causing these people to have psychotic episodes?"

Vega looked him in the eyes. She really wanted to see if he looked guilty when she answered. "Yes. I do."

To her surprise, Ryker didn't immediately blow her off like everyone else had, and he didn't look guilty either.

"And what leads you to this conclusion? Other than a couple of coincidences. Do you have a theory about why this might be happening?"

Was he fishing to see how much she knew?

"No, not yet. But there's a connection. I'm sure of it."

"Have you researched how many people have psychotic episodes yearly in the area? Where else these people have been before they had the event? What else is going on in their lives that may impact their mental health? Have they had mental health issues in the past? How much research have you done, Ms. Swift?"

"No. I didn't think about all that. I've been looking for the key file so I could see if they were all—"

"That file is only available to personnel on a need-to-know basis. And you are not on the list."

"But you have access."

"Of course."

"Will you show me?"

Ryker ignored her question. "I can't imagine there is any evidence these psychotic events are linked to the MYND device. Drexel and Daphne do follow-ups after every test. I'm sure they would have notified me of any anomalies. Did you ask Drexel?"

"Yes, I did. He said exactly what you did. That everyone was fine, and he couldn't share their information with me."

"Good. He's right, of course."

"I thought I could convince him."

Ryker nodded and looked away. "I understand you two have gotten quite close since you've joined us."

"I guess we have. But this isn't about that. I have a legitimate concern. The file would help me prove my theory."

"Or not."

"Yes, or not."

"If you had any real proof, I'm sure Drexel would do another check on the participants. I usually pride myself on being fairly open-minded, but I see nothing but conjecture here."

Vega's shoulders slumped. She was getting nowhere, and Ryker had not revealed an ounce of guilt. *Or maybe she simply couldn't read people well?*

"Was there anything else?"

"No. Thank you. At least you listened to me. Everyone else thinks I'm crazy."

"I'm sure they don't think that. Your work alone proves you have a very logical mind."

"Thank you."

"Just perhaps, not in this instance."

"Just when I thought you were giving me a compliment."

Ryker swirled his chair back to his screen.

Was that a blush she just saw on his face? Surely not.

"I guess I'll let you get back to work. I've got to go to a meeting with the product rollout group."

"On your way then."

Vega was confused. She was sure he was behind it all, but he looked so innocent. *How did he do it? Was she the only one incapable of lying with a straight face?*

But she wasn't ready to let it go yet. Now she was more determined than ever to convince Drexel she needed access to those files.

52

Vega was doing her best to keep her mind on her work to get everything ready for the rollout. But as she left the hospital after visiting her mother, she was upset about how bad Miren looked. She was supposed to have gone home three days ago. The doctor had put the feeding tube directly into her stomach, but she had continued to try to pull it out, and an infection had sprung up at the insertion site. The antibiotics were making her nauseous, and the hunt was on for an effective one she could tolerate. More complications and more things to add to the already ridiculously high hospital bill.

But through all her mother's issues and Vega's car troubles, she couldn't quit thinking about how Jenny had died. It gave her the shivers, and since she still didn't know what was causing the psychotic side-effect, it scared her to think she might perpetuate it with her program even though there were no problems with it yet. She needed to find that damn customer key file so she could correlate the participants of the trials to their real names. Then she could confirm her suspicions and see if others were affected.

It was a typical autumn day in the PNW. A light drizzle was falling from the low gray clouds, so she pulled up her hoodie as she walked across the parking lot from the hospital. Once inside the car, she debated. *Home to a nice quiet day by herself or go to Neilmann and play detective?* She steered the wheel towards Seattle.

The lobby was quiet as Vega walked through it, and she took the elevator up to her office. She opened her computer and logged onto the Neilmann cloud. She didn't know where else to look, so she started back with the file directory for the MYND headband specification documents where she had already searched several times before.

But after hours probing around in every directory and file she could think of related to the MYND project, she still hadn't found any documents that looked like a customer key file.

She needed a break. She pulled out her phone and texted Trent.

```
You busy?
Yes. Final touches for gallery opening 2nite
```

"Shit!" Vega had been so caught up with everything she'd totally forgotten about Trent's gallery opening.

```
Right.
U forgot didn't u?
No.
Don't lie
Yes. But it's not because I don't love you!
Uh huh. R u at work?
```

```
Yes.
U r coming aren't u?
Of course! I wouldn't miss it!
U better leave soon then. It starts at 6
```

She looked at the time on her computer screen: 4:23. *Holy cow! Had she really been here for three hours?* She slammed down the lid of her laptop and replied.

```
I'll be there.
What did u need?
Nothing. It can wait. I'll see you tonight.
OK
Love you.
U 2. C U later
```

Vega felt like the most horrible friend ever. She would arrive on time, even if it meant running over every car on the road.

* * *

Steering her car out of the Neilmann parking garage, she was thankful that at least it was Saturday, and the traffic was fractionally less busy. Luckily, she already had on something decent, because she had no time to go home and change first.

She jumped into her car and headed toward Bothell. She was so excited for him. He had been trying to get a solo exhibit for years. Eventually, he wanted his works to be in a gallery in downtown Seattle, but the Tsuga Fine Art Gallery in Bothell was a great place for a first exposition. It featured only local artists of the Pacific Northwest area and drew in sizable crowds, especially on the weekends. The town was known for its thriving art community and well-attended art walks, which were held seven times a year.

She took 405 to 522 west and exited toward Bothell. Turning into the cute downtown, she parked in front of the Tsuga gallery on the corner of 101st and 1st Street and freshened up her lipstick. She checked her hair in the visor mirror, took a deep breath and told herself to relax and enjoy the evening. It was Trent's night.

Through the locked glass doors, she could see Trent inside talking to the gallery owner, Ken. Trent was pointing to a painting and articulating something with his hands. Her watch said five twenty-one. The show hadn't officially started yet. She knocked on the glass, and Trent glanced over. She waved at him, and he said a few more words to Ken and came to the door.

They gave each other a kiss on each cheek, and he said, "You made it! And with time to spare. I'm so glad!"

"Are you kidding? I wouldn't have missed this for the world. I'm so proud of you!"

"It's not Seattle."

Vega waved him off. "Seattle's overrated. I bet you'll get more people here. This is where all the local artists are."

"Thank you. I have to admit, I'm excited."

"You should be, Trent! And, wow!" she exclaimed, looking around. "Your work looks fantastic!"

"You've seen it before."

"I've seen some of it. But not *all* your work. And not all together like this. It's bold! It's imaginative! It's textural. It's everything! I bet you sell a lot of pieces tonight."

He was beaming. "Thank you. I hope so."

"Can I look around? Before the masses arrive?"

"Sure! Would you like some wine first?"

"Yes, please!"

Trent led her to a table covered in a white tablecloth with a selection of white and red wines. A man and woman dressed in black jackets and bow-ties were standing behind the table ready to serve.

"Take your pick. Ken and I have some last-minute things to do before the doors open. Feel free to look around."

"Thanks. And good luck," she said, squeezing his hand before he left.

Vega turned back to the table and chose a mild white wine. She sipped the buttery smooth beverage and walked around. The gallery wasn't huge, but every spare space was covered with Trent's boldly colored artwork. They even had bags, cards and prints created with images of his paintings on them. A piney sandalwood aroma filled the air, and minimalist music played softly in the background. It was a pleasant explosion to her senses.

On the floor were tall partitions she could walk around completely to see the artwork hanging on both sides. And everywhere she looked, it was all Trent's work. She didn't know how he did it. He once told her it was a lot like what she did—that they were both creators—creating something from nothing. She did it with code, and he did it with paint.

But Trent didn't just use paint. His pieces were called mixed-media, and he had let her watch his process many times. Sometimes he used fabrics like burlap or lace, other times, metal pieces from a hardware store or even found objects from a garage sale or thrift store. She had even seen him put jigsaw puzzle pieces in his paintings. He may have thought she was creative, but she would have never dreamed of using the things he did in a painting. And yet somehow, the end results always looked amazing. Trent loved color, and he played with it fearlessly in his works. She stood there, took it all in and was blown away. She was proud to have such a talented friend.

At six on-the-dot, the doors opened, and people started filing in. Vega took her time looking at each piece and reading the plaques next to them which described the materials used to create the painting and the story or inspiration behind them. A few of his pieces hung on her wall at home—those that Trent had been nice enough to give to her. She loved them. But she wished she could really support him and afford to actually buy one.

She rounded another corner and stared at a painting of a forest. It was three-dimensional, and it was huge—at least five feet tall and three feet wide. To take it all in, she had to stand back. It made her feel like she was there, walking on the forest trail. It was vibrant but somehow still dreamy, like a foggy but saturated fairytale forest. She couldn't quite describe it. Beside it, the plaque read *Hidden Message*. Under the title, was a description: *Mixed-Media: acrylic paint, magazine paper, natural bark, sand, pebbles, metal bolts.*

"Do you like it?"

Startled, Vega jumped and turned to see Trent behind her.

"I love it! But shouldn't you be mingling with other people? Don't you have potential investors to woo?"

"Aren't you a potential investor?"

"I can't afford any of your pieces. You know that."

Shaking his head, Trent said, "I don't want your money, silly! Just pick one you like, and it's yours."

"No. I wouldn't do that to you."

"You're not doing it to me! I want you to have one!"

"Nope. Not going to happen. You deserve to be paid for your work."

"I have already sold three pieces," he said, unable to wipe the huge grin off his face.

"Wow! You've only been open for what, about thirty minutes? That's fantastic!"

"Thank you. You like *Hidden Message*?"

"Yes! I feel like I'm there, in the woods on the trail. But better. It's like, I don't know—a dream forest. But why did you call it *Hidden Message*?"

"You need to get closer."

"But then I can't see it all."

"Yes, but you'll understand the title."

"OK."

Vega stepped right up to the painting and looked closely. Then she saw it. The big image was created from thousands of little images of torn out pieces from magazine pages. And right in the middle was a teeny tiny string of words, obviously cut out from sentences in magazine articles. It read, *What was once hidden will be revealed.*

"Trent! That is so clever!"

"Thank you, ma'am."

Then she had a spark. "Oh, my god! You're a genius!"

"I know that, but—"

"Just a second! I have to…" she pulled out her phone and typed a note to herself then gave him a big hug. "I just don't want to forget. Thank you!"

"I don't know what I just did, but, you're welcome?"

Vega took a deep breath and relaxed. "I'll tell you later. It's your night." She gently pushed him away and said, "Now, leave me alone, and go sell the rest of your paintings!"

Trent gave her a small wave as he went back to schmooze more buyers. Vega walked around the rest of the gallery trying to enjoy herself, but she had a hard time concentrating. She could hardly wait to get back to the office and try out her idea.

53

The next work day Vega was so busy with all the rollout preparations, she hadn't yet had a chance to search for the customer key files. Now it was almost time to go home, and she was eager to try again. Trent's *Hidden Message* painting had given her an idea of how to find them. She hadn't even thought to look for a hidden file. All computers had the capability of making files hidden so they wouldn't show up in a general search command. But unless they were also password protected or encrypted, all she had to do was enter a special parameter in her search to reveal them.

She opened her computer, navigated to the directory for the focus-group results' documents and then pressed the command, shift and period keys simultaneously, to expand the results and reveal all the hidden files and folders. Four layers deep inside, she found a directory named *Miscellaneous.* Opening it revealed several files labelled *focus group trials* followed by a date. She was about to click one open just as Drexel came to her door. She quickly shut the lid of her computer and turned to face him.

"Hey, you're still here," he said.

"Yeah, well, you know. Busy, busy."

"Making any headway?"

"Yeah. It's all about the rollout now."

"That's great. No more concerns?"

Vega hesitated.

"So, yes."

She shook her head. "No, I don't know. I think I'm over it." *Why didn't she want to tell him?*

"Glad to hear it. Want to have lunch tomorrow?"

"Sure. Sounds good."

Drexel checked the hallway and then gave Vega a peck on the cheek. "See you tomorrow."

Vega smiled and thought, *Maybe I should look at these at home?* She copied all the files to her phone. She was hopeful. Maybe now she could finally find the proof she needed.

* * *

After work, Vega found herself standing in front of Trent's door.

"Hey, you."

"Hey," she replied. "Yeah, sorry for the short notice. You're not too busy?"

"No. Now that the show's over, I can like relax for a while."

"How many pieces did you end up selling?"

A huge grin came over his face. "All of them."

"What? No way!" She squeezed him hard. "I'm so proud of you! That's awesome!"

In a strangled voice, Trent said, "OK, OK. Let me go. I can't breathe!"

She released her bear hug. "That is so good! And your first show! What's next?"

"I do it all over again. I have lots of pieces I didn't include in the show, and I'm working on new ones, of course."

"Can I see them?"

"Not yet. It's too soon. I'll let you know."

"OK."

"Oh, and the owner of Garner Art Gallery called me."

"Where are they?"

"Downtown Seattle," Trent said with a smile.

"You got another show already?"

"No. Not yet. But it's looking good."

"That's wonderful! You're going to be so famous."

"We'll see. Anyway, what's up?"

"I made a discovery today. Want to look at some files with me?"

"Did you go snooping again?"

"Yes. I finally found those customer key files I've been searching for. I thought you might want to look through them with me."

"What about your NDA?"

"It's not programming secrets. It's just a list of names."

"That you're not supposed to know, right?"

"Yeah, well…"

"I don't care if you don't. Beer?"

"Please."

Trent went into the kitchen while she settled back on his couch. She picked up the remote and turned on the TV, then started her screen-sharing app so her phone mirrored its image onto the large screen.

Sitting down beside her, Trent handed her a beer, and they watched the screen as she opened her file app. She navigated to the four files she'd copied labelled *Key-1, 2, 3* and *4.*

"These are the ones."

She opened the *Key-1* file. It was a multi-column spreadsheet of information containing exactly the data she'd been searching for.

"This is it! It's got everything—the subject's first name, their surname, address, contact numbers! It's all here! Oh my god! This is the proof I've been looking for!"

"Don't get too excited yet. Right now, this is just a list of names. You need to check them against the people who've gone psycho."

"You're right. I'm getting ahead of myself. Let's see if any of the names in all those news reports and obituaries are in here."

"Do you know what names you're looking for?"

"I've been keeping a list."

Vega opened a notes app on her phone and checked the names. "The first one is Ben Marshall."

They looked through the list.

"He's not here. Who else?"

"Dave Byrne."

"Nope."

"Marie Castle?"

"No."

"Damn it! OK, how about Jenny Black?"

"No, she's not here either."

Vega felt defeated.

"Maybe they didn't start doing whatever it is that's hurting people until later?" Trent offered. "Open the next one."

Vega opened the file labelled *Key-2* and started scanning through the names. "There! Ben Marshall!"

"Who's he? I don't remember you mentioning him before."

"He's the one I read about in a news article before I even started working at Neilmann. I didn't know if he was involved in a study or not, I just remembered the article because it was so sad. And it said something about him having a psychotic breakdown. So I saved it, just in case. I'll Google his name. You'll see."

She pulled up the article about Ben Marshall, and they read through the news report saying he had stabbed his son to death and then slit his own throat with the same knife.

"That is so sad," Trent said.

They went back to the customer key file.

"And there," said Vega. "There's David Byrne. I always wondered about him. It was such a long time from when I saw him to when I read his obit. Oh, but look! He's in here again. He came in for an individual test after being in a group one!"

"So?"

"He committed suicide, remember? I told you about him before. Shot himself in the head. I'm beginning to wonder if it only affects people who are in the individual trials. Wait, was Ben Marshall in an individual or group test?"

They searched back through the file.

"Group test," said Trent.

"Damn! Oh well, so much for that theory."

"But that's two of them anyway. Open the next file."

Vega clicked on the *Key-3* file, and both Marie Castle and Jenny Black were on the list.

"Holy shit!" exclaimed Trent. "Everyone on your list is in these files. But what about all the other people? I wonder what happened to the rest of them?"

"Maybe they're OK? Maybe they fixed it? Or maybe it only affects certain people? Drexel did tell me not everyone responds the same way."

He looked at her with raised eyebrows, "And maybe they just haven't made the news."

"We should do a search on some of them. See if we can find anything."

After searching for news on several of the other names, they could only find information on two of them, and only one of them was dead. But they didn't know why because the obituary didn't list a cause of death, and Vega couldn't find their name anywhere else, not even on the genealogy website.

"I think I've proven my theory," she said. "What am I going to do now?"

"Go to the police! Duh!"

"I don't know. Maybe they don't even realize what's going on?"

"Who's they?"

"Drexel? Ryker? Astrid? I don't know. Ms. Neilmann?"

"Vega! You've got to be kidding. Doesn't anyone follow-up on these people? Someone must know."

"Drexel does the follow-ups."

"Then shouldn't he know?"

"I guess."

"You guess? No, the answer is *yes*."

"But he said he checked on them. Maybe it happened after?"

Trent shrugged. "Yeah, OK. That could be an explanation. You trust him?"

"Yes, I do."

"But maybe, just in case, you should go to the police?"

"No. They wouldn't understand the data."

"Vega."

"Trent. I'm just thinking about all the people who work there. Will they shut the whole company down, or will they just concentrate on the people responsible for the MYND project? I hate the thought of putting anyone out of a job. Not to mention, me."

"I think you've got your priorities wrong. You're talking about the difference between people's jobs and people's lives."

"I know. But, not to sound heartless or anything, but the people who participated in the tests, it's too late for them. But we can stop using the headband. And we can stop the rollout of my program. If it's not released, the public will never use it. They'll be OK."

"Why not call Drexel? You just said you trust him."

Vega thought about it. "I guess."

"Why are you hesitating? Hasn't he been there for you every time you've asked for his help?"

"Except for this."

"Yeah, but like you said, now you have proof."

"True."

"He picked you up after your accident, and he was your first lay in a long time. And he must be good because you keep going back for more."

"Trent!"

"It's true, isn't it?"

Vega rolled her eyes. "Yes. You're right. I'll try him again. I'll give him another chance to do the right thing."

54

Vega stopped the screen sharing app and called Drexel.

"Hi."

"Hi, Vega? This is a happy surprise. Do you know what time it is? You're not drunk, are you? Please tell me this is a booty call," Drexel said.

She had been so absorbed in everything she hadn't even noticed it was already close to midnight.

"God, I'm sorry. I didn't realize it was so late. Did I wake you?"

"No, it's fine. I was watching a movie. Trying to wind down. What's up?"

"I'll get right to the point. I found the key files."

"Key files?"

"The ones that match the trial participants' real names to the numbers given to them during the testing."

"What do you mean, you found them? I told you, you don't have the authority to look at those files."

"Is that why you had them hidden?"

"Yes. I guess I should have put a password protection on them as well."

"I'm sorry I looked at them, but it was worth it. I was right. Now I have proof that at least some people are messed up after they take part in the studies. And I bet it's from the stimulation."

"Please don't tell me you're back on this conspiracy thing again?"

"I know you don't believe me, but people are dying, Drexel! It's not just a theory anymore. I have proof now!"

"I don't know what you think you found, but Ryker checked on all the participants afterwards. He assured me there was nothing to worry about."

"I thought you said you did the follow-ups."

"Oh, right. I did say that. But I lied. I was supposed to do them, but Dr. Fedorov practically demanded that he do them. He said the MYND headband was his creation, and he wanted to be the one to make sure there were no unpleasant side effects. I didn't want to cause a big fuss about whose job it really was, so I let him do it, but I told everyone I did. The only thing that matters is they were done. And he didn't find anything."

"But then he should have uncovered what I did. These reactions were a little more than unpleasant."

"But why would he lie?"

"I don't know. Maybe he's trying to sell the technology to Seichō?"

"Why would he do that?"

"Didn't you know he's from Japan?"

"Yes, I knew. You think because he's half Japanese, he's a traitor?"

"I know it sounds horrible, and I don't have any proof he's behind it, but I think he's the one who tampered with my brakes. I overheard him on the phone the other day. It sounded like he was going to try something again since I lived through the first attempt."

"Vega! Why didn't you tell me?"

"OK, he never actually said my name, but I'm almost positive he was talking about me."

"Oh."

"Anyway, it doesn't even matter who's behind what right now. All that matters is finding out what's happening to these people and making sure we stop it."

"If you have their names, you can follow up with them. I'm sure they're fine."

"I did, Drexel! That's what I'm telling you. And several of them are dead! And some of them killed other people! I don't think their brains are normalizing after the trials."

"You keep saying."

"Why aren't you more concerned about this? I'm telling you there's a direct correlation!"

Drexel was quiet for a moment and then asked, "And you think Ryker is behind it all? Surely, he would have said something."

"I don't know. I could be wrong. Maybe he doesn't know? Maybe the side-effect takes longer to develop into full psychosis? Let me show you what I've found. I guess that's the only way I'm going to convince you. If we don't do something soon, Ms. Neilmann is going to roll my program out to the masses, and I know it hasn't had any problems yet, but I'm not positive it won't. And for all I know, she's in on it! She's so obsessed about being number one again, who knows what she'd be willing to do? You have to help me stop it! I think we should destroy everything—program files, headbands. All of it!"

"I'm starting to really worry about you."

"Then let me show you."

Drexel sighed, "You know I care about you, right? And because of that, I'm willing to see what you've got. I suppose you want to do this right now?"

"Yes, please. The sooner the better."

"OK. Once we're through looking over your data, and I've convinced you everything is OK, maybe we can do something a little more fun?"

"Drexel, this is serious!"

"I know you think that. All right. I'm sorry."

"I'll meet you at your place."

"No, not my place. Let's do it at Neilmann. I'll meet you in the basement."

"Why go to Neilmann? I can come over to your place and show you what I have. I would send it to you in an email, but I don't feel comfortable sending it over an unsecured network."

"I'm going to give you the benefit of the doubt, for now. If things are as bad as you say they are, there are some things we'll need to do to stop the focus group trials tomorrow."

"And stop the project."

"Yes, and stop the project. Might as well already be at Neilmann, just in case."

"Yes! Good idea. Thank you!"

"Not that I think we'll be doing that, but… And once we look at whatever it is you think you've found, if I can convince you it's nothing, you have to promise me you will drop all of this."

Vega hesitated.

"Vega?"

"OK. But I have to warn you, it's going to take a hell of a lot of convincing."

55

The night was cold and damp, and nebulous halos glowed around the streetlights as Vega steered her car off 520 and headed south toward downtown Seattle. She couldn't believe it had taken so much persuasion to get Drexel to look at what she'd found. She felt like she was living in another universe where no one cared about the plight of innocent people. But she knew he would understand once he saw the files. Then they would either destroy the headbands and the application together or come up with another plan to halt the project.

She pulled into the dark parking garage and made her way through the lobby and down to the basement level. When the elevator doors parted, Drexel was already waiting for her in the hallway.

"Hi."

"Hi." He took her into a hug. "I still think you're wrong, but let's see what you have."

"I'm right. I promise."

Vega followed Drexel into one of the conference rooms, and they sat down. She pulled out her phone, navigated to the documents and passed the phone over to him, pointing out the correlation she'd found between the participants and the events in the news. Then she told him about what had happened at Jenny's viewing.

She looked at Drexel. "Do you believe me now?"

Drexel read through the files, flipping back and forth between the key files, obits and news stories. He took a deep breath and looked over at Vega. "Did you fabricate these customer key files?"

Jerking her head back, she stared at him with a shocked face, not quite believing what he had just said. "What? Of course not! I took these off the Neilmann cloud. Don't you recognize any of the names? Why would I make this up?"

"Hell, if I know. Maybe you're hoping to sue Neilmann? Get a bunch of money to help you take care of your mom."

"Drexel! I thought you knew me better! I would never do something like that."

He just shrugged. "Where did you say you found them?"

"They were in the MYND project directory under a folder labelled miscellaneous. The folder was hidden, like I said. I don't understand. Didn't you create it?"

He looked away and shook his head. "I was really hoping it wouldn't come to this, but I can see you are never going to let it go."

"Come to what?"

He set the phone down and pushed his chair away from the table. Pacing behind her, she turned her chair around to face him.

"It was all going so smoothly," he said.

"What was?"

"After Ryker changed the headband to stimulate the nucleus accumbens, I noticed an anomaly in my follow-ups."

"Wait? You *did* do them?"

He simply smirked at her. "Of course I did them."

"But you said Ryker—"

"Yeah, well," he smiled. "I lied. Again. I noticed a lot of the subjects were complaining of headaches and flashes of light in their vision, but most people were fine. I thought about telling him right away, but I wanted to see how they fared after more time had passed."

"And?" Vega asked.

He gestured to her phone. "I think you already know the answer to that question."

Vega gasped. "You knew this was happening? All this time? You knew? You knew, and you let it go on?"

He ignored her accusation. "I have no idea why the headband is messing some people up. I'm sure you or Ryker could figure it out. Doesn't matter anyway. It serves my purpose, regardless."

"Drexel! We have to do something!"

"Oh, don't worry. It doesn't seem to affect everyone to the same degree. Otherwise, the whole thing would be useless to me. The correlation would be too obvious. But it screws up enough people that it's going to make an impact, that's for sure."

"You want people to die?"

"None of this was something I planned. I was given a gift, Vega. It fell in my lap like mana from heaven. And like I said, I certainly don't want *everyone* to die. That would defeat the purpose. But I am looking forward to a few fallouts."

"Fallouts! You're talking about killing innocent people!"

Drexel shook his head as he looked at her. "Why couldn't you have just kept your nose out of it?" He lifted his hand and stroked her hair. "I tried so hard to distract you, to win you over. It would have made everything so much easier."

She brushed his hand away. "I think it's time for me to go now," she said as she tried to scoot her chair back and stand up.

But his firm grip held her down.

"Let me up."

"I don't think so."

"Get away from me!" Vega pushed hard out of her chair and sprang up, accidentally cracking Drexel's chin with the top of her head. She turned to face him and saw blood dripping out of his mouth. He had bitten his tongue.

"Oh god, I'm so sorry. I—"

His face twisted into an ugly snarl, and he backhanded her. Vega's head whipped left at the impact, and she put her hand up to her cheek as she stumbled back down into the chair.

"I'm sick of listening to you! Why can't you just shut the fuck up?"

She looked up at him, shocked. It was like watching a Dr. Jekyll and Mr. Hyde movie. Realization hit her, and she gasped. "It was you! You cut my brake lines, didn't you?"

His face showed a hint of satisfaction before he revealed the truth. "Oh, please. I wouldn't crawl under your filthy car," he snorted. "I paid some kid to do it."

"What's wrong with you? I don't even know who you are anymore!"

"You never knew who I was."

"Then tell me. Tell me who you are," she said, trying to divert his attention away from her.

Drexel laughed and rolled his eyes, and Vega took her chance. She jumped out of the chair and ran for the door. But he grabbed her by the arm and yanked her back. He held her tight and wrenched her other arm down when she tried to pull away.

He looked straight at her, his eyes wide. "Think about it. Getting people to buy what you want them to is low fruit on the tree. Can you imagine what I could do with this technology? Who cares about a few deaths along the way? I can bury those." He laughed as he realized the double entendre. "And now that these stimulations can be done wirelessly, thanks to you, it can be everywhere! We can make them all respond the way we want!"

With Vega still in a vice grip, he barely looked at her as he chuckled to himself. "Of course, we'll tout it as a marketing tool, but just imagine. We could change the way people vote! And can you even fathom how much the military would pay for a product like this?"

She tried to remove herself from his grasp, but he wouldn't let go. "You've lost your mind, Drexel! Let me go!" she screamed as she struggled against him.

He titled his chin back and let out a snort. "I guess this means you're not interested in joining me?" he asked, as he pulled a needle out of his pocket. "Too bad. Might have been interesting having a partner-in-crime. Not to mention the sex benefits."

Vega's eyes widened when she saw the syringe. "No. Drexel, don't. Please!"

He plunged it into her arm.

"Time for a little nap."

"No!" Vega screamed as she watched the syringe empty its contents into her. She pulled her other arm loose and reached for his face. The last thing she saw before she lost consciousness was the trail of blood on his cheek left behind from her fingernails.

56

Her eyes were heavy, but she forced them open and slowly lifted her head. She felt weak and groggy and tasted some kind of metal in her mouth before she realized it was her own blood. She had bitten her tongue. *Now we have matching tongues,* she thought vaguely, trying to come up from her fog. She tried to stand up, but her legs wouldn't support her, and she fell back on the floor and leaned against the wall. Her head was pounding. Looking around, she realized she was in one of the testing labs, alone. *I have to get out of here!* Just as she tried to stand again, Drexel came through the door holding a MYND headband.

"Ah, you're awake. I was worried I'd misjudged the dosage."

Vega's vision was blurry, but she could still make out the scratches she had left on his face. She smiled.

"What are you smiling at?" he sneered.

"I was jus' enjoyn' my handiwork," she slurred.

Drexel laughed. "Oh, that little scratch? You are one feisty little bitch."

"Whuz wrong wi you?"

"There's nothing wrong with me. But there will be something wrong with you in a few minutes."

"You're 'n asshole!" She screamed, trying to stand up again and step towards him. "I'm goin' to—"

Drexel easily pushed her backwards, and Vega's world spun. Trying not to throw up, she almost hit her head on the floor, but Drexel caught her and guided her roughly into a chair.

"Woah! Don't want to mess up your pretty little head." He smiled. "Not yet, anyway. You just sit down here for a second. I'm going to make a slight adjustment to your attitude. Then, perhaps I'll let you go."

"I don' get it," she said, squeezing her eyes and concentrating on making her words clear. "What happen' to you? I cared 'bout you! Why are you doin' this?"

He gave her a big grin. "Just securing my place in the upper echelon of the world. And as a happy side benefit, I'm teaching someone a lesson."

Vega took some slow deep breaths and tried to clear the drug from her system. "Is it bcuz of your dad?"

Drexel laughed. "My dad? The only reason John cares about me at all is to keep the Hicks' legacy alive at OneVision. He blames me for Sarah, my dear, lovely adoptive bitch-mother, leaving him. Says I was a mean kid, and reminded me of that every time he swung his belt. She left us and never looked back, and John will never let me forget it. Screw him! I don't give a fuck what he thinks. This is for me!"

"Both of your mothers abandoned you," Vega whispered.

"Fuck 'em! I never needed them anyway."

"Drexel, people are dyin'! What's the point?"

"Besides becoming the hero of this shit show? I'm bringing the bitch who is my real mother, down. At least I get to fuck up one of them."

Vega turned her head to check her equilibrium, but the room did a somersault. Drexel grabbed her before she fell off the chair.

"Careful there," he said.

"She doesn't even know who you are!"

"She will before I'm done with her. It's a two-for-one deal. Money and revenge. You'd think I planned it all."

"But why? I thought you were waitin' for the right time to tell her? What's she done to make you hate her so much?"

"Did you forget already? She abandoned me. Gave me away the second she squeezed me out of her crack. She's just one part of my ultimate goal. I have bigger plans now. But I'll certainly be happy to see her crash and burn on my way up."

Vega found if she didn't move her head, she was pretty much OK. So she kept as still as possible and tried to focus. "How do you know she did it voluntarily? Maybe her parents forced her to give you up?"

"Are you kidding? It's obvious she doesn't have a maternal bone in her body. I bet she never thought about me again."

"That's not what Astrid told me. She said Katya was devastated. She told me she's been looking for you."

For a second, Drexel's face looked shocked, but then he recovered and shook his head. "How would Astrid know? That bitch would never tell Astrid she'd given up a kid. It's not like they're buddies or something. And I was able to find her, so why hasn't she found me? Whatever she told you, she's lying. Doesn't matter anyway. It used to be my main motivation. But now it's just a little cherry on the top."

Vega didn't believe him. Astrid wouldn't have lied about something like that. "Isn't this a bit overkill? Why hurt so many people? This isn't you! I know it isn't!"

He ignored her and put the MYND device on her head.

"I may not know why this thing isn't causing everyone who wears it to lose their minds, but I bet if I amp up the voltage a little, I can make sure it works on you."

Vega gasped. *Shit! He was probably right.* She reached up, pulled the headband off and threw it across the room.

Drexel picked it up and gently placed it back on her head. He stood in front of her and pulled his hand back, ready to hit her. "Don't," he growled. "Don't make me hit you again. I don't want to have to explain my bloody knuckles," he snickered.

She gave in and left the headband on. *She had to distract him. There must be something she could do to get out of this mess.* She tried to keep him talking—give herself more time to recover from the drug and figure something out.

"So, what's your big plan?"

"Not that it's any of your business, but what the hell, you won't be around much longer. I expect you'll be visiting a mental facility soon," he smirked. "Once your program rolls out to the masses, and the psychotic episodes become a little more obvious, I'll show everyone the evidence I *just* discovered. I'm expecting a big promotion."

"That's it? All you want is a promotion?"

"That's just the beginning. I'll put all the blame on my bitch of a mother—of knowing everything and not caring, just so her precious company can be number one again. It should be easy then for Seichō to take us over."

"But doesn't that put your planned promotion in danger?"

His face sneered. "Who do you think promised me the promotion? Along with a very large jump in salary, I might add."

"Oh." *So he's the one who was selling us out all this time, not Ryker!*

"Once we roll out your app, I'll present the idea of putting the technology everywhere—stores, schools, businesses, the military."

"But what if Seichō can't fix the problem? What if people keep having breakdowns?"

"Pffft," he flicked his hand at her. "I'm sure someone will figure it out. How hard could it be? I'll be rolling in dough, and Katya and her empire will be gobbled up."

"You're crazy!"

Drexel walked up to Vega and almost slapped her again, but his hand stopped in mid-air. She jumped back in the chair at his outburst, preparing herself for another blow.

"Shut the fuck up! I am not crazy! I'm a fucking genius!" he screamed, spit flying from his mouth.

What had happened to him?

"I'm sorry! I didn't mean crazy. Of course you're not crazy. You're just…just upset and sad. And why wouldn't you be? She abandoned you."

Drexel backed away and paced around her chair.

"That's right. She did! Now she's getting hers, and I'm getting mine."

"I… I could help you, Drexel. Let me help you."

Drexel laughed. "Yeah? And what are you going to do for me?"

"I'll help you find another way. A way to get back at her that won't hurt people."

He smiled as he understood. "Oh, of course. You think I care about those people, don't you? I don't. And I hate to burst your bubble, but I never cared about you either. Although I must admit, you were pretty good in bed. If you'd just stayed in your lane like a good little girl, things wouldn't have gotten so messy. But here we are."

He's a sociopath, Vega thought. *He must be. How can he not care that he's killing innocent people? And just to get back at his mom for giving him up for adoption? Just for more money? Does he really think he'll get away with this?*

"Enough talking. Time to get this party started."

All she could do was watch as he took his phone from his pocket and pressed the *Power* icon. The green light on the back of the headband flickered on and Vega's breath caught in her throat. Her heart started to race.

"Drexel, please! Don't do this!"

"There's no need to worry. You know this is a painless procedure. Of course," he said, his face brightening, "I'll be turning your signal up a bit more than usual. So…no guarantees."

Vega jumped up from the chair and ran at Drexel, grabbing for the phone. But she was still a little dizzy, and she missed. He slapped her backhanded, and she stumbled over the chair, her shoulder smacking on the floor as she fell. She pulled herself up and leaned against one of the chair legs, grabbing her painful shoulder.

"I tried to be nice," he said as he hit the *Stimulate* icon. "I wouldn't try that again if I were you," he said calmly. "We'll start with just a normal signal and work our way up from there. I really don't want to kill you right now. Everything would go much smoother if you just had a little breakdown later."

"Drexel," Vega moaned. "Please!"

His face showed no concern as he leaned down and wiped a tear from her cheek. "Why don't you quit fighting it?"

She reached up to take off the headband, and he pulled his hand back. She dropped her hand down to her lap.

"Don't touch the fucking headband again," he said. "Give it up. There's nothing you can do now."

She screamed, "Help me!"

"No one is here, Vega. It's one o'clock in the morning. There's no one down here but us."

She quit struggling. She was so tired. And he was right. They were probably all alone. Why would anyone else be here at this time of night?

Her head and shoulder hurt, and even though the drugs had almost worn off, she knew she couldn't fight him. He was too strong. And she was all out of ideas.

"Let's go a little higher, shall we?" He moved his finger along the level indicator of the stimulation signal.

Vega started to feel better. In fact, she realized, she almost felt happy. She smiled.

"That's more like it."

Then she remembered what was happening and forced herself to frown. She'd read about this in the reports—the temporary euphoria. The other side effect was damaging the nucleus accumbens area which could cause temporary or even permanent psychosis.

She screamed again, not caring if anyone heard her or not. She had to try. And if nothing else, she wanted to annoy the hell out of Drexel.

"Help! Help me!"

"Jesus, Vega! Shut the fuck up!"

Drexel walked over and slapped her again, slamming her head against the leg of the chair. Her teeth sliced against her cheek, and she tasted more blood in her mouth. She sucked in her breath and stopped screaming. She was shocked. *How could she have been so wrong about him?*

"Time to hit the high notes," he said as he adjusted the headband's signal and set his phone down on the table. "We'll just let that run for a while, shall we? I think another dose of sedative might be in order," he snickered. "My slapping hand is getting tired." He took a syringe and vial out of a drawer and pulled the drug into the barrel.

Vega started to laugh, then cry. She was happy. She was furious. She saw her mother standing in the corner of the room, smiling at her. That shocked her back to reality, because she knew it couldn't be real. She forced herself to concentrate on staying sane, staying in the real world. And then she remembered.

The headband had a kill switch.

She reached toward the back of the headband and long-held the power button three times in succession. The headband powered off.

Checking the dosage in the syringe, Drexel hadn't noticed. Yet. And she needed to keep it that way. She had to keep him talking—keep him focused on her.

Vega pretended to still be in pain. She screamed at him, "Drexel! Please look at me! Help me!"

"I'll look at you," he said, smiling. "If just to watch you lose your mind."

He walked over and looked into her eyes, his face filled with curiosity.

And Vega went for it. She jumped up and head-butted him right on the bridge of his nose. The loud crack as it broke made her flinch. Drexel stumbled back, grabbing his nose as the blood spewed out and trickled down his chin. She kneed him in the groin as hard as she could.

He screamed, doubled-over and dropped to his knees, the blood from his nose flinging red streaks across the floor. The syringe fell from his hand, and Vega scrambled on her hands and knees to grab it. She spun around, stabbed it into his leg and pushed the plunger all the way down.

Still crouched over in pain, he screamed again. Vega climbed on his back and pushed his face onto the floor with all her strength.

He tried to buck her off. "Get off me! I'll kill you, you bitch!"

Grabbing his hair, she yanked his head back, ready to slam his face into the floor if she had to. She held onto his hair and pushed all her body weight into his low back and yelled, shocking herself with her ferocity. "Stop it! I'll bash your head in! I swear I will!"

Drexel tried to grab her from behind and pull her off, but the drug was kicking in fast.

"I'm goin' to kill you!" His promise turned into a mumble as the tranquilizer overtook him. He tried to fight it, but his head dropped to the floor, and finally, his body relaxed.

She was breathing hard. Her shoulder was killing her, but she pushed him down, staying on top of him, ready to react, just in case he was bluffing.

And then the door opened, and Ryker walked in.

"What the–? What's going on here?" asked Ryker as he took in the scene. "Vega! What are you doing? Get off him!"

Vega stood up and stepped away from Drexel's limp body.

"Drexel and I had a little disagreement," she said, wiping her hand, dripping with his blood on her jeans.

"What?" Ryker ran over to Drexel and tried to shake him awake. "What did you do to him?"

Vega laughed.

"He's out cold." Ryker stood back up and finally took a long look at her. "What happened to your face?"

"It's a long story. And I'll tell you in a minute, but right now I need to find my phone."

"But what about Drexel?"

She nudged him with her foot. "I think he's going to be out for a while." She looked around the room. "Where is it?"

"Why?"

Ignoring him, she leaned down, dug through Drexel's pockets and found her phone in the back pocket of his pants.

"Here it is!"

"We can't just leave him here like this!" he said, kneeling down beside her to check on Drexel.

"He'll be fine." She stood up, wavering a little, and pulled him with her. "Now, come on. I've got to get my brain back together. I need some coffee!"

* * *

Bouncing off the walls, Vega lurched toward the break room, pulling Ryker behind her.

"Vega, are you OK?"

"Yeah. I'm fine. I thought the drug had worn off, but I guess not."

"What drug?"

She ignored him and bee-lined for the break room. She leaned against the counter, popped a pod into the coffee machine and flipped it on. As she turned to look at Ryker, the world tilted for a second, and when her eyes refocused, Ryker was staring at her.

"Are you sure you're OK?"

Vega shook her head. "I don't know. I think so. But here," she said, handing him her phone. "Just in case, maybe you better hold on to this."

"Are you going to tell me what happened here?"

She took in a deep breath and let it out slowly. "Remember when I told you I thought the headband was making people have psychotic breaks?"

"Yeah."

"I have proof now. It's all right there in my—" The room spun, and she grabbed onto the edge of the counter.

Ryker rushed over and caught hold of her arm to hold her up. "I don't think you're as OK as you think you are. Why don't you sit down?"

Vega shook her head. "No, it's just temporary. Drexel used the headband on me and—"

"Used the headband on you? What do you mean? That shouldn't make you dizzy."

She laughed. "Oh, it does a lot more than make you dizzy. Check the customer key files. They're on my phone. All the proof is in there. Drexel amped up the signal on me, so I don't know—" The floor flipped up, and the walls twirled sideways. And this time, Vega's knees buckled, and her world went black.

57

Low rumblings. Voices. But she couldn't tell whose. Rubbing alcohol and some kind of cleanser wafted up her nose. *Ammonia?* Her head and shoulder ached, and her throat was so dry and scratchy she felt like she'd swallowed a cactus. Her eyelids were heavy, but she forced them open slowly and tried to get her bearings. The bright light was harsh, and it took Vega a moment to adjust.

She was in a hospital bed. She looked over and saw Ryker in a chair on her left, eyes closed. Trent was next to him, looking at his phone. Glancing down at herself, she saw a thin intravenous tube snaking out of her left arm. Her other arm was in a sling. Slowly, she sat up and reached for the pitcher of water sitting on a rolling tray beside her bed, trying not to pull out her IV. But she missed and knocked over the already full paper cup. Water flowed across the tray and dribbled onto the floor.

Trent jerked his head up. "You're awake!"

Ryker woke and looked over. "Vega!"

"Hi guys. Sorry. I made a mess. I'm so thirsty."

"I'm so glad to hear your voice! Here, let me," said Ryker.

"I've got it!" Trent said, jumping up and reaching over Ryker to pour her some water. Ryker gave it up and started cleaning up the mess she'd made with some paper towels from the bathroom.

Trent handed her the cup and smiled. "I'm so glad you're awake!"

Vega took several long gulps of the soothing cool water.

"How long have I been asleep?"

"Two days," Trent and Ryker said simultaneously.

"Two days! Really?" She sat up straighter and rubbed her eyes. "I can't believe it."

"You passed out the other night," Ryker said. "The doctors said your blood pressure was dangerously high. They've been trying to counteract the effects of the headband ever since Drexel, uh, you know."

Trent enclosed her in a soft bear hug, careful not to hurt her. "You scared the hell out of me, girl! I'm so glad you're back."

"I've really been asleep for two whole days?"

"Well," said Ryker, "more like in a coma. We were really worried."

"But the doctors did an MRI," Trent added. "They said you're lucky. No permanent brain damage."

"Thank goodness," said Ryker. He dropped his eyes. "I'm really sorry."

Vega looked at his guilty face. "For what?"

"For not getting there sooner."

"Why are you sorry? You didn't even know we were there, or that I was in trouble." She took another sip of water. "Speaking of which, why did you come to the lab? I didn't think anyone else was even in the building."

"I was looking for my pen."

"In the middle of the night?"

"It's my favorite fountain pen. It's a Montblanc. A Meisterstuck Agatha Christie, to be exact. It's an expensive pen. I was so worried about it, I couldn't sleep."

"Oh."

"I know I shouldn't carry it to work, but I can't help myself. It's just such a pleasure to write with and to look at. Anyway, I thought I had left it in the lab, and I was afraid it was going to disappear."

"You thought someone was going to steal your fountain pen and just happened to walk in on me pounding the hell out of Drexel? I can't imagine what you thought."

"It was quite a shock. I didn't know what was going on. For that matter, I still haven't heard the whole story about what went down that night."

"Did you find your pen at least?"

Ryker pulled a polished black pen with silver finishings out of his front pocket and showed it to Vega. "It was on my desk at home. Under a writing tablet."

She smiled and chuckled. "Well, I'm glad you found it."

"And by the way," Ryker continued, "I'm sorry I didn't believe you about my headband causing psychotic episodes. I still have a hard time believing it."

"It's OK. No one else believed me either."

"But you didn't come back and show me once you found proof."

"Honestly Ryker, I thought you were behind it all."

"Me? Why?"

"You invented it. And if anyone knew how to tweak it to make it do something it wasn't supposed to, it was you. And well, I'm sorry, but part of the reason was because you're from Japan."

"Huh?"

"Seichō? Our main competitor? I thought maybe you were selling the technology to them or something and didn't care about the side effects. Maybe your loyalties laid with Japan and not the U.S. At least that was my logic at the time."

Ryker just shook his head. "You don't know me very well."

"That's an understatement. I'm obviously not a good judge of character. I trusted Drexel."

"We were all fooled by him."

"That's true. But Ryker, I also didn't think you liked me that much."

Ryker jerked his head back.

"Vega," Trent interjected, "maybe now is not the time."

"No, I want to hear. Why not?"

Vega shook her head. "The only time you ever talked to me was when we had to work together. You never said anything unless you absolutely had to. And I can count on one hand the number of times you were nice to me. Well, until I finally got my program working."

"I see."

Vega shook her head. "And that phone call? I really thought you were the one who cut my brake lines."

"Cut your brake lines?"

"Yeah. Remember that accident I had? The mechanic was pretty sure someone had cut the lines."

"Vega! You never said anything. And you thought I did it?"

"I heard you on the phone down in the lab one day, not long after, talking about something not working out as planned. You said you would have to try something else. That I wasn't going anywhere."

"I don't know what you're talking about. Are you sure I was talking about you?"

"OK, you never actually said my name, but you said something about, uh, like a new way to take her out. You may not have said my name, but it was obvious who you were referring to."

Ryker's face contorted, and he burst out laughing. Vega stared at him. "What's so damn funny?"

After composing himself, he replied, "Now I know what you're talking about. I remember that conversation. I've never told you this, but I run my dog in agility trials. A few sponsors have signed up to help me with the costs, and I had just come in second place. Jason from MeatMatch, my dog food sponsor, was giving me tips about how to get my dog to start out faster. It was about where I was standing at the start, the lead out. I was going to change the way I took her out."

Vega didn't know what to say. She wanted to bury her head under the covers and go back into a coma. "God, Ryker! I'm so sorry."

To Vega's surprise, Ryker's face turned red. He looked down at the floor. "And as far as me not liking you, nothing could be further from the truth. I liked you."

"You did?"

"No, I mean, I *really* liked you. Like you."

It took a moment for Vega to get his meaning.

"Oh! Astrid was right all along."

"What?"

"But then, why did you ignore me? Why didn't you ever say anything? Why did you act like you hated me?"

Trent couldn't take it anymore. "Vega! Are you really such a doofus? He's shy! He obviously didn't know how to approach you."

Ryker took a deep breath and glanced sideways at Trent, then back at Vega. "I'm sorry it came across that way. It's certainly not what I intended. But you're a little intimidating. Trent's right. I didn't know what to say to you to get your attention. On me, I mean."

"Wow! Thank you, I guess. I don't know what to say. I feel bad for reading you so wrong."

"Don't. It's my fault. I'm just glad you're OK. Do you think you could fill in a few blanks for me about that night? I'm still not clear exactly what happened."

"Yes, please! Holy crap!" exclaimed Trent. "We've been waiting for two days to hear how you managed to ride Drexel like a pony!"

"Trent!" But Vega laughed and told them the saga of events.

"Wow! This is a lot to take in," said Ryker.

"I didn't realize you were such a bad ass!" Trent declared. "You go, girl!" he said, trying to give her a high-five before he saw she might struggle with it with an IV in one arm and the other in a sling.

"Thank god you added that kill switch, Ryker. It probably saved my life."

"You remembered it?"

"Yes. It was very clever of you. I added one to my program too. But I hope mine never has to be used."

"Trent told me you two have been a regular dynamic duo," said Ryker. "And Drexel being Katya's son? That was a shocker. It's hard to fathom how much hate he must have been harboring all these years."

"What about the MYND program?" she asked.

"It's been suspended, for now."

"Just suspended? I can't believe they didn't cancel it! It's dangerous!"

"Yes, but it's also very powerful," Ryker said. "Your program could change the world."

"That all depends on who's running the show, and that my program doesn't cause the same problems as the headband."

"You're right. But I'm sure we can figure out what's wrong."

"You don't know that. I don't know why Ms. Neilmann would keep the project going after everything that's happened." Vega took a sip of water and asked, "What happened to Drexel?"

"The police arrested him for attempted murder and manslaughter," offered Trent. "And obviously, Katya fired him."

"By the way, Astrid sends her best," said Ryker. "She would be here, but she's with her sister. They're getting the news today about the results of her chemotherapy treatments."

"I hope it's good news," Vega said.

"Oh, and the only thing the police and the reporters know is that Drexel tried to kill you with the headband. They don't know anything about your program."

"I see. But we're not using the headband anymore, right? This must be a public relations nightmare."

"We're not using the stimulation command anymore. Not until we figure out what's wrong. But Ms. Neilmann still believes in your project. I think she thinks any publicity is good publicity. She also is positive we can fix everything, even still make an end-of-year push for your program. And she's been picking our brains about possible medical uses for it."

"Really? But Neilmann isn't a medical company."

"Not yet. But think about it. What if instead of just making people want to buy things, we could actually help them? Wouldn't you want to pursue that?"

"Of course. I've been thinking about the same thing. But... Are you sure I'm not still hallucinating?"

58

Ryker, Trent and Vega continued their catch-up until a nurse came into the room.

"How's our patient this afternoon?" the nurse asked.

"Better," Vega answered. "Shocked, though. I can't believe how long I've been asleep."

"You woke up. That's what's important."

The nurse busied herself taking Vega's vitals and then said, "Oh, I called the police to let them know you're awake. There's a detective waiting outside who wants to talk to you if you're feeling up to it. And the doctor should be in to see you shortly."

"Oh, OK."

The nurse left, and soon, there was a knock on the door.

"Yes?" asked Vega.

A man poked his head in. "Ms. Swift? I'm Detective Green with the Seattle police department. Mind if I come in?"

Vega looked down and made sure she had all her important bits covered with her flimsy hospital gown before she replied. "Sure."

A tall man dressed in a dark suit walked in, and Vega got a glimpse of a gun under his jacket. He held out his hand. "Darren Green. Nice to meet you."

She attempted to shake his hand, but was too encumbered. So she simply nodded. "You too."

Detective Green looked over at the others, and they got the hint.

"We're going to go grab some coffee in the cafeteria," said Ryker. "We'll be back. Don't go anywhere."

"Not a problem. But hopefully, I'll be dressed and ready to get out of here by then."

"Oh! I almost forgot. You may need this," Ryker said, pulling her phone out of his back pocket.

"Thank you! Is everything still there?"

"I didn't touch a thing."

Vega nodded, and after a round of hugs, found herself alone with the detective. He scooted a small chair over to her bedside.

"I just want to get your story about what happened a couple of nights ago. How you ended up in here. Are you feeling up to it?"

"Yes. I'm fine. But are you sure you wouldn't rather wait until I'm out of here?"

"No. I've been waiting for you to wake up. I like to get the details as soon as possible. While your memory is still fresh."

"You mean as fresh as it can be after two days of being unconscious?"

A smile came over the detective's face, and he handed her his card. "If you think of anything after we're done, just give me a call."

"OK. Fair enough."

Darren pulled out his phone and opened his *Activity Log* app.

"I thought you guys used memo pads."

"You've been watching too many old cop shows. We switched to electronic logs years ago."

"Oh."

"Goes right to our central database. So much faster. And now everyone shares their data. Helps us track repeat offenders or quickly find similarities in crimes."

"Huh. That makes sense. I never would have thought of that."

"Most people wouldn't have a reason to."

She nodded. "I have to warn you, there might be a few blank spots in my memory."

"That's understandable. Just start from when this whole thing began, and tell me everything you can remember."

"Do you want me to start with why I was there in the first place?"

"Whatever you think is relevant."

Vega took a breath and said, "This may take a while."

"I'm not in a hurry."

"OK." Vega went through the details of how she became concerned about the MYND headband's effects in the first place, trying to tell him as much as she could without violating her NDA. Then she went through her encounter with Drexel. At least everything she could remember before he drugged her, and after she woke up and he used the headband on her.

"There's a headband that reads people's minds? Sounds like a science fiction novel."

"No, it reads their brain waves. It's kind of like getting an EEG."

"I'm gonna be honest, and admit I know nothing about this mind science—"

"Neuromarketing."

"Right, neuromarketing. So, why was Drexel trying to kill you?"

"He wasn't trying to kill me, exactly. Just mess up my brain."

Vega continued on with the story of Drexel's scheme. When she finished, Darren asked, "So he wanted to bring down Ms. Neilmann because he wanted her job?"

"Because she's his mother."

His face looked puzzled as he flipped through some info on his phone. "I didn't see that in his records."

"She doesn't know."

"How would she not—"

"Yeah, I wondered the same thing," she said. "She was only sixteen when she had him. Her parents made her give him up. Apparently, it's been bothering him his whole life. He thought she never wanted him in the first place."

"I see. No one told her?"

"No. And I know it's none of my business, but maybe we should keep it that way. It was a closed adoption. He was never supposed to find out who she was. And considering everything he's done, maybe it's better if she never knows. I'm not sure how she'd feel, seeing how he turned out."

The detective nodded. "Yes, probably so. But not really my call. So, you're saying he wanted Neilmann Corporation to fail so Ms. Neilmann would go down with it?"

"That's right."

Darren nodded. "But what was that you said about psychotic episodes?"

"The headband has a problem. Drexel was the one who did the follow-ups with our test participants. But he never told anyone about the side-effects, so no one realized there was an issue."

"Well, everyone knows there's one now."

59

Vega sat between Astrid and Ryker in the first row of the Neilmann theater waiting for the all-hands meeting to begin. A five-minute video played on a huge screen touting the history and successes at Neilmann Corporation. When the video ended, Katya walked to the center of the stage and began.

"Good morning everyone! And thank you for taking time out of your busy schedules to attend our quarterly meeting!"

Ryker leaned over to Vega and whispered, "Like we had a choice."

She gave him a grin and snickered.

"I know a lot of you don't know this, but Neilmann has been number two in the industry ever since Seichō took over our number-one spot seven years ago." Katya clicked a button on the remote, and a huge number one displayed on the screen. "But this year, we passed them up and left them in the dust!"

A round of applause broke out from the audience.

"As of the beginning of this second quarter," Ms. Neilmann continued, "we are again in the number one spot in the world of neuromarketing!"

The audience clapped again, and a few hoots rang out from the crowd. Katya waited before holding up her hand to calm them down. "And one of the big reasons behind our move up, is the great work many of you did on ensuring the new MYND app rolled out last year in time for the holiday buying spree. So, thank you!"

Ms. Neilmann clapped out to the audience as another round of applause boomed.

"And none of this would have been possible without the impressive talents of the creator of the MYND application, Ms. Vega Swift! Stand up, Vega."

Her face blushing bright red, Vega stood up and gave a small wave. The crowd clapped until Ms. Neilmann calmed them down again. "And of course, working closely with her to ensure its success, Dr. Ryker Fedorov and Dr. Astrid Montgomery. Please stand up so everyone can get a good look at you!"

Ryker and Astrid stood up beside Vega, and when the applause finally died down, they sat down, and Ms. Neilmann clicked the remote. The screen switched to a graph showing the steady increase of sales over the last quarter. Katya used her laser pointer to bring attention to the numbers. "As you can see, our sales increased exponentially soon after the holidays, and for the last quarter, have moved from a low of…"

The review of financials went on for another thirty minutes, and Ms. Neilmann couldn't wipe the smile off her face throughout the entire presentation. She had finally gotten her number one position in the industry back.

Sitting at a table in the cafeteria after the meeting, Vega, Astrid and Ryker were happy to get out of the spotlight.

"You know," Astrid said to Vega, "I still feel bad about not believing you when you kept telling me there was a connection between the headband and the psychotic episodes in the area."

"I didn't believe her either, Astrid," said Ryker. "Wasn't just you."

Vega shook her head at them. "Stop it, you guys. I know I sounded like a crazy person. Drexel never told us. And he didn't know why the headband was causing issues, he just took advantage of it."

"Tell me again what was wrong with the headband?" asked Astrid. "I know you told me before, but…"

"It was the electricity. The headband sent an electrical signal to the nucleus accumbens to stimulate the users to click on the ads, but even though the amperage was small, the electricity had an unexpected effect. The signal jumped through the LFP—"

"Wait," Astrid interrupted, "what's LFP again?"

"It's an acronym for local field potential. It's the space between neurons. So, the signal jumped around in the limbic system from the nucleus accumbens to the amygdala and septal nuclei. Stimulation of these areas can create a feeling of overwhelming fear. So the electrical signal bouncing around in that region of the brain eventually resulted in the subjects experiencing a psychotic break."

"But why didn't it affect everyone?"

"I'm not really sure. My theory is that some people are simply more sensitive. Or perhaps there were a few plancks of difference between these areas in their brains. The distance was too far for the signal to make the jump from the nucleus accumbens, so it died out before it caused any damage."

"Planks?"

"Plancks. P-L-A-N-C-K-S. It's the smallest unit of measurement we know of—today, anyway. And I'm just theorizing. I really don't know why some people were more affected than others."

Ryker jumped in. "Doesn't matter. It was all my fault. And I didn't even realize it was happening. Drexel did all the follow-ups. Never told me there was an issue. He said everyone came out of those tests with flying colors. I was so pissed off when I found out." He shook his head. "I should have never trusted him. People died."

Vega put her hand on his arm. "Stop it, Ryker. It was not your fault. How could you know? He didn't tell anyone. As soon as the problem showed up, he took all the follow-up calls away from Daphne and did the rest of them without her. He purposefully hid everything. He didn't care who he brought down in the meantime."

"But then tell me again why your MYND app doesn't cause the same problem?" asked Astrid.

"Her application doesn't use electricity, remember?" answered Ryker.

"Right. I used magnetic stimulation. No electricity involved at all."

Astrid nodded. "I remember now. I'm going to write that down somewhere, so I quit asking you about it."

Vega laughed. "By the way, how's your sister doing? She still OK?"

A huge smile came over Astrid's face. "Yes! Shelly is still in remission, and she just got a job in pharmaceutical sales. She met her new boss in the hospital when she was getting treatments. Can you believe that?"

"That's fantastic!" Vega exclaimed.

"Oh! I almost forgot to tell you. She's selling her car—for cheap. An electric Cabrio. It's a convertible. The company is giving her a brand-new car. They're paying for everything—gas, reimbursement for mileage, insurance—the works. I told her she should sell it to you."

"That's really nice of you. But there's no way I could afford a Cabrio."

"I know you're still taking the bus into work, and Trent is carting you around for everything. You can't keep doing that forever. And I think you can afford this. They're cute. But they're tiny, and they're not that expensive. She needs to get rid of it quickly. She doesn't want to keep paying the insurance on it since it's just sitting there not being used. You should at least talk to her."

"Really? OK. I'll be surprised if I can swing it, but—"

"You can. I'll make sure she gives you a great deal."

"Enough chit-chatting," said Ryker. "Don't we have another project to go work on?"

60

Miren Anne Walker (Swift)

A wonderful daughter, mother and wife, Miren Swift grew up in the small town of Monterey, California, where she learned to love the beach and spent hours looking at the ocean. She always said staring at the waves was her therapy.

She went off to college at the early age of 17, moving to Washington State, and attending UW where she got her Master's in Education and met her husband Cyrus Swift. They fell in love, got married in Maui and later moved to the lovely town of Redmond.

Miren was as devoted a teacher to her kids at Risdon Elementary as they were to her. She won the Teacher of the Year award three years in a row. But she was not a pushover and told her kids, "If you think I'm tough, just wait until you get a real boss."

Ten years into her career, she took a break from teaching and popped out her daughter, Vega Grace Swift. The family spent many a vacation at the ocean, renting houses right on the water and pretending they lived there.

In her spare time, Miren loved modern art and color and painted with those two passions in mind. Her best friend once told her, in the most loving way possible, that her paintings looked like clown vomit, which made Miren very happy indeed. She passed along her love of the ocean to her daughter along with her love of modern art. Cyrus never understood it and once told her some of her most beloved pieces looked like one of her school kids had painted it. This made Miren happy as well because in her mind, it meant the artist was still unhampered by the insipidness of adulthood.

She was a fighter, and although she was struck by early-onset Alzheimer's at the age of 52, she refused to let it bring her down, always putting her family before herself.

Vega quit typing, closed the document and shut the lid of her laptop. She looked out at her back yard. The dogwood trees were blooming, and the soft pink flowers were striking against the bright blue spring sky.

She shook her head as she smiled at the beautiful scene and thought about her life which had taken a one-eighty in the last few months. After being stubborn for so long, she had finally given in and called Miren's sister, Sharon, in England. She had come through without hesitation, happy to aid with Miren's care expenses and a little pissed off that she had not been kept abreast of her condition. With the extra money Sharon was now providing, Vega had finally been able to move her mother to a facility that provided higher quality, round-the-clock care with resident on-site doctors—exactly what Miren needed now. Heart House cared for only twenty patients at a time, and everyone working there seemed genuinely happy. The staff even took time out of their normal care routine to play games with the residents, mainly to help them maintain muscle tone, but also to keep their spirits up. Her mom had finally completely recovered from the devastating UTI, and Vega hoped in her moments of clarity, she would even be able to have a little fun there.

For the first time in years, she felt like she could relax. And she didn't feel the least bit guilty about not being with her mom twenty-four hours a day. Instead, she felt relief for both herself and her mother.

At Neilmann, Katya had surprised everyone when she split the MYND project off into two different departments —one to oversee the continued maintenance and upgrade of the MYND app and another to investigate its possible medical applications. Vega was now leading a group to work on a new application called MYNDSET (Marketing Y-bit Near Disseminator Synapse Emergence Technology). She was adapting her original program to reroute synapse communication links in the brain to help victims of Alzheimer's and other brain-damaging diseases. If it was successful, the app would run continuously on smart phones, rerouting signals in real-time from damaged areas of the brain to more stable ones so patients could live a normal life for as long as possible. She had gotten Miren approved to be one of the first test subjects. She knew it wasn't a cure, and it might be too late for her mom, but she was hopeful it would give some patients a few more years of cognizance and memory. The first trial was scheduled to start in three months.

Other members of her group focused on selling her original MYND application, installed on smart-phones and tablets, to hospitals so they could easily monitor non-critical patients. It would eliminate the need to connect them to numerous, large, and much more expensive cumbersome machines. It would also allow the patients to go home earlier, since the doctors and nurses could monitor their conditions remotely.

Of course, Ms. Neilmann was not totally altruistic. She had made deals to share users' personal information with several drug companies. For example, if a user's data revealed they consistently had high blood pressure, that data, along with their contact info, was sent to whatever company Neilmann had an agreement with that sold high blood-pressure medication. Vega was sure more similar deals were in the works. She supposed it was a good thing. It could, hopefully, save people's lives. But she would be happier if Neilmann shared the data with doctors, free of charge.

Neilmann was also selling all the brain wave and biometric data gathered from the MYND application, to insurance and research companies. The users probably didn't even realize it, because after all, how many people actually read all the fine print in those agreement forms when they installed an application? At least in that deal, Katya had promised anonymity.

Vega had quit worrying about what her MYND program was doing to people. At least she knew it wasn't hurting anyone, and now that Ryker led the group, and she knew him better, she trusted him to keep things as ethical as possible.

But today she wasn't going to think about Neilmann. This weekend, she was taking some much-needed time off.

She jumped when her phone's ring split through her thoughts.

"Hey," said Trent.

"Hey."

"Did you hear the latest news?"

"No, what now? More lawyers coming to defend Drexel?"

"No. Maybe. I don't know about that. But guess what?"

"I don't really care."

"So, you don't want to know where he is now?"

"No."

In a sing-song voice, Trent teased, "I think you do."

Vega sighed. "OK, you're right. I'm curious. Where is he?"

"The judge claimed him mentally unfit for trial. The *Seattle Times* said the psychologist diagnosed him with narcissistic, paranoid and antisocial personality disorders. Apparently, Drexel has been working hard all his life to make sure he fit in and seemed normal. The doctor admitted him to the Johnson Mental Hospital in Bellevue." Trent said with a chuckle. "Maybe they'll give him shock treatments?"

"It's called electrotherapy now."

"Doesn't have quite the same ring. But it would be fitting, don't you think?"

Vega couldn't help but laugh.

"Did Detective Green ever find a law against using the headband?" he asked.

"No. He said he still has calls in to some of his lawyer connections, but I don't think there are any laws on the book against what they're doing. Or should I say what *we're* doing? I am one of them. At least I know it's in good hands now."

"Ryker's hands are good, huh?"

"Trent!" But she had to smile. "Yes, his hands are very good. But enough about all that. What about your new show?"

"I'm booked at the Garner Art Gallery in downtown Seattle in two months!"

"That's fantastic! I knew they would want you once they saw how well you did at the Tsuga opening. Congratulations!"

"Thanks."

"Will you be ready? Do you have enough new pieces finished?"

"Are you kidding? I have so many new things going. This fiasco of yours gave me a ton of ideas. So, thank you!"

Vega laughed. "Wasn't expecting that. But, yay?"

"Not quite the muse I was looking for, but whatever works!"

"I knew you'd be famous one day. Don't forget me when you're living in your mansion on the hill."

Trent laughed. "Not possible."

"The mansion, or forgetting me?"

"Both. Who wants to live in a mansion? Too big. I'd get lost. And can you imagine the upkeep?"

After a little more chit-chat, she hung up and looked over at Ryker.

"Trent?" he asked.

"Just giving me the latest."

"And?"

She smiled. "I'll tell you everything after we get there. I don't want to think about it right now. Ready?"

Ryker picked up the suitcases by the door and said, "Ready when you are."

"Got the instructions for us to get into the house?"

"Yes. The rental place sent me all the details, along with a map of Whidbey Island."

"All-righty then. Let's go to the beach!"

Vega walked out to her Mini EV Cabrio-Plus and ran her hand slowly down the candy-apple red hood. "I love my new car."

"Couldn't have asked for a much better deal than what you got."

"I'm a lucky girl," she said, smiling at him. "In more ways than one." She tossed him the keys. "But today, I want to sit back and relax. Be careful with her."

The roof on the convertible was down, the sun was shining, and Ryker's border collie, Stella, followed them out to the car. The black and white dog jumped into the ridiculously tiny back seat when she opened the door, and Vega gave her a quick ruffle on her head as she dropped into the passenger side. Ryker took the wheel and guided the car to the main road.

Vega was so used to gray and clouds that the bright sun made her squint even with her sunglasses on. The heat of its rays permeated the top of her head, so she tied on a scarf to keep her scalp from burning and her hair from tangling. Hanging her arm out the window, she let the breeze catch her hand, making little waves in the wind as they drove toward the ferry dock in Mukilteo.

As they got closer to the water, she heard the low drone of a ferry horn signaling its docking. They pulled into line to wait for boarding, and Vega caught the comforting smell of pine trees and the salty scent of the nearby water permeating the air.

She couldn't remember the last time she had felt so free.

ACKNOWLEDGEMENTS

This book was a long time coming. Years of writing, not picking it up for months, procrastinating and then more writing, while my ideas had a hard time keeping up with the advancements in neurology, smart devices and mobile apps. I've always loved books and movies that merged medical themes, technology, mystery and drama, and I had a lot of fun doing the huge amount of research required to try and make this book as believable as possible.

I'm sure I wasted more than a small amount of time venturing down rabbit holes while searching for medical and technological information relevant to Alzheimer's, neurology, neuromarketing and smart device capabilities. Without the plethora of scientific and medical information and articles so easily available on the internet, this book would have taken a hell of a lot longer to complete. Although I was a programmer in my past life, I never studied or worked in the medical field, and I needed all the help I could get.

I owe a huge debt of gratitude to Dr. Mark del Rosario and

his better half (his words), Dr. Nichole Bisquera, for taking the time to proofread my book for medical goof-ups and believability. When I met him, Mark was in his residency in neurology before switching to radiation oncology — zapping tumors with magic rays, as he put it — and now specializes in brain and spine radiosurgery. Oh, and he also happens to be the owner of Kasama which offers fountain pens proudly crafted in the Philippines. Color me impressed!

I met Mark purely by accident at the Seattle Pen Club all the way back in 2016, when the idea for this book was just beginning to form in my brain. He was nice enough to listen to me pitch my concept instead of doing what everyone else was doing—looking at and writing with beautiful fountain pens and playing with inks and papers. He has also kept in touch with me throughout the years, while I continued to promise to finish my book one day.

Mark and Nichole's knowledge and expertise in neurology and medical science, ensured I didn't make a complete fool of myself and write a book that no one would ever believe. Any errors are completely my own doing.

I also have to send out a huge thank you to my other alpha-readers, Karen Horn, Carla Kessler and Bill Pennabaker. They all offered extensive spelling and grammatical assistance, pointed out any mistakes in my timeline, revealed areas that needed clarification or editing, and simply gave me feedback on the general story and whether it was even worth reading or not. I am very thankful for their graciousness and service.

Thank you also, to the user, *Placidplace,* on Pixabay who provided a starting point for my book cover image. A few tweaks here and there, and it was exactly what I wanted.

And of course, to my wonderful husband, Gil, who proofreads, lets me bounce ideas off him, feeds me, supports me and loves me unconditionally throughout all my hours of writing, re-writing and editing. I would be lost without him.

I hope you, the reader, got some enjoyment from this book and found it at least a little bit entertaining. A lot of the smart device capabilities and technology presented here already exists today. Let's hope some of the scarier ones I imagined never will.

ABOUT THE AUTHOR

Teresa Widdowson is a self-published author who currently lives in Redmond, Washington. She is an avid mystery reader, but loves mixing it up with different genres. With the release of her first book, *The RH Factor*, she fulfilled her life-long dream of writing and publishing a novel. The completion of *MYND Control* continues her writing adventure and combines her love of medical and technological thrillers with a bit of murder thrown in.

She made her living as a computer programmer and high-tech sales rep but eventually refocused her career and completed a Masters in Digital Cinema. Leaving the corporate world behind, she worked as a TV producer, teacher and short-film writer and director.

Even though she's now retired, her other numerous passions sometimes make it hard to find the time to write. But she plans to continue her quest to get her stories out to the world. When she's not writing, she can be found journaling, making music, creating colorful paintings, hiking or playing with her fountain pens.